A FIRST-CLASS MURDER

KEITH FINNEY

VINCI
BOOKS

By Keith Finney

Rex and the Dowager

A Posh Murder

A Spiffing Murder

A Dapper Murder

A First Class Murder

The Norfolk Mysteries

Dead Man's Trench

Murder By Hanging

The Boathouse Killer

Miller's End

Dead... Again

A Yuletide Mystery

Double Cross

The Lavender Killer

Murder RSVP

For Joan

Vinci Books

vinci-books.com

Published by Vinci Books Ltd in 2026

1

This work is a work of fiction. Names, characters, places and incidents are the product of the author's imagination or are used fictitiously. Any resemblance to actual persons, living or dead, places and incidents is entirely coincidental.

A CIP catalogue record for this book is available from the British Library.

Paperback ISBN: 9781036716479

The EU GPSR authorised representative is Logos Europe, 9 rue Nicolas Poussion, 17000 La Rochelle, France

contact@logoseurope.eu

Chapter One

ALL ABOARD

I stepped from the boat-train onto the rain-slicked Southampton dockside. Beside me, the massive hull of the RMS Britannic Star loomed above us like a steel mountain through the haze. Sulphurous coal smoke mingled with steam, creating a peculiar tang that caught in my throat.

"Mind your footing, Arthur dear," HG called out as the detective inspector almost lost his footing on the slippery concrete. His oversized coat flapped in the bitter December wind, giving him the appearance of a dishevelled crow.

"Got it." Whipple grumbled as he clutched his bowler hat to his head. "Bloomin treacherous, this place."

A porter materialised through the throng of fellow passengers; his brass buttons gleaming. "Luggage, milady?"

"Indeed." HG's tall figure cut an elegant path through the chaos. "Though I daresay we'll need rather more assistance than one pair of hands, young man. There are eight trunks to manage."

The porter's eyes widened. "Eight, milady?"

"A lady must be prepared for all eventualities." She fixed

him with a warm smile. "When one travels with Scotland Yard's finest detective, one never knows what may occur." The young lad looked at Whipple in awe.

Whipple coughed. "Perhaps we shouldn't broadcast the—"

"Oh nonsense, Arthur. Half the first-class passengers are likely criminals of one sort or another. I'm sure we'll have our work cut out."

The porter's cheeks flushed as he drank in this latest revelation, before loading his sack truck and scurrying through a morass of humanity.

As we made progress to the first-class gangway, the crowd parted; their faces reflecting awe and curiosity. This did not surprise me - the Dowager Duchess of Drakeford's presence had that effect on people.

"Tide nor time tarrieth no man," HG announced.

Whipple lifted his damp bowler and scratched his forehead. "You mean—"

"I know what I mean, Arthur. It's a mediaeval English version of Saint Marher's idiom. To whit, we need to get our skates on or we'll be swimming across the Atlantic.

At the foot of the gangway, HG produced our first-class tickets with a flourish. "Rex, do keep an eye on Arthur. He looks rather pale already and we haven't yet boarded."

"I'm alright," Whipple protested, though his complexion suggested otherwise.

The thundering sound of the ship's horn blared, its vibration inducing base note dampened by the heavy sky. A plume of greyish steam fought to make its way skyward, only to be thwarted by the incessant drizzle dissipated its energy.

A daunting ascent to a world of luxury lay before us. HG strode forth with a regal air, her winter coat trailing like a velvet curtain. I hurried along, eager, yet nervous. Behind me, Whipple hung back, looking miserable.

As I placed my foot on the first step, the worn planks beneath felt slick. In an instant, my footing betrayed me. I stumbled, collapsing to my knees with an undignified thud. Whereupon my hands found purchase in the rich folds of HG's winter coat.

"Much easier to manage the gangway standing up," she said, amused by my pained expression.

Whipple guffawed. "Oh dear," he muttered, his face pinched with mirth.

I scrambled to my feet and dusted myself off with an exaggerated flourish. My action earned a smile from HG. “It’s all part of the adventure,” she declared, as we reached the top of the gangway.

The promenade deck stretched before us; an endless pathway of teak decking with black corking between each board to keep things watertight. Brass fittings did their best to stand out in the grey, wet afternoon, with wind-driven sleet assaulting exposed flesh, forcing passengers to scurry inside to escape the onslaught.

“It’s a long way down,” complained Whipple as he peered over the hardwood-capped deck railing.

“Not as far down as the Titanic slipped after it sailed from there,” I replied blindly as I pointed to berth 44, less than one-hundred feet from our own position.

Whipple froze as he fixated on the squat iron bollards that held the fated ship’s mooring lines before its tragic voyage. There they sat in an immoveable row, lining the dock’s edge, black, still, as if still in mourning dress.

“Thank you for that pearl of wisdom, young fella. I’ll be sure to ask your advice next time I need cheering up.”

A senior steward in a crisp white uniform, holding an

enormous open umbrella in his right hand, approached to inspect our tickets.

"What? Again?" Whipple grumbled under his breath, yet, I suspected, pleased to have his attention drawn away from Titanic's awful fate.

The steward threw HG a cautious glance.

"Take no notice of my ill-mannered companion. It is his queasiness that speaks. You see, the fellow is a poor sailor. Perhaps we should leave him on deck to take advantage of the fresh air, rather than you advising us where we might find our accommodation."

Whipple pulled his heavy collar about his ears and harrumphed.

The steward maintained his composure and offered HG a polite nod, while shielding her with the umbrella from the worst of the weather. "If Your Grace would be so kind as to follow me to the first-class lounge where hot chocolate and pastries await."

Mention of refreshments had an immediate effect on Whipple's countenance.

As we followed the senior steward into first class territory; a realm of plush carpets and lavish furnishings, Whipple sighed. "Where's the hot chocolate, then?"

HG surveyed our surroundings. "Now, Rex dear, do keep your eyes peeled for any suspicious characters."

"Suspicious? I thought our voyage a holiday?" I said, casting a confused glance around at our fellow passengers.

"More of a busman's holiday if you ask me," chuntered Whipple. "All I know is that wherever we go, trouble isn't far behind."

"Or merely waiting to be discovered, dear Arthur. Think of it as an adventure!"

The heavy doors opened into a luxurious first-class

lounge, a stark contrast to the gloomy weather. White-uniformed stewards served champagne in crystal glasses.

I paused at the threshold, overwhelmed for a moment by the grandeur. Rich wood panelling and ornate mirrors reflected the soft chandelier light. Hand-painted pastoral scenes, framed by gilded mouldings, adorned the ceiling. Velvet-upholstered settees and wingback chairs invited patronage in intimate groupings throughout the vast space.

"Your Grace!" A barrel-chested figure in a gleaming uniform strode towards us; bushy eyebrows rising like twin caterpillars above his ruddy face. “It is an honour to welcome you aboard the Britannic Star!"

Captain Hardwick's voice boomed across the lounge, causing several well-coiffed ladies to turn their heads in mild alarm. He seized HG's gloved hand and bowed over it with theatrical flourish, while casting Whipple and me a dismissive glance, as though we were peculiar luggage she'd insisted on bringing aboard.

"Captain Hardwick," HG acknowledged with perfect composure. "How kind of you to greet us personally."

"Nothing but the best for the Dowager Duchess of Drakeford!" He puffed out his chest. "I've arranged the finest suites on B Deck, port side for your party. The Admiralty Suite, no less!"

"How thoughtful," HG replied, extracting her hand with practiced grace. "May I present Detective Inspector Whipple of Scotland Yard, and my ward, Rex?"

The captain’s enthusiasm dimmed. "Ah. Scotland Yard, is it?" His eyes narrowed. "Not expecting trouble, I hope? Had enough bad luck this season without police involvement."

"Merely a holiday," HG assured him, though the gleam in her eye suggested she hoped otherwise. "The Inspector rarely travels without his credentials, much as I rarely travel without my pearls."

Around us, America's nouveau riche mingled with England's aristocracy in a choreographed dance of wealth and status. An elderly lady of the landed class sniffed disapprovingly at a steel magnate's wife's diamonds, while a young lord shared cigars with a Hollywood producer. Stewards weaved between them all, invisible yet indispensable.

"Splendid, splendid," the Captain muttered, clearly unconvinced. "Well, I must attend to other matters. The weather, you know. Bit of chop expected."

As he retreated, I caught Whipple's eye. "Charming fellow," I murmured.

"Indeed," HG said with a wry smile. "And about as competent as a fellow riding a bicycle with his back to the handlebars."

As Captain Hardwick departed, a moment of awkward silence hung in the air like a thick fog. I caught Whipple's eye just as he spotted the buffet table across the lounge, its surface burdened with the finest foods.

Before he could make a beeline for the feast, First Officer Greyson approached us, his expression bordering on anxious. He bowed excessively, nearly losing his balance.

"Your Grace," he said, straightening up with an embarrassed cough. "A pleasure to see you aboard."

HG smiled graciously. "And you, Mr Greyson. I trust the ship is well prepared for our journey?"

“Ah, yes,” he stammered; flustered in her presence. “The captain mentioned that there may be a few white horses along the way.”

I glanced at Whipple; the colour drained from his cheeks as if someone had siphoned the very life from him.

His earlier enthusiasm for indulging in the buffet evaporated.

"Horses?" Whipple repeated weakly. "You mean a stampede of stallions?"

Greyson's gaze flickered away momentarily, revealing his concern before he composed himself. "Nothing we cannot manage, Detective Inspector," he insisted, though a tremor in his voice belied his bravado.

"Weather always has its moods," HG interjected with an air of calm authority that seemed to bolster Whipple's spirits a little. "It is not uncommon for ships to dance a little upon leaving Southampton."

"Indeed," Greyson murmured hastily, his eyebrows shooting up involuntarily as if caught in an unfortunate miscalculation. "I assure you all precautions are taken."

"And what would those precautions be?" I couldn't help but ask.

"Lifeboats and such," Greyson replied, waving a hand dismissively before catching himself and adjusting his posture.

Whipple looked distinctly ill at ease now, far removed from his initial eagerness to explore culinary delights. HG observed him with an amused twinkle in her eye.

"You appear positively pale, Arthur," she said lightly. "Shall I fetch you a plate of something? Or perhaps a life vest instead?"

He managed a feeble grin that looked more like a grimace as Greyson excused himself with another overly deep bow.

"All will be well," HG assured us once he was gone. "A few boisterous waves never hurt anyone."

"So you say," Whipple moaned under his breath.

HG's laughter chimed amidst the surrounding chatter.

Their playful talk made me grin, but I kept glancing at the buffet, wanting something to eat and take my mind off the trouble ahead.

Mesmerised by the grand display of culinary delights before me, I hesitated. Suddenly, loud voices disrupted the calm atmosphere of the lounge.

"Have you lost your mind, Blythe?" a voice boomed, sharp and cold. I turned to see two men engaged in an animated argument. Sir Edmund Blythe, resplendent in a tailored suit that struggled to contain his portly frame, faced off against Klaus von Ritter, whose tall, lithe figure exuded an air of chilling confidence.

“Your threats mean nothing to me,” Blythe sputtered, his walrus moustache quivering with indignation. “You may fancy yourself untouchable here, but I know what you’ve done.”

Von Ritter smirked, icy blond hair gleaming under the chandelier light. “Oh dear Sir Edmund, your bluster is as transparent as your intentions. Have you not learned that one does not play games with fire unless one is prepared to be burned?”

HG arched an eyebrow at their exchange. “It seems our dear industrialist has found himself outmatched,” she mused quietly.

“Do you know them?” I asked, trying to glean some insight into this peculiar spectacle.

“Blythe is infamous for his cutthroat dealings,” she replied. “As for von Ritter…let us say he possesses an exquisite talent for using words as weapons.”

Whipple shuffled closer, leaning in as if he might gather strength from HG’s presence. “I’ve heard whispers about Blythe’s escapades; blackmail and the sort.”

“Quite,” HG nodded knowingly. “And von Ritter? A

diplomat who thinks himself above reproach while playing chess with people's lives."

The argument intensified; Blythe gesticulated wildly while von Ritter maintained his superior composure. My curiosity deepened; what could have ignited such passion?

"Perhaps we should intervene?" Whipple suggested half-heartedly.

HG shook her head with a smile playing on her lips. "Let them dance a while longer. I fear the entertainment has only just begun."

"Entertainment?" Whipple scoffed softly under his breath. "Seems more like a circus act."

"I daresay they could use a ringmaster." My remark earned me a gentle nudge from HG and a muted chuckle from Whipple.

Just then, Blythe leaned closer to von Ritter, lowering his voice conspiratorially, yet the tension between them was palpable enough to cut through the air like a knife.

"What are they arguing about?" I wondered aloud.

"I suspect it pertains to business dealings gone awry," HG speculated. "Or perhaps something far more personal."

Whipple adjusted his collar as we continued to observe the unfolding drama, a scene rife with intrigue amidst the glamour of our surroundings, hinting at deeper mysteries to play out on our voyage across the Atlantic.

The first-class dining room of the Britannic Star dazzled beneath a constellation of crystal chandeliers. The air shimmered with the clink of cutlery and the low hum of anticipation. Waiters in crisp white jackets glided between tables, the scent of roast duck trailing in their wake.

At the centre, beneath a vast painted dome, stood the captain's table, around which sat an eclectic gathering of the rich and famous.

Captain Ian Hardwick presided, his white uniform immaculate, gold braid gleaming. Beside him, sat HG, resplendent in a gown of deep violet silk, her diamonds catching every flicker of light. Her posture was regal, her gloved hands resting lightly on the table, her eyes sharp beneath a halo of white feathers.

Other guests included Sir Edmund Blythe, showing no sign of his unpleasant exchange with Von Ritter. To the captain's right, sat Miss Penelope Chase, the famous heiress. Her wide-eyed nervousness seemed at odds with her wealth, which the young lady tried hard to cover up with charm and elegance. I noted, too, that she avoided eye contact, or conversation with Sir Edmund. I assumed arose out of nervousness at having witnessed his verbal altercation with the German fellow.

I sat opposite HG, and more than a tad surprised to receive an invitation to the top table. To my right sat Madam Zelda; her hair draped in black lace quite out of keeping with the jolly occasion. Around her neck rested a prominent crystal pendant, as if to reinforce her somewhat mixed reputation as a psychic to polite society.

As the first course arrived, the captain launched into tales of storms weathered off Cape Wrath and a near-mutiny in the South Atlantic. He described, with a flourish, how he'd once navigated the Britannic Star through a channel so narrow "you could have tossed your hat onto the rocks and had it returned by the wind." Sir Edmond guffawed, Miss Penelope gasped, while HG offered a polite, if sceptical, smile.

Wine flowed, laughter rang, and the orchestra played

popular tunes in the background, its strains mingling with the distant, rhythmic thrum of the engines.

Within ninety minutes of pleasant company, dessert plates were cleared and the last toast made; a subtle shift ran through the room. Glasses trembled, chandeliers swayed imperceptibly. The captain paused mid-sentence, his eyes narrowing. A low, rolling shudder passed beneath their feet; the first warning of the storm's approach. The mighty ship began to pitch as the sea rose to meet it. Hardwick's voice had a quality that discouraged questions before they had formed.

Conversation faltered, replaced by a collective, breathless awareness. Outside, the horizon vanished into darkness. The captain, ever the showman, raised his glass and declared, "Your Grace, my Lords, Ladies and gentlemen, tonight, the Britannic Star dances with the North Sea herself!"

The words tumbled from Madame Zelda's lips, her crystal pendant swinging with the ship's motion. "Death rides the white horses." Her dark eyes searching for an invisible horizon through the dining room's grand windows, where foam-capped waves rose like spectral stallions in the blackness.

I might have dismissed her pronouncement as mere theatrics, but something in her tone sent a chill through me that had nothing to do with the weather.

HG's hand found my arm as we rose from the table. "Shall we brave the corridors, dear boy?" The ship's pronounced roll made even her graceful movements appear uncertain.

We navigated our way past other diners, many of whom clutched at chairs and tables with varying degrees of dignity. Sir Edmund Blythe stumbled past, his ruddy complexion now distinctly green. Miss Penelope Chase fared better as her hands slipped from chair to chair.

"I wonder where our dear Inspector has hidden himself?" HG mused as we reached the grand staircase. Stewards positioned themselves at strategic intervals, ready to catch any passenger who might lose their footing.

"Not at dinner, that's certain. The weather must have driven him to his cabin." I replied.

A particularly violent pitch sent us careering towards the mahogany-panelled wall. HG laughed softly. "Poor Arthur. The man can examine the ghastliest crime scenes without flinching, yet the mere suggestion of rough seas reduces him to a quivering wreck."

We passed the ship's faux English country house library, where Sir Edmund's secretary clutched a pile of papers to prevent their escape, his face drawn with anxiety. Through the elegant doorway, I glimpsed Madame Zelda again, arranging her tarot cards on a felt-topped table that prevented unwanted movement.

"The white horses," I murmured, remembering her words.

"What was that, Rex?"

"Something Madame Zelda said about death and white horses. Rather dramatic, don't you think?"

"Perhaps." HG's tone held a note of consideration I'd learned to recognise. "Though in my experience, those who deal in dramatics occasionally stumble upon truth."

We spent the next two hours or so in comparable company as we toured the public areas of our prestigious surroundings. Polite conversations were had and observations internally digested. “What a strange lot they are,” I observed to HG.

“You see here, Rex, conspicuous wealth effortlessly

combined with loathing, jealousy, and fear. Yet all appears well and rivals smile at each other. The class conventions must be upheld in public, you see. Anyway, I grow tired of the charade. My sleeping draft and a comfortable bed awaits."

My mentor's admission concerning the use of Bromidia, or similar, shocked my senses. I had not known HG used such liquids to aid sleep. HG picked up my demeanour in seconds.

'You misunderstand, my dearest boy. Do not mistake a glass of port and several Huntley & Palmers Water Biscuits for a medicinal compound poured from an amber bottle."

HG's correction made me feel foolish, though soon soothed by her warm smile and kind eyes.

We parted ways at her stateroom door, a magnificent suite befitting her status. "Sleep well, dear boy. Let's hope Neptune tires of his game by morning."

I made my way down the corridor to check on Whipple, rapping on his door. "Inspector? All well?" The silence from within spoke volumes. Poor chap, probably wrapped in blankets, clutching his basin like a lifeline. The mental image brought a smile to my face.

My own stateroom, while not as grand as HG's, still breathed luxury. Rich mahogany panels lined the walls, complemented by brass fittings that gleamed in the electric light. A thick carpet in deep burgundy cushioned my feet. The bed, dressed in crisp white linens, dominated the space, flanked by built-in drawers and a small writing desk. A decorated water pitcher and bowl in the Chinese style sat atop a marble-topped washstand, the water within sloshing with each roll of the ship.

I changed into my silk pyjamas, a Christmas gift from HG, who insisted a gentleman should dress properly even for sleep. The storm continued its assault; waves crashed against the porthole, creating abstract patterns of water on the thick glass. Beyond lay absolute darkness, broken occasionally by the white foam of massive waves caught in the ship's lights.

The bed welcomed me with the embrace of expensive springs and down pillows. I lay there, allowing the ship's movement to rock me towards sleep. The boundary between consciousness and dreams grew delightfully fuzzy. In that twilight state, the storm's voice transformed into a symphony: the deep bass of the engines, the soprano whistle of wind through unseen cracks, the percussion of waves against steel.

A shout pierced my pleasant reverie.

"Murder! Murder!"

The cry came again, closer this time, unmistakable despite the storm's cacophony. My eyes snapped open, heart pounding. The voice belonged to Sir Edmund's secretary; I'd recognise that high-pitched tremor anywhere.

The peaceful limbo between sleep and wakefulness shattered. Reality crashed back with the force of the waves battering our vessel.

A new reality.

A life taken.

A murderer at large.

Chapter Two

CAN IT BE?

I threw back the bedding and squinted at my bedside clock: one in the morning. The ship's violent motion almost sent me sprawling as I grabbed my quilted dressing gown, fumbling with the silk cord while yanking open the door.

The corridor buzzed with activity. Passengers in various stages of undress clustered in doorways, their faces pale under the electric lights. Sir Edmund's secretary, Matthews, crouched against the wall; his head buried in trembling hands.

"There, there." Penelope Chase knelt beside him in a pink silk wrap, patting his shoulder. "Someone fetch him a brandy."

"What he needs is to tell us precisely what happened." HG's voice cut through the growing murmur. She swept down the corridor in a magnificent burgundy velvet night-gown, her silver hair perfectly arranged despite the late hour. "Stand aside, please."

The crowd turned to acknowledge my mentor. Even in

the middle of the night, HG commanded the same authority she wielded during daylight hours.

"Now then." She fixed Matthews with her penetrating gaze. "Where is Sir Edmund?"

"His cabin." Matthews lifted his head, revealing red-rimmed eyes. “I called to deliver some urgent papers he requested before retiring. Upon my arrival, my knock on the door went unanswered. Given the importance of the papers, I tried the door…it creaked open, and…when I entered, I… His voice cracked.

"Take your time," HG said, though her tone suggested he'd better not take too much of it.

"He sat at his desk, slumped over, as if he'd fallen asleep. I called out, but he gave no answer…no movement. I touched his hand..." Matthews swallowed hard. "He was… cold, and there was blood."

A collective gasp rippled through the onlookers. HG caught my eye and nodded; we both knew this would be no peaceful voyage.

"Someone bring the ship's doctor," she commanded. "Rex, might you fetch Inspector Whipple? I dare say seasickness will be the least of his concerns now."

I made my way to Whipple's cabin, expecting to find him hunched over a basin. The inspector answered the door in his pyjamas and a dressing gown. His face bore none of the greenish pallor I'd expected.

"Heavens, Inspector. You look as fresh as a daisy."

"Seasickness, my boy? Conquered it." Whipple patted his chest. "The quack provided a most effective tonic. Tasted like horse liniment but worked wonders. What's all the commotion?"

I explained the situation as we hurried back toward Sir

Edmund's cabin. "I rather thought your indisposition might hold until we reached New York."

"Nothing clears the head like murder, Rex," Whipple replied, his professional demeanour falling into place with each step.

The corridor remained crowded when we arrived. HG raised an eyebrow at Whipple's miraculous recovery but said nothing. Matthews still sat slumped against the wall, despite someone providing the fellow with a glass of brandy.

First Officer Grayson rounded the corner; his face edged with concern. "I hear there has been an unfortunate accident?"

Whipple addressed the first officer. "Whether by accident or design, a man is dead. Time will tell which of the two scenarios plays out."

He approached the half-open door to Blythe's stateroom and peered inside, careful not to disturb anything. After a moment's assessment, he turned to those assembled in the corridor.

"Until I declare otherwise, this area is now a crime scene, and I must ask you all to return to your cabins. I shall speak to each of you in due course." His voice carried unexpected authority despite his nightwear. “Mr. Grayson, please arrange for barriers to be placed at least twenty feet away on each side of the cabin. Oh, and I'll share my early impressions with the captain and you as soon as we finish here.

"Of course, Inspector," he replied. "And thank you for that."

I followed HG and Whipple into the cabin, using my handkerchief to close the door behind us. The room lay in half-darkness, lit only by a small desk lamp casting long shadows across the luxurious furnishings. A sickly, metallic odour hung in the air; the unmistakable scent of stale blood made my stomach tighten.

A work table, washstand, wardrobe, and a bed complete with side table furnished the simple room. I thought the sparse accommodation odd for such a wealthy man, yet, perhaps, in keeping with his frugal ways? It appeared his only vice amounted to cigars resting in an exquisite leather pouch, which sat with its lip off on the bedside table.

"Perhaps more illumination might be beneficial, Rex?" HG suggested, her voice steady despite the grim tableau before us.

Whipple nodded. "Yes, but let us be methodical. Rex, would you mind?"

I located the wall switch and flicked it on, revealing Sir Edmund slumped forward at his desk. His silver hair lay matted with crimson at the back of his head; a dark pool of blood had collected beneath his cheek on the polished mahogany surface. What struck as peculiar was the pristine state of the cabin. The bed remained made; the crystal decanter stood at the ready on the sideboard. Not a single item appeared disturbed or out of place.

"No sign of a struggle," I observed quietly.

"Indeed," HG agreed, her keen eyes surveying the sad interior. "Either Sir Edmund knew his attacker, or he never saw them coming."

Whipple investigated the wound on the body. His earlier seasickness forgotten as he slipped into his professional role.

"A stiff blow to the head," he pronounced after a moment. "No sign of a weapon."

"The assailant must have taken it with them," I suggested.

HG circled the desk, her burgundy dressing gown

almost touching the carpet. "Or disposed of it elsewhere. The ship offers countless opportunities to rid oneself of incriminating evidence...including that porthole."

Whipple and I turned to inspect the heavy brass frame, bolted tight shut against the inclement weather beyond.

"I'll inspect that later. For now, I'm more interested in the timing of events, "Whipple mused. "Most passengers would have been asleep, or at least in the cabins, and the corridors largely deserted."

"Yet Matthews was still about," I pointed out. "And who knows how many others might have been wandering the passageways?"

"The storm provides excellent cover for nefarious activities," HG added, glancing toward the porthole. "The noise, the distraction, the general discomfort made sleep elusive for many."

Just then, a muted knock on the door announced the doctor, Ambrose Livingstone.

'You requested that I attend?' the doctor announced in a well-spoken Scottish accent. The tall, thin fellow stood rigid and unsmiling, waiting to be invited in by Whipple.

'Thank you for coming so soon. I need your advice about this unfortunate fellow," Whipple pointed to the frozen figure of Sir Edmund. "You know, probable cause of death, time, and, of course, a death certificate."

Doctor Livingstone declined to respond. Instead, he approached the body without speaking or changing his demeanour. The cabin fell silent as he loomed over the body. Several seconds later, he reached into the leather bag he'd brought and retrieved a silver spatula and pulled on a pair of latex gloves.

I noticed a pang of jealousy in Whipple, which, I

suspected, lay in his inability to gain police access to the newfangled hand coverings.

Livingstone once again bent over Blythe's lifeless corpse. He brought the spatula to bear on the wound-site, parting the bloodied hair with precision.

"Blunt trauma," he announced. "A heavy object brought down with considerable force. The perpetrator is right-handed. Judging by the blood splatter pattern, the murderer landed the blow, then continued his sweep in the fashion of a golfer swinging his club. One blow was all that it took. Whoever did this knew what they were doing; not crazed rage or sloppiness, just a cold intent to kill."

Whipple straightened up, his face grim. "We must secure this room. I'll inform the captain that we have a murderer aboard his vessel. HG, would you like to join me? Rex, can you stand guard outside the cabin until I arrange for one of the captain's trusted stewards to relieve you?

Doctor Livingstone placed the spatula on a bleached cotton fabric square. Removing his gloves, he folded the bloodstained item and put it in his leather bag.

"My conclusions are, of course, preliminary, pending a full postmortem in New York. I should like to secure the body in the ship's mortuary as soon as possible, and no later than noon."

I glanced at my watch; 3.30 am.

"I'll let you know as soon as I'm able to release the body," replied Whipple.

The two men locked eyes, before Livingstone turned to HG. "Your Grace." With that, he left the cabin without uttering another word.

"Not one to pass the time of day with," I offered.

“Isn't it better than someone who talks endlessly about his or her work?” replied HG. Whipple appeared in a world of his own as he studied the body and cabin in minute detail. HG and I knew better than to interrupt this phase of the detective's investigative journey.

I stood guard outside Sir Edmund's cabin for an hour before a steward with a grim expression and a ship's officer's authorisation relieved me. By then, the storm had abated, leaving the ship riding more easily on the calmer sea. Dawn was breaking as I returned to my cabin for a hasty wash and change of clothes.

At breakfast, the first-class dining room hummed with subdued conversation. The news of Sir Edmund's demise had spread like influenza through a boarding school. Passengers whispered among themselves, eyeing our isolated table.

"Extraordinary how quickly gossip travels," HG remarked, delicately buttering a piece of toast. "I've already overheard three contradictory accounts of how poor Sir Edmund met his end."

Whipple nodded, his face drawn from lack of sleep. "The captain has agreed to make an announcement after breakfast, confirming only that there has been a death aboard. Nothing more."

"Very wise," said HG. "The less information, the fewer fabrications."

A steward approached with fresh coffee, his movements mechanical, his eyes darting nervously around the room. Watching him retreat, Whipple leaned forward.

"Rex, I wonder if you might track down Sir Edmund's personal steward. He might have noticed something unusual in the victim's behaviour yesterday."

"Certainly," I replied. "What will you two be doing?"

"The captain and first officer require a more detailed briefing," HG said. "We shall bring them up to speed while you conduct your inquiries."

After breakfast, I began my search for Sir Edmund's steward. None of the staff I questioned seemed willing to divulge his whereabouts until I encountered a maid emerging from one of the first-class suites.

"You'll be wanting Charlie Peabody, I expect," she said, wiping her hands on her apron. "Try the linen store on D Deck."

Martha Briggs introduced herself with a no-nonsense nod. She was a squat woman with iron-grey hair pulled back severely from a face that had seen decades of service. Her shrewd eyes missed nothing.

"Been with the line twenty-seven years, I have," she informed me proudly. "Seen everything there is to see on the high seas, and then some."

I made a mental note to cultivate Martha's acquaintance; such sources of information were invaluable.

Following her directions, I located the linen store. Inside, Charlie Peabody sat on an upturned bucket, staring at the white-painted steel wall. He seemed to count the rivets, his gaze unfocused, fingers trembling.

"Charlie?" I said in a quiet tone. "I'd like to ask you a few questions about Sir Edmund Blythe."

Charlie Peabody turned towards me, his shoulders hunched as if carrying an invisible burden. The steward was a slight man, no taller than five foot six, with thinning brown hair combed across a balding pate. His uniform, though immaculate, draped on his frame, suggesting recent weight loss. The skin around his eyes had the papery translucence that comes from sleepless nights, and a nervous tic pulled at the corner of his mouth.

He offered no greeting, only a vacant stare from watery blue eyes. The silence between us strained as I closed the linen room door with a soft click.

I approached him with deliberate casualness, the way one might a skittish animal. The clean-smelling room, filled with crisp white linens, contrasted with our grim situation.

Lowering myself to a crouch before him, I placed my hand on his forearm. The muscles beneath his sleeve were taut as bowstrings.

“This is tough for you, Charlie,” I said. "Sir Edmund was in your care, and now this has happened. I'm here to help in any way I can."

At the mention of Sir Edmund's name, a visible tremor ran through the steward. His eyes, until now unfocused, snapped to mine with alarming intensity.

His voice, breaking like ice, he whispered, “I saw nothing.” "Nothing at all, sir. I swear it."

I hadn't accused him of anything, which made his defensive response intriguing. Fear emanated from him in palpable waves, his hands fluttering like wounded birds in his lap.

"No one is suggesting you did," I assured him. "But perhaps you noticed something unusual about Sir Edmund yesterday? His mood, his visitors?"

Peabody's gaze darted to the door, then back to me, then to the small porthole as if calculating escape routes. Was this the nervousness of a man who knew too much, or the panic of one who had done something unforgivable? The distinction was crucial, yet impossible to determine from his demeanour alone.

"I just do my job, sir," he said, his voice barely audible. "That's all I ever do. Just my job."

I tried a different approach, still crouching next to the nervous steward.

"Tell me about your family, Charlie. Do you have anyone waiting for you back in Southampton?"

The change of subject worked like a charm. His shoulders relaxed, and a small, genuine smile replaced the anxious grimace.

"Yes, sir. My Bethany and our two little ones. We've got a small, terraced house in Millbrook, just a ten-minute omnibus ride from the docks."

"How old are your children?" I asked, watching his expression soften further.

"Alfie's ten now, sir. Smart as a whip, always with his nose in a book. And little May just turned six last month. She's the spitting image of her mother."

As Peabody continued, pride clear in his voice, I noticed the tremor in his hands had subsided. He lit up, describing Alfie winning a spelling bee and May aspiring to go to sea like her dad.

When I judged him at ease, I steered the conversation back to the matter at hand.

"About last night, Charlie. Could you walk me through your duties? Anything at all might help us understand what happened to Sir Edmund."

He nodded, more composed now. "Nothing unusual, sir. I made my rounds at eight, checking that all cabins were ready for their occupants' return. Fresh towels, turned-down beds, water carafes filled. Sir Edmund's cabin was no different from any other I entered..." He paused, a shadow crossing his face. "Except that..."

I fought to keep my expression neutral, though my pulse quickened. "Except for what, Charlie?"

The steward retreated inward again, weighing his words. After what felt like an eternity, he continued.

"Earlier, as I was checking the cabin next door to Sir Edmund's, I heard raised voices. Coming from his cabin, I mean."

"Could you make out what was being said?"

"No, sir. It's not my place to listen in on passengers' private conversations." He straightened his uniform jacket. "I've been with the company twelve years. Discretion is part of the job."

"Of course," I assured him. "But anything you recall might be important."

"I was called away by a junior steward, sir. New lad, needed showing how to make proper hospital corners on the beds." Peabody's brow furrowed in concentration. "As we passed Sir Edmund's cabin, I did catch one phrase clearly: 'You will, or I'll...'"

"Was it Sir Edmund speaking, or the other person?"

Peabody shook his head. "Couldn't tell you, sir. The young steward was chattering away about his aunt in Liverpool. Couldn't hear properly over him."

The Dowager's accommodations put my own modest cabin into context. Rich wood panelling and plush crimson velvet furniture created a luxurious atmosphere. HG and Whipple were already deep in conversation when I arrived, having just returned from their meeting with the captain and first officer.

"Ah, Rex," HG greeted me with a raised eyebrow. "I

trust your conversation with Sir Edmund's steward proved illuminating?"

I recounted my interview with Charlie Peabody, including the overheard fragment of conversation.

"Interesting," Whipple mused, tugging at his collar, which seemed perpetually too tight. "The steward's account aligns with our suspicion that Sir Edmund may have been a blackmailer…or he was the victim of blackmail."

"Why do you say that?" I asked.

Whipple sank into a plush armchair reminiscent of the Georgian style. "You'll recall Sir Edmund's argument with von Ritter yesterday? Considering the captain's slip just now, and your contribution, I postulate that someone is selling secrets.

HG gave me a warm glance as I pressed Whipple about their meeting, and how the captain and first officer had held themselves.

"As a matter of fact, most peculiar. Hardwick and Greyson expressed appropriate concern for the deceased, of course. However, there was a definite reluctance to engage beyond superficial cooperation. As for the cigar Captain Hardwick chewed on; ugh, certainly not one of Havana's finest, that is for sure…although it did look familiar. I'm sure I've seen that brand somewhere."

"As if they feared what our investigation might uncover," HG added, with an exaggerated sniff, while pouring tea from a silver service.

"The first officer did confirm one useful measure," Whipple continued. "He's ordered the telegraph room closed to all passengers. No news of Sir Edmund's death will reach shore until we determine it should do so, which means we must solve this dreadful riddle before we dock in New York."

HG's lips curved into a mischievous smile. "How fortunate the captain's second-in-command thought to secure communications. I wonder why such an elementary precaution didn't occur to Scotland Yard's finest?"

Whipple's nose received a vigorous scratch as his eyelids fluttered at remarkable speed. "Yes, well, moving on," he stammered, accepting a china cup from HG with unsteady hands. "We must contemplate our next steps."

I reminded Whipple that he'd mentioned a slip-up by the captain.

"Ah, yes. On the surface, an innocuous phrase, yet in the current circumstances, most telling. Hardwick noted that expecting reliable service aboard the ship was unrealistic.

HG noticed my confused air.

"Arthur means the captain is a bully, no matter how he appears before passengers. The steward who served us looked terrified."

For the next hour, we reviewed what little evidence we'd gathered. A mysterious cabin visitor, odd officer replies, and a public argument between guests added to the mystery. The timing of events painted a picture with crucial scenes missing.

"I suggest we interview the other prominent passengers after luncheon," HG declared. I find Penelope Chase to be most observant, and Madame Zelda's prediction feels unsettlingly accurate."

Whipple nodded. "And Klaus von Ritter. Yesterday's argument with Sir Edmund makes him our prime suspect.

I hesitated at the entrance to the Winter Garden restaurant. The magnificent space rose to a glass ceiling, which would have shown the sky if the storm's renewed fury hadn't obscured it. Potted palms created small islands of privacy between tables draped in pristine white linen.

Crystal lighting cast a warm glow over the assembled diners, making the silver cutlery gleam.

All eyes turned in our direction. Some guests wore expressions of exaggerated sorrow, as if mourning a distant relative whose inheritance they coveted. Others appeared anxious, their gazes darting about like startled fish in a pond. I wondered what each was thinking; more importantly, what each knew of the murder.

We took our seats at a table near the centre of the room. Lunch was perfunctory, everyone trying hard to appear 'normal'. The room was almost silent except for silver cutlery landing on fine china plates. Talk was limited, as if we were a church congregation waiting for Sunday Service to begin.

All remained subdued until Madame Zelda rose from her table. As she made her way to the exit, she meandered around several tables, delivering a white envelope to specific guests. Chatter in the restaurant increased as first one, then a second envelope changed hands, then a third. This continued until the woman reached our table.

"Your Grace," Madame Zelda said in a dour tone as she delivered a crisp white envelope into HG's hands. Then she was gone, her black dress trailing behind her like a shadow.

HG studied the envelope's surface before opening it to retrieve a simple card. "How extraordinary," she murmured. "The invitation requests our presence at a seance tonight at 10 pm."

Whipple dismissed the invitation with a wave of his fork. "A waste of time. They're all fake."

"That may be so," HG replied, her eyes twinkling with amusement, "but who knows what may come of the gathering? If nothing else, it shall be fun."

Whipple shook his head and took another bite of his

sausage. I noticed his complexion had improved since the previous evening; the ship dealt admirably with the rough seas, though the occasional lurch of the enormous vessel still sent waiters scrambling to steady themselves.

"I rather think we should attend," I whispered. "People often reveal more than they intend in such... theatrical settings."

At 9:55 pm, HG, Whipple, and I arrived at the smoking room, transformed for Madame Zelda's seance. The normally jovial, masculine retreat now exuded an unsettling atmosphere. Heavy curtains blocked any glimpse of the stormy night beyond, after someone drew them across the portholes. The room's elegant electric lights were extinguished. Instead, a dozen black candles flickered, casting grotesque shadows upon the wood-panelled walls. In a far, dark corner, a terrified steward observed unfolding events, unlucky enough to have been placed on fire watch against the naked flames.

Incense burned in brass holders, filling the room with swirling grey smoke. Their sickly sweet perfume, a mix of sandalwood and an overpowering exotic scent, permeated the air, causing my nostrils to twitch in discomfort.

A circular mahogany table, covered in blue velvet with silver symbols, was in the room's centre. The surface held several disturbing items: a skull topped with a lit candle, a glass-eyed raven, and ancient books made for an unsettling experience.

"How theatrical," HG whispered, her eyes twinkling with amusement.

We took our seats in the gathering. Klaus von Ritter sat rigid, his Teutonic features unreadable in the flickering light. Penelope fiddled with her pearls; Captain Hardwick stayed calm despite the strange surroundings. Matthews, Sir

Edmund's secretary, looked ill, his face ashen. First Officer Greyson completed our circle, leaving one chair empty.

Before this vacant seat sat a crystal ball upon an oak plinth, capturing and refracting the candlelight into eerie patterns. Beside it lay a deck of tarot cards, their edges worn from frequent handling.

Madame Zelda circled the room, trailing joss-sticks that left ribbons of smoke in her wake. Her lips moved in an unintelligible chant, her eyes unfocused as though peering into another realm. Her black dress seemed to absorb what little light existed, making her pale face float disembodied in the gloom.

Finally, she took her seat. Acknowledging none of us, she closed her eyes and drew a deep, lingering breath. The silence that followed was absolute.

"Join hands," Zelda commanded, her voice strangely distant and hollow. "The veil between worlds grows thin."

I felt HG's cool, steady fingers close around mine on one side, while Whipple's damp palm reluctantly clasped my other hand. He clearly found the spiritualist performance far less appealing than a confrontation with hardened criminals.

"We must form an unbroken circle," Madame Zelda continued, her eyes still closed. "Only then may the spirits cross over."

Captain Hardwick cleared his throat. "I say, is all this absolutely—"

"Silence!" Madame Zelda's eyes snapped open, fixing him with such intensity that the captain's protest died in his throat. "Doubters disturb the spirits."

The candle flames dipped, as though a collective breath had passed through the room. A curious sensation crept up my spine, as if sensing unseen eyes upon one's back.

"Does anyone from the spirit world wish to speak?" Madame Zelda intoned, her head tilted towards the ceiling.

The silence gnawed. I caught HG's eye; she raised a single eyebrow, her expression conveying amused scepticism. Then, without warning, the table beneath our hands gave a violent shudder.

Penelope Chase let out a small shriek. "What was that?"

"The spirits grow restless," Madame Zelda whispered.

As if in response to her words, one of the portholes burst open with a bang, allowing a gust of rain-laden wind to invade our sanctuary. The candles flickered, some extinguishing entirely. The crystal ball caught what remained of the light, glowing eerily in the semi-darkness.

"Ah, you're here," Madame Zelda breathed. Her body now rigid, fingers digging into the hands of those beside her as a cold, damp wind filled the room; its shrieking tone enough to chill the spine.

First Officer Greyson made to rise to secure the porthole, but Madame Zelda's sharp command froze him in place.

"Do not break the circle!"

The wind howled through the opening, sending papers flying and curtains billowing. Madame Zelda's breathing grew laboured; her head rolled back, exposing the pale column of her throat.

"I see him," she gasped. "Edmund! Edmund speaks!"

A fearsome gust of wind scattered the tarot cards. HG squeezed my hand hard. She pointed to von Ritter. One card had wedged itself under his port glass. I discerned the dreadful imagery: a skeletal knight in black armour astride a white horse, surrounded by figures who kneel in surrender...the symbol of death.

Madam Zelda's body shook. Matthews whimpered beside her; his face drained of all colour.

"He says... he says..." Her voice rose to a shriek. “Beware. Not every face belongs to one soul. There are those who wear a second mask, and before Liberty arises, their true selves may be the death of us all.”

With these words, she collapsed forward onto the table, her forehead striking the crystal ball with a dull thud. The ship chose that precise moment to pitch, plunging us into total darkness as the remaining candles surrendered to the storm.

Chapter Three

AN EAGLE EYE

Chaos reigned in the darkness. I heard Penelope Chase's frightened gasp, Matthews' continued whimpering, and the scrape of chairs as several people stood. Someone struck a match, illuminating Captain Hardwick's stern face as he relit two candles.

"Everyone, please remain calm," he ordered, moving to secure the flapping porthole.

In the restored half-light, Madame Zelda remained slumped across the table, her dark hair spread dramatically over the scattered tarot cards. Dr. Livingstone, who had been passing in the corridor, strode into the room.

"Merely fainted," he pronounced after a cursory examination. "The excitement, no doubt."

As First Officer Greyson escorted the shaken medium to her cabin, HG rose gracefully to her feet.

"I believe that concludes tonight's entertainment," she announced. "I suggest we repair to the Ascot Cocktail Bar. A restorative tot of rum or the like seems in order."

Ten minutes later, we were making our way through

the ship's corridors, the vessel pitching and rolling beneath our feet. The storm had intensified, forcing us to brace against the walls occasionally to maintain balance.

"What utter balderdash," Whipple muttered, steadying himself against a handrail. "Spirits indeed. The woman's a charlatan."

"Perhaps," HG replied, "though one must admit her timing with the porthole was rather impressive."

I chuckled. "You can't possibly believe she summoned Sir Edmund's ghost, HG."

"Of course not, dear boy, but consider this: charlatans often make excellent observers of human nature. They must be convincing."

Whipple snorted. "The only thing she observed was an opportunity to create hysteria."

"And yet," HG countered with a mischievous glance, "how curious that the death card should land before von Ritter, with whom Sir Edmund quarrelled so publicly."

"Coincidence," Whipple insisted as we rounded the corner.

"There are no coincidences in murder investigations, Arthur," HG replied. "Only patterns we have yet to recognise; you taught me that."

Whipple harrumphed and grabbed a handrail to steady himself.

The bar presented a welcome haven from both the storm and the evening's unsettling events. Panelled in rich mahogany with brass fixtures polished to a mirror shine, it exuded quiet luxury. Art deco candleholders allowed their charges to cast a warm glow over leather armchairs and intimate alcoves where passengers conversed in hushed tones. A pianist played softly in the corner, the gentle melody…no mean feat as a counterpoint to the storm's fury.

We settled around a small circular table in a quiet corner. Despite the late hour, several other passengers had sought refuge here, including the American steel magnate Cornelius Harrington and his much younger wife.

A steward in a crisp white jacket came toward our table, silver cocktail tray balanced well despite the ship's motion.

"Good evening. What may I bring you?"

"I'll have a whisky and soda," Whipple ordered, relaxing slightly now that we were away from the seance.

"A dry martini for me," HG said, "and perhaps a brandy Alexander for Rex?"

I nodded my agreement, settling into the plush leather armchair. The steward departed with our orders, navigating the tilting floor with practised ease.

"What do you make of von Ritter's reaction to that death card?" I asked, keeping my voice low.

"He certainly turned a shade paler," HG remarked. "Though whether from guilt or mere superstition remains to be seen."

Whipple leant forward. "I'm more interested in why Hardwick attended. Ship captains rarely participate in passenger entertainment, particularly something as frivolous as a seance."

"Perhaps he wished to keep an eye on proceedings," I suggested. "A murder aboard is hardly good for the shipping line's reputation."

Our drinks arrived, each presented with a flourish. Whipple eyed his whisky and soda with satisfaction while HG raised her martini glass in a silent toast.

The tranquil moment was interrupted by a tipsy Lily de Vere, the actress whose presence aboard had caused quite a stir among the male passengers. She wore an outlandish flapper outfit of emerald silk that clung to her figure, leaving little to the imagination.

"Well, hello there," she purred, her gaze fixing on me with predatory intensity. "Room for one more?"

Before anyone could answer, the ship lurched violently. Miss de Vere stumbled forward with a theatrical cry and collapsed onto the banquette beside me, pressing herself against my side.

"Oh my! How fortunate I landed somewhere soft," she giggled, making no effort to restore a proper distance between us.

I felt heat rising to my face and glanced helplessly at HG, who merely sipped her martini with a sphinx-like smile.

"The, um, weather is quite awful at present," I stammered, shifting awkwardly.

Lily giggled again, somehow managing to press even closer. "I know I'm safe with a strong, good-looking man like you!"

"The events of last night were quite a tragedy," I tried, changing the topic.

Lily's playful demeanour faltered. "Sir Edmund? I hated that man. Was always leering at me." She stretched a gloved hand toward my untouched brandy Alexander. "Mind if I have a sip? I'm simply parched."

As she reached across, I noticed her white glove was torn at the wrist, and what appeared to be a dark stain marred the delicate fabric. Our eyes met, and something flickered behind her theatrical charm; cold and calculating.

I stared at the stain on Lily's glove, my sleuthing instincts stirring despite her overwhelming proximity. Before I could formulate a tactful question about it, the cocktail bar's door swung open.

"There you are, Lily! If you turn any more heads, darling, they'll have to give us our own deck."

A slender young woman with a fashionably bobbed haircut and a silver beaded dress that caught the light with every movement sashayed toward us. Her kohl-rimmed eyes sparkled with mischief as she slipped an arm around Lily's waist, planting a tipsy smooch on her cheek.

She turned a teasing smile on me. "Careful, sweetheart. This one's the bee's knees, and twice as dizzy after champagne!"

Lily giggled, rising from her seat with the grace of a performer. "You're just jealous I found him first, Dottie. She leaned, putting her lips on my cheek in a drawn-out kiss; I was unable to move. "Until next time, handsome."

The pair meandered out of the bar, arms linked, leaving behind a cloud of expensive perfume and the echo of their laughter. I remained motionless, my cheek burning where Lily's lips had touched it.

HG dissolved into peals of laughter, her shoulders shaking as she tried to maintain some semblance of decorum. Whipple, meanwhile, narrowed his eyes at the departing women, studying them with the same intensity he reserved for prime suspects.

"I believe you've made quite an impression, Rex," HG managed between chuckles. "Though perhaps not the sort you'd hoped for in your role as an amateur detective."

I cleared my throat, straightening my dinner jacket. "She had a stain on her glove. Dark, possibly—"

"Blood?" Whipple interrupted, suddenly alert.

"Or red wine, or lipstick, or any number of things," I admitted reluctantly.

HG's laughter subsided, though her eyes still danced with amusement. "Perhaps you should fortify yourself after such an ordeal. Your drink remains untouched."

I glanced down at my glass and without thinking, downed the sweet concoction in one continuous gulp. The potent mixture of brandy, crème de cacao and cream hit my throat with unexpected force, sending me into a fit of coughing.

"Bravo," HG said, with gentle mockery. "I don't believe I've seen anyone dispatch a cocktail with such determination since the Prince of Wales at the Derby last summer."

I got my composure back step by step, dabbing my mouth with a napkin while silently cursing my lack of sophistication. My embarrassment faded as I noticed Whipple's sudden alertness, his gaze fixed on a point beyond my shoulder. His posture had stiffened, resembling a pointer dog that had detected a scent.

HG caught my eye with a subtle glance. "It's von Ritter," she murmured. "The timing could not be better."

Before she finished speaking, Whipple was on his feet, moving with surprising agility for a man of his build. I resisted the urge to turn around; in polite society, one did not gawk like a curious schoolboy. Instead, I watched from the corner of my eye as Whipple intercepted von Ritter halfway between the entrance and the bar.

"A whisky for Herr von Ritter," Whipple called to a passing steward, then gestured toward the table with an inviting sweep of his arm.

Von Ritter followed, his face impassive. He was immaculately dressed in evening attire that emphasised his tall, lean frame. A duelling scar across his left cheek became apparent as he approached.

"Your Grace," he greeted HG with a formal bow. "It's a

pleasure to see you again." His English was impeccable, betrayed only by the slightest Germanic precision in his consonants.

He gave me a brief greeting before pulling up a chair from a nearby table and joining our circle. The steward arrived with his whisky, which von Ritter accepted with a curt nod.

"A dreadful crossing so far," he remarked, directing his comment to HG, "Though I understand the weather should improve soon."

"One can only hope," HG replied pleasantly.

Von Ritter took a measured sip of his whisky. "And this terrible tragedy with Sir Edmund. Most distressing."

"Indeed," HG agreed.

"I didn't know the man well," von Ritter continued, rotating his glass slowly between long fingers. "I am saddened for his family, if he has any."

HG's expression remained composed, but I recognised the gleam in her eye; it was the same look she wore when setting a trap at chess.

"Yet you knew him well enough to have a blazing row with the fellow in public," she said, her tone conversational but with steel beneath the velvet.

Von Ritter's hand paused mid-rotation. For the briefest moment, something flickered across his face; then his composure returned, smooth as polished marble.

"Ah," he said softly. "You observed our minor dispute."

"A disagreement, yes," von Ritter conceded. "Business matters can become heated, particularly when large sums are involved."

HG raised an eyebrow. "Such a disturbance was hard for anyone in the vicinity to be unaware of."

Von Ritter tilted his head playfully. "True, but still, I did not know the...how do you say...chap, well. One mustn't confuse business with friendly relations."

I glanced at Whipple, noting his increasing agitation. His fingers drummed silently against his thigh, yet he seemed oddly reluctant to join the verbal sparring match unfolding before us. I couldn't understand his hesitation; this was precisely the opportunity we needed.

HG took another sip of her cocktail without taking her eyes off von Ritter. The crystal glass glinted as she lowered it, her movements deliberate and unhurried.

"How is your homeland doing?" HG asked pointedly.

Von Ritter, the epitome of decorum, replied without hesitation, "It is in pieces, as I'm sure you know, Your Grace. The fools who condemned Germany to penury at Versailles two years ago continue to gloat at my country's expense. However, new voices are beginning to speak for my country, and those that now berate us shall change their opinion one day."

His somber tone gave way to something lighter. "But why are we being so serious, when things go so well for our class?" Von Ritter held his tumbler towards HG as if making a toast.

HG's glass remained resolutely in her lap. Her expression cooled several degrees, though her voice maintained its cultured calm. "I find it curious that you speak of class, Herr von Ritter, when your own background is somewhat... shall we say, recently elevated?"

The German's face became hard for an instant before he composed himself. I sensed we had touched a nerve, though I couldn't determine whether it was relevant to our investigation or merely wounded pride.

"Your Grace has been misinformed," he replied in an

even tone. "The von Ritters have held estates in Bavaria since the sixteenth century."

"How fascinating," HG murmured. "And yet I recall meeting a merchant named simply Klaus Ritter in Berlin before the war. The resemblance is quite remarkable."

The silence that followed was broken only by the distant sound of the ship's engines and the muffled crash of waves against the hull. Von Ritter's smile remained fixed, but something cold and calculating had entered his gaze.

I could stand Whipple's inaction no more. The detective continued to be oddly reticent, leaving HG to conduct what was essentially a police interview. I leant forward, fixing von Ritter with what I hoped was an authoritative stare.

"What exactly was the nature of your business dealings with Sir Edmund?"

Von Ritter ignored me for a second or two while he sipped his drink. His deliberate discourtesy made my cheeks burn. At last he talked without glancing at me.

"Only the young and inexperienced might ask such an impertinent question."

I was stumped. The casual dismissal left me floundering for a response that wouldn't sound childish or petulant. HG stepped in smoothly.

"Yet none-the-less valid?"

Von Ritter calmly placed his drink down. "As you say, Your Grace. As you would expect, the matter concerned money, a debt, owed by the titled gentleman to me. If you must know, he insisted on trying to pay me back in German Marks instead of British Pounds. You know my country's currency is worthless due to the interference of several nations, including yours, Your Grace. Do you realise my countrymen now take their Marks stacked in wheelbarrows just to buy a loaf of bread? Can you imagine that happening in London, or Paris, or New York? The man took me for a fool and—"

"Paid the price," HG interrupted.

Von Ritter's eyes narrowed. "A poor choice of words, Your Grace. I merely meant he owed me a considerable sum, and I required payment in a currency of actual value."

"Enough to kill for?" I blurted out.

A ghost of a smile played across von Ritter's scarred face. "My dear young man, if I eliminated everyone who owed me money, half the aristocracy of Europe would be in their graves." He stood, straightening his immaculate dinner jacket. "Now, if you'll excuse me, I find this line of questioning tiresome. Good evening, Your Grace."

With a bow to HG, he departed, leaving his half-finished whisky on the table.

"Well," I said, deflated, "that was hardly illuminating."

HG's eyes followed von Ritter's retreating figure. "On the contrary, Rex. Our German friend just revealed a great deal more than he intended."

I turned to Whipple and asked why he'd remained silent.

"Diplomatic immunity," he replied through gritted teeth.

"You see, Rex," HG said. "Had Arthur said anything that sounded as an official enquiry, Klaus von Ritter would have closed up like a clam, and we should have discovered nothing."

"But we didn't."

"Oh, but we did, Rex. The diplomat laid bare his reason for killing Sir Edmund."

I stared at HG, astonished. "What motive? He denied any involvement

"Precisely," HG replied, her eyes twinkling with that familiar gleam I'd come to recognise when she'd spotted something significant. "He protested rather too emphatically, wouldn't you say?"

Whipple nodded thoughtfully. "The matter of the German currency. Worthless paper instead of solid British Pounds."

"And there's our motive," HG concluded, sipping her tea. "Financial ruin can drive even the most civilised men to desperate acts."

A figure appeared at our breakfast table. Lily de Vere stood swaying, clutching the back of an empty chair. Her complexion had a distinctly greenish tinge, and her usually immaculate hair hung limply around her face.

"Good morning," she mumbled, blinking rapidly in the bright light. "I was hoping I might—"

"Sit down before you fall down, my dear," HG interjected, gesturing to the empty chair.

Lily collapsed into it with visible relief. She turned towards me, batting her eyelashes in what I assumed was meant to be an alluring manner. I became aware of the heat rising to my cheeks.

"I wanted to apologise for my behaviour last evening," she began. "It was most unladylike to—"

Her words were cut short by the arrival of a steward bearing our breakfast meals on a silver tray. The rich aromas wafted across the table: smoked salmon for HG, kedgeree for me, and a full English breakfast for Whipple, complete with mushrooms and black pudding.

Miss de Vere's pale face turned positively ashen. She made a strangled sound and attempted to stand, only to crumple in a heap at my feet.

I knelt beside her, my heart racing. “Lily? Can you hear me?"

HG reached calmly into her clutch bag and withdrew a small glass bottle. "Wave some of this under the gal's nose," she instructed, handing it over. "Never fails."

I removed the crystal stopper and wafted the pungent contents beneath Lily’s nose. The effect was instantaneous. She jerked upright, coughing and spluttering.

"There we are," I said, taking her hand and patting it gently.

"She's not a dog, Rex. Put her down at once," HG said drily.

I ignored the suggestion, gazing into Lily’s striking blue eyes. "Are you quite well?"

She offered me a tremulous smile. "I am now with you as my protector, and things always seem less alarming, once one accepts they cannot be changed”.

"Ye gods," HG groaned.

Whipple, meanwhile, had not allowed the drama to interfere with his breakfast, and remained content working his way through a second sausage partially wrapped with fried egg.

A stern-looking woman in her early forties strode into the restaurant with a wheelchair, guided by an officer from the ship. Her crisp white uniform and no-nonsense demeanour marked her instantly as the vessel's nurse.

"I understand there's been a fainting spell?" She asked, her voice clipped and efficient.

"Miss de Vere appcars to be suffering from the effects of the sea," I explained, still kneeling beside Lily.

The nurse assessed the situation with clinical detachment. "Sir, would you kindly assist me in getting Miss de Vere into the wheelchair?"

I slipped an arm around her waist and helped her to her feet. She leant against me, perhaps more heavily than strictly necessary, her perfume enveloping me in a cloud of jasmine and something more exotic.

"I believe this gentleman should escort me to my cabin," Lily murmured, her fingers clutching at my lapel. "I'd feel so much safer with him."

The nurse's expression hardened. "That would be most inappropriate, My dear. I am perfectly capable of seeing to your needs."

"But—"

"No arguments, please. The motion sickness tablets I have will set you right in no time."

I couldn't hide my disappointment as Lily settled into the wheelchair, her forlorn expression following me as the nurse wheeled her briskly from the restaurant.

"My, my," HG remarked, watching me return to my seat. "That was quite a performance from our Miss de Vere. And you, my dear boy, looked like a puppy denied its favourite bone."

"I was merely being polite."

"Is that what they're calling it these days? In my time, we called it 'making calf eyes'."

Whipple pushed his empty plate away and took a final, noisy slurp of tea. "I intend to search Sir Edmund's cabin more thoroughly this morning. Would you care to join me?"

His question came so out of the blue, so disconnected from the previous fifteen minutes, that HG and I exchanged amused glances. Whipple had clearly been inhabiting his own world, oblivious to the minor drama that had just unfolded.

"We'd be delighted," HG replied, folding her napkin precisely.

Minutes later, we stood outside the cabin. Whipple extracted a key from his waistcoat pocket and inserted it into the lock. He turned it, then frowned.

"The door is unlocked. How curious."

I perceived a peculiar sensation as we entered the room; a cold tingle shooting down my spine. Something felt strange, wrong somehow. The curtain obscured the port-hole, casting the compact space into semi-darkness, as though in mourning for its last inhabitant.

"Be careful not to disturb anything," Whipple reminded us, his voice hushed in the gloomy cabin.

HG nodded and moved towards the wardrobe, while Whipple returned to the table where Sir Edmund had met his end. I drifted to the bedside table, drawn by its mundane ordinariness in this room of death.

"Anything of interest in there, Rex?" HG asked, her gloved hands carefully rifling through the pockets of Sir Edmund's evening wear.

"Nothing yet," I replied, sliding open the small drawer beneath the tabletop. "Only a Gideon Bible."

I closed the cabinet harder than I'd intended, producing a hollow thud. The sound caught everyone's attention.

"What was that?" Whipple asked, looking up from his examination of the writing desk.

"I'm not certain," I admitted. "It sounded like something fell."

Whipple approached the bed, his brow furrowed. He dropped to his hands and knees, peering beneath the iron bed frame. After a moment's consideration, he stretched his arm under the bed-base, grunting with the effort.

"Anything?" HG inquired, abandoning her search of the wardrobe.

Whipple extracted himself with considerable effort, his

face flushed. "I'm getting too old for this," he muttered, now on his knees beside the bed.

He held the object delicately between his handkerchief-covered finger and thumb.

"Well, well," he said. "I wonder how this ended up behind the headboard."

HG and I moved closer. Whipple carefully unfolded his handkerchief to reveal a small brooch. Even in the dim light, I could see dark stains on its ornate surface.

"Is that blood?" I asked, leaning in for a better look.

"I rather think it is," Whipple replied. "And unless I'm very much mistaken, this is no ordinary piece of jewellery."

HG adjusted her spectacles. "That is the Royal Prussian Eagle, if I'm not mistaken. What on earth was Sir Edmund doing with a German military decoration?"

The brooch gleamed in Whipple's handkerchief, its golden wings splattered with what could only be Sir Edmund's blood.

Chapter Four

DANGEROUS DOCUMENTS

I stood at the railing, watching the sea's violent dance with a strange fascination. The Britannic Star rose and fell with each swell, her steel hull groaning in protest against nature's onslaught. Whipple had declined our invitation to "experience the invigorating sea air," as HG had put it. He muttered something about paperwork and the purser's office as he retreated below decks.

"He's missing a magnificent display," HG remarked, linking her arm through mine. Several hatpins secured her hat, creating the unsettling impression that they had passed through her skull.

The grey sky bled into the churning waters, creating a disorienting monotone world where the horizon ceased to exist. Droplets of icy spray lashed our faces, each one feeling like a tiny needle against my skin.

"Bracing, isn't it?" HG shouted over the wind's howl, looking most jubilant. While all other ladies of her station had retreated to the comfort of the lounges, the Dowager thrived in this elemental chaos.

"If by 'bracing' you mean 'thoroughly unpleasant,' then yes," I replied, though I couldn't help smiling at her enthusiasm.

We crept around the stern, clutching the rail with gloved hands. As we rounded the corner, the wind's assault stopped, creating an unexpected pocket of calm.

"How curious," I noted, releasing my death grip on the railing. "The ship's structure creates a perfect blind spot."

HG nodded. "Naval architecture at its finest. Even fury has its limitations."

We stepped into a small alcove, protected from the worst of the weather. I extracted my handkerchief and dabbed at my face, removing the salty residue that stung my eyes.

A violent wave crashed against the hull, sending spray over the railing and into our hidden bolthole. HG remained unperturbed.

"What of Madame Zelda?" I suggested. "Her prediction about death riding white horses seems uncannily prescient."

"Theatrical frauds often cultivate an air of prescience, Rex. Though I grant you, her performance at the seance was remarkably well-orchestrated. Almost as if she knew precisely what would unfold."

"And Lily de Vere? Her fainting spell this morning seemed—"

HG's lips curved into a small smile. "Women of her ilk have elevated fainting to an art form. Though I wonder if her pallor suggested something beyond mere theatrics…and alcohol."

She turned with sudden purpose. "We must speak with Matthews again. Sir Edmund's secretary will know his employer's business affairs intimately. And I should like to examine Sir Edmund's papers before the fellow does something rash; perhaps in an attempt to protect his former employer."

As HG and I prepared to return inside, I opened my mouth to suggest we speak with Matthews straightaway, but the words died on my lips. A peculiar heaviness had settled over me, quite unrelated to our investigation.

"Are you quite alright?" HG asked, studying my face. "Is the ship's motion too much for you?"

I shook my head, meeting her concerned gaze. "I know it sounds ridiculous, but I've been thinking about my father quite a lot recently."

HG's expression softened. She guided me back to the sheltered alcove. "There's nothing ridiculous about that, Rex."

The sea spray continued its assault on the deck beyond our sanctuary. "It's this voyage, I suppose. I've always wondered whether he went to America."

HG endured, giving me space to continue.

"I remember so little of that evening," I said, my voice barely audible above the wind. "Just the cold, the gates of your children's home in London, and his slumped outline as he walked off into the fog."

"You were very young," HG reminded me gently.

"I know. But lately I've been wondering if he fled to escape his troubles, whatever they were." I straightened my shoulders, embarrassed by this uncharacteristic display of sentiment. "Perhaps he started a new life in America. People do, don't they?"

"It's possible," HG conceded, though her tone suggested she thought it unlikely. "What I can tell you is that your father was a man of integrity and kindness. Traits abominably exploited by unscrupulous persons around him. We've spoken before about what a talented actor and magician he was, and the money he'd accumulated. Left cheated and destitute, it took bravery and a deep love to give up his son, rather than allow you to experience heaven knows what as the son of a debtor. Think of your father fondly, dear Rex. If he still lives, who knows, perhaps one day he may walk back into your life."

Her frankness was refreshing; HG never patronised me with false comfort.

"The not knowing is the hardest part," I admitted. "I've built a thousand different stories in my head over the years."

"And in each one, I imagine, he had an interesting reason for his actions."

I nodded, unable to deny it.

"That speaks to your character," HG said. "You've grown into a fine young man, Rex. Your father's wretched decision proved to be the correct one, wouldn't you say?"

Emboldened by HG's close attention, I summoned the courage to ask a question that had troubled me for years but felt I could not ask. "And he never wrote to the Horizons Children's Home, or yourself?" My gaze dropped for fear of censure for breaking her trust.

The ship lurched, shattering the moment. HG gripped me with surprising strength. The moment for answers had passed.

"Now," she said, resuming her usual brisk manner, "we have a murderer to catch, and I believe Matthews may hold several of our missing pieces. Shall we?"

I struggled to pull the teak door against the wind, feeling as though I were wrestling a bear rather than mere wood and brass. With a last heave, HG and I tumbled inside, the door slamming shut behind us with a resounding thud. The sudden stillness of the interior corridor felt almost unnatural after the tempest outside.

Yet I felt HG's gaze settle on me. Would she have answered my question had the Atlantic Ocean not intervened?

"Heavens," HG remarked, patting her immaculate coiffure with practiced nonchalance. "One might think Neptune himself had a personal vendetta against this vessel."

We mopped our foreheads, the contrast between the howling gale outside and the plush interior of the ship almost comical. The corridor's gilt-framed mirrors betrayed our bedraggled appearance.

"Time for a nice cup of Earl Grey, wouldn't you say, Rex?" HG suggested, straightening her jacket. "Nothing settles the nerves like properly brewed tea."

"Capital idea," I agreed.

A familiar figure caught my attention. Inspector Whipple was close to a large aspidistra, mumbling to himself, while looking at his notebook with unusual excitement.

"Are you quite well, Arthur?" HG called out, her tone gently teasing. "You look rather like a man who's found sixpence and lost a shilling."

Whipple's face lit up. "Ah, there you are." He hurried toward us, clutching his notebook. "I have information that simply cannot wait."

The Palm Court was quiet, caused by most passengers having retreated to their cabins to wait out the storm. A piano quartet endeavoured to play the latest tunes. I thought their rendition of Zez Confrey's hit, *Stumbling*, apposite, given the ship's movement. Amused, yet respectful of their sterling efforts, we settled at a table near a porthole, where the tumult lashed against the glass with rhythmic fury.

A steward appeared soon after, taking our order with the efficiency that defined first-class service. HG requested Earl Grey with a slice of lemon. I asked for the same, while Whipple opted for what he called "normal tea, none of that smelly stuff, if you don't mind."

Once our tea and iced fancies arrived, HG fixed Whipple with an expectant gaze. "Well, out with it, Arthur. What have you to tell us?"

Whipple's hands encircled his teacup as though drawing warmth from its contents. The ship lurched, sending a splash of tea onto the pristine tablecloth. He dabbed at the spill absentmindedly with his napkin.

"I had the most enlightening conversation with the purser this morning," he began, his voice lowered despite our relative isolation. "Fellow named Barrington. Frightfully stuffy at first, all 'ship's regulations' this and 'passenger confidentiality' that."

Whipple's nervousness around rich people vanished when he discussed his successful investigations, no matter how small.

"Then I noticed a photograph on his desk. The man in his cricket whites, you see. Turns out he played for the Hampshire Second XI before the war." Whipple's eyes gleamed. "Once we got talking about the 1913 county championship and Woolley's batting average, he became positively garrulous."

HG stirred her tea with practiced elegance. "And I presume this cricketing camaraderie yielded more than just sporting reminiscences?"

"Indeed, it did." Whipple leaned forward, his voice dropping further. "The purser's office contains a safe where first-class passengers store their valuables. Barrington maintains a ledger of everything that goes in and out."

"Did Sir Edmund make use of this service?" HG asked.

"Oddly, no. But several of our suspects did." Whipple flipped open his notebook. Zelda declared the crystals were potent. Barrington thought they looked like fake gems.

I suppressed a smile as Whipple continued.

Lady Penelope Chase kept three hatboxes. She called them "emergency millinery" for when she had to go to social events unexpectedly, and she changed them every day.

HG's eyebrow curved. "Emergency millinery? One wonders what constitutes a hat emergency at sea."

"Most interesting," Whipple continued, "von Ritter deposited a locked leather portfolio just hours before Sir Edmund's murder. Withdrew it the following morning looking, in Barrington's words, 'as nervous as a cat in a room full of rocking chairs.'"

Rex noted how Whipple's typical class-consciousness disappeared when in professional mode. The inspector forgot himself, animated by the chase.

"Did the purser happen to mention whether anything unusual was placed in or removed from the safe yesterday?" HG asked.

"That's just it." Whipple tapped his notebook. "According to Barrington, Matthews—Sir Edmund's secretary—came to deposit something after dinner. A large manila envelope, sealed with wax. Curiously, he returned for it before breakfast this morning."

HG set her teacup down with deliberate precision, the fine china making scarcely a sound against its saucer. "Then we must discover what lies within that envelope."

"Matthews strikes me as the jumpy sort," I offered.

"Corner him too directly, and he might well destroy whatever evidence it contains."

"Quite right. The man practically vibrated with anxiety when we encountered him after the murder. One wrong word, and he may panic."

Whipple consulted his notes again. "Barrington mentioned that Matthews's cabin is on B Deck, starboard side. Number B-47."

"A frontal approach would be foolish," HG said. "We need him away from his cabin, preferably somewhere public where he cannot simply flee."

The ship lurched, sending our teacups sliding. I steadied them before continuing. "What if we summoned him under official pretences? Whipple could request his presence in the captain's quarters for a formal statement."

"Too obvious," Whipple countered. "He'd grow suspicious immediately, might dispose of the envelope on the way."

HG's expression brightened. "Rex, you mentioned the steward Charlie Peabody has disappeared?"

"Martha said he was ill, though she seemed rather unconvincing about it."

"Perfect." HG leaned forward conspiratorially. "Rex, you shall express concern for young Charlie's welfare to Matthews. Play the sympathetic gentleman worried about the fellow. Suggest Matthews accompany you to the crew quarters to enquire after him."

I understood my task only too well.

"While you're gone, Arthur shall conduct a swift but thorough search of Matthews's cabin." HG turned to Whipple. "Can you manage a locked cabin door?"

The inspector blushed. "I, well, that is to say—"

"Come now, Arthur. Surely Scotland Yard provides instruction in such necessary skills?"

Whipple coughed into his fist. "There was a course. *Lock-picking for the informed detective*. It felt rather underhanded, but yes, I can manage most mechanisms, although without a warrant, technically I'm committing—."

"Excellent," HG cut in, her smile positively feline. "Rex, keep Matthews occupied for, shall we say, half-an-hour? That provides ample time for a proper search."

"And if Matthews refuses to accompany me?" I asked.

"Then you must make it up as you go, dear."

Within ten-minutes I stood outside cabin B-47. I straightened my tie, took a breath, and knocked on Matthews's door; my knuckles hammering against the wood. The corridor remained still, save for the whisper of the ship's movement beneath my feet. After what felt like an age, footsteps shuffled behind the door, and the cautious click of a latch sounded.

Mathews appeared, a dishevelled figure clad in a crumpled suit, hair askew from sleep. His eyes, bleary and bloodshot, blinked several times as though attempting to chase away a stubborn dream.

"Apologies for the intrusion," I began, imbuing my voice with an earnest concern. "There's an urgent matter I must discuss with you."

His brow furrowed in confusion but, to my relief, he swung the door open, gesturing for me to enter. I stepped into the small cabin, plainly furnished, feeling the closeness of the air, thick with the scent of musty books and shoes in need of a deodoriser. Mathews plonked himself on the ruffled bed cover, the springs creaking in protest.

"What's this about, then?" His voice carried a hint of irritation, but I soldiered on.

"It's Charlie Peabody," I replied, my gaze sweeping the cabin as I paced, noting the scattered ledgers. "The fellow has vanished. It's imperative we find him before the higher-ups realise he's abandoned his post."

Matthews's frown deepened, lines etching themselves across his brow. "And what does that have to do with me?"

"Well," I hesitated for dramatic effect, "I had a word with Charlie after all the…unpleasantness with Sir Edmund, and he mentioned you." I fixed him with a look of earnest admiration. "Had much to say about what a sound fellow you are, how you've conducted yourself with such dignity under trying circumstances."

A flicker of something akin to pride crossed Matthews's weary features. He wriggled, shuffling his limbs. Despite himself, I could see a sliver of satisfaction beneath his cautious exterior.

"Charlie said that, about me?"

"Took it upon himself to sing your praises," I assured, my tone one of confiding warmth. "Helped him cope with things, I think, seeing you so stalwart in the face of tragedy."

The tension in the room eased, lessening whatever barrier his waking confusion had thrown up.

"All right," Mathews sighed, resignation mingling with the satisfaction. "I'll help you. It can't hurt to make sure the rascal hasn't gotten himself into mischief."

Together, we left the cabin; the door closing with a soft click, and Mathews' attention to ensuring the lock engaged with a swift turn of the key.

After I spent half an hour taking poor Mathews on a long and pointless search of the ship, we went back to his room. Once inside, we commiserated with each other concerning Charlie's likely punishment when the captain found out. I congratulated myself for maintaining the lie, but the sham bothered me...something HG wouldn't have approved of.

I scanned the small cabin, hoping to find some clue that Whipple had been there. A book out of place , perhaps, or a drawer left open. Anything to show he'd investigated the matter. To my relief, everything appeared untouched. The inspector had been thorough; I inwardly congratulated him on his expertise.

"Well, thank you for your help, Matthews," I said, moving toward the door, eager to rejoin Whipple and discover what he'd found. "I'm sure Charlie will turn up in time."

Matthews remained rooted in place, his expression troubled. The man's haunted eyes revealed shadows and spoke of more than fatigue.

"Are you quite all right?" I asked, stepping back from the door. "You mustn't worry about Charlie. It's not your responsibility, after all."

He shook his head. "It's not Charlie that's bothering me."

Something in his voice—a tremor of dread, perhaps—caught my attention. I returned to the centre of the room and lowered myself into the small desk chair.

"What is it, then?" I asked. "Something seems to be troubling you greatly."

Matthews regarded me with a long, penetrating stare, as though taking my measure. The ship pitched, but neither of us looked away.

"If there's anything I can do to help..." I prompted.

Breaking eye contact at last, Matthews turned toward the porthole, his gaze fixed on the heavy curtain that covered it. I watched, intrigued, as he stepped over to the fabric, ripped at a seam, and withdrew a large manila envelope.

"That's a nice trick," I said, genuinely impressed.

Matthews glanced down at the envelope in his hands, then back at me. "I hid it between the curtain and the lining. A couple of quick stitches is all it took to keep its contents safe."

He extended the envelope toward me. I paused before accepting it, feeling its substantial weight.

"What's so important?" I asked, running my thumb along the sealed edge.

"You'll see," Matthews replied, his voice barely above a whisper. He glanced nervously at the door, then back to me. "No one must know I had it, or it will surely cost me my life. The inspector must see the contents. What he does about matters is for him to judge."

The envelope grew heavier in my hands. Whatever lay within, Matthews believed it worth risking his life to preserve—and now he'd entrusted that risk to me.

I knocked on HG's stateroom door, waited a moment, then entered to discover a rather dismal tableau. Whipple sat hunched in a wingback chair, his expression thunderous. A half-empty decanter of whisky stood sentinel on the side table. HG perched on the edge of her bed, a sherry glass balanced between her fingers, the beginning of a concerned frown creasing her aristocratic features.

"Ah, Rex," HG said, her tone carefully modulated. "Do come in."

"How did your search of Matthews' cabin go?" I asked Whipple, closing the door behind me.

Whipple huffed, rubbing a crystal tumbler between his palms as though hoping to conjure a genie. "Waste of my time," he muttered, then tossed back the remaining whisky in one swift movement. "Not a blessed thing of interest. Either Matthews is innocent, or he's cleverer than I gave him credit for."

I couldn't suppress a smile as I produced the manila envelope from inside my jacket with a flourish.

Whipple's eyes widened comically. His mouth fell open, then snapped shut with an audible click.

HG's lips curled into a delicious smile. "My dear boy, what have you got there?"

"I think this is what evaded you?" I said to Whipple, unable to keep a hint of triumph from my voice.

"Crikey" Whipple spluttered. "How on earth—"

"Matthews gave it to me," I explained, relishing their astonishment. "After our wild-goose chase, he seemed to reach some kind of decision. Had it hidden inside the lining of his curtains. Quite ingenious, really. Said it might cost him his life, but you needed to see it."

Whipple stared at me, then at the envelope, then back at me again.

"Are you going to hand it over, or shall we admire the thing all evening?" HG asked, her tone dry but her eyes dancing with amusement.

I passed the envelope to Whipple, who accepted it with reverent hands.

"Still sealed," he observed, turning it over.

I nodded. "Thought it best to leave that honour to you."

Whipple sliced the envelope open with a silver letter opener HG provided. He tipped the contents onto the counterpane of HG's bed as she leaned forward, her curiosity clear.

Four small envelopes tumbled out first, all already opened, their flaps ripped. Whipple arranged them in a neat row before extracting a legal document folded lengthwise.

I moved closer, making out the words "Last Will" printed in Gothic Script across the top margin as Whipple laid it beside the letters.

HG's eyes gleamed with the satisfaction of a predator catching the scent of prey. "Well, well," she murmured, reaching for the nearest envelope. "What have we here?"

HG plucked the letters with a gloved hand, while Whipple unfolded the document he held, smoothing its creases against the bedspread. The room fell silent except for the distant wail of the storm outside. Their expressions shifted from curiosity to astonishment as they devoured the contents.

"Blackmail!" HG suddenly exclaimed, wafting the gaggle of envelopes in the air like a winning hand at bridge. At that exact moment, Whipple looked up from the larger document, his face flushed with discovery.

"Fraud," he announced solemnly.

A stunned silence fell between us, heavy with implication. The ship lurched beneath our feet, but none of us moved, transfixed by the gravity of what we'd uncovered.

"Well," I ventured, breaking the moment, "who's going first?"

HG struggled to contain herself. She perched on the edge of her chair; letters clutched in her elegant fingers like precious artefacts.

"These letters are from our erstwhile actress, Lily de Vere, to Madame Zelda and speak of blackmail." Her eyes gleamed with the thrill of discovery. "Rather explicit, too."

Intrigued, I leaned forward. "What leverage could Lily possibly have over Madame Zelda?"

"The letters do not explicitly spell anything concrete

out. However, they make clear Lily knows something that Madam Zelda might wish to remain secret. Something so disastrous that Lily's target would suffer ruination."

HG and I eyed Whipple, who still clutched the legal document.

"Does it corroborate the letters?" HG asked, her tone crisp with anticipation.

Whipple shook his head; his brow furrowed in confusion. "No, yet I'm convinced Sir Edmund having these documents in his ownership cost him his life. Mathews did well to hand the curse over to us."

Chapter Five

INVISIBLE THREATS

I followed HG and Whipple out of the Palm court, my mind whirling with the implications of what we'd discovered. The ship's corridors seemed more menacing now, as if the very walls were listening for our secrets.

"Do you think Matthews knows what's in the envelope?" I asked, keeping my voice low.

"Undoubtedly, no matter what he told you." HG replied. "The question is whether he knows who killed Sir Edmund. "You will find," HG added, "that silence is rarely accidental."

We continued our discussion as we made our way to the library. HG had expressed a keen interest in attending a lecture by a visiting professor of physics. His lecture was to be about manned flight. However, I suspected her true motive was to observe more of our fellow passengers in a neutral setting.

The library was everything one would expect from a first-class liner. Mahogany shelves lined the walls, housing leather-bound volumes that gleamed in the soft lamplight.

Plush burgundy carpeting muffled our footsteps as we entered. The air hung thick with the unmistakable aroma of expensive cigars, their smoke forming lazy spirals toward the ornate ceiling. The setup of comfy leather chairs in little groups reminded one of a men's club rather than a ship's facility.

As we entered, I noted our fellow attendees; a sparse crowd of only four, much to the irritation of HG. An elderly woman had succumbed to slumber in the corner, her feathered collar swaying in perfect rhythm with her gentle snoring. Beside her, a middle-aged man buried his nose in a massive tome, ignoring the lecture unfolding before him.

The remaining two audience members, who comprised a father and son, judging by their resemblance. They leaned forward, nodding encouragement as the professor delivered his presentation. The lecturer himself cut a concerning figure: tall and thin, he teetered as he gestured toward a complicated diagram of an aeroplane wing pinned to an easel.

We settled into vacant chairs at the back. I observed the professor's gaunt complexion, his sallow skin stretched over prominent cheekbones. Beads of sweat dotted his forehead despite the cool temperature of the room. His hands trembled as he pointed to various aspects of his diagram.

"Rather ill-looking chap, isn't he?" I whispered to HG.

The young man with his father snapped his hand up, causing the professor to pause mid-sentence.

"Excuse me, sir," he called out, his voice carrying across the room with youthful confidence. "Do you foresee a time when aeroplanes will displace the great ocean liners for international travel?"

The professor's eyes brightened, his expression one of unmistakable relief as he lowered himself onto a wooden chair beside his easel. Once he sat down, the trembling in his hands decreased somewhat.

"An excellent question, young man," he replied, dabbing his forehead with a handkerchief. "I cannot see a time when aeroplanes will carry enough passengers, or fly over long distances safely, to displace a leviathan such as the Britannic Star."

The professor leaned forward, warming to his subject. "You see, as a plane gets bigger, it becomes heavier, requiring more engines. No matter how clever our engineers are, they cannot break the laws of physics.

The young man's father nodded, while his son looked crestfallen.

"Perhaps," the professor continued, "the German company DELAG's efforts to build a larger gas balloon may carry, say, one hundred people. But again, physics will place a natural limit on size and range. The future of international travel, ladies, and gentlemen, remains firmly with the great ships."

The young man offered gracious thanks, though his disappointment was clear. I wondered what the world might look like in twenty or thirty years. Would we still be crossing oceans in massive vessels like this one, or even larger once weighing 75,000 tons, or even 100,00 tons?

Beside me, Whipple shifted and leaned toward HG. "My feet are staying firmly on the ground," he whispered. "This ship is bad enough."

I couldn't help giggling at Whipple's contradiction. The sound escaped before I could suppress it.

HG nudged me with her elbow. "Quiet," she murmured, though I caught the slight quirk of her lips that betrayed her amusement.

The professor continued his lecture, but my attention

drifted to the elderly woman in the corner, whose snoring had grown more pronounced, her feathered collar flapping with fury. I wondered if any of the people in this room knew Sir Edmund, or perhaps harboured secrets that might connect them to his murder.

The professor brought matters to a sudden stop as he raised a hand to his mouth and bolted from the room, leaving his diagram on the easel flapping in his hurried wake. HG chuckled, amusement clear in her eyes. "It seems our learned friend has another appointment that demands his immediate attention."

Whipple wore an expression of puzzled bemusement, his crumpled features furrowing until HG's meaning dawned on him. "Ah," he whispered, with a conspiratorial nod. "The necessary; the toilet."

As the professor plunged through the library exit, he almost collided with Madame Zelda. The incident seemed to ignite her temper, for she unleashed a torrent of colourful invective in his direction. I observed HG as she extended a curt yet dignified nod to Zelda.

"I do apologise, Your Grace," Zelda said, recovering swiftly from her affront, her voice dripping with theatrical remorse. "Such an uncouth fellow."

HG's demeanour was composed as ever. She gestured toward a vacant chair, inviting Zelda to join us. "Be assured," HG remarked, her eyes twinkling, "the fact that he fled spared you from a forceful emesis."

Puzzlement clouded Whipple's countenance, leaving him floundering. I leaned nearer, a touch smugly. "Shc means...tossing his biscuits all over you."

Madame Zelda's eyebrow arched in exaggerated disbelief as she settled herself beside HG. The seating arrangement around our little circle of armchairs felt lively with the addition of Zelda's vibrant presence. Light chatter ensued about the ship's grandeur and notable passengers. The tempestuous weather occupied our conversation, interwoven with sly observations about fellow travellers.

HG seized the brief lull in discourse to mention the curious case of missing letters. Her question quickly wiped away Zelda's earlier camaraderie, leaving a flicker of surprise in her eyes. Zelda recomposed herself with subtle grace and air, although the brief pause betrayed her discomfort.

"Missing letters? It does sound quite mysterious," she mused with a pensive glance, sweeping the carpet with her gaze. "I'm sure all sorts of correspondence and documents vanish without a trace on such a large ship. Why do you ask?"

Whipple leaned forward with newfound purpose. "A simple mention of letters was all HG said. Why do you make reference to documents?"

Zelda's demeanour shifted in an instant, her form going rigid as if ensnared by invisible threads. Her hand pressed against her temple whilst her other stretched into the void, appearing to engage with ethereal forces. Her voice emerged in a haunting cadence, rich with portent. "Beware strange words that lie. Neptune knows all; he will have his way before liberty holds out her flame."

The spell seemed to break as Zelda flopped once more into her chair. Then she startled us by leaping up as though alight with newfound energy. Zelda darted from the library with an agility akin to a cat in the thralls of some mysterious reverie. HG offered a weary sigh.

"What is it about this room that compels people to flee with such haste?" She observed, a bemused shake of her head as we absorbed the latest spectacle in our mystery.

The father and son duo ambled past our position, together with the man who'd been reading, pausing only to offer the most curious of looks in our direction. This left only us, and the snoring lady with the billowing feathers in our snug accommodation. Even the cigar smoke seemed to have evaporated.

"I must say, Zelda's antics were rather peculiar, wouldn't you agree?" HG opined, folding her hands demurely on her lap. Her eyes, however, were anything but demure. They sparkled with an intensity that suggested the wheels in her head were turning with new ideas.

"She's a charlatan, that's all," Whipple replied. His hand dismissed the idea with a flick of his fingers. "Her reference to 'documents' might have been nothing more than an artistic flourish to dazzle the gullible."

The phrase 'artistic flourish' bounced around my mind like an unwanted relative at Christmas; the idea wouldn't leave. "Yet, her reference to 'words that lie'. Isn't that telling?" Silence hung briefly, allowing us to ponder the implications.

HG nodded, her expression firm. Her voice adopted a thoughtful note. "Yes, Rex. Why warn of letters being untrue unless she knows more than she's letting on?"

Whipple appeared to reconsider his earlier dismissal, chewing on his lip. "It was indeed an odd association," he conceded. "Perhaps she's playing the victim in a plot we haven't fully unearthed."

We sat with our thoughts a moment longer. Whipple rubbed his eyes as if to scrub away trifles clouding his mind.

"It's time for a break," he announced with a resigned sigh. "I'm heading to my cabin to mull over today's events."

"Splendid idea, Arthur," HG agreed, her voice maintaining a note of her usual enthusiasm. "I'm rather looking forward to a brief repose myself."

They moved to depart, their figures growing smaller as they vanished down the corridor and around a corner. I decided a stroll through the first-class rooms might prove fruitful, or perhaps just a mild distraction.

As I ambled along the corridor, a loose tie on my shoelace ensured the speed of a turtle. Kneeling to fix the offending cord, I noticed the First Officer emerging from a crew-only area. His wayward gait drew my attention as I watched Mr Grayson limp toward me, attempting to avoid eye contact with a respectful tip of his officer's cap. His eyes found fascination on the floor tiles.

"That looks painful," I called, stepping up to him with a sympathetic air.

Grayson winced as he stopped. "Yes, it is. Stupid of me, really," he muttered, glancing up just enough to catch my gaze. "I bumped into a fire hydrant below deck on my evening rounds last night."

"Oh, that's unfortunate," I lamented, assured he would echo my sentiment. Our brief exchange concluded, he nodded and limped away.

As I continued my walk, a thought prodded at my mind. He wasn't limping when I caught a momentary glimpse of the fellow as HG and I returned from the promenade deck earlier today.

I ambled down the corridor, pondering Mr Grayson's limp and the inconsistencies it presented. Just as I processed the thought, a strangled cry fractured concentration.

Penelope Chase.

I sprinted toward the source, rounded a corner, and spotted Penelope bolting from her cabin, her pallor resembling a frightened doe. Her distress propelled her into my arms.

"My room…someone has been in there," she gasped, pointing a shaky finger back at her open cabin door.

The corridor livened with interest. Curious heads emerged from doorways like turtles cautiously peering from shells, only to vanish just as swiftly.

"Let's have a look, then," I said, doing my best to assure her, though unease gnawed within.

I approached the cabin door, every instinct warning me against disturbing whatever evidence lay within. Carefully, I pushed the door open with my sleeve.

Chaos reigned within. Clothing lay scattered across the floor as if a whirlwind had passed through. Drawers hung ajar, spilling their contents in disarray. The scene spoke of desperation. It betrayed the actions of someone with little time and less finesse, tearing through personal effects in pursuit of treasure.

"Stay here," I urged Penelope, stepping gingerly over articles as I entered.

Surveying the disorder, I pondered the perpetrator's aim. What might they have sought amidst this destruction? Valuable items untouched begged further questions.

A glint snagged my gaze; a whisper of fabric caught on the jagged edge of a trunk's corner. I crouched, the shred of cloth offering the only tangible clue amid the devastation.

I turned, beckoning Penelope inward. She hesitated on the threshold; reluctance etched upon her features. With gentle encouragement, she agreed, slipping her arm through mine. Her nearness intensified my awareness of her fragile state.

"Does this belong to you?" I asked, proffering the scrap.

She leaned in, inspecting the cloth with an expression

mingling intrigue and revulsion. "No, I do not own such a garment," she replied.

Here lay the first inkling within our investigation; a possible new thread in the tapestry of this mystery. A clue tangible in its existence, yet lacking identity. I removed the satin morsel and folded it in a handkerchief. HG and Whipple were sure to find the exhibit electrifying.

"Best leave this as is," I suggested gently, nodding toward the chaos in Penelope's cabin. "Inspector Whipple will want to see it as it stands. Let's lock up, and I'll take you for a snifter to calm your nerves."

Penelope gave me a demure glance, her lashes fluttering in a way that suggested both relief and gratitude. "That sounds...lovely," she murmured, her voice tinged with a soft vulnerability.

As we left the cabin, the key turned with a resolute click, sealing the disarray from prying eyes. Penelope clung to my arm as we navigated the corridor, each step measured as if the floor might give way at any moment.

The cocktail bar proved to be a welcome refuge from the outside mayhem; its warm lights casting an inviting glow over plush seating and polished wood. We found shelter in a snug corner, shielded from the thoroughfare. I made sure Penelope was comfortable in an overstuffed chair, so I could sit opposite her and have a view of every entrance and exit of the intimate space.

A steward approached, his presence quiet and unobtrusive as he awaited our order. Penelope looked at the drink list and ordered a stylish Sidecar, while I chose a Rob Roy, which felt familiar and reassuring given how uneasy I was.

I leaned forward across the petite round table. "Got any other favourite concoctions, or have your wanderings introduced you to the best club in London?"

Her lips quirked as she considered the question; some of her apprehension dissipating like morning fog. "Well," she confessed, tucking a loose strand of hair behind her ear with relaxed deliberation, "I have a taste for a good Gimlet on occasion, though nothing compares to the atmosphere of the Black Cat Club."

I feigned astonishment, sparking a glimmer of deeper amusement in her eyes. "Ah, I've heard the rumours. True or no, that their singer has a voice to rival any nightingale?"

Penelope's laughter was pure and musical, washing over her previous tension. "Entirely true," she assured me, nodding with enthusiasm.

Our drinks appeared as if conjured by wish alone. Raising my glass, I offered a toast. "To the voyage. May the seas be calm and the company lively."

She clinked her glass against mine, her earlier smile blossoming into laughter once more. "You've got a crazy sense of humour," she teased.

"It made you smile, didn't it?" I replied, the connection between us unspoken yet palpable.

The moment hung suspended as we each took a sip, the exchange drawing us closer.

I watched Penelope carefully, using the pause as she studied her drink as an opportunity to broach the subject that had been nagging at me. I kept my voice low to maintain the intimacy of the situation.

"Penelope, do you have any idea who ransacked your room? Or what they were looking for?"

Her eyes flicked up from her cocktail, a shadow of wariness crossing her features. Yet there was no hostility, just a guarded sort of trust.

"I don't know," she replied softly, her fingers tracing the

glass rim. "Nothing seemed to be missing, at least not anything obvious."

I considered this for a second or two, taking care with my next words. "Could it have been money, or jewellery maybe?"

She let out a delicate snort, shaking her head. "Jewellery? As if I'd have anything worth taking. My parents are rich, true, but they keep me on a tight leash."

Amusement in her voice, but beneath it lay a thrum of understanding, a shared knowledge of the world they both inhabited. I pressed on.

"Whoever it was, they wouldn't take such a risk without a good reason. If it's not a case of mistaking the cabin number...then what?"

She paused, took another sip of her Sidecar, then looked me square in the eye, a nervous tick emanating from one corner of her mouth. "I need to tell you something. During the seance, I took something from Madame Zelda's."

"But you were terrified at the seance, why filch one of her props... if that's what it was?"

Penelope's cheeks coloured, a touch of embarrassment soaking through her reticence. "I know, it's silly. I was too embarrassed to say anything when you found me."

Her words held a truthfulness that drew me in, a sense of genuine vulnerability I respected. She lifted a petite shoulder bag onto her lap, unzipping it with care.

From within, she extracted a small metal tube that was about one inch in diameter. I watched as she pulled at one end. To my surprise, the tube elongated to two feet.

"Perfect, isn't it? Allows Madame Zelda to perform her little tricks, touching legs under the table without being noticed."

I mulled his fact over. "A torn piece of dress fabric, and a sham psychic's prop... I think we both know who ripped through your cabin?"

Penelope nodded, a flicker of fear in her eyes. "And now I'm terrified she'll do something to stop me from exposing her." Her voice trembled with the admission, yet her gaze remained steady, finding reassurance in my presence.

The cocktail bar's cosy atmosphere, previously untouched by drama, suddenly sparked with tension, as if the air held its breath. Madame Zelda's voice rose resonant and indignant.

"Look," I urged Penelope, my gaze flickering past her shoulder toward the source of the commotion. Her features mirrored confusion, but she chose not to turn.

The scene unfurled before us. Madame Zelda stood at a distance, her posture rigid, every line etched with seething intensity. Her arm was outstretched, finger pointing like an accusatory blade.

“You are a devil,” she spat, her voice ringing with a conviction that made several passengers start. “Words may be your armour, but a bauble will be your undoing.”

Klaus von Ritter stepped away from a small knot of onlookers, his tall frame and effortless composure lending him an air of unruffled superiority. He appeared entirely unmoved by Zelda’s venom.

“At least, madam, I am not a fraud,” von Ritter replied, his tone a polished mixture of charm and mild derision. The remark slipped from him with the ease of long practice. Without breaking stride, he made for the bar and requested a drink, dismissing Zelda as though she were no more than an inconvenient draught.

For a moment, Zelda faltered. She stood quite still, her eyes swirling with indignation and something darker, a flicker of agitation that suggested a private exchange with unseen companions only she could perceive.

Her gaze snapped suddenly to Penelope, fixing her with such sharp intent that even I felt the atmosphere tighten.

Penelope stiffened, the colour draining from her face. Although her back was turned to Zelda, some instinct, however irrational, compelled her to turn. When she did, her expression altered at once, as though a shadow had swept straight through her.

Zelda's voice rose, carrying across the cocktail bar with disquieting clarity.

"Beware those who steal from the spirits," she intoned, her voice so laden with dark resonance that even I sensed Penelope flinch beside me, "for they shall be visited by the spirits, and their wrath laid upon them."

Penelope gripped the table, the last of her confidence draining from her face. Zelda lingered a fraction too long, her stare unsettling the room more than her words had. Rex felt a cold draught at his back and, sceptic though he was, even he had to admit that the atmosphere had shifted.

Chapter Six

THE ELUSIVE STEWARD

I observed Penelope scurry away, clutching her bag close, with Madame Zelda's icy stare following her retreat. The encounter left a chill that lingered well into the evening hours.

Dinner that night was a sparkling affair. Calmer seas had encouraged most of the first-class passengers to venture from their cabins. The dining room sparkled with crystal-lit adornments. The ladies' finest evening wear contrasted with the men's formal attire. This created a tableau of post-war elegance that seemed determined to push back the shadows of a dreadful period.

I spotted HG and Whipple at our usual table and hurried over, barely containing my excitement.

"You won't believe what happened today," I began, words tumbling out faster than propriety allowed. "First, I ran into Grayson limping down the corridor, though he wasn't limping earlier when I saw him on deck. Then I found Miss Chase in quite a state after someone tore through her cabin. And at the cocktail bar—"

"Rex," HG smiled, raising an eyebrow as she adjusted her beaded evening wrap, "do lower your voice and restrain your exuberance. The walls have ears, particularly on a ship where a murder has occurred."

"Sorry," I muttered, cursing myself for my amateurism.

Whipple, meanwhile, glowered at the menu card in his hands. "Blasted thing's in French again. What's wrong with English roast beef and potatoes?"

"It's poulet roti, Arthur," HG translated smoothly. "Roast chicken."

Whipple grunted his thanks while I continued in hushed tones.

"As I was saying, I found Penelope Chase quite strained. Someone had searched her cabin rather thoroughly. In the cocktail lounge, she admitted to taking something from Madame Zelda during the seance; a metal tube that extends, perfect for fake spirit tapping under tables. Then we witnessed a most extraordinary scene between Zelda and von Ritter. She called him a devil, he called her a fraud, and then she turned on Penelope with some ominous warning about stealing from the spirits."

HG's expression sharpened. "Interesting. Our cast of suspects grows more theatrical by the hour."

"Theatrical or not," Whipple murmured, "one of them is a murderer."

As the discussion continued, HG and Whipple whispered words about Penelope's theft and Zelda's ominous warnings. We were all so absorbed in our musings that I almost didn't notice Henderson approaching our table, his dinner suit a size too large, lending him a particularly dishevelled air. It seemed a near-accomplishment to make Whipple appear well-tailored by comparison.

Henderson hovered with an air of affected nonchalance.

"Good evening, fine company of sleuths," he greeted with exaggerated cheer, his eyes twinkling with mischief. "Mind if I join for a moment?" Without waiting for an invitation, he settled in, eyes dancing between the three of us.

HG and Whipple offered polite smiles, though I noted the restrained warmth in their greetings. It was no secret Henderson wasn't particular about selling his grandmother for a juicy headline, let alone a friend.

"Detective Inspector Whipple," Henderson began with a confidence that only a desperate journalist might possess, "I hear the winds have brought quite the scandal to our nautical doorstep. Tawdry tale, isn't it? Certainly, a death in these deep waters has caught the public imagination."

Whipple nodded, expression inscrutable. "Tragic," he said, though the word carried no real weight.

Undeterred, Henderson pressed on, eyes gleaming with the relentless hunger of someone seeking a scoop. "Rumours abound, you know," he said, voice low and conspiratorial. "About Sir Edmund's untimely demise, is it true that our victim threatened vengeance on the esteemed diplomat, Mr von Ritter? A dangerous thing to do, wouldn't you say?"

It was a testament to Whipple's skill that he only nodded again, his expression giving away nothing. "Rumours are the territory of idle tongues," he said flatly, "not facts."

After a few more unsuccessful probes, Henderson relented, though his smile didn't falter. "Well then," he said, rising, "I'll leave you to your dinner. Do enjoy the evening."

"Pleasant evening to you," HG replied politely.

Once Henderson sauntered away, Whipple let out a noise that was half laugh, half growl. "Slippery as an eel, that one."

HG chuckled, a lightness returning to her gaze. "Come,

Arthur," she teased, "you know as well as I that your profession isn't above enlisting their help when required…or, dare I say, feeding them false information to see what rabbits may be set running."

Whipple gave a sharp sniff, as if catching a scent of hogwash. "That's different," he insisted.

Her laughter tinkled like a bell. "I'm glad you think so," she said, her eyes twinkling with amusement.

As the last notes of conversation between ourselves and the journalist drifted away on the soft hum of dining room chatter, I noticed our table steward hovering at the edge of my vision. He stood at a respectful distance, his demeanour alert but patient. It was only after Henderson's departure that the steward aligned himself with the table, offering to fill our water glasses, and offer bread. The timing was so precise, I couldn't help but respect the man's professionalism.

With the menus before us, we began the delicate dance of selection. Whipple, who had by now surrendered any pretence of French fluency, nudged his menu towards HG with a look of resignation. "Poulet roti it is," he mumbled, folding the card.

Once the table steward departed with our selections, a man of discerning pallor approached; the sommelier, his presence marked by a serviette draped with purposeful elegance over his shoulder. The sommelier performed his role with great ceremony; one Whipple was noticeably reticent about engaging in. He leaned back, giving the selection process over to HG.

HG made short work of choosing a fine wine for each course, then dispatched the sommelier with a graceful nod and a "Thank you, good sir," that could have befitted royalty.

As our food was prepared, and the clattering orchestra of cutlery, dish-ware, and chatter continued, HG, ever thrumming with energy, turned to Whipple and me with a considered look. "I propose we take stock," she stated, eyes flicking between us. "Reassess where we stand in this twisted saga."

Whipple's expression of contentment from earlier dissipated like a shot of fog. He cleared his throat. "We have a tangled web, no doubt of it," he began cautiously, as if speaking the words aloud risked sealing their truth. "Sir Edmund was undoubtedly involved in something underhanded. Blackmail, likely, given the letters we found. His fateful dinner companions seemed a mixed bag of potential quarrels: von Ritter with his Germanic connections, Madame Zelda and her predictions of doom, and Lily de Vere with her swoons and distractions."

HG inclined her head. "Yet it's more tangled than that, isn't it? Penelope was found in distress, her room ransacked. But she managed to diagnose Madame Zelda's fraudulent means."

"Yes, though we must consider Zelda's motives," I offered. "her theatricality has me sceptical of a person who enjoys meanings more than facts. Then again, her warnings are uncanny enough to warrant notice."

"Correct," Whipple continued, pushing the discussion onward. "We've observed strange behaviours from more than one corner of this ship. Matthews' shifty-eyed toss of the envelope and Miss Chase's stolen trinket. And Grayson's limp is conveniently inconsistent."

"It's a performance none can assist but truth itself," HG mused, her eyes narrowing as if catching sight of something elusive. "Last evening's seance, for whatever it's worth, cast another shadow; have Penelope and von Ritter given something away…knowingly, or by mistake?"

I interjected, voice pitched low against the rising crescendo of our surroundings. "Is there more to this ship than the passengers let on?"

Whipple paused, a contemplative heaviness hanging between us. "It seems many passengers…and, perhaps, staff, guard secrets. Some of those secrets brush dangerously close to Sir Edmund's fate. Furthermore, given the angst we continue to observe in some quarters, perhaps Sir Edmund's murder may not be the last killing we shall see on this voyage."

A moment of silence passed as Whipple's terrifying assessment sank in. Above the din, Herzog's heedful presence reflected a complex entanglement. Which path to tread, which loose ends to pull taut.

"Then tonight," HG lifted her glass, capturing the room's crystal glow, "We gather pieces of this terrible puzzle; our measured approach continues."

With silent accord, we welcomed our meals. For a few moments, at least, the mystery of Sir Edmund's murder lay at rest.

For the next hour, we enjoyed the type of experience passengers on any normal voyage might reasonably expect. Light-hearted conversation flowed…as did the wine. HG's selections had hit the spot, such that even Whipple gave forth with an occasional titter as he observed his fellow guests.

"And now for the evening's formal entertainment. We shall promenade to the first-class lounge and put ourselves in the hands of Mr Fenwick, the Britannic Star's most esteemed musical director."

Whipple's demeanour sobered in a jiffy. I knew him not

to be a fan of upper-class reviews, which I presumed was to be our fate.

"Come, Arthur," HG began, "it will be splendid, and you never know, some clue may reveal itself to give clarity to our cause."

"I'm not sure about the review, HG," Whipple said, straightening his bowtie with clumsy fingers. "We've very little time to waste on musical numbers while a killer roams free."

"You have another plan, I presume?" HG raised an eyebrow, her gaze keen and assessing.

Whipple nodded. "I think I ought to revisit First Officer Grayson. That limp comes and goes most suspiciously. Plus, I'm determined to track down Charles Peabody; that steward knows more than he's letting on."

"You believe he withheld information?" I asked.

"People rarely tell us everything in a first interview," Whipple replied, dabbing his mouth with his napkin. "Particularly when they're afraid. And young Charlie was certainly afraid of something."

HG considered this for a moment, her fingers tapping against her silver chain purse. The soft glow of the dining room lights caught the emerald on her finger, sending tiny green flashes across the white tablecloth.

"I suppose you're right, Arthur. However, I think it prudent for Rex to accompany you."

I opened my mouth to protest; I'd quite fancied hearing the ship's orchestra. But HG's expression brooked no argument.

"Two heads and all that," she continued. 'And Rex has the knack of getting people to talk to him with his impish ways."

Whipple nodded. "The boy does have a knack for it."

"I'm hardly a boy," I muttered, though neither of them paid me any mind.

We rose from our table, making our way toward the exit. Just as we reached the doorway, I felt a light tap on my shoulder. Turning, I found myself face to face with Penelope Chase, looking particularly striking in an evening gown of midnight blue.

"Rex," she smiled, her voice musical. "I was hoping you might escort me to the review. I find these social events so dreadfully dull without pleasant company."

I glanced helplessly at HG, caught between duty and desire. Her expression softened at my obvious conflict.

"I'm afraid Rex will not be able to accompany you," HG said smoothly. "I have given him one or two little jobs to do. However, you are most welcome to join me."

Penelope's smile faltered as she glanced my way. The disappointment in her eyes was unmistakable, and I felt an answering pang in my chest.

"Perhaps another time," she said softly.

Before I could respond, HG had taken Penelope's arm, whisking her away. The last thing I saw was Penelope glancing back over her shoulder at me, her expression unreadable in the dimly lit corridor.

It didn't take long for Whipple and me to reach the First Officer's base, although more than one curious passenger enquired about the investigation in transit. Whipple, skilled in such things, offered generalised replies without revealing specifics. "The investigation continues along its course," you'd hear him say, leaving listeners with not a crumb.

Giving a polite tap on the door, I heard a calm voice bid us enter. Inside, the office was a model of maritime efficiency, with no wasted space. The desk barely interrupted the flow of wood panelling that lined the room, and a single lamp cast its warm light over immaculate charts pinned to the walls.

As Grayson met our gaze, the calm rapidly faded, replaced by a slight twitch of nerves. "Please, gentlemen," he said, gesturing to the simple wooden chairs opposite his desk. We sat, the chairs unexpectedly comfortable in their utilitarian design.

I fixed him with what I hoped was a look of polite curiosity. "I couldn't help but notice earlier, sir, your limp," I began, adopting a flatness to my voice. "Feeling better now?"

He glanced down at his leg as if surprised by its very existence. "It comes and goes," he mumbled, eyes flickering for a moment to Whipple.

Whipple pounced on that. "Indeed. How did it happen, if you don't mind my asking?"

Grayson hesitated before replying. "An accident on deck a few days before setting sail. Slipped while inspecting a lifeboat."

I leaned back, keeping my face neutral. The inconsistency between this tale and Mr Grayson's previous recital tickled my suspicions.

"And how does that happen, especially for someone of your experience?" Whipple's tone remained cordial, yet it carried weight. Grayson shifted, clearly sensing it.

The first officer waved a dismissive hand. "It's the sea, Inspector. Must watch it every moment or it'll have you on your back."

I cut in, changing tack. "And aside from the...unfortunate incident with Sir Edmund, how fares the voyage generally speaking?" Vague interest laced my words, calculated to appear routine.

Grayson shrugged, easing back into his chair. "Much the

same as any other. First-class passengers griping over a lack of 'service' at four instead of five-star levels. Chef's souffles not rising to expectation. A gentleman unhappy with champagne at dinner being served a degree too warm. You know how it is aboard these liners."

He exhaled like a man pleased to have weathered an interrogation. But then he eyed us cautiously. "This is all most cosy. But why, exactly, have you troubled to call?"

Whipple and I exchanged a brief glance. I knew that look; it meant the inspector was about to strike.

"You're quite right, Mr. Grayson," Whipple said, adjusting his posture. "We do have a specific reason for calling. I was wondering if I might glance at the ship's log."

Grayson's eyebrows shot up, his composure momentarily shattered. "The ship's log? Whatever for? I assure you that the vast majority of entries are merely routine weather reports and staff matters."

Whipple nodded, his expression placid. "Yes, I understand the legal requirement to keep such a routine record," he said, his voice measured and even. "But you said the majority, not all entries."

I leaned forward, offering what I hoped was a reassuring smile. "It's all a matter of routine, Mr. Grayson. Any morsel the inspector can pick from the log may help with our enquiries. You understand how these investigations work; every detail counts."

Grayson hesitated, his gaze flicking between us as if calculating some invisible equation. After a few seconds, he reached into the breast pocket of his uniform and extracted a small key. The metal caught the lamplight as he inserted it into his desk drawer. The lock turned with a soft click.

The first officer withdrew a black leather-bound volume from within. He placed it on his desk with reverence, as if handling a sacred text, then slid it across the well-polished surface toward Whipple.

Arthur accepted the log with a nod, opening it carefully. His eyes began scanning the neat columns of handwritten entries, fingers occasionally tracing a line or pausing at a particular notation. The soft whisper of turning pages was the only sound in the otherwise silent office.

While Whipple investigated the log, First Officer Grayson fixed his stare on me. His eyes narrowed, studying me with an intensity that made me want to fidget. I held his gaze steadily, refusing to be the first to look away. There was something in that stare, something beyond mere annoyance at our intrusion. Was it fear? Calculation? Whatever it was, it confirmed my suspicion that Grayson knew more than he was letting on.

The silence stretched between us like an elastic band pulled taut, ready to snap at any moment.

Whipple's request to borrow the logbook hung in the air like fog settling over London Town. For a moment, Grayson stared as if the inspector had asked to abscond with his soul. The first officer's face contorted with disbelief, shaking his head emphatically.

"I'm sorry, Detective Inspector, but that is impossible," Grayson replied, voice suddenly firm. "The logbook is the ship's legal record. If anything happened to it on my watch, I'd lose my career."

Whipple breathed heavily through his nasal cavity, fixing Grayson with an unwavering stare that was equal parts sombre and earnest.

"Mr. Grayson, you have my promise as a gentleman and senior police officer. I shall keep it under my personal supervision every moment it's with me."

Grayson hesitated, balling his hands into fists upon the

desk's surface. I could almost hear the gears of his mind grinding: risk versus duty, desperation clashing with necessity. There was reluctance etched deep in the first officer's features, but slowly he relented with a nod, providing a tacit agreement. Whipple placed the logbook inside his dinner jacket; its presence lending an unusual rigidity to his frame.

Our task was interrupted by a sudden opening of the office door without ceremony. Captain Hardwick barged in. His gaze, sharp and suspicious, flitted to Whipple and me, then settled on Grayson with an intensity that seemed to pierce straight through the man.

The exchange between captain and first officer carried dreadful tension, a pleasant facade barely masking the evidence. Grayson's reaction was unmistakable; thinly veiled fear rippled across his countenance. Hardwick, all false joviality, declared that Grayson was needed on the bridge.

It was our cue to leave. Whipple, careful not to reveal the slight bulge beneath his jacket, mustered a somewhat awkward posture as he pulled open the door.

"We shall take our leave, gentlemen," Whipple announced, politeness coating every syllable while he ushered me out.

I shut the door behind us, closing the chapter on what felt like an alternate reality laden with whispered secrets. As we stepped away, nearing the end of the corridor, voices erupted through the now-closed door. Hardwick and Grayson were shouting, their latent conflicts surfacing with volcanic fury.

Whipple leaned closer, comparing our thoughts to the muffled cacophony. "Let's leave them to it. I'll secure the log in my cabin before we seek Peabody."

His suggestion met with my silent agreement. The

farther we moved from the senior office's echoing tempest, the better our prospects for finding our next quarry.

Once out of Whipple's room, where he secreted the ship's log, we descended the stairwell behind a mahogany panel delineating a change from the grand trappings of first class, into a utilitarian maze. The ship's belly thrummed with activity as Whipple and I entered the depths, one set of metal stairs after another. The opulence above transformed to raw function beneath. Each step resonated sharply, drowned swiftly in the unrelenting din of the lower decks. It was like traversing the heart of a mechanical behemoth, pulsing with a life of its own.

We reached the laundry room, a cathedral of organised chaos. The enormous washing machines clanked rhythmically, a chorus that crashed like ocean waves against the hull. Overhead, the thunderous whirl of a hydro-extractor shook the ground beneath us. Lining the austere walls, drying cupboards hummed with heat, exuding the faint scent of steam and soap.

Within this chaos, I followed a hunch. Charlie Peabody had once emerged from these mechanical entrails, and now I needed to dig him up from the linen labyrinth. I beckoned Whipple to follow, weaving through the madness, seeking the sanctuary of a quieter corner where sheets of domesticity cloaked the utilitarian roar.

We slipped behind a wall of neatly folded bed linen and snow-white tablecloths. Towels stacked to my chin formed an impromptu barrier against the din. Here, hidden amongst the ship's fabric maze, we found him. Charlie Peabody sat perched on a small stool, engrossed in the Daily

Mail from the day of our embarkation. The paper crinkled in his hand, though his face was a picture of repose amidst the clamour.

I caught Peabody's eye as I stepped forward, interrupting his tranquillity. At first, a flash of alarm crossed his features, concern shadowing the easy air. But realisation quickly dawned upon recognition; the slight tension around his eyes dissolved into welcome.

"Ah, you've found me again, young fella," Charlie said, a grin broadening into familiarity. He winked slowly, a touch of mischief lingering in his gaze, and tucked the newspaper under one arm as if to make space for conversation.

Whipple, hands tucked behind his back, regarded Charlie thoughtfully. The informality of the working man, juxtaposed against the fastidious detective, seemed to lighten the atmosphere even amidst the droning machines. Charlie leaned back, waiting for us to get to the point, unconcerned by the machinery's orchestra.

Charlie's grin, teasing at the edges, mirrored my own as I crouched beside him, lowering myself into the realm of camaraderie. Whipple remained the paragon of duty, standing as stiff as a starched collar, extracting his notebook and pencil with an air of resolute intent.

"That looks official," Charlie observed, nodding towards Whipple, a mischievous glint in his eye.

"Our detective here is never off duty, know what I mean?" I said, easing the tension with my words. Charlie chuckled, his trust in me growing.

"Er, I am here, you know. Now, let's get down to business," Whipple interjected, his tone unable to pierce the casual bubble we had created. I caught the muscle in Charlie's jaw twitch instinctively. I felt his walls rising. He'd clam up faster than a Venus flytrap and spin us a yarn that would lead Whipple and me nowhere fast.

"Why don't you head back upstairs, Whipple? I'll join you shortly," I suggested, hoping my voice conveyed that I had it under control.

Whipple hesitated, considering my words before conceding gracefully. "Right, do carry on," he said, his reluctance barely concealed, and left.

With Whipple's departure, it was just the two of us, a private enclave amid roaring machinery, hidden from other watchful eyes behind billowing sheets.

"Can't stand coppers," Charlie confessed, the tension slipping away. "Your detective seems alright, but I've met too many bad 'uns to trust any of the blighters."

"That's understandable," I replied, empathy threading through my words. "They're not a bad lot in general, but I'm with you. Southampton must feel like a world away from this sort of thing."

Charlie nodded, a half-smile tugging at his lips, opening the door to the life he'd left behind to work aboard floating cities. Through his words, I glimpsed the bustling docks of Southampton, where the Solent whetted the appetite for adventure and stable wages. He spoke of his wife, Bethany, a local girl who grounded him with her laughter, her eyes always shining with mischief and warmth. Their oldest son, Alfie, was just like his dad, full of energy like he was ten. Little May acted like her mother, her laughter bright as she played near the washtub and wringer.

"Our Alfie's started learning the cornet. Not sure if it's music yet, but he gives it his best." Charlie chuckled, the warmth of family lighting up his features.

Slowly, but purposefully, I steered the conversation back toward Sir Edmund's murder.

"Let's go over that night again, Charlie. Anything else come to mind since we last chatted?" I leaned towards him, maintaining the easy connection we'd formed.

He paused, pulling details from the shadows, then sat up straight as a realisation dawned. "Well, I did see Mr Grayson, you know, the First Officer. Come to think of it, he was loitering outside that bloke's stateroom. I never give it a thought, but…"

The revelation landed heavily, a puzzle piece unsettling in its implications. Why indeed would one of the ship's most senior staff be hanging about a passenger's cabin in the dead of night? The peculiar limp Grayson had sported also needled at the corners of my mind. Secrets had a habit of clinging to the very fabric of this ship. But how to make sense of it all?

Chapter Seven

THE BUNKER

I tapped softly on HG's stateroom door, my knuckles barely grazing the polished mahogany. Whipple stood beside me, his face drawn with fatigue after our separate nocturnal investigations. The door swung open to reveal HG in her dressing gown, looking remarkably fresh despite the late hour.

"Come in, both of you," she beckoned, ushering us into her opulent suite.

HG's quarters remained the epitome of first-class luxury; velvet drapes framed the porthole, Persian rugs adorned the floor, and brass fittings gleamed in the soft lamplight. Near the chaise lounge, a silver tray displayed decanters and a plate with odd dark snacks.

"You look as though you could use a nightcap," HG remarked, pouring amber liquid into crystal glasses. "Help yourselves to Devils on Horseback."

Whipple eyed the dark, glistening appetisers with undisguised suspicion. "What exactly are they?"

"Prunes stuffed with a savoury filling and wrapped in bacon," HG explained with a smile. "Quite delightful."

"A good old sausage would have been better," Whipple muttered, though he tentatively selected one.

I settled into an armchair, gratefully accepting both drink and delicacy. "What news from the evening's entertainment?"

"Rather eventful," HG said, sinking gracefully onto the chaise. "Doctor Livingstone was called upon mid-performance when an elderly lady experienced a frightful coughing fit after her wine went down the wrong way. Quite a commotion ensued."

HG took a measured sip of her liquor. "When the lights came up during the chaos, I observed von Ritter making a hasty departure, followed moments later by Lily de Vere. Most interesting, wouldn't you agree?"

"Indeed," Whipple nodded, warming to the prune concoction despite himself.

"I also caught sight of someone I hadn't previously encountered; the Chief Officer, Mr Lucian Bowthorpe."

Whipple nearly choked. "Bowthorpe? No one mentioned this gentleman to me. Who is he?"

“I, too, was unaware of his presence until tonight," HG replied, arching an eyebrow. "A refined gentleman seated to my left explained how peculiar it was to see him. Apparently, Bowthorpe is usually quite visible about the ship and known for being an amiable fellow who always has a kind word for those who approach him."

"And yet we haven't seen hide nor hair of him until now," I mused. "Curious timing for him to appear, wouldn't you say…and why have not the captain or first officer mentioned the fellow?"

"I shall seek the fellow out in the morning," Whipple said, brushing bacon crumbs from his lapel. "Seems rather suspicious that we're only learning about him now."

I nodded, finishing my drink before sharing our findings. "Charlie Peabody had quite the revelation for us tonight. He claims to have seen First Officer Grayson lingering outside Sir Edmund's stateroom on the night of the murder."

"Most peculiar," HG replied, "especially given his inconsistent explanations about his injury."

Whipple leaned in, his voice lowered despite our private surroundings. "The captain and Grayson were having quite a row after we left them. Something about responsibility and keeping things in order."

"I've yet to go through the ship's log," began Whipple. "Though Grayson was reluctant to let us see it. And I suspect the fellow keeps a second, personal log, perhaps to record matters he thinks may be useful at some future point. Anyway, I delve into the official record when I get back to my cabin—Grayson will need it back pronto, tomorrow."

HG considered this with a thoughtful expression. "We've accumulated several threads, but the pattern remains elusive. Von Ritter with his Prussian connections, Madame Zelda's foreknowledge, Penelope and Lily's suspicious behaviour, and now the officers themselves."

"Let's not forget this mysterious Bowthorpe," Whipple said through a stifled yawn. "However, I think we've done all we can for tonight."

The lateness of the hour weighed upon us all; even HG's usually perfect posture had softened against the chaise.

"Shall we reconvene over breakfast?" I suggested, rising from my chair. "The observation lounge should be empty early in the morning. We could speak freely there."

"An excellent idea," HG approved with a nod. "I'll have my personal steward arrange for a light breakfast to be served. Eight o'clock should give us ample time before the other passengers appear."

Whipple checked his pocket watch and grimaced. "Not many hours of sleep to be had, but needs must. Eight o'clock it is."

We bade each other goodnight, and I stepped into the corridor, my mind churned with questions. For now, I just wanted my bed.

I woke to a gentle rap at my cabin door, reminding me I'd requested an early call. The night had passed mercifully without further drama, though my sleep had been broken by dreams of Prussian eagles and shadowy figures lurking in corridors.

After a quick wash and shave, I made my way to the Observation Lounge. The storm had finally abated overnight, allowing sunshine to stream through the vast windows that curved around the forward section of the ship. The view was magnificent; endless blue stretched to the horizon, unmarred by clouds.

"How refreshing to see a clear horizon," I remarked as HG and Whipple arrived, "and not be forced to grab onto the nearest chair or fitting to remain upright."

The stewards had prepared our private breakfast table with meticulous care. Crisp white linen draped to the floor, polished silver cutlery caught the morning light, and fresh flowers provided a splash of colour. HG's personal steward, Graham, stood several feet away, attentive yet unobtrusive, watching to ensure we had everything we required.

"Will there be anything else, Your Grace?" Graham asked, making a final adjustment to the food press.

"No, thank you, Graham. This is quite splendid," HG replied with genuine warmth.

Graham tilted his head slightly in acknowledgment before quietly withdrawing, leaving us to our privacy.

The press was a marvel of culinary delights: fresh croissants, Cumberland sausage, scrambled eggs, grilled tomatoes, and a selection of preserves. Whipple immediately gravitated toward the heartier options, piling his plate with sausages and eggs. HG selected a croissant and a modest serving of fruit, while I helped myself to a bit of everything.

We settled at our table, deliberately keeping our conversation light as we enjoyed our breakfast.

"The chef has outdone himself with these sausages," Whipple commented, his mood considerably improved from the previous evening.

"Indeed," HG agreed. "The quality of cuisine aboard the Britannic Star is quite exceptional."

I nodded, savouring a bite of perfectly prepared eggs. "Captain Hardwick may have his secrets, but he certainly knows how to run a ship's kitchen."

Our casual banter continued until we had satisfied our immediate hunger. Only when HG reached for the elegant silver teapot did our focus shift.

"Assam," she announced, pouring the fragrant brew into delicate bone china cups. "Now, back to work."

"I'll focus on catching up with Chief Officer, Lucian Bowthorpe," Whipple said, carefully setting his teacup down. "But first, I need to return the ship's log to Grayson and have another chat."

"A chat?" HG picked up on his phrasing, one elegant eyebrow raised. "That sounds ominously casual, Inspector."

Whipple offered a thin smile. "I found several inconsistencies in the log. Plus, there was a reference to a matter that may have led to the captain's sharp words with Grayson after Rex and I left the first officer's office."

He paused, clearly for dramatic effect. HG and I stared at him, waiting for the fellow to continue. The inspector took a deliberately slow sip of his Assam tea, eyes twinkling with the knowledge that he had captured our complete attention.

"Well?" I prompted, unable to contain myself. "What did you find?"

"There's a vague log entry about a technical matter in the boiler room," Whipple finally revealed, placing his cup down with precision. "Nothing precise, which I find odd. A ship's log should contain detailed accounts of any mechanical concerns, especially on a vessel of this calibre."

"I wonder if that's why the captain and first officer appeared to be at loggerheads," I said, recalling their heated exchange.

"And perhaps why this mysterious Chief Officer Bowthorpe has been conspicuously absent until now," HG added thoughtfully. "Could he be involved with whatever's happening in the boiler room?"

Whipple nodded. "My thoughts exactly. A senior officer suddenly appearing mid-voyage, having been steadfastly absent from public view raises questions."

"I recommend you add the first officer to your list of people to interview," HG suggested, refilling her teacup. "His behaviour has been inconsistent at best, suspicious at worst."

"And what will you be doing, HG?" I asked.

She straightened her napkin with a purposeful motion.

"I intend to track down Lily de Vere and see if I can tease out why she appeared to chase after von Ritter last night."

After a pleasant thirty minutes partaking of our breakfast, HG brought events to a close by suggesting we should be about our agreed tasks. Within minutes we spotted First Officer Grayson locking his office door. Whipple called out quietly so as not to attract attention to ourselves. Grayson turned to face us.

"I have something for you." Whipple added.

Grayson nodded, unlocked his office again and invited us in. "I've no doubt you've read more interesting things?" Grayson opined to Whipple, as he accepted the log being held out by the inspector.

'If you mean case files, then yes, I read my fair share of gruesome documents. However, there is one entry I should like to ask you about. Something about a technical problem in the boiler room. The entry relates to the two days before we departed Southampton. Rather vague for a ship's log, wouldn't you say?"

I watched Grayson's face carefully. A muscle twitched near his right eye, and his shoulders stiffened as he unlocked the drawer in his desk, placed the log inside and re-locked the drawer.

"Standard procedure," Grayson replied, his voice tight despite his attempt at nonchalance. "Minor maintenance difficulties do not require exhaustive documentation."

"I see." Whipple's tone remained conversational, but I recognised the subtle shift in his demeanour; this was top-notch detective at work. "Twenty years in the force has taught me that vague documentation often hides something significant underneath."

Grayson sauntered from his desk to the far wall, putting distance between himself and us. "Detective Inspector

Whipple, with all due respect, maritime protocol differs from police procedure."

"Perhaps," Whipple conceded. "But human nature remains consistent across all professions. People obscure details when they have something to hide."

A flash of anger crossed Grayson's face. "Are you accusing me of making a false log entry; calling me a liar?"

"Not at all. I'm simply making an observation about the peculiar lack of detail in an otherwise meticulously kept log." Whipple paused. "Especially curious when coupled with your heated discussion with the captain yesterday."

Grayson's gaze flicked briefly to the locked drawer. "The captain and I occasionally have professional disagreements. Nothing unusual there."

"And Chief Officer Bowthorpe?" I asked suddenly. "Where does he fit into these professional disagreements?"

The colour drained from Grayson's face. For a moment, he appeared to struggle with what to say next. When he spoke, his voice was low, almost a whisper.

"Our chief officer is my immediate superior and a man of the highest integrity. He dealt with the issue, which, as I say, was of a minor nature, and briefed me on what to enter into the log. All perfectly normal practice."

Whipple gave Grayson a whimsical look. "Did I suggest Mr Bowthorpe to be anything other than an honourable gentleman? Unless, that is, you wish to tell me something. Nevertheless, it is strange that the first sighting of your illusive superior was as recent as last evening, is it not?"

Whipple's approach entranced me. In two short sentences, he had opened Grayson up like a segmented orange.

Grayson looked trapped. "I have not," said Grayson, as he walked to back of his chair and gripped the object as if his life depended upon it. "The technical issue was nothing that affected passenger safety at the time, or now, I assure you. As for when and where the Chief Officer was seen, he holds a position of the utmost importance to the safe running of the ship and must concentrate his efforts where the captain and he agree they should be placed. Anyway, shouldn't you both be focussing on Sir Edmund's murder and leave ship operations to those qualified to manage them."

I thought it a desperate attempt to divert Whipple's devastating asset on his account of recent matters.

"Two investigations need not be mutually exclusive," Whipple replied. "I've done this job long enough to recognise that even events or facts, seemingly unrelated, have a knack of informing one another. As for Mr Bowthorpe concentrating on important issues, I, of course, concur. However, it is telling that you frame that importance as one of 'safety.'"

Grayson's face hardened. "If you don't mind, I have duties to attend to," Grayson said, pointing to the office door.

The dismissal was clear. Whipple nodded politely, turned and winked at me as we moved toward the door.

"One last thing," Whipple said, turning back. "Where might we find Chief Officer Bowthorpe?"

"Hc's hiding somcthing. Thc rcaction whcn I mcntioncd Bowthorpe wasn't normal."

"Indeed," Whipple agreed, checking his pocket watch. "Let us see if we can find this mysterious chief officer."

Our search proved frustrating. The engine control room

contained only junior officers, who claimed Bowthorpe had just left. The bridge crew (who we spoke to from the threshold, since we were not allowed to enter without the captain's express permission) directed us elsewhere. Each location yielded similar results; Bowthorpe was perpetually one step ahead or behind us, like chasing a ghost through the vast metal labyrinth.

"This is becoming rather tiresome," Whipple muttered after our fourth unsuccessful attempt. "Let's try the engineering section."

As we passed from the luxury of the passenger area, through a heavy metal door into the crew's domain, I followed Whipple down several narrow staircases, deeper into the ship than I'd ventured before. The growing rumble of machinery grew louder, and the environment grew grubbier. A black substance soon surrounded us. Every surface bore a coat of coal dust.

I was the first to admit, silently, that we had taken a wrong turning. The passages had narrowed, the air grown thick and damp, and the steady throb of the ship's heartbeat now pressed in from all sides. Pipes ran low along the bulkheads, sweating faintly, while the electric lights burned weakly behind wire guards, their yellow glow doing little to soften the gloom.

Whipple stopped abruptly.

Ahead of us, a door stood half-open. From within came the scrape of cutlery, the low murmur of voices, and the unmistakable smell of coal dust, grease, and boiled meat. Heat rolled out in a suffocating wave.

I glanced at the stencilling on the bulkhead and felt a small tightening in my chest.

STOKERS MESS

We had no time to retreat.

Three men sat at a rough iron table just inside, hunched over tin plates. Their shirts had blackened almost to the original cloth, and soot streaked their faces so deeply that it seemed part of their skin. Coal dust clung to hair, brows, and eyelashes. Even their hands, thick, scarred, and powerful, left black smears on the cutlery as they ate.

All three looked up at once.

For several seconds, no one spoke.

The ship's engines thundered unseen beyond the bulkhead. A drip echoed somewhere in the pipework overhead, mixing with the coal dust where it fell to form a glutinous mush.

The men stared, disbelief giving way to suspicion, then to something colder.

Whipple stood his ground, shoulders squared. I was acutely aware of how out of place we were, clean collars, polished shoes, breathing air meant for other men entirely.

The largest of the three stokers slowly put down his knife and fork.

He was immense, thick through the neck and shoulders, arms like coiled rope beneath the grime. His eyes, pale and watchful beneath a heavy brow, never left Whipple's face.

He leaned back in his chair and growled, voice low and dangerous.

"What you two doin' down 'ere?"

He glanced pointedly at the doorway behind us.

"This is our place. Not passengers'."

A pause. Long enough to be deliberate followed.

"Get yourselves out of here," he added, "before I shift you."

For a moment, Rex was certain the man meant to rise.

The stoker's chair creaked as he shifted his weight forward, heavy boots planted wide beneath the table. One of the others slid his plate aside, not looking at Whipple now, but at me, as though judging how hard he might hit. The third man's hand disappeared briefly below the tabletop and returned empty, yet the movement alone was enough to give me a start.

Whipple raised a hand.

"Easy," he said quietly.

The word carried, not in volume, but in certainty.

"I'll not pretend we belong here. We've taken a wrong turning, and for that I apologise."

The big stoker snorted.

"Wrong turning's a habit of yours, is it?"

Whipple met his gaze evenly.

"Detective Inspector Arthur Whipple. Scotland Yard," Whipple announced with quiet authority.

That, at least, caused a stir. One of the men straightened. Another frowned. The big stoker did neither. He merely leaned back again, arms folding slowly across his chest.

"And 'I'm?

Whipple looked at me and put a hand on my shoulder. "I suppose you might call him my apprentice."

I took Whipple's explanation as a compliment. Also, if it stopped me getting a walloping from the three giants, all the better.

"Is he," growled the huge stoker before snorting out a black concoction from his nose into a filthy neckerchief. "This ain't your patch," he said.

"No," Whipple agreed. "But there's been a death aboard. And until that matter is settled, every part of this vessel is my concern."

Silence returned, altered now, less hostile, more watchful.

"We are looking for the chief officer. Mr Bowthorpe.

The name landed heavily.

One of the stokers glanced at the others. The smallest of the giants frowned and looked down at his scarred hands. The big man's jaw moved, as though grinding grit between his teeth.

"Bowthorpe's a fool, and a coward," he said at last.

"Really? Why do you say that" Whipple asked.

"Thinks he knows everything. The problem is that the man understands nothing."

A humourless curl touched Rex's mouth, but he said nothing.

Whipple nodded.

"Then we'll leave you to your meal. Again—my apologies for the intrusion."

He turned, signalling the end of our encounter.

"Hang on."

Whipple stopped.

The stoker unfolded his arms and leaned forward, forearms on the table, voice lower now, less guarded.

"If you're lookin' into things…there's summat you ought to know."

Whipple turned back.

"Yes?"

The stoker hesitated, then jerked his chin toward the bulkhead, as though the words were reluctant to travel.

"Coal bunker number three is on fire."

Rex stiffened.

"On fire?" Whipple repeated evenly.

"It's deep down. Hard to stamp out proper 'cos there's 500 tons of best Welsh steam coal in that bunker."

"How long?" Whipple asked.

The stoker's eyes flicked briefly to the others, then back again.

"Best part of a week."

"A week," Rex echoed. "And no report?"

The muscle-bound stoker shrugged his shoulders and gave an exaggerated sniff. "We reported it. The chief officer knows. He just said to get on with our jobs. The fool doesn't understand what can…will happen if we don't empty the bunker and get the hot coals in the boiler."

I didn't want to think about the repercussions, but Whipple did.

"Has it spread?" Whipple asked.

The stoker's mouth twisted.

"It ain't spread…yet. Bowthorpe's betting on us getting to New York before the balloon goes up."

Whipple let the word hang.

"Thank you," he said at last. "That was the right thing to mention."

The man grunted, unconvinced.

"Just don't have it comin' back on us. It'll cost us our jobs if it does.

'What about your lives?" Whipple asked.

The stokers exchanged glances, then shrugged their shoulders.

"We have families to feed," said their leader.

A knowing silence fell.

"It won't," Whipple said. "I promise you."

As Whipple and I withdrew into the passage, the heat followed us like a living thing. I didn't speak until the door was well behind them.

"A fire," I said quietly. "Kept quiet for a week or more."

Whipple's expression was grim.

“And the Chief Officer…and captain has known about it all the time.”

He glanced back toward the direction of the stoker's mess.

“It wasn't wrong turning at all as things turned out, eh, Rex?” Whipple added. “Not in the least.”

Chapter Eight

A CONFESSION

I caught up with HG as she took a turn about the promenade deck in the late morning haze. The sea was calm and the breeze light. As if to provide further proof of a welcomed change in the weather, smoke billowed towards the stern from three huge funnels.

"We're making excellent time after the storm," HG commented, pointing to the fizzing water passing along the hull.

I didn't notice because I was too busy wanting to update HG on our discoveries.

"One of the coal bunkers is on fire," I said, keeping my voice low. "Has been for almost a week, according to one stoker. Both Bowthorpe and the captain know about it."

HG listened, her expression serious yet measured.

"Solid progress, Rex, but an unwanted distraction from our murder case, unless a link exists and you can prove it."

We both looked out to sea as I changed the subject.

"Any luck finding Miss Lily?"

HG harrumphed. "I could not find the woman, or von

Ritter for that matter. It's almost as if they're deliberately avoiding—" She stopped mid-sentence. "Well, talk of the Devil, there he is."

I turned to watch the diplomat saunter along the teak deck, without a care in the world. He wore a light grey three-piece suit with subtle pinstripes, polished oxfords, and carried a walking stick with a silver handle. A Homburg hat completed his ensemble.

"Good morning, Your Grace, young Rex," said von Ritter, doffing his hat.

We made small talk about the weather, and then HG asked, "Have you seen Miss Lily De Vere, our young actress, this morning?"

The diplomat thought for a second before saying he hadn't.

HG sighed. "I wish to return the item she left on her chair from the Variety Review last evening." She paused. "Speaking of which, I noticed Miss De Vere pursued you at close quarters as you left the entertainment."

Von Ritter looked out to sea, then back at HG. "Last night?"

The exchange had me on high alert; von Ritter's manner and the ease with which he played at disinterest piqued my curiosity. The man seemed to glide over HG's probing like an ice cube on glass.

"That lady can be quite persistent when she tries," von Ritter continued with a nonchalant wave. "Yes, she attempted to engage me in conversation when I finally reached the smoking room. Do you know, she rushed in like a rabbit escaping a greyhound. Caused quite a stir. Is there nowhere a man might have a little peace?"

HG's eyes twinkled with mischief, and she lifted an eyebrow. "Indeed, such an intrusion. Are we asking too much when we let you men escape life's demands for just a moment?" Her voice hinted at teasing, knowing too well von Ritter's type.

Von Ritter chuckled, a soundless laugh a diplomat would use, as they talked about the nicer weather.

"Do you know," von Ritter remarked, leaning on his stick with both hands, "the Kaiser Wilhelm II won the Blue Riband for the fastest return crossing in 1904? Quite an achievement, don't you think?"

HG barely missed a beat. "And now he spends his days chopping firewood in Holland...The Kaiser, I mean, not the ship!" Her smile was one of an aristocrat amused, yet acknowledging deeper undercurrents at play.

I watched von Ritter as HG brought up a sore spot from his country's history. He did not flinch, as if he were completely detached from the affair. Instead, he turned his gaze to the wide expanse of sea shimmering beneath the winter sun, which now gained ascendancy over the thinning clouds.

"Ah," he said, a note of acceptance in his voice, "such is life."

In that moment, von Ritter's resilience, or perhaps his careful play at nonchalance, revealed itself once more. The fellow was skilled at turning the conversation to safer waters without so much as batting an eyelash. His calm exterior masked whatever it was he truly thought or felt about the former Kaiser, and perhaps recent events on the ship, too.

HG, with her penchant for people-watching, likely enjoyed the game as much as I did. She knew the diplomat wouldn't take the bait, yet her pressing offered insight into his personality.

"And did she remain?" said HG.

Von Ritter turned, "No, no. Alas, The Empress died in early April last year...so sad."

HG displayed a rare touch of indignation. "You know well I meant Miss De Vere, and not her late Majesty. You let yourself down, Herr Ritter."

Von Ritter bit, "What is gone is gone. My country is in turmoil in no small measure because of your country, and others. One should be careful in demanding too much of the vanquished. A fox in a corner will bite back, will it not?"

HG and von Ritter glared at each other, neither willing to give ground. Eventually, von Ritter's facial features softened until he broke out in a soft smile.

"Come, Your Grace. Let us not argue. Has there not been enough of such things between the Great Powers in recent years? Please accept my apologies for teasing you, which was most uncalled for. Can you forgive me?"

I watched the unfolding events with astonishment; how two such powerful people played with one another over the most serious of world events. The pair danced around each other like seasoned fighters, testing defences, withdrawing when necessary. The dialogue exemplified aristocratic verbal sparring.

HG offers a nod. "You are correct, of course. Let us not argue. Instead, we shall be friends, although our friendship will be all the stronger if you consider my earlier question in the manner I asked."

Von Ritter snapped his heels together in military style and gave a sharp bow of his head. "Of course, Your Grace...or may I address you as Eleanor, now that we are to be firm friends?"

HG offered her hand, palm downwards, which von Ritter kissed.

"That is the spirit, Klaus."

I watched the diplomat's face. Something flickered behind his eyes that I couldn't quite place, satisfaction perhaps, or calculation. The diplomatic exchange shifted from out-and-out hostility to polite friendship in mere moments. However, I couldn't shake the feeling that neither revealed their hand.

"Now, as to your question," von Ritter continued, his tone lighter but guarded, "Miss De Vere did not remain in the smoking room long. She approached me and began to…how do you say…ah, yes, rummage about in her handbag. However, whatever it was she searched for, her efforts remained unfulfilled. After that, she simply looked at me for a few seconds, then left without looking to her left or right. Most peculiar behaviour, even for an actress, do you not think?"

"Indeed. Most peculiar," HG replied.

"If you'll excuse me," von Ritter said with another slight bow, "If that is all, I have important correspondence to attend to before luncheon."

After a further dip of the head, the fellow turned and strode off with a purposeful stride.

I turned to HG. "Do you believe him?"

"Not entirely," she murmured, watching his retreating figure. "But even lies can reveal truths, Rex. Remember that."

I wandered the first-class areas alone, mulling over von Ritter's exchange with HG. Something about it nagged at me. Perhaps the diplomat's too-smooth transition from antagonism to cordial friendship?

The promenade deck stretched before me, now bathed

in winter sunlight as passengers emerged to enjoy the calmer seas.

A soft whimper broke through my thoughts. I paused, unsure if I'd imagined it until I heard it again; a stifled sob coming from somewhere nearby. The sound led me to a hidden alcove, out of sight from the main path, behind a decorative column.

There stood Penelope Chase, her elegant figure hunched forward as she dabbed at her eyes with a silk handkerchief.

"Miss Chase?" I kept my voice low. "Are you quite alright?"

She startled, looking up with red-rimmed eyes. As she moved her hand away from her face, I noticed a thin trickle of blood running across her knuckles.

"You're bleeding," I said, stepping closer.

"It's nothing." She tried to tuck her hand away but winced.

"Excuse the double-negative, that doesn't look like ‘nothing’. What happened?"

Her lower lip trembled. "I was just—" She broke off, fresh tears welling. Before I could react, Penelope moved toward me, arms sliding around my waist as she pressed her face against my chest.

I froze, confounded. My hands dangled at my sides while my mind raced. This close, I caught the scent of her French perfume mingled with salt tears.

"Miss Chase, I—"

"Plcasc," shc whispcrcd. "Just for a momcnt."

Compassion tugged at me, yet caution held me back. A tearful woman on a previous case, an error that almost cost HG her reputation, had duped me before. Was this genuine distress, or calculated manipulation?

I glanced nervously at the alcove entrance. If anyone discovered us in this compromising position, it would ruin both our reputations.

Trapped in this tiny space with a crying, bleeding woman who might well be involved in a murder, I knew I had to act. I placed my hands on her shoulders and created a distance between us.

"Your hand needs attention," I said firmly. "Then you must tell me what happened."

I understood that Penelope's appearance, with tears and a bleeding hand, could attract attention she didn't want. A discreet exit to HG's stateroom seemed prudent.

"Miss Chase," I murmured softly, "I suggest we continue our conversation somewhere more private. Perhaps you could pretend to search for something in your handbag as we walk. You know, to hide your injury."

Penelope nodded, her face pale but understanding. She rummaged through her handbag as we made our way down the corridor, the colourful carpet absorbing the sound of our footsteps. My heart thudded with each step, mind a whirl. What could have driven her to such visible despair? And more pressing, would HG be in?

Thankfully, the corridor remained deserted as we reached HG's stateroom. I knocked, pressing a silent prayer to the skies. Please be here, HG.

Moments later, the door swung open to reveal HG's elegant figure. Her brows furrowed with concern as she took in Penelope's dishevelled state and my tight expression.

She caught my gaze.

"What happened, my dear boy?"

I could only shrug, my shoulder shrug a clear admission of ignorance.

"Come in," HG said, ushering us inside the warm,

inviting stateroom. The scent of lavender hung in the air, soothing in its familiarity. She settled Penelope into a plush armchair and turned her attention to the young woman's condition.

"A brandy, I think," HG said, pouring a generous measure from the decanter on an elegant mahogany table. Penelope accepted it with a trembling hand, then surprised us both by downing it in one swift motion. I shared a wide-eyed glance with HG; neither of us had anticipated such fortitude.

Once Penelope appeared calmer, HG knelt beside her and gently examined the raw knuckles. "Who have you been walloping?" HG's tone held a teasing lilt designed to ease the tension in the room.

Her levity had precisely the opposite effect. Penelope's composure shattered once more as a fresh wave of sobs emerged, leaving HG and I exchanging looks of consternation. Without words to soothe, I closed my eyes for a brief, weary moment as we waited for Penelope's storm of tears to abate. What was it that lay behind such distress?

HG allowed Penelope's distress to unfold for a short while, her presence calming in its decisiveness. She placed a hand on each of Penelope's shoulders, anchoring the young woman once more.

Penelope's eyes met HG's with a flicker of defiance. HG whispered, but with resolution. "Time to explain, dear girl. Such distress must not continue. Remember your upbringing...where is that stiff upper lip? Now, another brandy, if you promise not to knock it back in one and pass out on Rex and I. Come, let us gather our emotions."

The magic of HG's words unfolded before my eyes; the mere mention of 'stiff upper lip' seemed to rekindle a flame within Penelope. She sat up straight, as if playing a part, she knew well from years of practice, and her calm demeanour was like a comfortable cloak. Her tears vanished, a transformation both astounding and unsettling.

I'd not experienced such societal training as a child. I marvelled at the power an upper-class upbringing held. My own childhood lay a world apart from the polished façade presented by Penelope. I knew I'd never truly fit that aristocratic mould. This, despite HG's plucking me from the children's home she endowed and making me her Ward.

HG poured another brandy and handed it to Penelope, watching as she accepted with a tentative smile. "Now, my dear," HG began, "tell us plainly what troubles you so."

Penelope drew a shuddering breath, then looked more certain. "Someone visited my cabin early this morning. I was still in bed," she confessed, voice subdued yet unwavering. "They took nothing, rearranged nothing, yet left behind a sense of...violation. As though a warning."

HG and I exchanged a look, understanding the implications.

"Did you see anyone?" I inquired, maintaining the calmness HG had inspired in the room.

"No," Penelope admitted, her eyes momentarily dimming with fear. "But I felt a presence...I"

"All will be well, dear girl," HG interjected, a warm smile softening her features. "We'll get to the bottom of this."

Whipple soon appeared at the stateroom door, his usual ill-fitting suit doing him no favours. The fabric hung loose on him, giving him a perpetually dishevelled appearance. As I opened the door wider to admit him, his bored expression shifted to eager intent the moment his eyes settled on Penelope. It reminded me of a leopard spying its lunch.

Penelope stiffened, her hands tightening around her

glass. Yet, before any awkwardness could form, HG's soothing voice cut through the sudden tension.

"Do come in, Arthur. I'm sure Miss Penelope won't mind, will you, dear?" HG's words were a balm; her tone relaxed.

Penelope's training kicked in as she offered a forced smile, though I noted the tightness lingering around her eyes.

Whipple plopped himself into one of the luxurious armchairs, looking out of place amidst the opulence. As if sensing the collective curiosity in the room, HG addressed him.

"What brings you here at this time of day? I thought you had urgent matters to attend to."

Whipple grimaced with frustration. "I did, but the captain is unavailable because of a safety drill with the crew." If you ask me, it sounds a bit fishy, considering he's got a chief and first officer for such matters."

Settling in, Whipple reached into his jacket pocket with familiar intent. I watched him with detached amusement, guessing what he sought from the distinct rustle of paper. True to form, out came an Everton mint. Whipple unwrapped it, slid the mint into his mouth, and nursed it with customary care.

As he sucked on the sweet, I pondered whether it served as a sort of comforter for him. Something that bridged childhood security into the stress-laden demands of grown-up life. He invariably reached for mints when anxiety or stress gripped him, a revealing habit.

HG leaned back, sipping her brandy as she studied Whipple with a mix of interest and empathy. "Well, Arthur, at least we have some time to assist Miss Penelope with her conundrum."

I heard the distinct sound of the Everton mint colliding with Whipple's teeth as this new piece of information sparked his interest.

"A conundrum?" offered Whipple. His brow furrowed with the alert curiosity that transformed him from rumpled bureaucrat to keen detective in an instant.

HG briefed him succinctly. "Miss Chase believes someone entered her cabin this morning while she was still abed. Nothing was taken or disturbed, yet she feels it was deliberate, perhaps a warning."

Whipple fixed Penelope with such an intense stare that she shifted in her seat. He had forgotten he was supposed to be offering a sympathetic ear, not interrogating a suspect. I suppressed a smile, remembering the maxim I'd heard so often around Scotland Yard: 'Once a policeman, always a policeman.'

HG noticed too. "Arthur, do behave," she scolded gently. "Miss Chase is distressed, not under suspicion."

Whipple looked confused for a second before understanding dawned. His features softened , though the transition appeared almost mechanical, as if he were adjusting a mask.

"My apologies, Miss Chase," he said with more warmth. "But I must ask, how do you know someone entered your room when nothing was disturbed? Was your cabin locked when you checked?"

Penelope tensed again.

"Inspector Whipple wants to find out what happened to better protect you," HG explained calmly.

The reassurance worked. Penelope's shoulders relaxed as she looked at Whipple with renewed trust.

"I just know," she said softly. "I cannot explain it logically, Detective Inspector. The door was indeed locked, both when I retired and when I rose. Yet I felt a presence, a disturbance in the air. Like the atmosphere when you enter a room recently vacated, that lingering warmth of another person." Her voice grew steadier as she continued. "I've lived alone since my father died three years ago. One develops a sensitivity to intrusion, even subtle ones."

Whipple nodded. The mint clicked against his teeth again as he considered her words.

"Instinct shouldn't be dismissed," he conceded. "Did you notice anything at all out of place? Even something minor might help."

Penelope's calm veneer shattered before us.

"None of you believe me," she wailed, her voice rising to a pitch that made me wince. Tears streamed down her face as she hugged herself tightly. "Someone did get into my room. Or something did."

We exchanged alarmed glances. Whipple's Everton mint fell from his open mouth.

"It must have been a ghost," Penelope continued, her eyes wild and unfocused. "Sir Edmund Blythe from the spirit world. He tried to blackmail my father just before he died. Now Blythe has come back to haunt me. He wants something from me..."

I felt a chill run through me that had nothing to do with the temperature of the stateroom. Her accusation hung in the air like a physical presence, impossible to ignore.

Where had this flood of words come from? Was this a secret Penelope had been bottling up since boarding? The implications were horrendous if she had joined the ship knowing Sir Edmund was a passenger. Perhaps she had boarded specifically because of him.

HG moved first, crossing to Penelope and guiding her gently back to her seat. She spoke in hushed, soothing tones while I remained frozen, unable to reconcile the composed society girl with this frightened creature before us.

"My dear, breathe deeply," HG murmured, her hand making small circles on Penelope's back. "No spirits will harm you while we're here."

Whipple cleared his throat awkwardly. He retrieved his mint from the floor, examined it sadly, then slipped it into his pocket.

"Miss Chase," he said carefully, "what exactly did Sir Edmund hold over your father?"

HG shot him a warning glance, but Penelope had begun to settle. Though still tense, her breathing grew more regular. Her hands shook, making the brandy HG gave her move around in the glass, like a small, stormy sea. Her gaze darted toward the door. Whether she feared something coming in or was planning her escape, I couldn't tell.

Penelope clutched her brandy glass. The wildness had left her eyes, replaced by something more controlled, more calculated.

"My father never revealed the nature of his problem," Penelope said at last, her voice steadier now. "In the last few months of his life, he became reclusive, withdrawn. It wasn't like him at all; he was always so outgoing, so full of life."

HG nodded encouragingly. "Was he ill perhaps?"

"Not that I knew of," Penelope replied, absently tracing the rim of her glass. “Our family doctor mentioned no ailment serious enough to cause such distress.”

She paused, took a small sip of brandy, and continued. "In his last days, he asked to speak with me privately. He told me never to be frightened of anyone, and never to be duped by tales of quick money in foreign parts."

"Curious advice," Whipple remarked, his eyes narrowing.

"I found it deeply worrying," Penelope admitted. "Our family estate was, and remains, entirely solvent. Father had no need of money, nor financial concerns I was aware of." She looked up, her gaze moving between us. "I could only conclude he spoke of protecting my reputation rather than financial matters. Integrity and reputation meant everything to Father. Another strange thing he said to me was that the truth was not always in the written word. I don't know what he meant, I'm afraid."

"And how did he pass away?" HG asked gently.

Penelope's expression clouded. "A massive heart attack took him, or at least that is what his doctor said, "yet no autopsy took place. Something in her tone suggested doubt.

We exchanged concerned glances. The implications were devastating. Blackmail, mysterious warnings, a wealthy man's sudden death…and a murdered passenger?

Whipple leaned forward, his elbows on his knees. "Miss Chase," he said carefully, "did you know Sir Edmund was to be a passenger on the Britannic Star when you booked your ticket?"

The room fell silent. Penelope's gaze dropped to the floor; I could see her mind working, weighing her options. Her expression remained composed, almost defiant, when she finally looked up at Whipple.

"Yes."

That single word changed everything. I felt my breath catch, watching as Whipple's face hardened. The gentle questioning atmosphere evaporated.

"You are aware," Whipple stated sternly, "that the things you've told us make you a top suspect in Sir Edmund Blythe's death?"

Penelope didn't flinch. She placed her glass down on the side table, her movements deliberate and controlled. The trembling had stopped; her earlier distress seemed almost theatrical now in retrospect.

"I suspected as much," she replied coolly. "But if I'd killed him, Inspector, why would I voluntarily tell you about our connection? Surely that would be rather foolish of me."

HG placed a restraining hand on Whipple's arm before he could respond. "Let's not get ahead of ourselves, Arthur," she cautioned, though I noticed her own expression had grown more guarded. "Miss Chase came to us in distress. Something frightened her this morning, ghost or otherwise. We should address that before casting accusations."

I struggled to reconcile the sobbing, frightened woman I'd found on the deck with this composed, almost challenging figure before us now. Which was the real Penelope Chase? And more importantly, how did she hurt her hand?

Chapter Nine

NOTHING TO LOSE

The air felt fresher here, away from the warren of first-class compartments. A gentle breeze carried the lingering scent of salt and varnish as I ambled through the shaded promenade towards a quiet spot, seeking solitude after the whirlwind of recent revelations. Yet my solitude was brief, for there stood Baron von Ritter, appearing at ease, as if the murder that rattled our voyage were merely a footnote in his leisure.

Glimpsing me, he extended a greeting, his smile an elegant enigma. "Ah, young Mr. Rex, indulging in a breath of fresh air, are we?"

"Trying to, Baron." I replied, wary of the undercurrents beneath his calm surface.

He gestured to the bench beside him, and I obliged, noting how relaxed he seemed. It was as if even the grim affair of Sir Edmund's demise could neither disturb his composure nor crease the pleats of his impeccably tailored suit. I tried to discern whether his calm was an affectation or genuine indifference.

"You strike me," von Ritter began, tone as smooth as polished mahogany, "as someone who might appreciate the difference between influence and integrity."

The mention seemed benign on its face, but his words carried weight. They ran deeper, almost like the anchored hull beneath our feet. I sensed an oblique reference to Sir Edmund, the catalyst for our silent dance of words.

"The Dowager instilled in me a preference for the latter," I remarked, aware von Ritter was testing the depth of my understanding.

He laughed softly, a sound unobtrusive and yet somehow resonant. "Indeed, a philosophy many extol, but few practice when their interests face a challenge."

I anticipated the arrival of a thrust, some pointed query to unseat me, but he was all languid grace, these barbed impressions intangible yet unmistakable. His conversation pirouetted like a dance of smoke, always indicating but never directly accusing.

Still, I felt scrutinised, and what more might his gaze quantify? My knowledge or perhaps anticipated retaliation? Was this an evaluative prelude, a strategic gauging of loyalties? I matched his coolness, exchanging words, untroubled in outward demeanour while attempting to decipher each layer he laid down.

Yet above all else, his poise was striking. It bespoke of a man who carried his own innocence with the certainty of a burden hoisted elsewhere, an athlete unburdened, knowing full well when this race concluded, the finish line's shadow would fall not upon him, but another, one ensnared unawares in the wake of his confidence.

Von Ritter ran his fingers along the polished rail, his gaze fixed on the horizon where sea met sky in a perfect, untroubled line.

"Sir Edmund," he said, the name emerging with deliberate precision, "was not the reckless fool many assume. He operated with...shall we say, a certain latitude? Men like Blythe rarely navigate dangerous waters without some manner of protection."

I watched von Ritter's profile, noting how the man seemed utterly unconcerned about discussing a murder victim so openly.

"Protection is rarely accidental, wouldn't you agree?" Von Ritter continued. "Someone must extend it. Someone must maintain it."

"I imagine Sir Edmund had many connections," I offered cautiously, measuring each word.

Von Ritter's smile tightened. "Connections. Yes, that's the English way of phrasing it. So delicate, so proper." He turned to face Rex fully. "Your Sir Edmund had arrangements that would make even your aristocracy blush. His death was not random, nor was it unexpected in certain circles."

I felt a chill that had nothing to do with the ocean breeze. Von Ritter spoke with the assured certainty of someone privy to information he shouldn't possess. There was no overt threat in his words, but something far more unsettling – absolute confidence.

"You seem remarkably well-informed about a man you claimed to barely know," I observed.

Von Ritter chuckled softly. "Information is currency, young man. And I am, by nature, a wealthy individual." He adjusted his cufflinks – gold, with small diamonds catching the light. "Your English respectability is quite the façade, isn't it? All those impeccable manners concealing the most... uncomfortable arrangements."

"Every society has its secrets," I countered.

"Indeed. But yours are particularly fascinating when exposed to daylight." Von Ritter straightened his already immaculate jacket. "When the truth emerges, and it always does, I simply wish to be properly positioned to observe the spectacle."

I suddenly understood. Von Ritter wasn't concerned with justice or even with clearing his own name. He was anticipating the scandal, the revelation of whatever tangled web Sir Edmund had woven. The German diplomat was settling in to watch respected reputations unravel, perhaps even to profit from their destruction.

"You'll excuse me," von Ritter said, offering a military-style nod. "I believe I've said quite enough for one morning."

As the baron walked away, I remained still, troubled not by what had been said, but by the calculated pleasure with which von Ritter had said it.

I found HG waiting for me at our usual table in the Palm Court restaurant. Beams of sunlight slanted through the glass ceiling, casting dappled light across the white linen. She wore a slate-grey dress with subtle embroidery around the collar, the very picture of aristocratic composure.

"You look troubled," she remarked, setting aside her menu as I took my seat.

"I had an encounter with von Ritter," I explained, keeping my voice low despite the clink of silverware and murmur of conversation that provided cover.

As the waiter served our consomme, I recounted the entire exchange. HG didn't interrupt. She watched me with unwavering attention, her spoon poised midair. What struck me was how she focused on aspects I'd considered incidental.

"His posture was relaxed throughout?" she asked.

"Completely at ease." I nodded, buttering a roll. "He seemed almost pleased about it."

HG sipped her water, her eyes narrowed in thought. Within ten minutes, the waiter returned with our Dover sole, perfectly filleted table-side. She waited until we were alone again before speaking.

"Rex, men like von Ritter are dangerous not because they lie, but because they offer partial truths. They reveal just enough to disturb the waters while remaining safely on shore."

"You believe he knows something concrete about Sir Edmund?"

"Without question. But knowledge isn't the same as culpability." She placed her napkin across her lap with precise movements. "Such men flourish in uncertainty; they position themselves close to truth without caring where it leads, provided they remain untouched."

A chill ran through me despite the restaurant's warmth. "Then what is his game?"

"Perhaps he wishes to witness the fallout. Perhaps he seeks to direct it. What matters is that he feels removed from consequence." She leaned forward, her voice dropping. "Remember this, Rex. A man untouched by fear or consequence is capable of watching great harm unfold without lifting a finger. Indeed, he may even take pleasure in the spectacle."

Whipple arrived as we finished our dessert, looking somewhat more rested than he had earlier. His suit remained as rumpled as ever, but there was a sharpness in his eyes that spoke of renewed determination. He slid into the chair beside HG with a nod of greeting.

"I trust I haven't missed anything significant?" he asked,

signalling for his usual plate of sausages, mashed potatoes, and garden peas.

"Rex had an interesting encounter with our German friend," HG replied, dabbing her lips with a napkin.

I recounted my conversation with von Ritter once more, watching Whipple's reaction with interest. His expression remained largely impassive, though I noticed a tightening around his mouth when I mentioned the baron's apparent foreknowledge of Sir Edmund's precarious position.

"What do you make of him?" I asked.

Whipple sighed, stirring sugar into his newly poured tea with more attention than the task required. "Diplomatically speaking, he's an inconvenience."

"An inconvenience?" I echoed, somewhat taken aback by his dismissive tone.

"We've nothing concrete against him, Rex," Whipple explained, setting his fork down with deliberate care. "Insinuations and cryptic remarks don't constitute evidence. The man holds diplomatic status; without something substantial, pursuing him would create complications far beyond this ship."

HG agreed. "The Foreign Office would become involved; there would be questions in Parliament. All manner of political considerations would overshadow our investigation."

I understood their perspective, of course. Procedure and jurisdiction were the foundations of Whipple's work; international diplomatic immunity presented genuine obstacles. Yet I couldn't shake the feeling that we were missing something important about von Ritter.

"There's something about him," I insisted, searching for the right words. "He doesn't fit neatly into our assessments of motive or opportunity. He speaks as though positioned above consequences."

"Many diplomats cultivate that precise impression," HG replied, her tone not unkind but firm. "It's part of their professional armour."

As the conversation moved to other aspects of the case, I found myself troubled by how easily von Ritter had been set aside. Perhaps that was his greatest protection; to be dismissed as a diplomatic complication rather than recognised as a genuine threat.

I excused myself after the meal concluded, promising to meet HG and Whipple later for further discussions. My mind kept returning to Penelope, her wounded hand, her tearful confession. Concerned for her wellbeing, I sought her out in the ship's library, where a steward had mentioned seeing her.

The library stood almost empty at this hour, weak sunlight filtering through tall windows onto polished tables and leather-bound volumes. Penelope sat alone in a corner armchair, a book open but unread in her lap. She looked up as I approached; her smile faltered and then reasserted itself.

"How's your hand?" I asked, taking the seat opposite her.

"Better, thank you. The Dowager's ministrations were most effective." She flexed her fingers.

I hesitated, uncertain how to broach my concerns without causing further distress. "I wanted to ask you about something. Earlier today, I had a rather strange conversation with Baron von Ritter."

The effect was immediate. Colour drained from Penelope's face; her shoulders tensed. She closed her book with a sharp snap.

"What about him?" Her voice sounded tight, controlled.

"He seemed to know things about Sir Edmund, things that suggested a closer connection than he's admitted."

"I've had no dealings with that man," she insisted quickly, too quickly. "None whatsoever."

I leaned in, keeping my voice gentle. "Penelope, I'm not suggesting you have. I simply wondered if you might know something about their relationship."

She shook her head, yet her eyes darted around the room as if seeking unseen listeners. What struck me wasn't fear of accusation but something more fundamental; fear of implication, of being drawn into something beyond her control.

"Sir Edmund," she finally said, her voice barely above a whisper, "moved among men who frightened me. Men like von Ritter. They're part of a system where rules bend for those with influence."

"You're safe here," I assured her, though my words felt hollow.

"Am I?" Her smile turned bitter. "These men, they have connections, systems that protect them. I think Sir Edmund understood this."

I wanted to reassure her, to promise protection, but what guarantees could I offer? Looking at Penelope's frightened face, I understood something crucial. Her fear wasn't irrational; it related to the impersonal machinery of power that men like von Ritter represented, systems that could crush lives, even amongst the aristocracy, without even acknowledging their existence.

I left Penelope to her troubled thoughts, my mind turning to another enigma. As I walked the corridor back towards my room, a memory resurfaced; something I'd noted but not processed during my exchange with von Ritter.

Lily de Vere had been there, not ten yards away, concealed behind a lifeboat station. She was perfectly positioned to overhear our entire conversation, but she didn't approach or acknowledge her presence. Her stillness had been deliberate, almost professional in its execution.

The more I considered it, the more this pattern of behaviour revealed itself. At the captain's dinner, when tensions flared between Blythe and von Ritter, she'd spilled wine with such precise timing that it redirected the entire conversation. In the smoking room, she'd watched the seance unfold with calculated detachment. During breakfast discussions and corridor encounters, she lingered just within earshot yet contributed nothing beyond social pleasantries.

What struck me now was that Lily had spoken barely a word about Sir Edmund, despite their apparent acquaintance. She didn't speak about his personality or who he knew, even though others shared their thoughts and memories. Such disciplined reticence seemed increasingly deliberate.

Perhaps her power lay not in what she said, but in what she heard; not in the information she provided, but in what she collected. Like a spider sensing vibrations in its web, she gathered intelligence through patient observation.

I paused by a porthole, watching whitecaps form on the grey Atlantic. Intelligence gathering served a purpose beyond mere curiosity. Knowledge required application to hold value. If Lily collected secrets and confidences, what conclusions had she already drawn about Sir Edmund's murder? About the passengers and crew? About me?

Most concerning of all, what decisions might she make based on these conclusions? While we scrambled to uncover the truth, she might already possess it, weighing its value against her own interests. Her silence now seemed less like disinterest and more like calculation, a measured assessment of when and how to deploy what she knew.

I paced the length of my cabin, recalling each encounter with von Ritter since Sir Edmund's death. The German diplomat's behaviour had been striking not for what it revealed, but for what it lacked. Where others displayed shock, distress, or at least appropriate solemnity, von Ritter had shown nothing beyond mild irritation.

When news of the murder first broke, passengers gasped and whispered. Madame Zelda clutched her pearls; Penelope nearly fainted. Even the hardened sailors looked disturbed. Yet von Ritter merely frowned, as if someone had spilled coffee on his newspaper.

At breakfast the following morning, when the captain had circulated the formal procedures for a death aboard ship, von Ritter checked his watch twice. Not the gesture of a man concerned with justice or propriety, but of someone impatient for an inconvenient matter to conclude.

During HG's subtle questioning at luncheon, his responses were perfectly composed, his eyes never widening, voice never trembling. He discussed a brutal murder with the emotional investment one might give to discussing a delayed train.

I recalled how he'd sighed when informed the investigation would delay certain shipboard activities. "These English procedures," he'd muttered, "always so tediously thorough." As if murder were merely an administrative burden.

What troubled me wasn't just this emotional absence; it was the calculation behind it. Von Ritter wasn't suppressing normal human reactions. He simply didn't possess them.

The death meant nothing to him beyond its impact on his schedule, his comfort, his plans.

HG once told me that the most dangerous people aren't those who act from passion or anger, but those who feel nothing at all when causing harm. Anger burns hot but often burns out; indifference has no natural limit.

Von Ritter's cool detachment wasn't evidence of innocence, as I'd initially assumed. It might instead be the hallmark of someone who viewed human lives as mere pieces on a chessboard, to be sacrificed without regret when strategy demanded it.

I shivered despite the warmth of my surroundings. Perhaps this was what truly separated killers from ordinary people. Not the capacity for rage, but that of indifference.

I needed clarity, direction through the murk of motives. Only one person aboard could provide it. I found myself knocking on HG's stateroom door just as dusk settled over the ship, casting long shadows through the portholes that lined the corridor.

She admitted me with a nod, already dressed for dinner in a gown of midnight blue silk that captured the fading light. The scent of lavender mingled with a warmer fragrance, a restrained pairing I connected with moments of deep thought.

"I've been expecting you," she said, gesturing toward a chair. "You've had time to consider our German friend's performance."

"Performance is precisely the word," I replied, settling into a comfortable armchair. "Everything about him seems calculated, rehearsed."

HG poured two small glasses of brandy from a crystal decanter, handing one to me before taking her seat opposite.

The amber liquid caught the light from the desk lamp, creating miniature constellations in the glass.

"Men like von Ritter present a particular challenge to investigators," she began. "They operate at the periphery of culpability, always positioned to observe rather than act directly."

I sipped the brandy, feeling its warmth spread through my chest. "He knows things about Sir Edmund's death; I'm certain of it."

"Undoubtedly," HG agreed. "But knowledge isn't the same as guilt. Von Ritter cultivates information the way a gardener cultivates rare orchids, with patience and selective attention."

HG fixed me with her penetrating gaze. "Listen carefully, my dear boy. Men with nothing to lose often speak truths that others avoid. They can afford to be cavalier with facts that might destroy reputations or upend lives."

"You think he might actually lead us toward the truth?" I asked, surprised.

"I think he might point toward certain truths, yes," she replied. "But never mistake his revelations for justice or concern. Von Ritter serves only his own interests. Any illumination he provides is incidental, perhaps even calculated to obscure larger truths."

Her words crystallised something I'd felt but couldn't articulate. "He doesn't care who's harmed in the process."

"Precisely. His detachment isn't merely diplomatic; it's fundamental to his character. He observes human frailty with the clinical interest of a scientist watching bacteria in a petri dish."

I contemplated this as the ship rolled gently around us. Outside, twilight had given way to darkness, the portholes reflecting only our own images against the black night.

"Listen to him," HG continued. "Note what he reveals but never accept his conclusions. The facts he offers may be genuine. However, the narrative he constructs around them serves his purposes, and his purpose only."

"How do I separate truth from manipulation?" I asked.

HG smiled, the expression both kind and knowing. "By remembering that truth rarely serves a single master. von Ritter's revelations will align too perfectly with his worldview, his prejudices. The real truth is messier, more contradictory."

I nodded, understanding dawning. von Ritter might indeed offer valuable pieces to our puzzle, but the picture he suggested would distort reality to serve his ends.

As I left HG's stateroom, the corridor lights seemed dimmer than before. The ship's familiar creaks and groans now carried notes of warning rather than comfort. Something had shifted; not just in my perception of von Ritter, but in my understanding of our investigation.

Chapter Ten

THE NATURE OF INFLUENCE

HG's appearance at my cabin door after our discussion did not surprise me. The ship's social calendar showed nothing scheduled until late evening, leaving a rare pocket of muted reflection.

"Walk with me," she suggested, and we found ourselves in a secluded corner of the promenade deck. The grey Atlantic stretched beyond the rail.

After we had settled away from curious ears, HG asked me, "Tell me, Rex, do you believe people always exercise power openly?"

I considered this. "I suppose there are several ways in which influence may present itself. Direct actions with visible consequences by one who has power over another, or many people, for example?"

HG nodded, her gaze fixed on the horizon. "That's natural enough. But perhaps too limiting."

"How do you mean?"

She explained that people often apply the most effective pressure without direct instruction. Sometimes, just a look, a word, or even silence can make people act, and you don't have to be involved in what follows.

I recalled Captain Hardwick, First Officer Grayson, Matthews receiving the envelope, and Penelope's frightened expression when they discussed von Ritter.

"Like a chess master," I ventured, "moving pieces without touching them."

"The powerful rarely dirty their hands with direct action when they can achieve their aims through others."

My understanding shifted, rearranging the patterns I'd observed throughout our voyage. Conversations took on new significance; casual remarks revealed potential manipulation.

"So the person responsible for Sir Edmund's death might never have entered his cabin," I intoned.

"It's possible. Someone might have pressured or tricked the person who used the weapon into thinking they were doing the right thing.

The realisation settled over me like a cold fog. "Influence may be more dangerous than violence," I murmured, "because it leaves no trace, no evidence to follow. The guilty party might walk away unscathed while another pays the price."

HG's approving nod confirmed I'd grasped the lesson she'd intended to teach.

"I had a rather peculiar conversation with Penelope this morning," I said, leaning against the ship's railing. "She seemed more forthcoming than before, though still hesitant."

HG turned to face me, her grey eyes sharp with interest. "Go on."

"She mentioned something about Sir Edmund's manner that struck me as significant. She had raised the question of her father with Blythe. He never made direct threats when speaking with her about her father's situation."

"This is new information, Rex. She didn't mention this when we soothed her distress in my room?"

"No, I asked her the same thing when I escorted Penelope to her cabin. She had a moment of clarity once the pressure she felt in front of Whipple had eased off."

HG tilted her head to one side. What did the girl tell you?"

I frowned, recalling Penelope's exact words. "She gave him a stiff smile and said matters were 'seen to' without his involvement. He'd added things like 'unfortunate circumstances tend to find those who resist' or 'some situations have a way of resolving themselves.'

"Classic intimidation through implication," HG remarked.

"Penelope said what frightened her most was that he never raised his voice or showed anger. He spoke of ruination as casually as one might discuss the weather, with absolute certainty that his wishes would be carried out."

HG nodded. "Did she provide specific examples?"

"When her father refused to sign the codicil, Sir Edmund remarked that he should consider his daughter's reputation. Three days later, a journalist approached her with questions about fictional indiscretions. Sir Edmund never claimed responsibility; he asked her father if he'd reconsidered his position."

"Coercion based on expectation rather than force," HG said.

The pieces aligned in my mind. "That's it, isn't it? Sir Edmund relied on others, maintaining perfect deniability. He created an atmosphere where people anticipated his desires and fulfilled them without direct orders."

"A system of implicit commands," HG agreed. "The perfect shield against accusations."

I stared out at the darkening sea. "Which means the person who struck the fatal blow might have been acting on perceived expectations rather than explicit instructions. Sir Edmund's genuine power wasn't in what he did but in what others believed he might do."

"And it puts Penelope in Arthur's sight as the prime suspect when he hears this news, just as he warned the girl. Is that why you failed to tell us when you returned to my room after finding Miss Chase in the library?" HG added.

HG's comment hit me like iced rain. I realised what I had done. Instead of sharing vital information, I'd allowed my feelings for Penelope to cloud my judgement without even realising the consequences.

"I…I suppose I—"

'You suppose nothing, my darling boy. You know what you did," HG began. She placed a hand on my cheek and held it as a mother might calm her child. "Let this be a lesson. Emotions cloud our judgement, something we cannot allow when we are on an investigation. How do you think Arthur will react when he finds out, as he will?"

I knew that HG's words were not those of a reprimand. However, she was telling me what my responsibilities were, without speaking the words.

"You're right, and it's my responsibility to tell him."

HG's smile encircled me with the safety and love that only she could provide. I had learned a valuable lesson in my journey to emulate my mentor's investigative prowess, and, perhaps, a wider insight into trust.

"I'll speak to Arthur before dinner," I promised, feeling both chastened and grateful for HG's gentle correction. "He deserves to know everything I've learned, without delay."

"Good lad," HG said, patting my arm. "Now, I must attend to some correspondence. We'll reconvene before dinner to compare notes."

As HG departed, I remained at the railing, watching the gentle procession of waves. My thoughts focused on Sir Edmund Blythe, his comportment during the period between embarkation and his murder. Something about it nagged at me; a discordant note I hadn't identified until now.

Blythe seemed very confident, almost too much so, from the moment he entered the first-class lounge. I'd attributed this to his status and wealth, the natural confidence of a man accustomed to power. But understanding his methods clarified the hidden elements.

Blythe walked around the Britannic Star like he didn't have a worry in the world, even though he had upset or threatened others. He'd argued with von Ritter in public. The fellow had also made veiled threats at dinner; he'd moved through the ship's social spaces without a backward glance or moment of caution.

This wasn't just the confidence of privilege. Protection emanated from the man's assumed invincibility. But shielded by whom? And why would he feel so secure in the middle of the Atlantic, confined to a ship with his enemies?

The fire in the coal bunker, Matthews' anxious behaviour, von Ritter's puzzling comments, and how he bullied Penelope. These all pointed to a shape I couldn't yet define.

I gripped the railing tighter as the realisation gnawed at my mind. A man like Blythe, who crafted systems of influence and manipulation, would never place himself in genuine danger. He was right to be confident; He believed himself protected by the very web of relationships and secrets he'd constructed.

Whatever had happened in Sir Edmund's cabin that night had shattered his protection. He succumbed, unaware of the impending blow.

I found Whipple in the ship's library, hunched over a rough sketch of the first-class deck plan. His usually rumpled appearance had deteriorated further; his collar askew, and his hair stood at odd angles where he'd run his fingers through it.

"Arthur," I said, settling into the chair opposite him. "I need to tell you something."

He looked up, dark circles under his eyes. "What is it?"

"I've inadvertently kept information from you. About Penelope Chase." I recounted our conversation, including her revelations about Sir Edmund's methods of intimidation. "She described how he never made direct threats; he simply created an atmosphere and felt intimidated into action."

Whipple listened without interruption, his expression unchanging. When I finished, he sighed and returned to his deck plan.

"That's all fascinating, Rex, but it doesn't change our approach."

"But Arthur, don't you see? It speaks to how Blythe operated, how he might have enemies we haven't identified."

Whipple tapped his pencil against the paper. "I need to find out who entered Sir Edmund's cabin the night he died, between 10:30 PM and midnight."

"But what if the killer was an individual who felt forced

into action? Perhaps believing they had no choice...like Penelope?"

"That might affect the court's leniency, but not my methods," Whipple said, marking another X on the cabin layout. "Motives are messy, Rex. Access, timing, physical evidence; these are what solve cases."

I watched him work through his timeline, marking movements and locations. His approach was meticulous, tested by years of successful investigations. Yet I couldn't shake the feeling that something vital remained beyond its reach.

HG concentrated on spheres of influence; Whipple focused on concrete facts and physical possibilities. Both were necessary, I realised, but perhaps insufficient alone.

As Whipple continued his mapping, I wondered whether the truth of Sir Edmund's murder might lie somewhere between his procedural rigour and HG's intuitive understanding of how power truly operated in that shadowy space where influence became action, and suggestion manifested as violence.

I followed HG and Whipple into the cocktail lounge, a vision of refined opulence with its polished mahogany panelling and art deco light fixtures. Crystal chandeliers cast a warm glow. Plush crimson velvet armchairs were arranged in clusters around low marble-topped tables. The bar itself was a masterpiece of craftsmanship, with a brass rail gleaming beneath arranged bottles of premium spirits.

We settled into a quiet corner, Whipple signalling a white-jacketed steward who navigated between tables with practiced grace. The room hummed with the sophisticated murmur of first-class passengers. Crystal glasses tinkled against silver cocktail shakers.

"Gin rickey for me," HG said, smoothing her evening gown. "Arthur?"

"Scotch and soda, thank you," Whipple replied, his collar already beginning to wilt after a fine dinner.

"Whisky neat," I added.

As the steward departed, I noticed several passengers casting furtive glances our way. The murder of Blythe had transformed us into objects of fascination; respected yet feared for what we might uncover.

"They're wondering if we've made progress," HG murmured, following my gaze. "People fear uncertainty more than the truth."

Across the room, Lily de Vere held court among a circle of captivated listeners. The emerald dress matched her look, with her detailed hairstyle perfectly framing her face. Everything about her seemed calculated for impact.

"You didn't know him as I did," she was saying, voice pitched precisely to carry without appearing to do so. "Sir Edmund always demanded attention; it wasn't confidence so much as arrogance. Men of his sort measure their worth by the discomfort they create in others."

Her audience agreed, happy that she made Blythe's nature uncomplicated, even common.

"She's quite skilled," HG observed, accepting her drink from the returning steward. "Watch how she's reshaping their memories."

Lily's companions were sharing their memories of Blythe, but they were now coloured by Lily's version of events. What might have seemed commanding was now overbearing; what appeared as assurance was recast as entitlement.

"A bit of revisionist history," Whipple muttered. "Though I suppose the dead can't defend their reputations."

"It serves her purpose," I said, sipping my whisky. "If Blythe was merely an arrogant bully rather than a confident power broker, it diminishes him. Makes his murder seem less significant."

HG nodded. "And by extension, makes whoever killed him seem less dangerous, perhaps even justified."

I watched as Lily shimmied to another group, leaving her previous audience nodding in consensus. Within minutes, she had them laughing, the tension of discussing a murdered passenger dissolving under her social alchemy.

"She has a remarkable ability," I said, "to transform discomfort into acceptance."

"A valuable skill indeed," HG replied, her eyes never leaving Lily. "One wonders where else she might have applied it."

I was about to respond when Klaus von Ritter appeared beside our table, looking immaculate in his dinner jacket. His posture remained rigid despite the ship's gentle roll.

"May I join you?" he asked, gesturing to an empty chair.

HG nodded. "Please do, Baron."

Von Ritter settled himself with fluid ease, acknowledging Whipple with a nod before signalling the steward. "Courvoisier, if you please. Not that Brandy de Jerez, again, please."

"You prefer the Cognac of Napoleon rather than what Spain has to offer?"

Vo Ritter laughed, "On sent tout le soin qu'on y a mis."

Whipple scrunched his eyebrows at me. "One can taste the care that has gone into it," I whispered.

"That is correct, young Rex. I see the mark of your patron upon you."

I blushed; HG took the compliment.

We chatted about nothing in particular until his drink arrived. Von Ritter took a precise sip, his expression revealing nothing.

"I see our actress friend is holding court," he remarked, glancing toward Lily de Vere. "She possesses remarkable skill for someone of her background. One might almost believe she was born to it rather than merely playing a role."

"Miss de Vere is certainly gifted," HG replied neutrally.

Von Ritter smiled through thin lips. "Indeed. Your countrywoman understands how to deploy charm like a weapon. It's quite effective against English gentlemen who prefer to maintain their illusions of propriety."

The comment hung between us, deliberately provocative.

"I've always been intrigued," von Ritter said, swirling his drink, "by the English way of using others instead of acting directly."

His words were light but pointed, like a fencing expert making delicate touches with deadly intent.

"We find that civilisation often depends upon restraint, Baron," HG countered smoothly.

"Ah yes, restraint," he replied with a small smile. "Though I wonder if that restraint merely conceals a more calculated approach. Maintain a convenient distance, such perfect deniability. Perhaps not so different from our German methods after all, merely less honest about its nature."

He finished his brandy in a single elegant motion and stood. "Please excuse me. I promised the captain I would join his table this evening."

As von Ritter departed, I watched his back, noting the confident set of his shoulders.

"He understands the game well," I said.

"Too well," Whipple muttered.

For all his critique of English methods, von Ritter recognised the architecture of influence. He might disdain our approach, but he understood its power to perfection.

The evening wore on as the ship's gentle vibrations formed a constant backdrop to our conversation. After von Ritter's departure, we remained at our table, our drinks untouched.

"He's toying with us," I said, keeping my voice low. "Practically admitting he knows more than he's letting on."

Whipple tapped his finger against his glass. "But is that because he's involved, or merely enjoying the diplomatic immunity that allows him to act without consequence?"

"Both, perhaps," HG replied. "Men like the Baron cultivate ambiguity. It provides them with room to manoeuvre."

I glanced across the lounge where Lily de Vere now sat with Captain Hardwick, her hand occasionally brushing his arm as she spoke. The captain's expression had softened; the stern authority he usually projected now diminished.

"She's working him," I murmured. "Look at how she's positioned herself; close enough to suggest intimacy but not so close as to create scandal."

HG followed my gaze. "Observe how she laughs at precisely the right moment; not at his jokes, mind you, but when he needs reassurance."

Whipple shifted in his chair. "Surely that's just social grace?"

"It's calculated," I said. "Watch how she tilts her head, always maintaining eye contact at crucial moments. She's reading him, adjusting her responses to whatever he needs most."

HG smiled. "You're learning, Rex."

Around us, the evening's social choreography continued, a series of carefully managed impressions and subtle influence. First Officer Grayson watched Lily and the Captain, and I saw a look of concern or maybe envy on his face.

"I believe I'll retire," HG announced, finishing her drink. "Tomorrow promises to be most illuminating."

Whipple nodded, rising to his feet. "I'll accompany you, if I may. There are several points I'd like to discuss regarding the ship's log."

They departed together, leaving me alone with my thoughts and half-finished whisky. I watched the room with fresh eyes, seeing beyond the social veneer to the currents beneath. Penelope Chase sat alone, pretending to read while stealing glances at von Ritter's table. Matthews hovered near the door, his nervous energy barely contained. Madame Zelda observed everything from a corner, her heavily ringed fingers drumming silently against her thigh.

I finished my drink and stood, deciding to take a turn around the promenade deck before retiring. The night air was brisk but refreshing after the warm confines of the lounge. Stars scattered across the clear sky, and the moon cast a silver path across the dark water.

HG's words returned to me as I walked. True power operates through subtle influence rather than direct action. I thought of Sir Edmund Blythe, murdered despite his apparent confidence and position. Someone had decided his influence had become a liability rather than an asset.

Looking back at the illuminated windows of the cocktail lounge, I could see shadowy figures moving within. Passengers and crew engaged in their nightly rituals of sociability and service. Among them moved the invisible threads of influence.

Who aboard had woven those threads around Sir Edmund Blythe? Who had calculated that his death would serve their purpose better than his continued existence? The answer lay not in who had struck the physical blow, but in who had created the circumstances that made that blow inevitable.

As I turned toward my cabin, I felt a subtle shift in my perception. The way things were affecting each other on the ship was clear, like a web sparkling in the night. And like all such patterns, once recognised, they could never again fade from view. I knew I would never see the world quite the same way again.

Chapter Eleven

WHO'S INTERESTS ARE SERVED?

I woke before dawn, my mind still circling the web of influence I'd glimpsed the previous night. Unable to return to sleep, I dressed and made my way to the ship's library, surprised to find Whipple already there, surrounded by notes.

"You're up early," I said, sliding into the chair opposite him.

Whipple looked up, tired eyes suggesting he'd been there for some time. "I haven't slept. Something von Ritter said kept nagging at me."

"About intermediaries?"

"Indeed." Whipple pushed a sheet of paper towards me. "I've been mapping who benefits from Blythe's death."

I examined his methodical notes. "Von Ritter tops your list."

"With Blythe's demise, and from what HG tells me about von Ritter's German industrialist 'friends', they stand to gain power in several markets. Our victim was blocking their expansion efforts."

"And Madame Zelda?" I asked.

"Blythe knew something about her past. I applied a little police pressure on Mathews. In the end, he confirmed his boss kept a dossier of her activities in Paris before the war."

Whipple continued down his list: Penelope Chase's family reputation preserved; Lily de Vere's blackmail letters recovered.

"Everyone had something to gain," I murmured.

"And that's what troubles me," Whipple said. "Too many beneficiaries, too many motives."

I followed his logic, but something felt off. The columns of beneficiaries and motives seemed too neat, too rational for the messy business of murder.

"What if we're approaching this wrong?" I suggested. "We're looking for someone who deliberately killed Blythe for personal gain. But what if the benefit was incidental?"

Whipple frowned. "Explain."

"HG said true power operates through subtle influence. What if someone created conditions where Blythe's death became inevitable, without doing it themselves?"

"A catalyst rather than a direct agent," Whipple mused.

The morning light crept through the library windows as we sat in silence. Outside, the sea stretched to the horizon.

"The most dangerous person aboard," I said finally, "might be someone who benefits from chaos itself rather than any specific outcome."

A realisation struck me then, chilling in its clarity: one need not intend the death of another to profit from it. The web of influence I'd glimpsed was more complex than I'd imagined, with strands connecting in ways perhaps no single person had designed.

"What about Penelope Chase?" I asked, my thoughts gravitating back to her tear-stained face.

Whipple flipped through his notes. "Her motive seemed straightforward. Blythe was blackmailing her father, who died of a heart attack."

"Yes, but what did she actually gain from his death?" I traced the edge of the table with my finger. "The damage to her family was already done. Her father is dead. Whatever Blythe knew, he could have told others. Killing him doesn't guarantee silence."

Whipple paused, considering. "You have a point. She gains nothing tangible."

"And she's been genuinely frightened since we found the body," I added. "Not the behaviour of someone who's accomplished their goal."

"Perhaps her tears were genuine after all," Whipple conceded.

A quiet relief settled over me. I'd been drawn to Penelope's vulnerability from our first meeting; the thought that she might be innocent comforted me more than I cared to admit.

"So if not Penelope," Whipple said, returning to his notes, "then who?"

The library door opened, and Captain Hardwick entered, nodding to us before selecting a book and departing without a word.

"Did you notice?" I asked once the door closed.

"His hands," Whipple replied. "Trembling slightly."

"And he's avoiding eye contact."

"A guilty conscience, perhaps?"

I leaned forward. "Or fear. Remember what the stokers told us about the coal bunker fire? Hardwick has more immediate concerns than a passenger's murder."

"A captain responsible for hundreds of lives concealing a potentially catastrophic fire," Whipple mused. "That's motive enough to silence someone who discovered his secret."

"What if Blythe learned about the fire?" I suggested. "He was known for exploiting weaknesses. Perhaps he threatened to expose Hardwick."

"A captain facing disgrace and criminal charges," Whipple nodded slowly. "That's a powerful motive indeed."

The pieces were shifting, rearranging themselves into a new pattern. Suspicion was now directed away from the passengers with personal issues and toward the man responsible for our safety and security.

I stared out the library window, watching the morning light dance across the waves. "Von Ritter benefits from Blythe's death, but can we prove it?"

"The diplomat's fingerprints are nowhere to be found," Whipple agreed. "Only suggestions and implied involvement."

"That's what makes him dangerous," I said, turning back to face Whipple. "He's comfortable with ambiguity."

Yesterday's conversation with von Ritter replayed in my mind. His casual demeanour when speaking of murder, the veiled references to arrangements and connections. There had been no shock in his manner, no outrage at the crime committed aboard. Instead, he'd seemed almost expectant, as though Blythe's death were an inevitability rather than a tragedy.

"I've encountered men like von Ritter before," Whipple said, gathering his notes. "They cultivate an aura of mystery and knowledge. Makes people believe they're pulling strings when they're merely observing from the shadows."

"But what if he is pulling strings? HG said true power works through others."

"Then we need to find those others," Whipple replied firmly. "Speculation without evidence is dangerous, Rex."

I nodded, acknowledging the wisdom in his words. "It's easy to be led astray by suspicion alone."

We left the library together. Passengers strolled along the promenade deck, their laughter at odds with the grim reality of murder that underlay our voyage.

Von Ritter himself appeared on deck, nodding as he passed. I watched him engage another passenger in conversation, his manner calibrated to inspire both trust and respect.

"Look at him," I murmured to Whipple. "He moves through the ship as though nothing has happened."

"Or perhaps," Whipple countered, "as though everything has happened exactly as planned."

I considered his words. Casting von Ritter as the mastermind, the spider at the centre of the web, would entice. But I remembered HG's gentle rebuke about my judgment of Penelope. How easily I'd been led astray by my feelings.

"We need evidence," I said finally. "Not intuition, nor suspicion. Otherwise, we're just weaving our own web of assumptions."

Whipple nodded. "Now you're thinking like a detective."

We made our way to the observation lounge where HG awaited us, her elegant figure framed by the vast expanse of ocean beyond the windows. She listened intently as we shared our suspicions about Captain Hardwick and the coal bunker fire.

"A captain concealing such danger," she mused, stirring her tea thoughtfully. "It's certainly plausible."

"But something doesn't quite fit," I said, frowning. "If Hardwick killed Blythe to protect his secret, why hasn't he taken steps to silence the stokers?"

HG's eyes gleamed with appreciation. "An excellent point, Rex."

Whipple nodded. "The stokers present a far greater threat to him than Blythe ever did."

"Perhaps we're overlooking something more fundamental," HG said, setting down her cup. "Have you noticed how quickly order has returned to the ship? The initial shock and disarray following the murder have subsided remarkably fast."

I glanced around the lounge. Passengers chatted, the orchestra played a gentle waltz, and stewards moved efficiently between tables. Even the weather had calmed.

"It's as if," I began, "the murder itself was a storm that needed to pass before calm could return."

"Precisely," HG replied. "Sometimes stability itself is a beneficiary of sudden violence. The removal of a disruptive force can restore equilibrium."

"Sir Edmund was creating tensions throughout the ship," I recalled. "His argument with von Ritter, his barely veiled threats at dinner, his blackmail schemes."

"And now?" HG prompted.

"Now the voyage continues without him, and everything seems more...settled." I suggested.

Whipple frowned. "You imply his death served some greater purpose beyond individual gain?"

"Sometimes the removal of one piece allows the entire game to continue," HG said. "Without benefit to any single player."

I stared out at the endless horizon, feeling unsettled by this perspective. The murder had cleared the air somehow, dispersing conflicts and allowing the Britannic Star to sail on untroubled.

"If that's true," I began, "then how do we identify a killer whose only motive was to restore peace?"

I stared across the lounge, watching passengers engage in the mundane rhythms of shipboard life. Ladies gossiped over tea, gentlemen discussed business, couples strolled arm in arm. The murder that had dominated conversations just days before now seemed forgotten.

"It reminds me of removing a splinter," I suggested. "The pain is sharp at first, but once extracted, relief comes quickly and the body heals as if nothing happened."

HG's eyes sparkled with approval. "An apt metaphor, Rex. Sir Edmund was indeed something of a splinter in the side of this voyage."

"Are we suggesting," Whipple asked, "that the murder itself was a...correction? A means of restoring social harmony?"

I considered this. "Not necessarily premeditated that way, but perhaps that was its effect. Look around us; the atmosphere has lightened considerably since his death."

My gaze fell upon Captain Hardwick, who was laughing heartily with a group of passengers. His earlier trembling hands now gestured with life. Even von Ritter seemed more at ease, no longer scanning the room with suspicion.

"Sir Edmund created ripples of discomfort wherever he went," I continued. "His absence has allowed everything to settle, like a pond after a stone is thrown."

"Which makes our job considerably more difficult," Whipple muttered. "If everyone benefits from his absence, how do we narrow our suspect list?"

HG sipped her tea. "We look at who had the most to

lose from his continued presence, not just who gained from his absence."

As we talked, I felt a strange sensation creep over me. Sir Edmund's absence had become its own presence, a negative space that shaped everything around it. The ship sailed on, passengers dined and danced, crew members performed their duties, all of them orbiting around this absence, defined by it.

I realised with sudden clarity that Sir Edmund's influence had not diminished with his death; it had merely transformed. His absence exerted as powerful a force as his presence once had. The thought chilled me. How does one investigate a murder when the victim's very disappearance serves as its own motive?

I was noticing the quietness of the ship when Lily de Vere came toward us, using the deliberate grace I'd seen her use before. Her silk dress whispered against the polished floor as she stopped beside us.

"What a lovely morning," she remarked, her gaze sweeping across the placid ocean visible through the windows. "The waters are finally calm; it's as though the sea has decided to grant us peace for the remainder of our journey."

HG offered a polite smile. "Indeed, Miss de Vere. Nature has its own rhythm, quite separate from human affairs."

"Just as this ship has found its rhythm again," Lily continued, running a gloved finger along the back of an empty chair. "I must say, the initial unpleasantness has given way to such a delightful atmosphere. Everyone seems so much more at ease."

I noticed how she described Sir Edmund's murder as

'unpleasantness,' as though discussing spilled tea rather than a brutal killing.

"Some might find it curious how quickly tragedy is forgotten," I ventured.

Lily's smile never faltered. "Not forgotten, Rex; simply absorbed into the greater fabric of our journey. Life continues; it must. Sir Edmund would hardly expect us to spend the entire voyage in mourning."

"Particularly those who found his company challenging," HG observed.

"Which was nearly everyone," Lily laughed lightly. "I do believe we're all breathing a bit easier now. Even you, Detective Inspector," she nodded toward Whipple, "must appreciate the return to order."

After Lily glided away to join another group, I watched the other passengers. They nodded and smiled, not doubting her version of what happened. Sir Edmund's death, though unfortunate, had fixed the problems on their journey.

"It's remarkable," I said. "How readily people embrace comfort over discomfort, even when that comfort is built upon a foundation of violence."

"People will accept almost any narrative," HG replied, "if it allows them to continue their lives undisturbed."

I stared at the passengers laughing and chatting, their faces betraying no hint that a man had been murdered just days before. I thought about how easily people choose comfort over truth, and how quickly we create delightful stories to hide what's not so good. And somewhere among these smiling faces was a killer who had provided everyone with the perfect excuse to look away. Remarkably, he, or she, had also convinced everyone else that all danger had ended.

The easy camaraderie of the surrounding passengers

struck me. Their laughing faces, their animated conversations. Sir Edmund's presence evaporated, his existence erased and forgotten from the world.

"I still don't understand how you can see design in this," Whipple said, breaking into my thoughts. "Murder is rarely so philosophical. People kill for simple reasons: jealousy, greed, fear. Not to restore social harmony."

HG studied him with patient affection. "Arthur, you know as well as I do that human behaviour rarely conforms to neat categories."

"The evidence suggests otherwise," Whipple insisted, pulling out his notebook. "Every murder I've solved came down to hard motives. People don't kill for abstract concepts like 'restoring balance.'"

I felt a growing distance between us, not physical but philosophical. Whipple saw the world as a series of logical connections, cause followed by effect. A man had evidence of blackmail, so someone killed him to stop exposure. Simple, straightforward.

But I sensed something more complex at work aboard the Britannic Star. The way Lily moved through the passengers, reshaping their perceptions. How von Ritter spoke of English methods of employing intermediaries. How Captain Hardwick maintained his authority despite the trembling of his hands.

"What if," I ventured, "the killer never intended to restore order? What if they simply removed Sir Edmund for their own reasons, and this atmosphere is merely a fortunate consequence?"

"That's what I've been saying," Whipple replied, satisfied. "Simple motives, not grand designs."

HG's eyes met mine across the table, and I caught a

glimmer of something there, perhaps understanding, or approval.

"Either way," I continued, "someone has benefited enormously from this new atmosphere. The question is who possessed the skill to capitalise on it so effectively?"

We sat in contemplative silence, watching the passengers move about their temporary world. Yet someone had done more than just remove Sir Edmund; they had reshaped the very reality of the Britannic Star.

I observed HG as she turned her teacup in a slow, deliberate circle. Her silence spoke volumes; she disagreed with Whipple's assessment but chose not to challenge him.

"Perhaps we might consider both perspectives," she finally said. "The practical motivations Arthur identifies, alongside the more subtle social dynamics at play."

Whipple nodded, pleased that HG seemed to concede his point. But I caught her eye and recognised the familiar glint. She remained unconvinced.

"I should speak with the ship's doctor again," Whipple announced, closing his notebook with finality. "There may be forensic details we have overlooked."

After he departed, HG and I sat for a moment. Sunlight shone through the windows of the observation lounge, creating bright shapes on the floor.

"You disagree with him," I said.

HG smiled. "I believe Arthur's approach has merit, Rex. The tangible evidence must guide us. But I also believe there are currents beneath the surface of this case that conventional detection might miss."

"Like what happened with Lily just now," I replied. "The way she reshaped everyone's perception without them noticing."

"Precisely." HG took a small sip of tea. “Observe that she doesn't say Sir Edmund's death wasn't sad.”

I understood then why HG hadn't challenged Whipple. Sometimes direct confrontation only strengthened opposition. She respected him enough to let him follow his methodical path while she explored alternative approaches.

I thought out loud, "Murder investigations usually look at who had a motive, the ability, and the opportunity to do it," as I watched people walk by our table. "But this feels different somehow."

"Different how?"

I struggled to articulate the feeling. "It's as though we're investigating not just who killed Sir Edmund, but who orchestrated the aftermath. Who determined how his death would be perceived and used that perception to their advantage."

HG's eyes warmed with approval. "You're beginning to see the invisible architecture of power, Rex. Sometimes the most significant aspect of an event isn't the event itself, but how it's interpreted and remembered."

I surveyed the lounge again. Captain Hardwick chatted to passengers, his earlier trembling nowhere to be seen. Von Ritter sipped cognac alone, his face a mask of aristocratic boredom. Madame Zelda held court at a corner table, her audience rapt as she held court with a pack of tarot cards.

"So we're looking for someone who not only wanted Sir Edmund dead but knew exactly how to make use of his absence," I said.

"Someone who understands that true power lies in controlling the narrative," HG agreed.

"But how do we prove such a thing? There's no physical evidence of such an approach."

"We observe, we listen, and we pay attention to inconsistencies," HG replied. "Someone is being diligent in making Sir Edmund's murder appear to be a simple matter of personal vendetta. Our job is to determine why they need that story to be believed."

I felt a shift inside me, as though the investigation had transformed into something more complex than identifying who struck the fatal blow. We were now hunting for the author of a fiction, one that had constructed a killer to hide in plain sight among grateful passengers.

The Britannic Star continued its steady journey across the Atlantic. Meanwhile, someone on the ship was watching and waiting.

Chapter Twelve

THOSE WHO ISSUE ORDERS

The ship rolled beneath us as another day at sea unfolded. I watched the rhythmic pace of life aboard the Britannic Star. Passengers moved with ease along the promenade deck; their concerns confined to menus and game schedules.

It was then that I noticed a minor incident unfold near the starboard railing, one that might ordinarily pass without comment. A deckhand, informed by an officious chief steward that his duties in the grand salon were required, halted in his task. He seemed, just for a moment, torn between competing priorities.

"You'll obey," snapped the steward, brooking no dissent. The deckhand stopped. He straightened his shoulders and followed the man. An absolute, unspoken command underlay the interaction; a command obeyed without question.

My attention turned inward. Here, within the elegant confines of the Britannic Star, where each person seemed an actor in a choreographed dance, I sensed something deeper. Obedience, a subtle force, crushed like the ship's turbines.

At first, I dismissed my discomfort as ordinary unease, perhaps a residue from last night's mysterious theatre of shadows and schemes. But watching the interchange, realising how my attention lingered, stirred something. It swelled from within, a warning not formed. I felt exposed to invisible currents, the kind HG spoke of. After all, why was a steward ordering a deckhand about? Unless the task required specialist skills, deckhands could not enter passenger areas inside the ship.

HG often said power lived not in action but in implication, in directing others without overt gestures. I saw that truth here among us. Nothing was as simple as it appeared, neither the deckhand's compliance nor the orchestrated daily spectacle.

I glanced sidelong at HG. Her poise mirrored in her calmness. Eyes ahead, gauging where thoughts and movements converged. She'd recognised this truth long before; obedience was the invisible mariner guiding our ship. And on this sea, minor acts carried profound meaning.

The truth struck me as sharply as any revelation in our inquiries. As the Britannic Star cut through waves, I was learning to navigate a human tide, where actions whispered yet with weight.

My focus shifted to other passengers; a woman adjusting her pearls as a steward brought tea, accepting it without checking her order. The old man nodded at the purser without paying attention.

Throughout the ship, this pattern repeated itself. Officers gave orders; stewards executed them; passengers made requests; staff fulfilled them. Each interaction reinforced the hierarchy.

"Interesting, isn't it?" HG appeared beside me, her voice precise. "How easily we all fall into our assigned roles."

I nodded, watching a young stewardess rearrange flowers she had just arranged moments ago because an officer had made a casual comment.

"They never question," I murmured. "Not even when the instructions make little sense."

“Compliance without curiosity," HG agreed. “The foundation upon which power grows.”

A memory surfaced from my childhood in the home; the absolute authority of matrons whose word became law, whose approval we sought. This system of unquestioning obedience also shaped me.

"I wonder," I offered, "about Sir Edmund. Did he recognise the same pattern? Did he exploit it?"

"Almost certainly," HG replied. "Men like Blythe understand how to seek out and position themselves within systems of authority."

The ship's whistle sounded, signalling the approach to lunch. Passengers moved in response, a collective shifting like schools of fish changing direction.

"There's something unsettling about it," I confessed. "This willingness to surrender judgment."

"Is it judgment they surrender, Rex, or merely the burden of decision making?" HG's eyes held mine. "Perhaps what you're seeing isn't mindlessness but discipline. The question becomes: at what point does discipline become dangerous? When does following orders without question transform from efficiency to complicity?"

I considered her words as we joined the stream of passengers heading toward the dining room. The line between judgment and discipline seemed as thin and wavering as the horizon beyond the ship's rail.

Whipple came into view across the dining room. His expression remained impassive as I recounted the incident with the deckhand and steward.

"Interesting observation, but hardly relevant to our investigation," he said, carefully refolding his napkin. "Hierarchies exist on ships just as they do on land. One follows orders, life proceeds. Without such a structure, we'd have chaos. And with a vessel at sea, positively dangerous."

"But don't you see?" I pressed, keeping my voice low. "This blind obedience lets others manage things without being present themselves."

Whipple shook his head, the faintest smile crossing his lips. "Rex, you're becoming quite the philosopher thanks to HG's influence. However, Scotland Yard requires facts, not theories about human nature. We need fingerprints, not looking into the souls of men through their eyes."

'Goodness me, Arthur, I did not know you were a student of Tudor history?"

Whipple paused. "Eh?"

"Elizabeth I. she said, 'I have no desire to make windows into men's souls'. Of course, she framed her words in the religious settlement she sought after her half-sister, Mary's, reign. However, your interpretation fits the bill perfectly."

Whipple looked surprised, not knowing whether to regard HG's remark as a compliment or not. His dismissal of my hypothesis stung. I had glimpsed something important, yet Whipple could not or would not see beyond his methodical framework. The law required evidence, witnesses, means, motive, opportunity. It cared nothing about the subtle currents of power.

"Our murderer may have left no fingerprints," I countered. "What if they never entered Sir Edmund's cabin?

What if they simply created circumstances where someone else would act on their behalf?"

"Then we find that person and trace back the chain of events," Whipple replied, his tone gentle but firm. "But I cannot present theories of manipulated obedience to a prosecutor, nor can I arrest someone for being persuasive or manipulative."

HG observed our exchange with interest, saying nothing but nodding in my direction. The gap between us felt vast; Whipple sought what the law could punish, while I pursued what morality would condemn.

"The legal definition of guilt may not capture the true architect of a crime," I said finally.

"Perhaps not," Whipple conceded. "But it's the only definition within my power to enforce."

I fell silent, watching passengers order meals, crew members respond, officers patrol. The ship continued its steady progress across the Atlantic as New York neared. Yet now the Britannic Star seemed less a vessel of pleasure and more a floating mechanism of power, control, and dangerous compliance.

Someone aboard understood this mechanism well enough to orchestrate a murder without raising suspicion. As I observed the dining room's routine ballet, my unease grew. The killer might watch us too, comfortable knowing that the very structure of upper society protected them from discovery.

The afternoon light shifted as our conversation ebbed. I noticed how the staff served, their eyes rarely meeting those they served. Each encounter made the unseen divide between social classes, the powerful and the submissive, even stronger.

"Rex, crimes tend to happen more often in well-organised systems rather than in messy ones," HG said as she stirred her tea.

"How do you mean?" I asked.

She gestured to those around us. "Consider this ship. Every function regulated, every person assigned their role. With the hierarchy clearly defined, the boundaries rarely crossed. Such orderly systems provide perfect cover for those who understand how to manipulate them."

Whipple frowned. "That seems counterintuitive. Surely orderly systems prevent criminal activity through oversight and accountability."

"Quite the opposite, Arthur," HG replied. "The more predictable the system, the easier someone can identify and exploit its weaknesses. The clearer the chain of command, the easier to ensure blame falls elsewhere."

I felt a chill run through me as her words aligned with my earlier observations.

"Like Sir Edmund," I murmured. "He understood how to use the system as both a weapon and a shield."

"Precisely," HG nodded. "And his killer likely understands it equally well."

Whipple sighed, conceding the point. "Still, we must work within the framework of evidence and testimony."

As he spoke, I watched First Officer Grayson pass through the dining room, trailing junior officers who adjusted their posture in his wake. The officers then passed this subtle correction down to the stewards, who became more attentive to the passengers.

The realisation settled over me with disturbing clarity. In this floating hierarchy, obedience wasn't merely expected; it was the very currency of power. Those who commanded respect received it without question. Those who followed orders were absolved of responsibility for the consequences.

I understood then what made our investigation so challenging. The killer had used not just the physical architecture of the ship but its social architecture as well. They all used the same protection: doing what they were told without asking questions, regardless of their rank.

I stared at my half-finished tea, letting its warmth seep through the fine china cup into my fingers. The ship's rolling, which had become calm after the storm, felt normal and even soothing.

"What troubles your thoughts, young man?" Baron von Ritter's voice broke my contemplation as he paused beside our table. Without waiting for an invitation, he settled into the vacant chair next to me with fluid grace.

"Just considering the nature of authority aboard ship," I replied carefully.

Von Ritter's lips curved into what might have been a smile. "Ah, the English, and their beloved hierarchies. So very efficient, are they not?"

Whipple straightened in his chair. "It's a necessary system that ensures order and safety."

"The English are masters of creating order, where everyone knows their role…and place," von Ritter said.

HG's eyes narrowed. "You speak as though Germany operates differently, Baron."

"We have our hierarchies too," he conceded with a slight inclination of his head. "But the English have refined it to an art form."

I felt uncomfortable under his penetrating gaze. "Is there something wrong with clear chains of command?"

"Not at all," von Ritter replied. "It merely creates a certain...predictability. When a man knows his superior is above being questioned, he follows even questionable orders. When a captain speaks, officers obey; when officers command, sailors comply. No one asks why. No one considers alternatives."

He took a sip of his coffee, grimaced at its temperature, then stood. "It makes your society run smoothly, but it also makes it vulnerable in ways you rarely perceive. Good day."

As von Ritter departed, I watched his straight-backed figure navigate between tables. His words hung in the air. What bothered me most wasn't his criticism; rather, the recognition that he'd articulated the flaw I'd been circling. Our society's greatest strength. Yet its ordered efficiency created its most exploitable weakness.

His words persisted. The appearance of Lily de Vere, who approached our table with her customary graceful swagger, broke the uncomfortable silence.

"What a delightful gathering," she remarked, her gaze sweeping across our faces. "May I join you for a moment?"

"This table is beginning to feel like Liverpool Street station," Whipple muttered to no one in particular.

HG gestured to the chair von Ritter had vacated. Lily settled into it with a fluid motion, arranging her silk dress with practiced care.

"I couldn't help but notice the Baron speaking with you," she said, signalling a steward for tea. "Such a serious man; one wonders how he manages at social gatherings."

Whipple cleared his throat. "We were discussing shipboard matters, Miss de Vere. Nothing of consequence."

"Oh, but everything aboard the Britannic Star is of consequence," she replied, accepting her tea with a smile that never quite reached her eyes. "Don't you find it remarkable how smoothly everything runs? Even with that dreadful business about Sir Edmund, the ship's routine continues uninterrupted."

I scrutinised her. "You seem to admire efficiency, Miss de Vere."

"I admire anything that works as intended," she replied, stirring sugar into her cup. "This ship is a brilliant example of British innovation."

HG's expression remained neutral. "Even the finest watches occasionally need adjustment."

"Perhaps," Lily conceded with a light laugh. "But the Britannic Star seems to run perfectly regardless of what transpires. Even murder; nothing disrupts the essential rhythm. Breakfast is served at eight, lunch at one, dinner at seven. The sun rises, the sun sets, and we move inexorably toward our destination."

Her words carried a strange comfort, like a lullaby meant to soothe anxious children. I felt myself nodding in agreement before catching myself.

"Doesn't that strike you as odd, Miss de Vere?" I asked. "That not even murder disrupts our comfortable routines?"

"Odd? Not at all. Reassuring, I'd say." She smiled, touching my arm. "The ship continues its journey regardless of individual tragedies. There's something almost poetic about that constancy, don't you think?"

As she excused herself moments later, I watched her navigate between tables with the same practiced ease as von Ritter. Everyone she passed seemed to brighten at her attention, like flowers turning toward the sun.

The unexpected string of encounters left me with much to ponder. While I'd absorbed HG's lessons on influence and manipulation. However, aboard the Britannic Star, those dynamics were far more intricate than I'd imagined.

As I observed passengers move from table to exit, an unsettling thought took root: routine and power here were intertwined in a relentless dance. This vessel was more than a liner cutting through water. It reinforced high society's unyielding structures. Each participant an actor in a silent play of compliance and governance.

Waiting for HG and Whipple, I let the sights and sounds envelop me. The clatter of silver on china, the low hum of gossip, the wait staff moving with choreographed precision. The ship hummed in its own language of order, where deviations seemed a suppressed whisper among the harmony.

HG appeared beside me, her gentle touch grounding my wayward thoughts. Distracted as I'd been, her presence somehow shifted my internal compass back toward purpose.

"Rex," she said with her signature deliberation, "I believe you identified something crucial earlier."

I turned, meeting her gaze. "The idea that obedience makes exploitation possible?"

"Yes, precisely. It's imperative we uncover who manipulates that dynamic to cloak their actions," she continued, lowering her voice. "And more importantly, who stands to benefit once chaos reigns."

I nodded, feeling the weight of her words. Yet, just as our conversation deepened, a sudden clamour from the corridor beyond snared our attention. A harried steward appeared breathless before us, his urgency painting concern across his features.

"Begging your pardon," he began. "There's been an incident. The passenger library is in a right state. There are no officers around, and I didn't know who to tell."

HG arched an eyebrow. "It is quite alright. You made the correct decision. An incident, you say?"

"If you would follow me, Your Grace."

Upon reaching the library, the scene that unfolded confirmed the steward's disquiet. Books lay discarded, spines bent under careless feet. Chairs overturned like fallen soldiers. The entire room appeared a testament to some desperate search.

Whipple surveyed the scene, his expression, resolute as ever. The detective's training bathed this jumble of events in cool logic.

"Seems someone didn't just break routine," I muttered, surveying the disarray. "They shattered it."

Whipple moved between the scattered volumes, his experienced eyes cataloguing each detail of destruction. Someone had violated the library's usual serenity. Leather-bound classics lay splayed on Turkish carpets. Reading lamps toppled, and index card catalogues upended.

"This wasn't done in anger," Whipple concluded, crouching to examine a torn page without touching it. "There's method here beneath the apparent chaos. Someone was searching for something specific."

I studied the scene and noted that certain cabinets had been ransacked while others remained untouched. "It seems targeted, doesn't it?"

"Indeed," HG agreed, her gaze sweeping the room's perimeter. "But the question remains: was this the work of a passenger or a crew member? The distinction matters significantly."

Whipple straightened, frowning. "How so?"

"Passengers have limited time in public spaces, constantly observed by others. A crew member, however, might explain away their presence here, perhaps claiming to be cleaning or restocking shelves," HG explained. "They would arouse far less suspicion."

I navigated around a broken chess set, pieces scattered across the floor like fallen soldiers. "There's something theatrical about this destruction. It seems excessive for a simple search."

"Multiple participants, perhaps?" Whipple suggested, examining scuff marks on the polished floor. "These indicate at least two sets of movements, possibly three."

HG nodded. "Notice the periodicals table is completely overturned, yet the atlas collection remains perfectly arranged. Our intruder knew precisely which areas deserved attention."

"Could this connect to Blythe's murder?" I asked.

"It could be viewed that way," Whipple replied. "This level of risk indicates desperation. Something aboard this vessel has several people terrified, and I'd wager it relates directly to whatever Blythe possessed or knew. But let us not get ahead of ourselves."

The steward who had fetched us fretted by the doorway, uncertain whether to enter or maintain his distance.

"Young man," Whipple called to him, "Once we leave, I need you to secure this room immediately. No one enters without my explicit permission. Find the purser and tell him what I have ordered."

"Yes, sir," the steward replied, visibly relieved to have explicit instructions.

Whipple turned to us, lowering his voice. "We're running out of time. New York looms ever closer, and once we dock, our little community disperses. Unless I can establish an obvious motive for this destruction quickly, I may have to let this matter rest."

"You mean prioritise the murder investigation," I clarified.

"Precisely," Whipple nodded. "We cannot afford to be diverted by tangential incidents; however dramatic they appear."

HG's expression remained thoughtful as she surveyed

the destruction once more. "Perhaps that is exactly the intention of whoever did this."

"What do you mean?" I asked.

"Consider the timing," HG explained, her voice measured. "We're making progress with Blythe's murder. Suddenly, we're confronted with fresh chaos demanding immediate attention. It's rather convenient, wouldn't you say?"

Whipple's eyes narrowed. "A deliberate distraction?"

"It would serve multiple purposes," HG continued. "Not only diverting our investigation but perhaps destroying evidence we hadn't yet discovered. The library contains newspapers, reference materials, passenger logs from previous voyages. What might someone fear we'd find here?"

I felt a chill of understanding. "So, our murderer now fears discovery enough to create this scene."

"Or," Whipple added grimly, "they're executing preemptive moves before we dock. Either way, time is now our enemy as much as deception."

The steward returned with the purser, keys jingling in hand. As they secured the library doors, I couldn't shake the unsettling feeling that we were being manipulated. Drawn into an orchestrated game where each move revealed and concealed in equal measure.

Chapter Thirteen

SMOKE WITHOUT FLAME

The library's near destruction troubled me more than I cared to admit. Someone aboard the Britannic Star was growing desperate, which made people unpredictable.

As we departed the ransacked room, a faint acrid smell caught my attention. Nothing obvious, just a subtle wrongness hanging in the air.

"Do you smell that?" I asked.

HG lifted her chin, nostrils flaring in that aristocratic way I'd come to recognise when she was assessing a situation.

"Something's burning," she murmured.

Whipple frowned. "Coal dust perhaps?"

We paused at the foot of the grand staircase, where a steward whispered to a pair of uniformed officers. Their expressions remained neutral, but their body language betrayed tension. The steward nodded and left, as the officers got into place to direct people to the Palm Court.

"Curious," HG remarked. "No alarms, no announcements."

Whipple approached one officer. "Pardon me. Is there a problem?"

"Nothing for you to concern yourself with, sir," came the practised response. "Just a small matter below decks requiring attention."

"I'm Detective Inspector Whipple, Scotland Yard. What sort of matter?"

The officer's composure faltered. "A minor issue with one of the ventilation systems, sir. Captain's orders to redirect passengers temporarily."

More stewards appeared, offering complimentary refreshments in the Palm Court. The efficiency of their movement struck me. This was no improvised response but something rehearsed.

"The coal bunker," I whispered to HG and Whipple as we stepped aside. "It must have worsened."

HG's gaze followed a steward who dabbed perspiration from his brow. "Note how the crew is sweating while maintaining perfect smiles."

"Standard procedure on passenger vessels," Whipple observed. "Contain, control, and conceal until absolutely necessary."

We watched passengers being shepherded away, chatting and laughing, unaware. Life aboard the ship went on as usual: music, drinks, and kids running around with nannies watching.

I wove through the crowd, watching as crewmen directed passengers without spreading alarm. The entire operation ran like a well-oiled machine.

"I need to speak with someone from engineering," Whipple muttered.

“Then I shall leave you two gentlemen to your endeavours,” HG said as she waved us off.

We descended a narrow stairwell marked 'Crew Only,' ignoring the protests of a steward. Three flights down, the elegant carpeting gave way to utilitarian metal steps. The air grew warmer, heavier.

Near a service corridor, Whipple cornered a young man in oil-stained overalls. The junior engineer's cap was pushed back on his head, revealing a sheen of sweat across his forehead.

"Inspector Whipple, Scotland Yard," he announced quietly. "A word, if you please."

The lad's eyes darted to the corridor's end. "I shouldn't be talking, sir."

"Just clarification of the current situation," Whipple assured him. "Nothing more."

"It's...contained, sir," he answered. His fingers worried about the stain on his sleeve. "Been managing it since before Southampton, truth be told. But as I say, we've got it under control. Captain says we'll make New York fine, but might be delayed…have to reduce speed, you see."

"The coal-bunker fire? Is that what's causing this...situation?"

His eyes widened. "How did you...?" He swallowed. "It's contained, like I said. No passengers need worry about."

"But the crew is worried," Whipple observed.

"I've said too much already." The young engineer stepped back. "If Mr Bowthorpe sees me talking, he'll—"

"Don't worry, you're in the clear. Thank you," Whipple said, allowing him to escape.

The engineer's nervous departure left me unsettled. I exchanged glances with Whipple, whose usual stoic expression had given way to concern.

"We need to see for ourselves," I said. "The stokers' mess?"

Whipple nodded. "Lead on."

We hurried through the labyrinth of narrow corridors that formed the ship's underbelly. The temperature climbed with each level we descended until my collar clung to my neck. Gone were the polished brass fittings and plush carpets of first class; here, everything was utilitarian metal, pipes, and valves.

When we reached the stokers' mess, I half-expected to find the three burly men we'd encountered before. Instead, the space stood empty, abandoned mugs of tea still warm on the wooden table.

"There," I pointed to a closed bulkhead door across the mess. White stencilled lettering above it read 'BOILER ROOM - AUTHORISED PERSONNEL ONLY'.

Whipple nodded.

I approached the heavy metal door, grasped the large iron wheel that served as its handle and tried to turn it. The wheel refused to budge at first, coated in a vile mixture of grease and coal dust that made my hands slip. I removed my jacket, wrapped it around the wheel for better grip, and pushed with all my strength. The mechanism groaned in protest but finally gave way.

The door swung open, unleashing hell.

A blast of scorching air struck us like a physical force. The temperature must have been well over a hundred degrees, carrying with it the unmistakable stench of sulphur from the burning coal and human sweat. The noise was overwhelming, a cacophony of shovels scraping, coal tumbling, and flames roaring.

Before us stretched a scene Dante might have envisioned. Massive boilers lined the walls, their furnace doors glowing orange-red like demonic jaws. Men toiled before each one, stripped to the waist, their bodies gleaming black with coal dust and sweat that carved rivulets through the grime. Filthy trousers hung from their hips, and each wore a sodden neckerchief either around his neck or tied across his mouth.

In the centre of this inferno, a separate crew attacked what must have been bunker number three, shovelling coal away from the source of combustion. Their movements held the desperate energy of men fighting a losing battle.

The huge stoker, who'd spoken to us earlier, caught sight of our intrusion. His eyes widened in recognition before narrowing with fury. He hurled his massive spade to the floor with a clang that somehow cut through the din. The giant wiped his blackened face with a neckerchief so filthy it seemed to add rather than remove dirt and strode toward us.

He stepped over small mountains of coal awaiting the furnaces, each stride carrying the threat closer.

"What in blazes are you doing here?" he bellowed, his voice barely audible above the roar of the boilers. "This is restricted! Out! Now!"

He reached for my shoulder, intending to evict us from his domain.

"They know," Whipple shouted, standing his ground with surprising steadiness. "The passengers know something's wrong. You can smell burning up there."

The stoker's hand stopped, and his look changed from anger to a mix of fear and acceptance.

"How bad is it?" I asked, meeting his gaze.

The giant stoker shook his head, coal dust raining from his sweat-soaked hair. "Can't put it out while at sea. That's the devil of it."

"Surely there's a procedure for this," I said, struggling to be heard over the hellish roar surrounding us.

"Procedure?" He spat on the floor, his saliva instantly evaporating. "There's procedure and there's reality, young sir. We've got near 500 tons in that bunker. No space to get it all out at once." He gestured to the cramped confines. "And the more we dig, the more oxygen reaches the heart of it, see?"

As if to punctuate his point, a plume of acrid smoke billowed from bunker number three. Two men staggered back, coughing and shielding their faces from the inferno.

"And the captain knows this?" Whipple asked, his collar now wilted completely.

The stoker's laugh held no humour. "Oh, aye. Told him myself three days back. First Officer Grayson too. And that Bowthorpe fella." He lowered his voice, though the din made it unnecessary. "Captain wants full steam ahead, regardless. Says we need to maintain the schedule. It's madness, pure madness."

I watched the men working in relays, their bodies pushed beyond reasonable endurance. How much longer could they continue before exhaustion claimed them?

"What's the worst that could happen?" Whipple's question cut through my thoughts.

The stoker's gaze drifted back to the smouldering bunker before fixing Whipple with an icy stare. "Worst? The fire weakens the hull and adjoining compartments. Once it spreads beyond the boiler room, we're done for." He nodded toward the upper decks. "Then there's the toxic gas; that's what you're smelling up in your fancy quarters."

A violent flash exploded from bunker three. A gout of flame shot upward, greedily consuming available oxygen. Men scattered, diving away from danger.

"Close it! Close it now!" the stoker bellowed. His voice

carried an unquestionable authority that comes from life-and-death responsibility.

A team of men rushed forward with long-handled tools, manoeuvring a heavy metal plate to choke off the oxygen supply. Their coordination impressed, but wide eyes betrayed genuine fear.

The stoker turned back to us, wiping soot from his face. "See what we're up against? If this carries on, the lot will go up. We'll lose the ship."

I could feel the blood drain from my face. Hundreds of passengers lounged above, unaware of the inferno beneath their feet.

"What do you need?" Whipple asked urgently.

"Time. The captain must slow this beast down while we get the fire under control. Full steam means we're feeding these boilers constantly, can't spare men or space to tackle the bunker fire." He gestured to his exhausted crew. "We need time."

Whipple and I exchanged glances. The implications were clear.

"Leave it to me," Whipple said in a firm tone. "Expect to hear from the captain soon."

As we turned to leave, the stoker called after us, "One more thing, gents. If I were you, I'd make sure your life-jacket's close at hand. Just in case."

We pushed back through the bulkhead door, the relative coolness of the corridor a blessed relief. Neither of us spoke until we'd climbed two decks, putting distance between ourselves and that vision of hell.

"Is it stretching credibility to think Sir Edmund did find out about the fire, as we touched on previously?" I said finally.

"If he did, I've no doubt at all that he'd use the information to ruin the captain...unless he paid Blythe's price," Whipple conjectured.

After we'd bathed and changed into clean clothes, picking up HG on our way to the captain's quarters, I felt almost human again. The memory of the inferno below decks remained vivid. However, one thing I could not scrub away was the acrid smell embedded in my nostrils.

"We need to be direct but diplomatic," Whipple cautioned as we approached the officers' quarters. "The captain maintains absolute authority at sea."

"Diplomatic?" HG raised an eyebrow. "I rather think we're past that point, Arthur."

As we neared the first officer's cabin on our way to the bridge, raised voices spilled into the corridor. This represented an echo of what Whipple, and I had overheard the previous day. The captain's thunderous tones were unmistakable, though the words themselves remained indistinct.

Whipple paused for a moment before his demeanour hardened. "Right," he muttered, then strode forward with purpose, pushing the door open without ceremony.

Captain Hardwick and First Officer Grayson, surprised, looked at us. Their conversation died in an instant.

"What is the meaning of this intrusion?" Hardwick demanded, his bushy eyebrows knotting together.

HG stepped forward, her elegant figure filling the space with an authority that outmatched even the captain's. "The safety of this ship, Captain Hardwick," she said, her voice cutting like a shard of ice. Her eyes burned into his with an intensity that would have made lesser men weaken.

I shut the door behind us. Whatever came next, it wouldn't benefit from an audience.

Whipple wasted no time. "Captain, Rex and I have just come from the boiler room. We've seen the fire in coal bunker number three with our own eyes. Your men are fighting a losing battle while you maintain full speed."

"You had absolutely no right to be in that area!" Hardwick blustered, his face reddening. "It's strictly—"

"Captain." Whipple's voice, though quieter than Hardwick's, cut him off completely. "I suggest you calm yourself before I am forced to inform Scotland Yard by telegram that this vessel is in immediate danger. I've already notified the Yard and the American authorities about Sir Edmund's death. If you don't reduce speed, it will be a problem, since your crew is dealing with a dangerous situation.

Hardwick's mouth opened and closed several times, resembling nothing so much as a fish finding itself on dry land. "You've no right to interfere with the running of my ship!"

"Have you informed your principals of either the murder or the fire, Captain?" Whipple asked calmly.

"Now see here—" Hardwick's voice rose again.

"Be quiet this instant," HG commanded, employing that devastatingly effective tone that only generations of aristocratic breeding can perfect. The captain fell silent as though she'd thrown a switch.

As Hardwick gesticulated, something caught my attention…a subtle fragrance wafting from his uniform. I inhaled. Perfume? How odd that such a scent should cling to the captain's clothing.

Meanwhile, Grayson remained rooted to the spot, watching his superior being eviscerated by HG and Whipple. His expression betrayed a mixture of alarm and, unless

I was mistaken, a hint of satisfaction at seeing his tyrannical captain brought low.

The captain's face contorted through a range of emotions: shock, anger, and finally a trapped resignation. Before he could calm down, he faced Grayson, who looked pleased with the situation.

"What are you gawping at?" Captain Hardwick barked, his thunderous voice returning. "Get about your business! Go to the bridge and inform Chief Officer Bowthorpe to call for half-speed immediately."

Grayson snapped to attention, a lifetime of naval discipline overriding any pleasure he'd taken in his superior's dressing-down. "Yes, sir!" He hurried from the room, the door slamming behind him.

The captain's shoulders slumped once Grayson departed, though he maintained his rigid posture. The silence stretched until HG broke it with cool precision.

"Now we are getting somewhere," she said. "You will need to prepare a statement for the passengers. I care not what excuse you give for our delayed arrival in New York."

Hardwick closed his eyes for a moment as if to wish the dilemma away. "There will be hell to pay from my principal," he growled. "Not to mention the passengers with onward journeys planned."

HG sniffed the air, her nostrils flaring. "Would they rather this ship lie at the bottom of the Atlantic? Are memories so short-lived of other tragedies?"

Her reference to the Titanic hung heavy. The captain lowered his head, defeated at last. "You have no idea what you have forced me to do," he said in a muted tone.

Whipple, normally so controlled, suddenly flushed with anger. "Forced? None of this should have been necessary, had you fulfilled your duty! If your career is over, so be it.

You deserve nothing less." He paused, his eyes narrowing. "At least you will have more time to spend with your... how should I put this? 'Lady'."

The captain bridled, and I marvelled at the inspector having picked up on the perfume scent just as I had.

"And expensive it is, too," HG added, her refined nose apparently recognising the scent as well.

Captain Hardwick did not try to bluster. His face had gone a peculiar shade of grey, all the fight draining out of him. Without another word, he stormed from the room, banging the door closed behind him.

The three of us exchanged glances in the sudden stillness.

"Well, gentlemen," HG said with a satisfied smile, "I thought that went rather well. Bravo for catching on to the perfume; perhaps some men are not the blockheads they play at."

I couldn't help but grin. "I never claimed to be completely unobservant, HG."

"No, indeed," she replied, her eyes twinkling. "You're becoming quite the detective. Though I wonder whose perfume our captain has been enjoying?"

The room fell silent as we each considered what had just happened, and the implications it might have on our investigation. As we left Grayson's office, I broached a question I knew we had to answer.

"I wonder if we've been overly hasty in connecting the murder and the bunker fire…as far as blackmail goes, I mean?" I said as we made our way back towards HG's stateroom. The ship's motion had already lessened as the engines slowed. "The two may be entirely separate matters."

HG gave me a considered look. "Perhaps. Though coincidences make me nervous, particularly when they involve men like Blythe."

Whipple nodded. "I share your scepticism, Rex, but consider the timing. Sir Edmund died shortly after our voyage started, before he could make too many demands. However, if he discovered the fire and threatened to expose Hardwick..."

"It gives the captain quite the motive," I admitted. "Though bludgeoning a passenger seems a rather extreme response to an event, any capable captain should be able to explain away."

We settled into HG's stateroom. Graham appeared almost instantly with a tray of tea. The familiar ritual brought a welcome sense of normalcy after our confrontation with the captain.

"Let's take stock of what we know," Whipple said, once HG's personal steward had withdrawn. He pulled out his notebook. "Sir Edmund Blythe, a man with numerous enemies, is murdered on the first night at sea. Blow to the head, no signs of struggle, suggesting he knew his attacker."

"Or didn't perceive them as a threat," I added.

"Indeed. We have several suspects with clear motives: von Ritter and his German associates would benefit from Blythe's absence in certain markets. Penelope Chase feared him exposing family secrets; Madame Zelda was potentially being blackmailed. Lily de Vere had compromising letters in his possession."

“Perhaps also Captain Hardwick? If Blythe found out about the fire, and threatened to expose him for setting sail knowing the danger to everyone on board.”

"Yes," Whipple said. "A dangerous coal bunker fire, concealed from passengers and, I'd wager, from the shipping line as well. The captain was desperate to maintain speed despite the risk. Why? Do commercial considerations matter that much?"

"The perfume is curious," I said. "Do we think the captain is... involved with a passenger?"

HG's eyes glittered with amusement. "Oh, I recognised that scent immediately. Our captain has been keeping company with none other than Lily de Vere."

"Lily!" I exclaimed. "But she's been so publicly attentive to von Ritter."

"A clever diversion, perhaps," HG replied. "Though whether their association is romantic or something more calculating remains unclear to me."

Whipple tapped a pencil against his notebook. "We're making progress, but I fear we may be connecting dots that don't necessarily align?"

"The reduced speed works in our favour," I pointed out. "With our arrival in New York delayed by at least a day, possibly two, we have more time to unravel the case."

"Very true," HG said. "So, what's our next move, gentlemen?"

Whipple closed his notebook with a snap. "I propose we divide our efforts. Rex, you've established a rapport with Penelope Chase. See what more she might reveal about Blythe's threats. I'll approach Matthews again; as Blythe's secretary, he may know more that he's already told us. Perhaps he picked up his boss knew about the fire."

"And I," HG said with a mischievous smile, "shall make it my business to have a friendly chat with Lily de Vere. If she's romantically entangled with our captain. It certainly creates an intriguing additional dimension to consider."

"Splendid," I said, rising from my chair. "Shall we reconvene here before dinner to compare notes?"

Just then, urgent banging on the stateroom door shattered our plans.

Chapter Fourteen

A WOMAN WHO CONCEALS

Graham, HG's personal steward, opened the door to reveal Martha Briggs, the elderly maid we had met earlier. Worry drew her face, and her hands fidgeted with her apron.

"Begging your pardon, Your Grace, but there's trouble. Someone found Charlie Peabody, unconscious in the linen cupboard. Nasty blow to the head, poor lad."

Whipple was on his feet in an instant. "When was he discovered?"

"Not fifteen minutes ago, sir. The doctor is with him now. Thought you ought to know, seeing as how you'd been talking to him and all."

We exchanged glances. Charlie was the only witness who had placed Grayson near Sir Edmund's cabin on the night of the murder.

"Is he conscious? Can he speak?" I asked.

Martha shook her head. "Not making much sense, sir. They've moved him to the surgery."

After Martha departed, HG turned to us with concern.

"This is no coincidence. Someone didn't want Mr Peabody sharing what he knew."

"Or what else he might have remembered," Whipple added.

We hastened to the infirmary, only to find Lily de Vere already there, speaking with the ship's doctor. She turned at our approach; her face one of polite concern.

"How dreadful," she murmured. "A steward attacked. One wonders what the world is coming to."

"You seem particularly interested in a crew member's welfare, Miss de Vere," HG observed.

Lily gave a delicate shrug. "One hears things on a ship of this quality. The poor man mentioned something to the captain about Sir Edmund's death, I gather."

Whipple stepped forward. "And how would you know that?"

"The captain mentioned it over cocktails yesterday," she replied without hesitation. "He said the steward was being rather...imaginative in his recollections."

I studied her. Her tone conveyed no deception, but it lacked substance. Every phrase seemed calculated to acknowledge the facts, offering nothing beyond them.

"Very civic-minded of you to check on him," Whipple noted, with a neutral expression.

"We're all concerned for everyone's safety, Detective Inspector," she replied in a smooth tone.

Dr Ambrose emerged from behind a curtained alcove; his angular features set with professional detachment.

"The patient is stable but incoherent," he informed us briskly. "Blunt trauma to the posterior cranium. Delivered with considerable force."

"May we see him?" Whipple asked.

"You may, but go easy with him. Dr Ambrose drew back the curtain.

Charlie lay motionless on the narrow bed, his face ashen against the white pillow. A bandage wrapped his head, with a spot of crimson showing through at the back.

"Someone didn't want him talking," Whipple murmured.

Miss de Vere nodded to us all and glided from the room. I watched her depart, struck by her composure in the face of such violence.

HG caught my glance and, after the doctor withdrew, said, "Notice how economical Miss de Vere is with her emotions."

"How do you mean?" I asked.

"She exhibits precisely the minimum emotional response required for any situation. When we discovered poor Charlie had been attacked, she displayed mild concern, no shock, no distress."

I considered this. "She seemed the same when Sir Edmund was found."

"Exactly. No fear, despite a killer being aboard. No genuine surprise at the news. Only a measured regret, as if responding to a cancelled dinner engagement."

I recalled other moments: the seance, when Madame Zelda collapsed and the lights failed. While others gasped or cried out, Lily had remained still. During the argument between von Ritter and Sir Edmund, she had observed with the mild interest one might give a mediocre stage play.

"Even when she spilled wine on Sir Edmund at dinner," I said, "her apology seemed rehearsed rather than spontaneous."

"That's what makes her intriguing," HG replied. "One

expects an actress to be theatrical, expressive. Yet she maintains rigid control, never revealing more than she intends."

"Perhaps that's the key," I whispered. "Calm isn't the absence of emotion; it's control. Someone aboard this ship has the control to order a murder, arrange an attack, and maintain perfect composure throughout."

"And unlike poor Charlie," HG added, "they know exactly when to remain silent."

'The question is," began Whipple, "is Miss de Vere in control, or is someone manipulating her?"

Penelope entered the infirmary, pausing at the doorway to talk to someone in the corridor. Evidently, Miss de Vere still lingered. A presence that appeared to unsettle Miss Chase.

"Miss Chase," Penelope acknowledged with a polite nod. "Are you unwell? Perhaps the doctor might help with the headaches you mentioned at dinner."

"I'm perfectly fine," Penelope replied. "I heard someone was hurt."

Miss Chase stepped closer, her movements fluid and deliberate. It's a steward, dear. Nothing for you to concern yourself with," HG said.

"Charlie Peabody," I clarified. “An attacker assaulted him.”

Penelope's eyes widened. "The steward who—" She stopped herself.

"Who, what, Miss Chase?" Whipple prompted.

"Nothing. I simply recognised the name." Penelope’s fingers twisted the small handbag she carried.

After Penelope departed, Whipple cleared his throat. "Why did she come here? And for such a short time. She hardly looked at Peabody."

"That may be, but she almost let something slip. What was it she was going to divulge?" HG said.

Dr. Ambrose kept working on his patient and writing notes in his journal while the inspector's question lingered.

I turned to Whipple as we exited the infirmary. "I'm convinced Penelope was about to reveal something crucial."

"Agreed," he replied, "she caught herself just in time."

HG adjusted her hatpins with deliberate care. "Perhaps we should follow Miss de Vere. She departed with remarkable haste for someone who claims to be concerned about poor Charlie. That said, she lingered in the corridor long enough to give young Penelope the heebie-jeebies."

We tracked Lily's path through the ship, following discreet inquiries with passing stewards. One directed us to the Royal Bar, where first-class passengers gathered for intimate chats.

The Royal Bar occupied the forward section of A Deck, a sanctuary of polished mahogany and brass fittings. Crystal chandeliers cast a warm glow over the leather-upholstered armchairs and private booths. The ceiling featured hand-painted scenes of maritime glory, each panel bordered by intricate gold leaf. The room exuded exclusivity.

Lily de Vere sat in an end booth with Baron von Ritter. They conversed in low tones with their heads inclined towards each other. A fresh bottle of champagne stood between them. von Ritter had clearly been expecting his guest.

"How convenient," HG murmured. "Our two most interesting passengers, sharing confidences."

We selected a booth with a discrete, yet clear view of them, and a white-jacketed steward appeared at once.

"Gin and tonic for the gentlemen," HG ordered, "and a glass of the Château d'Yquem for me."

I watched as von Ritter leaned back in his chair, his posture relaxed yet alert. Unlike his usual bombastic manner, he treated Lily with a curious deference. When she spoke, he listened, his eyes never leaving her face.

"He's wary of her," I whispered.

Whipple nodded. "Like a man handling unexploded ordnance."

Our drinks arrived, and HG raised her glass in a silent toast. "Observe that she never gestures while speaking. Complete economy of movement. So at odds with her professional occupation."

Von Ritter burst into laughter at something Lily said, but the sound held no warmth. He signalled for a Cuban cigar, then glanced around the room. His gaze swept past us without acknowledgment, though I felt certain he'd registered our presence.

After twenty minutes, they rose to leave. Von Ritter escorted Lily to the door, his hand hovering near her elbow without touching it. Before departing himself, he stopped at our table.

"A pleasant day to you all," he said with a formal neck-bow. "Miss de Vere is most remarkable, is she not? She possesses a quality rare in women."

"And what might that be?" HG inquired.

"She knows when not to speak." His smile revealed nothing. "A talent many could benefit from cultivating."

"I doubt that was intended as a compliment," Whipple remarked after von Ritter had gone.

"On the contrary," HG replied, swirling her wine

thoughtfully. "From a man like the Baron, it's the highest praise he can offer."

"Sounds like diplomatic blather to me," Whipple grumbled.

HG smiled, but I noticed how carefully she tucked away the Baron's words, like a collector adding another specimen to a private cabinet.

We finished our drinks in contemplative silence. As we prepared to leave, I reviewed every interaction I'd witnessed between von Ritter and Lily. He was arrogant and rude to everyone during the trip, treating the captain and Penelope with disdain, and being mean to Sir Edmund. Yet with Lily, he maintained a cautious respect that struck me as telling.

The Baron feared very little on this ship, but he feared her.

We left the Royal Bar and strolled along the promenade deck. The sky had cleared, presenting a brilliant blue canvas above the Atlantic swells. Several passengers walked or lounged in deck chairs; their faces turned toward the strengthening sun.

"Something's been bothering me about Lily de Vere," I said as we found a relatively private section of rail. "Since we boarded, she's never once spoken directly about Sir Edmund."

Whipple frowned. "Is that significant?"

"Everyone else has mentioned him. The captain discussed his demanding nature. Penelope admitted her connection. Even von Ritter openly argued with him. But Lily? Not a word."

HG adjusted her gloves, her gaze following a gull that soared alongside the ship. "Perhaps she simply didn't know him."

"No, that can't be right," I countered. "Blythe had those blackmail letters from her. There must be a connection."

"She might have avoided the topic to prevent drawing attention to herself," Whipple suggested.

"Yet she's an actress," HG mused. "She thrives on attention."

“I thought about this. When the captain announced Blythe's murder, everyone showed different reactions. You know, like shock or confusion. Lily just kept drinking her tea.” I offered.

Whipple tapped his pocket, where he kept his notebook. "Absence of comment is hardly evidence, my boy. We can't build a case on what someone hasn't said."

"True," HG replied, "but absence can be revealing in its own way. In society, silence often speaks volumes. Consider the duchess who refuses to acknowledge a social climber at her table. She needn't say a word. Her silence communicates everything."

"Are you suggesting Lily's silence about Blythe is deliberate?" I asked.

"I'm suggesting," HG said carefully, "that we should consider what people choose not to discuss as carefully as what they volunteer."

A steward passed with a silver tray of coffee, and we paused our conversation until he was well beyond earshot.

"The question becomes," Whipple continued, "what does Miss de Vere gain from this calculated silence?"

"Distance," I replied immediately. "If she never mentions him, she creates the impression they were strangers. No connection means no motive."

HG grinned in consent. "Precisely, Rex. And what better way to appear innocent than to seem utterly disinterested in the victim?"

"Yet she kept those letters that connected them," Whipple pointed out. "Why not destroy them?"

"Insurance," HG suggested. "Or leverage."

I recalled how Lily had watched von Ritter across the dining room that first night. How she'd positioned herself to overhear conversations in the library. How she'd appeared at Charlie's bedside without being summoned.

"She's researching her subject," I said. "Watching reactions, measuring responses. But contributing nothing herself."

"A woman who withholds," HG murmured. "Dangerous indeed."

We sat in contemplative silence as the ship ploughed forward through the truculent waves. I couldn't explain why, but I felt certain that Lily's silence about Blythe wasn't just absence of evidence, as Whipple suggested.

"I can't dismiss what my eyes tell me," Whipple said, leaning against the railing. "Miss de Vere had the blackmail letters in her possession, which places her squarely in the realm of material evidence. No amount of theatrical behaviour changes that fact."

"Arthur, you're missing the subtlety," HG replied, her voice gentle but firm. "Consider how power truly operates. The most dangerous individuals rarely dirty their own hands. They exist in the space between action and consequence."

I watched a dolphin leap from a wave, catching the sunlight before disappearing back into the Atlantic. "What if Lily isn't our murderer, but someone who creates circumstances where murder becomes inevitable?"

HG's eyes lit with approval. "Precisely, Rex. She needn't have swung the murder weapon to be culpable."

"That's all very philosophical," Whipple said, "but a

court requires tangible evidence. A jury won't convict based on atmospheric influence."

"Then we must find where her influence intersects with physical reality," I suggested. "The blackmail letters prove she had leverage over Madame Zelda. What if she used that leverage to orchestrate something?"

Whipple tugged at his moustache. "We can't prove she compelled another passenger to kill Blythe without testimony or written instruction."

"True," I conceded, "but perhaps we're looking at this backwards. What if Blythe wasn't the primary target, but merely a convenient sacrifice?"

HG tilted her head. "Elaborate."

"Consider what we've learned about the coal bunker fire. The captain concealed a serious danger to protect his reputation. First Officer Grayson and Chief Officer Bowthorpe were complicit. If Sir Edmund discovered this secret..."

"He could have threatened exposure," Whipple finished thoughtfully. "But how does Miss de Vere factor into this?"

I shrugged. "I'm not certain yet. But she's been uncommonly interested in the ship's operations. Remember how she engaged Captain Hardwick last night? And her appearance at the infirmary seems too coincidental."

"The procedural difficulties remain formidable," Whipple cautioned. "We cannot arrest someone for creating an atmosphere conducive to murder."

HG tapped her gloved fingers against the railing. "Lily de Vere exists in a liminal space, Arthur. She understands how to position herself between instruction and execution. She navigates the territory between suggestion and action. That makes her dangerous, but also elusive."

A chill ran through me despite the warming sun. "Perhaps that's why von Ritter treats her with such caution. He recognises a fellow practitioner."

"Practitioners of what, exactly?" Whipple asked.

"The art of invisible control," HG replied. "The ability to shape outcomes without appearing to participate in them."

I contemplated HG's words. Throughout my training with her, I'd learned to observe physical evidence, to follow logical trails of inquiry. But this was something different—this nebulous realm where influence superseded direct action.

"So how do we proceed?" I asked. "If Lily orchestrated events rather than committed the murder herself, how do we prove it?"

"We follow the connections," HG said simply. "Among Miss de Vere and the people on this ship."

I nodded, finally grasping what HG had been teaching me throughout this voyage. Lily de Vere was in a dangerous spot, right where planning to kill became killing someone. Her power lay not in what she did, but in what others might do at her behest, while she remained untouched, watching from a calculated distance.

A sudden blast from the ship's horn caused several passengers nearby to jump, though Whipple was the only one of our trio who visibly startled, even though we had been pre-warned of the test. HG noticed his reaction and offered a private smile that was both reassuring and gently mocking.

"I believe our time might be well spent in a more systematic approach to Miss de Vere's connections," HG suggested as we continued our stroll. "Rex, you mentioned she's been uncommonly interested in the ship's operations."

"Yes," I confirmed, "particularly with Captain Hardwick. She charmed him thoroughly last evening."

Whipple consulted his pocket watch. "The captain should be completing his noon inspection about now. Perhaps we might accidentally encounter him on the bridge."

"Accidentally, Arthur?" HG's eyebrows arched. "How devious of you."

"I've learned from the best, HG," he replied with uncharacteristic cheekiness.

We made our way to the bridge, where, as Whipple had predicted, Captain Hardwick was concluding his inspection. His face soured upon noticing our approach.

"Detective Inspector Whipple," he acknowledged curtly, "I'm rather occupied at present."

"Of course, Captain," Whipple replied. "We merely wanted to inquire about Miss de Vere's interest in maritime operations."

The captain's expression flickered. "Miss de Vere? She's merely a curious passenger. Many first-class guests show an interest in the running of the ship."

"Indeed," HG interjected, "though not many spend quite so much time with the captain himself."

Hardwick's shoulders stiffened. "She's researching a theatrical role, I understand. A captain's wife in some nautical drama."

"How fascinating," I remarked. "Though curious she hasn't mentioned this role to anyone else."

"I wouldn't know about that," Hardwick replied, lifting his binoculars as his gaze drifted toward the horizon. "Now, if you'll excuse me."

As we descended from the bridge, I considered the

captain's defensive posture. "He's hiding something about Lily."

"Obviously," HG agreed. "But is it romantic interest, professional compromise, or something more sinister?"

"All three, perhaps," Whipple suggested. “Men in power can be easily tricked by pretty women who fain interest in their jobs.”

"Especially men like our captain," HG noted, "whose ego requires constant feeding."

We paused by a lifeboat, its canvas cover rippling in the salt breeze. "The ship docks in two days," I said. "Even with the delay caused by the fire, we're running out of time."

"Then we must be more direct," HG declared. "I propose we confront Lily directly."

"She'll deny everything," Whipple protested.

"Of course she will," HG agreed. "But denial requires explanation, and explanation often reveals what denial seeks to conceal."

Lily was in the first-class reading room, a temporary space after the library problem, reading poetry and acting like she wasn't interested. While others were anxious, she was calm, turning pages at a steady pace.

"Miss de Vere," HG began, settling into the chair opposite her. "We'd like to discuss your relationship with Sir Edmund Blythe."

Lily looked up, her face a perfect mask of mild surprise. "Sir Edmund? I scarcely knew the gentleman."

"Yet he possessed letters from you," I stated. "Letters used to blackmail Madame Zelda."

Her expression never faltered. "How interesting. Though I fail to see how that constitutes a relationship."

"Your lack of comment on his death has been conspicuous," Whipple added.

"Should I have wept dramatically, Detective Inspector?" A cool smile played across her lips. "Would that have satisfied your expectations?"

HG straightened her back "Miss de Vere, in my experience, silence is rarely neutral. It is a choice, and choices reveal intent."

"Sometimes," Lily replied, closing her book with deliberate care, "silence is merely the absence of anything worth saying."

As she rose to leave, I noticed how the room seemed to reconfigure itself around her movement. Without a word, the other passengers shifted in their seats, creating a path for her exit.

Later, in HG's stateroom, we discussed the encounter.

"She gave away nothing," Whipple grumbled.

"On the contrary," HG replied. "She demonstrated precisely what makes her dangerous. Some people change outcomes not by what they say, but by strategically choosing when to remain silent."

I nodded, understanding finally crystallising. "Withholding isn't passive at all. It's an active exertion of power."

Chapter Fifteen

A SATISFACTORY EXPLANATION

I spent some time reflecting on how rapidly the ship's rhythm had reasserted itself. The Royal Bar hummed with pre-dinner cocktail chatter. Ladies in evening attire glided past with practiced smiles. Gentlemen puffed cigars and discussed stock prices. The assault on Charlie Peabody might never have happened.

First-class passengers had absorbed the shock like a drawing room carpet absorbs spilled tea. Blotted, brushed over, and forgotten before it could stain the social fabric.

"Have you noticed," I whispered to HG as we occupied a corner table, "how everyone's pretending nothing's amiss? A man lies in the surgery, and they're debating whether Pimm's is passe."

HG placed her sherry glass on the small table between us. "Power requires stability, Rex. Those who hold authority tolerate disruption if they control it. When it erupts, they must contain it.

"Like the coal bunker fire," I murmured.

"Precisely like that," HG agreed. "Both literal and

metaphorical fires aboard this ship are being smothered with remarkable efficiency."

Whipple joined us, his face grave. "I've just come from speaking with Dr Livingstone. Charlie remains unconscious but stable. The doctor believes he'll recover, though when he'll wake is uncertain."

"Convenient timing for some," I observed. "His testimony about Grayson's whereabouts was becoming rather problematic."

"Yes, rather difficult to cross-examine an unconscious witness," HG remarked with a sardonic twist to her lips.

Whipple frowned. "I've stationed a crewman outside the surgery. If, when, Peabody brightens up, we'll be the first to know."

"If they allow it," I said, glancing around the room. "This ship operates like a small kingdom, with its own laws and hierarchies. We're merely visitors."

"Visitors with the authority of Scotland Yard," Whipple reminded me.

HG patted his hand. "Arthur, dear, even Scotland Yard's reach grows somewhat diluted several hundred miles into the Atlantic. We're floating in a curious limbo of jurisdictions."

"Which makes it the perfect location for murder," I concluded, watching as Lily de Vere entered the bar, her composure absolute, her timing impeccable. "No wonder she chose the middle of an ocean crossing."

"What exactly did Dr Ambrose say about Charlie's condition?" I asked Whipple, lowering my voice as a steward passed with a tray of cocktails.

Whipple glanced around before replying. "Concussion, of course. Significant bruising on the back of the skull and neck. The doctor believes something firm, but not rigid, struck Charlie.

"How severe?" HG inquired, her face betraying genuine concern beneath her customary composure.

"Serious enough to render him groggy, but not life-threatening," Whipple replied. "Dr Ambrose noted the precision of the attack. Whoever struck Charlie knew exactly how much force to apply."

"A professional, then," I concluded.

"Or someone with experience in such matters," Whipple agreed. "The doctor mentioned something peculiar. Charlie has gaps in his memory from before the attack. Not unusual with head injuries, but convenient for our assailant."

HG raised an eyebrow. "Do you believe this calculated intimidation instead of an attempt to silence him permanently?"

"Indeed," Whipple nodded. "A warning, perhaps. Or a message to others who might consider speaking to us."

"How reassuring," I remarked dryly. "One can appreciate the restraint shown in merely concussing the poor fellow rather than finishing the job properly."

HG suppressed a smile. "Your gallows humour is improving, Rex. Though perhaps not appropriate for the dining room."

"I've ruled out random violence or shipboard disagreements," Whipple continued. "Charlie is well-liked among the crew, keeps to himself, does his job without complaint. This was no drunken quarrel between stewards."

"Then it's connected to our investigation?" I replied.

"Without question," Whipple confirmed. "Charlie saw something, or someone, and paid the price for his observation. But our assailant wanted him frightened, not dead."

"Which suggests," HG mused, "that whoever attacked

him has no particular taste for unnecessary bloodshed. They're practical rather than passionate."

"Unlike Sir Edmund's killer," I noted. "That murder suggests anger, with a force beyond what that required."

"Two different people, then?" Whipple pondered.

"Or maybe one person, but in different situations," HG said, gazing at the doorway where Lily de Vere was, still looking around the room carefully.

I studied Lily as she surveyed the room with a calculating gaze. "She treats every entrance as if it's a stage appearance, doesn't she?"

"The world is her theatre," HG replied. "For women like Lily, every interaction is a performance with stakes higher than most understand."

Whipple frowned. "I find it peculiar she hasn't once mentioned Blythe's name since his murder. They clearly had a history, given those blackmail letters."

"A studied omission," HG said. "Speaking of studs…"

She paused as a steward passed before continuing in a lower tone. "What happened to Charlie is what I call a 'warning beating.' It's the language of power, Rex. Those who understand real influence rarely deliver threats themselves."

"You mean the captain?" I asked. "Or perhaps one of our first-class suspects paid someone to do their dirty work?"

HG gave me an indulgent smile. "You're thinking too conventionally. This isn't merely about wealthy passengers flexing authority through proxies. It's about a system where violence can be implied rather than stated, arranged rather than executed personally."

"Rather like Sir Edmund's blackmail approach," I observed.

"Indeed, Rex," HG nodded. "The truly powerful create

circumstances where others act on their behalf without explicit instructions. They establish conditions where violence becomes inevitable without their fingerprints appearing anywhere."

Whipple looked uncomfortable. "That makes prosecution damnably difficult."

"Which is precisely the point," HG sipped her sherry. "Charlie's attack was planned to send a message, while allowing the sponsor to deny responsibility."

"The hierarchical structure of the ship makes it perfect," I said. "Orders flow downward without question. The person who commanded the attack might never have met Charlie's assailant."

"And might never meet them," HG agreed. "The chain remains broken; the connection impossible to prove."

"Then how do we catch our murderer?" Whipple asked, genuine frustration colouring his voice.

"By understanding that whoever orchestrated Sir Edmund's death thinks differently than you or I." HG began. "They feel safe from consequences because they've covered up their deeds."

"Every fortress has a weakness," I began. "We simply haven't found it yet."

I stifled a yawn as I watched a steward fumble two tables away. The passenger's request for a different wine flummoxed the table fellow. Champagne glasses remained empty, even though the bottle was chilled in its ice bucket.

"The ship's service is like a clock with a missing cog," I observed. "Everything still functions, but not quite right. Passengers who never noticed Charlie are now unconsciously registering his absence."

"Most people remain invisible until they're gone," HG remarked. "The truly powerful understand this dynamic.

They know precisely which cogs can be removed without stopping the machine entirely."

We watched as a senior steward swooped in to correct the wine situation, his haste betraying the pressure below stairs. Another steward hurried past with napkins for a table that should have been set an hour ago.

"It's rather like London during the General Strike," I said. "The surface appears normal while underneath, everything's stretched to breaking point."

I noticed a hundred small deficiencies that would have escaped my attention yesterday. A water glass unfilled. A breadbasket forgotten. The slight delay between courses. The subtle anxiety on stewards' faces as they worked twice as hard to maintain standards.

"One invisible man," I mused, "and his absence ripples through the entire first-class dining room."

"Rather makes you think about all those invisible people holding our world together, doesn't it?" HG said with a knowing smile. "The Charlies of England, quietly ensuring everything runs without a hitch, never thanked because they're never seen."

Whipple looked uncomfortable, perhaps thinking of his own working-class origins. "Charlie was exceedingly good at his job. Sir Edmund specifically requested him as his personal steward for this voyage."

I paused, fork halfway to my mouth. "Did he indeed? That's the first I've heard of it."

"The purser mentioned it when I was inquiring about cabin assignments," Whipple replied. It seems Sir Edmund often sailed with the shipping line, so such requests are treated as a priority.

"Sir Edmund knew Charlie from previous crossings," I intoned. "He trusted him enough to request him specifically.

What if Charlie knew more than he initially told us? What if he had information about Sir Edmund that extended beyond this voyage?"

"Information worth silencing him for," Whipple concluded grimly.

HG dabbed her lips with her napkin. "Well then, gentlemen, I believe we must ensure Charlie receives the very best care aboard this vessel. His recovery has become even more essential to our investigation."

"And his protection more urgent," I said, glancing around at the dining room's elegant façade. I pondered which smiling face had ordered a steward's assault, and what other violence they might yet command before we reached New York.

After dinner, I escorted HG back to her stateroom, our footsteps cushioned on the carpeted floor. Whipple had gone to check on Charlie once more, promising to join us later. The gentle roll of the ship belied the chaos brewing beneath its elegant veneer.

"What I don't understand," I said as we walked, "is why someone would assault Charlie now. Why not immediately after he spoke with us the first time?"

"Perhaps our culprit only recently discovered Charlie had shared information," HG replied. "Or perhaps they've only now realised the significance of what he revealed."

Whipple arrived fifteen minutes later, his collar askew and his expression troubled. Graham brought in tea without being asked, a testament to his uncanny ability to anticipate HG's needs.

"No change in Charlie's condition," Whipple announced, accepting a cup. "Doctor Ambrose believes he'll be up and about after a good rest."

"Just in time for our arrival in New York," I noted.

"Precisely my concern," Whipple said, settling into an armchair. "I've developed a working theory about the assault. It connects directly to Blythe's murder and involves someone who fears exposure."

"Do elaborate, Arthur."

"The timing is crucial," Whipple continued. "Charlie witnessed First Officer Grayson near Sir Edmund's cabin on the night of the murder. But I believe the assault occurred because Charlie knows something even more damaging."

"About the coal bunker fire," I ventured.

Whipple nodded. "I'm increasingly convinced that's our pressure point. Sir Edmund discovered the fire and confronted Captain Hardwick about concealing it from passengers."

"Blackmail," HG murmured. "Sir Edmund's specialty."

"Indeed," Whipple agreed. "The captain faced professional ruin if news of the fire reached Southampton. Sir Edmund would have recognised the leverage immediately."

"But surely the captain wouldn't murder a passenger," I objected. "The scandal would be infinitely worse."

"Maybe not directly," HG added, "but we know power works through different levels."

Charlie's job allowed him to hear what the high-ranking officers were saying.

"And someone realised he knew too much," I concluded.

"Precisely," Whipple said. The coal bunker problem is the reason for the captain's anxiety and Grayson's contradictory statements.

HG placed her teacup on the side table. "One hesitates to accuse a ship's captain of murder, Arthur. The maritime tradition rather frowns upon it."

"I'm not suggesting he wielded the weapon himself,"

Whipple clarified. "But he may have created conditions where someone else felt compelled to act."

"The invisible hand of power," I muttered.

"You're learning, Rex," HG smiled. "Though I suspect your education will require considerably more than one transatlantic voyage."

Hardwick was going to be exposed, so someone got rid of the problem, and now Charlie is silent because he saw something important," Whipple offered.

"But who actually struck the fatal blow against Sir Edmund?" I asked.

"That," Whipple sighed, "remains our central question. But I believe the answer lies within the chain of command aboard this vessel."

HG regarded us both with an appraising eye. "We have approximately thirty-six hours before we dock in New York, gentlemen. I suggest we use them wisely."

The ship gave a sudden lurch, reminding us of the fire burning in her bowels, threatening to consume us all while polite society danced above.

I left HG's stateroom with thoughts swirling like the Atlantic beneath us. Dawn would bring our penultimate day at sea. The resolution I sought seemed near yet elusive.

The corridor stretched before me, silent save for the distant thrum of engines. I almost reached my cabin when a voice called from behind.

"Just the man I wanted!"

Henderson, our erstwhile journalist, leaned against the wall, notebook in hand, a gleam in his eyes that reminded me of a terrier spotting a rat. His collar was askew, his tie loosened, the dishevelled uniform of his profession.

"Rather late for an interview," I replied.

Henderson fell into step beside me. "Or early, depending on one's perspective. The journalist's day begins when others sleep, Mr Ward. When guards drop and tongues loosen."

"Mine remains firmly in place, I assure you."

"Oh, I wouldn't dream of asking about Sir Edmund's murder," Henderson said with a dismissive wave. "That's merely the appetiser in this feast of scandal."

I stopped walking. "I beg your pardon?"

"Come now, you're part of the Dowager's little detective club. Surely you've realised there's something far bigger than a murder happening aboard this ship." Henderson lowered his voice, though the corridor remained empty. "Wheels within wheels, Mr Ward. Reputations that won't survive this crossing."

"Whose reputations?"

Henderson's smile widened. "Now that would be telling." He tapped his notebook. "But consider this: why would a man like Sir Edmund travel on a vessel commanded by someone he could destroy with a single telegram to Southampton?"

The question struck me with unexpected force. I hadn't considered the relationship from that angle.

"Perhaps you should ask the captain," I suggested.

"Oh, I have. Three times. He grows more evasive with each attempt." Henderson's eyes narrowed. "Did you know our illustrious Captain served as a convoy commander during the war? Quite the hero, they say. Though heroes often have the most to hide."

"Everyone has secrets, Mr Henderson. Even journalists."

"Indeed! Though ours tend toward the prosaic. Too much whisky, unrequited love for actresses, the occasional gambling debt." He chuckled. "Nothing like the secrets that bind our fellow passengers."

"You speak as if you know something concrete."

"I know that Chief Officer Bowthorpe hasn't been seen for two days. I know that First Officer Grayson makes hourly inspections of the lower decks that don't appear in the ship's log. And I know," Henderson leaned closer, "that someone is very desperate to ensure certain truths never reach New York."

I maintained my composure, though Henderson's revelations aligned with our own discoveries.

"Fascinating theories. Do you plan to publish them?"

"Theories become facts with sufficient evidence, Rex. I'm gathering quite a collection." Henderson straightened his rumpled jacket. "When this story breaks, it won't be Sir Edmund's murder that shocks society. It will be the web that surrounded him."

"And you'll be there to catch the falling spiders," I observed.

Henderson laughed. "Poetically put! Yes, with my net at the ready." He glanced at his watch. "I should let you retire. Dawn approaches, and I have an appointment with a nervous steward who's suddenly flush with cash he can't explain."

He tipped an imaginary hat and strode away, leaving me standing in the corridor. Fresh questions buzzed through my mind like disturbed hornets.

I couldn't help but ponder the number of different investigations that had developed, and if any of us understood the full picture.

I returned to my cabin, but sleep remained elusive. Henderson's information complicated our investigation, making a confusing situation even harder to understand. I poured myself a small nightcap and sat by the porthole, watching the moonlight scatter across the restless Atlantic.

A soft knock interrupted my contemplation. Opening the door revealed HG, still dressed in her finery, despite the late hour.

"May I intrude upon your solitude?" she asked, entering at my nod. "I saw the light under your door."

"Henderson cornered me in the corridor," I explained, offering her the chair while I perched on the edge of my bed. "He knows about Bowthorpe's disappearance and Grayson's unlogged inspections."

HG's expression darkened. "That man collects information like a magpie collects shiny objects, with little concern for the nests he destroys."

"He seems to think the murder is merely one thread in a larger tapestry."

"And he's not entirely wrong," HG replied, accepting the small glass I offered. "However, Henderson represents a different sort of threat than Sir Edmund ever did."

"How so?" I asked.

"Blythe hoarded secrets, kept them locked away to use at his convenience. Henderson publishes them for early gain and reputation." She took a measured sip. "Sir Edmund's power came from the threat of exposure. Henderson's comes from actual exposure."

"But surely that makes him less dangerous? More predictable?"

HG smiled with the patient indulgence of a teacher correcting a promising but mistaken pupil. "Consider the pressure he creates simply by existing aboard this vessel, Rex. Everyone who possesses something to hide knows Henderson might discover it. His presence alone forces people into illogical actions they might otherwise avoid."

The truth of her observation struck me. "Including murder?"

"Including murder," she confirmed. "Particularly when combined with the pressure of that smouldering coal bunker. This ship has become rather like a pressure cooker with the safety valve removed."

"And we're all inside it," I murmured.

"Precisely. Henderson doesn't need to make explicit threats. His notebook and pencil accomplish that without a word being spoken."

I recalled the journalist's eager face. Also, his dishevelled appearance invited levity, while concealing a razor-sharp intellect.

"What concerns me," HG continued, "is whether Henderson himself understands how dangerous his position has become. Men who reveal secrets often fail to appreciate how desperately others will act to preserve them."

"You think he might be in danger?"

"Anyone with too much knowledge of this ship should be very cautious," she responded as she finished her drink. "Including ourselves."

I awoke to grey morning light filtering through my porthole, having slept fitfully after HG departed. The ship maintained its steady rhythm, pushing forward towards New York with determined purpose, as if nothing were amiss.

Over breakfast, I mulled over the parallels that had crystallised in my mind during the night. Sir Edmund wielded secrets like weapons, threatening to reveal them if his demands weren't satisfied. Henderson collected those same secrets, not for private leverage but for public consumption. Both men trafficked in other people's vulnerabilities, albeit for different purposes.

And Charlie Peabody, poor fellow, had witnessed something that made him dangerous to someone aboard. Something worth a calculated blow to the head.

"You're particularly thoughtful this morning," HG observed, buttering her toast with meticulous precision. "I can practically hear the clockwork turning behind those eyes."

"I'm troubled by the symmetry of it all," I confessed. "Blythe threatened because of the 'evidence' he held. Henderson threatens with ink. Charlie has been silenced. It's as if someone aboard is systematically managing information—violently, when necessary."

"Rather reminds one of government work," HG remarked with the faintest ghost of a smile.

"I'm not joking, HG. There's a pattern here. Knowledge is being controlled, channelled, suppressed."

Whipple joined us, looking haggard from a night spent keeping watch over Charlie. "Our steward remains unconscious, though the doctor reports his vitals are improving."

"Someone aboard understands the game," I continued, pouring Whipple a cup of tea. "They know exactly how much force to apply and where. A threat here, a bribe there, violence when subtler methods fail."

"Just like Parliament," HG quipped.

"Or Scotland Yard," Whipple added with surprising candour.

I glanced between them, chilled despite the dining room's warmth. "You speak as if this is normal."

"Oh, it is normal, Rex," HG replied, her eyes suddenly serious. "That's precisely what makes it so terrifying."

Chapter Sixteen

ANOTHER ONE?

I sat in silence for a moment, reflecting on the casual way both HG and Whipple accepted unnatural death and the machinations of the upper class as normal. Perhaps I was still naïve in some respects, despite HG's careful tutelage.

"We should speak with Henderson again," I suggested, returning to the practical matter at hand. "If he's pieced together so much already, he might have insights we've missed."

"A sound idea," Whipple agreed, though his expression remained troubled. "The man possesses a certain low cunning, despite his affectation of bohemianism and personal disarray."

We finished our snack and set out to locate the journalist. His absence from the dining room was unusual. Henderson seldom missed an opportunity to eavesdrop on the conversations of passengers.

"Perhaps he's pursuing some new lead," I offered as we knocked at his cabin door. The silence that greeted us proved disconcerting.

"Might he have gone below decks again?" HG wondered.

Whipple's expression darkened. "Let's check the service stairwells."

We descended into the territory between the opulent first-class spaces and the functional crew areas. These paths allowed entry to both places, ideal for a journalist looking for news or anyone wanting to go unnoticed.

The narrow corridor felt colder than our own, with harsh electric bulbs casting stark shadows against painted steel walls. Our footsteps reverberated in the confined space.

"What's that?" I pointed to a dark shape huddled at the foot of the next flight of stairs.

Whipple rushed forward. Henderson lay crumpled against the wall, his body still. The notepad that seemed always attached to his hand lay several feet away, with a few torn pages scattered like fallen leaves.

"Lordy Lord," Whipple murmured, kneeling beside the journalist. A perfunctory check confirmed what was already clear from the unnatural angle of Henderson's neck and the fixed stare of his eyes. "He's been dead for hours."

HG surveyed the scene with remarkable composure. "Our pressure cooker has claimed another victim."

"This wasn't an accident," I observed, noting the bruising around Henderson's throat. "Someone wanted him silenced."

"Two deaths on one voyage," Whipple said grimly. "This has escalated beyond scandal into something far more sinister."

"It's a containment kill," HG stated with clinical detachment. Henderson either knew too much or seemed to. Someone couldn't risk whatever revelations he might publish upon reaching New York."

I collected the scattered notebook pages, careful not to disturb any potential evidence. "Look here," I said, holding up a page filled with Henderson's messy scrawl. "Names, dates, connections. He was mapping the relationships between everyone aboard."

"Including us," HG noted, pointing to her name with an elegant finger.

Whipple straightened, his face grave. "This changes matters considerably. Sir Edmund's murder might have been explicable as a personal vendetta or blackmail gone wrong. But Henderson's death suggests something larger at stake. But why did the killer leave such riches?"

"Perhaps he or she feared discovery?" I offered. "We must notify the captain."

HG placed her hand on my arm. "Think carefully, Rex. If Henderson was killed to prevent exposure, we now possess the very information that made them dangerous."

I grasped the peril of our position, staring at the scattered notes. "You're saying we might be next."

"I'm saying," HG replied with grim certainty, "that we must be very careful about what we reveal, and to whom."

I gazed at Henderson's motionless form. The unnatural stillness of his normally animated features struck me with unexpected force. Just yesterday he'd been pestering passengers with that roguish smile. Now he lay discarded like unwanted luggage.

"We need to move quickly," I said, slipping Henderson's notebook into my jacket pocket. "Someone believed that whatever he discovered was worth killing for."

"The question remains whether Henderson actually knew something significant, or merely appeared to," HG mused. "Either would be a sufficient motive if someone felt cornered."

Whipple knelt to survey the scene, his experienced eyes cataloguing details I might have missed. "No sign of the murder weapon. Strangulation, most likely. A powerful grip from behind."

"A crime of opportunity, perhaps?" I suggested. "Henderson was always skulking about where he shouldn't."

"No," Whipple replied, rising with a grunt. "This stairwell is seldom used. Our killer would have had to follow Henderson here or arrange to meet him."

HG touched my elbow. "Rex, we need to examine these notes somewhere private. They may reveal what Henderson discovered."

The gravity of our situation settled upon my shoulders. "If we alert the captain now, we lose control of the investigation."

"And possibly our lives," HG added with characteristic bluntness. "Captain Hardwick has shown little enthusiasm for our inquiries thus far."

Whipple's bushy eyebrows knitted together. "We're withholding evidence from a murder investigation, HG. It goes against every principle—"

"Yes, yes," HG cut in, waving away his objections. "Principles are marvellous in theory but occasionally inconvenient in practice. I suggest we temporarily borrow Mr Henderson's final insights. Then report our grim discovery to the captain and Doctor Ambrose."

HG's talent for making the outrageous sound perfectly reasonable never failed to impress me.

"Very well," Whipple conceded reluctantly. "But we proceed with extreme caution. Two murders mean we're hunting someone both desperate and experienced. However, our plan may not work. Whoever uses these stairs after us will discover the body."

"That may be so," HG began, "but any time we can steal now may pay dividends in the long run."

As we retreated up the stairs, I felt the bulk of Henderson's notebook against my chest. The poor chap had been irritating, intrusive and indiscreet, but he'd been alive. Now his last observations might lead us to his killer, if we could decipher them before whoever silenced him decided we knew too much as well.

I hurried along the corridor, Henderson's notebook burning a hole in my pocket. HG and Whipple flanked me as we retreated to the relative safety of HG's stateroom.

"Two murders on one crossing," I murmured as HG closed her door. "Rather shatters the promotional brochures claiming, 'tranquil luxury at sea,' doesn't it?"

"Indeed," HG replied, her lips pursing upward despite the gravity of our situation. "Although I imagine 'murder on the high seas' might appeal to a certain adventurous clientele."

Whipple was in no mood for levity. He paced the stateroom carpet, hands clasped behind his back. "Henderson's murder confirms we're dealing with something far more significant than a personal vendetta."

"A pattern," I agreed, spreading Henderson's notes across HG's writing desk.

"Precisely," Whipple nodded, suddenly seeming taller, more authoritative. The uncertain, seasick inspector had vanished, replaced by the seasoned Scotland Yard detective. "Two murders, possibly linked, both victims possessing information that threatened someone aboard."

HG perused the scattered papers. "Our journalist was surprisingly thorough. Look here, he's traced financial connections between Blythe, von Ritter, and Hardwick."

"And this," I pointed to a hasty sketch of the ship. "He

marked the coal bunker area. Henderson also noted that 'Bowthorpe vanished after inspection.' Perhaps he'd discovered a connection between the fire and Blythe's murder?"

Whipple removed his notebook. "This event places me in a particular situation," Whipple said while scratching his forehead, as if conflicted over the situation.

'How so?" HG asked.

"Remember that I am merely another passenger on the Britannic Star. My superiors gave me no instructions, so my credentials are void. Unless the captain specifically requests that I investigate the journalist's death, I am no more than an interested party."

Whipple's disclosure shocked me to my core. I had assumed His Majesty's justice extended to British-registered ships.

"What about Sir Edmund's death?" I asked.

"The same, young Rex. Captain Hardwick has simply tolerated my…our, interference. At any time, he could have, and still can, call an immediate halt to our endeavours."

I looked at HG to see a confirming nod. "Of course, Hardwick will have reported the first death, and its circumstances, to his Principals. He may even have told them that a representative of Scotland Yard is on board as a passenger. Unless Arthur is invited by the company, or instructed by the Chief Constable to investigate, Arthur has no more power than you or I. As for your point about the vessel's British registration, it matters not, since we are in international waters. Only the captain's authority stands."

I pondered Whipple's dilemma for several seconds, then came up with an idea. "Perhaps you might send a telegram to the chief constable?"

Judging from his facial contortions, I realised the thought hadn't occurred to him. Perhaps living in a law-restrained world of strict order and formal procedures, Whipple had shut down the possibility.

HG gave Whipple a sympathetic glance. "It might be worth a try, Arthur. After all, What's the worst that can happen?" She spoke with a gentleness reserved only for those closest to her.

Whipple's stare hardened. "Oh, just a disciplinary hearing, that's all."

"Is that all?" HG said with a smile.

"It's alright for you, HG "But—"

HG held a hand up. "I apologise for making light of your predicament. What I should have said is that I will not allow such a situation to arise. Do we understand each other, dear Arthur?"

Whipple's frame relaxed as he looked to HG. Instead of speaking, he nodded. No words were required.

I knew Whipple wouldn't wait long to send his telegram. Within minutes of leaving HG's stateroom, he marched to the wireless room with a determined stride that brooked no argument.

He insisted on notifying Scotland Yard. "Two murders aboard a British vessel cannot go unreported," he said to me stiffly as we reached the wireless room door.

What we hadn't expected was how quickly Captain Hardwick would discover Whipple's actions. The captain's steward found us barely twenty minutes later, his face a mask of professional neutrality that couldn't quite hide his discomfort.

"Inspector Whipple," he announced stiffly. "The captain requests your immediate presence in his quarters."

Whipple glanced at HG and me. "We shall all attend."

"The captain specifically requested—"

"We shall all attend," HG repeated with a tone that rendered further discussion pointless.

The captain's quarters were impressive. A spacious room with polished wood panelling and nautical instruments mounted in brass frames. But the atmosphere within was far from cordial. Captain Hardwick stood by his desk, his face flushed with anger, a crumpled telegram form clutched in one fist.

"How dare you," he began without preamble, brandishing the form at Whipple. "I gave you full licence to look into Sir Edmund's death without making it official. And how do you repay my trust? By going behind my back to contact Scotland Yard!"

Whipple stood his ground. "A second murder demands official intervention, Captain."

"A second murder?" Hardwick's voice rose to new heights. "You concealed that from me as well?"

"We were coming to inform you when—"

"When what? When you'd finished sending telegrams to every authority in London?"

I watched Whipple's transformation with fascination. Gone was the rumpled-suited, uncertain man of our early acquaintance. His posture straightened; his voice hardened.

"Captain Hardwick, I represent the law, even as a passenger. It was my duty to—"

"Your duty?" Hardwick spat the word. "Your duty was to respect the chain of command aboard my vessel!"

The two men faced each other, neither willing to yield. The captain's desk between them might have been a battlefield's no man's land.

Then HG stepped forward.

"Gentlemen," she said in a muted tone, "this display is unbecoming."

Both turned to her, for the moment united in surprise at her intervention.

"Captain," she continued, "while you speak of a chain of command and respect, might I inquire about your duty to your passengers? The coal bunker fire, for instance. Still not fully extinguished, I believe, which puts this entire vessel and all souls aboard in mortal danger."

The captain's mouth opened, then closed without a sound.

"Perhaps," HG added, adjusting her gloves with deliberate care, "I should send a telegram to the Home Secretary to seek his counsel on these matters?"

The effect was immediate. The captain's face drained of colour. Whipple's eyes widened in astonishment. I felt a curious mixture of awe and admiration at HG's display of raw power, effortlessly wielded.

The silence stretched taut as piano wire.

Then, HG's demeanour softened. She smiled that smile I'd come to recognise as her bridge between confrontation and reconciliation.

"Now that order and common sense rule once more," she added, "let us sit and discuss matters as mature adults working for the same end."

She glanced around the cabin. "Perhaps, Captain, you might order some tea and iced fancies? You will find the combination most restorative."

The captain looked as though he'd been struck by lightning, then mesmerised by its afterglow. He reached for the internal telephone with mechanical movements.

"Tea for four," he said faintly into the speaker. "And...iced fancies."

The intervening few minutes were spent with the captain and Whipple exchanging suspicious looks. I glanced at HG, who offered the faintest of smiles, then winked at me. I suspected she rather enjoyed the situation.

A sharp rap on the door heralded the entry of the captain's personal steward, dressed as one might expect for his role.

I observed as the tray was laid out with meticulous care, the steward's movements precise and practiced despite the thick tension in the room. The silver teapot gleamed under the cabin lights, and the iced fancies sat in perfect formation on a bone china plate.

"I shall be mother," HG announced, her voice slicing through the awkward silence.

The steward hesitated, glancing at Captain Hardwick. The captain gave a curt nod, and the man retreated with obvious relief.

"How do you take your tea, Captain?" HG asked, her tone suggesting we were at a garden party rather than in the middle of a confrontation about multiple murders.

"Milk, no sugar," Hardwick muttered, his bushy eyebrows still knitted in displeasure.

HG poured with a delightful elegance, her hands steady despite the ship's gentle roll. She distributed the iced fancies with equal attention, placing a pink one on the captain's saucer with a smile that could have charmed a prison warden with a toothache.

We sat in silence for several minutes, the only sounds the clink of china and the distant thump of the engines. I caught Whipple's eye as he bit into his fancy. His expression suggested he found this teatime diplomacy as surreal as I did.

A sharp knock interrupted our curious gathering.

"Enter," barked the captain.

The door cracked open to reveal a wireless boy in a crisp white tunic. He couldn't have been older than sixteen, and his nervousness was palpable as he addressed the captain rather than any of us.

"A telegram for Detective Inspector Whipple, sir."

Whipple looked up from his half-eaten fancy, but HG was quicker.

"I shall take that, young man," she said smoothly, "and let me see what I have in my purse for you."

The boy's eyes never left the captain as HG rummaged in her handbag, finally extracting a silver shilling. The coin caught the light, and the boy's attention finally shifted from Hardwick to the gleaming piece of silver. HG placed it in his palm, and he handed over the telegram with a small bow.

The door closed behind him as he departed, still staring at his unexpected bounty.

HG unfolded the single sheet of paper within the envelope, her expression revealing nothing.

"Now," she said, smoothing the paper with an elegant finger, "let us see what news we have."

HG studied the note with that familiar gleam in her eye, the one that told me she had the upper hand and intended to play it with relish.

"You have permission to investigate both deaths formally, Arthur," she announced, her voice carrying a hint of triumph. "The note also requests that Captain Hardwick extend such assistance as you may require in expediting matters."

Before Whipple could react, a knock on the door interrupted things. The second postboy surpassed the first in confidence. He announced a telegram for the captain.

Hardwick urged the boy in and almost snatched the envelope before dismissing him with a wave of his hand. I observed his face darkening as he read the slip of paper, then screwed it up and dropped it onto the floor.

"I assume the note is from your Principals and confirms arrangements?" Said HG.

Hardwick scowled. "It does."

"Excellent, then no more angst between you two; we have much work to do before the vessel docks in New York tomorrow."

The two men stared each other out like prize fighters at the beginning of a round. I waited for someone to throw the first verbal punch.

HG sighed. "And that will be enough of that...unless you want me to treat you both as errant schoolboys? What is it to be, I knock your heads together...and I will, or the both of you grow up at once?"

Hardwick and Whipple saw sense, and the tension in the room eased.

"To business, then," Whipple announced.

The tension between Whipple and the captain dissipated like morning fog, though neither man looked pleased about it.

"Now," Whipple said, straightening his rumpled jacket, "regarding Mr Henderson's death. We need to secure the area immediately."

"I shall have my men cordon off that section of the service stairwell," Captain Hardwick replied grudgingly.

"And no one is to leave their cabins without being questioned," Whipple added. The familiar determination had returned to his voice. "We're dealing with a second murder aboard your vessel, Captain, not some regrettable accident."

Hardwick's eyebrows shot up. "Surely it could have been—"

"The marks on Henderson's neck were unmistakable," I interjected. "Someone strangled him."

HG placed her teacup down with a delicate clink. "I believe Arthur is quite correct in treating these deaths as connected, Captain. First Sir Edmund, then a journalist who was investigating Sir Edmund's activities."

Whipple nodded. "We need a list of every passenger and crew member who was in that section of the ship within the last six hours."

The captain bristled. "That's half the ship!"

"Then I suggest we begin straight away," Whipple replied calmly.

I watched the interplay between them with fascination. Authority sat easily on Whipple.

As we left the captain's quarters, HG fell into step beside me. "Rather enjoying this, aren't you?" she murmured, her eyes twinkling mischievously.

Whipple moved with purpose toward the stairwell where we'd discovered Henderson's body. Two crewmen now stood guard, grimacing at their assignment.

"Nobody has disturbed anything?" Whipple commanded.

"No, sir," the senior of the two replied."

Whipple knelt beside the body; his eyes narrowed in concentration. "As we know, Henderson was pursuing at least two separate matters," he said after a moment. "Sir Edmund's murder, certainly. But also, something else."

"The coal bunker fire," I suggested.

Whipple's expression tightened. "Yes. His notes made that quite clear."

"Expanding our circle of potential murderers considerably," HG observed.

"Indeed," Whipple murmured, carefully examining Henderson's pockets. "Anyone connected to either Sir Edmund or the ship's officers now falls under suspicion."

I watched as he scrutinised Henderson's clothing, removing a pencil stub, a pocket watch, and three shillings.

"Nothing else?" I asked.

"Nothing visible," Whipple replied. "But he knew something that made him dangerous to someone."

"Or to several 'someones'," HG added. "Journalists rarely limit their investigations to a single thread when multiple scandals present themselves."

Whipple frowned. "We need to speak with every passenger or crew member Henderson interacted with in the last twenty-four hours."

I thought of the many people I'd seen Henderson approach over the past day. His notebook always at the ready, his questions probing and often unwelcome.

"That's half the ship," I said, unconsciously echoing the captain's earlier protest. "We need to narrow our focus."

Whipple thought for a moment, before offering HG a glance. "You're right, of course. Perhaps the list of suspects is self-selecting? "Rex, I'd like you to speak with Penelope Chase. Henderson mentions her in his notes."

"And I," HG announced, "shall have a word with our German diplomat. Henderson's notes contained some rather intriguing observations about von Ritter's movements, did they not?"

"Very good," Whipple nodded. "I'll question Matthews again. Henderson noted a late-night meeting between him and First Officer Grayson that neither has mentioned to us."

I left HG and Whipple to their assigned tasks, winding my way through the first-class corridors in search of Miss Chase. The ship felt different now. Tense, as though the bulkheads were holding their breath. Two deaths had transformed our floating palace into something sinister.

I turned a corner and almost collided with Lily de Vere.

"Rex," she said, stepping back with perfect poise. "How fortunate. I was hoping to speak with someone sensible about this dreadful business. We've been told to remain in our rooms, but I simply cannot abide the atmosphere."

Her composure struck me as peculiar. Here stood Lily, as collected as if attending afternoon tea.

"You've heard about Mr Henderson, then?"

"Indeed." She adjusted her pearl necklace.

"You spoke with him recently?"

"He cornered me last evening." Her voice cooled. "Most impertinent questions about my acquaintance with Sir Edmund. He implied I might know something about his death."

"And do you?"

She laughed. "Only that the world is better without him. Henderson seemed determined to extract some form of confession from me. As if I would have anything to confess."

The words came too easily, like lines rehearsed in anticipation of being questioned.

"How unfortunate his curiosity led to such an end," I said.

"Quite," she replied. "Curiosity is often fatal…to cats and journalists alike."

The chill in Lily's voice lingered long after she'd glided away. I stood for a moment, considering the performance I'd just witnessed. For that's what it had been, calculated to the last syllable.

I continued toward Penelope Chase's cabin, my mind turning over Lily's strange composure. The corridor seemed longer than usual, the ship's gentle roll somehow more pronounced. A steward hurried past, his face pinched with worry.

When I knocked on Penelope's door, the response was immediate.

"Who is it?" Her voice wavered through the polished wood.

"It's me, Rex. May I speak with you?"

The lock clicked, and the door opened just enough to reveal her pale face. Her eyes were red-rimmed; her blonde hair hastily pinned.

"Come in," she whispered, glancing up and down the corridor before pulling me inside.

Her cabin was in disarray, with clothing scattered across the bed, and cupboard drawers half-open.

"Are you packing?" I asked, surprised given the captain's orders.

"I...yes. No, I don't know what I'm doing." She sank onto the edge of her bed. "They're saying someone killed that journalist. Is it true?"

"I'm afraid so."

"Dear Lord." She pressed her handkerchief to her lips. "It's happening again."

"Penelope, did Henderson speak with you recently?"

She drooped her head. "Yesterday afternoon. He asked about Father and Sir Edmund. He knew things, private things."

"Things?"

"About the financial arrangements between them. About meetings at our home." She twisted the handkerchief between her fingers. "He had a card, you see. A calling card with Sir Edmund's name. It had my father's handwriting on the back. A time and date."

I felt my pulse quicken. "Do you know where he got it?"

"He claimed he found it near the service stairwell." She looked up. "The same stairwell where they found him, isn't it? That can't be a coincidence."

I was about to reply when something caught my eye. A small white rectangle protruded from beneath her dressing table. I bent to retrieve it.

A torn calling card corner displayed the jagged edge with only the letter "E."

"Is this what he showed you?" I asked, holding it up.

The blood drained from Penelope's face.

Chapter Seventeen

DANGEROUS INFORMATION

Penelope's eyes widened as she stared at the torn fragment. She reached for it with trembling fingers.

"Where did you find this?" she whispered, clutching it like a talisman.

"Just there, beneath your dressing table. Penelope, I need to ask—"

"I didn't take it," she interrupted, shaking her head. "Henderson showed it to me, yes, but he kept it. I never touched it. You must believe me."

Her distress seemed genuine, but I had learned that appearances could be misleading aboard the Britannic Star.

"Then how did it find its way into your cabin?" I kept my voice gentle, without a hint of accusation.

"I don't know! Someone must have..." She trailed off, her gaze darting to the door. "Someone's been in here while I was at luncheon."

I pocketed the torn corner. "I need to fetch Inspector Whipple. Will you be all right for a moment?"

She nodded, though her hands continued to twist her handkerchief into knots.

"Lock your door behind me," I advised.

Whipple met me in the corridor outside Henderson's cabin. "Anything from Miss Chase?" he asked, producing a small brass key.

"Rather a lot, actually. Including this." I showed him the torn card fragment. "Henderson had it; now it's mysteriously appeared in Penelope's cabin."

"Interesting," Whipple murmured, unlocking the journalist's door. "Yet curious."

The victim's cabin revealed the man himself: energetic, scattered, and terrier-like. Papers covered every surface, some arranged in tidy stacks, others crumpled and discarded. Books lay open, marked with pencilled notes. A half-drunk cup of tea sat cold beside his typewriter.

"Not the tidiest chap, was he?" I remarked, surveying the chaos.

"On the contrary," Whipple replied, taking out the notebook I'd found earlier beside the journalist's body. "There's method in this muddle. Look here, he's organised his suspicions by person."

The notebook contained observations of passengers, crew members, and their interactions. Henderson kept tabs on von Ritter's meetings with Lily, saw Captain Hardwick was anxious, and drew a layout of Sir Edmund's room.

"He was thorough," I admitted. "Too thorough for his own good, perhaps."

"That's the trouble with journalists," Whipple said, leafing through the pages. "They gather facts without understanding their true weight. A dangerous habit when murder is involved."

I picked up a crumpled telegram form. "He was

composing a message to his editor. Something about 'corporate collusion' and 'international scandal.'"

"Ah," Whipple nodded sagely. "Henderson stumbled onto something bigger than a simple shipboard murder. Something that made him dangerous to more than one person aboard."

Whipple turned another page in Henderson's notes and whistled.

"He certainly had the captain's measure," he said, showing a passage. "Look here, 'Hardwick risked passengers for prestige, hiding coal fire at all costs. Shipping line reputation worth more than human lives?'"

Whipple held the notebook a little higher to catch the light. "Our journalist friend was constructing quite the expose."

"That's not all. His character study of Lily is remarkably astute: 'Beautiful and controlled, never wastes a gesture or emotion. Acts as though permanently on stage. What role is she truly playing?'"

Whipple handed the notebook to me. I flipped through the pages, discovering Henderson's observations of our entire cast of suspects.

"He watched von Ritter closely too. Talks about 'mysterious meetings' in the early hours. Also, 'suspicious familiarity with the ship's layout for a first-time passenger.'"

Whipple picked up a second notebook. "Henderson was thorough, I'll grant him that; financial information. This stuff, if true, is dynamite."

"Perhaps too thorough for someone's comfort," I replied, reaching for a folder marked 'CONNECTIONS.'

Inside were crude diagrams linking various passengers with lines and question marks. Sir Edmund was in the middle of a diagram, with lines going to Penelope's father,

Captain Hardwick, and some companies with German names.

"Our journalist was a conspiracy theorist," Whipple remarked dryly.

"Or he uncovered the truth," I countered.

A gentle knock interrupted us. HG entered.

"Anything worthwhile?"

Whipple handed her the diagram. "Henderson believed there were financial connections between our victim and several parties aboard."

"Hardly surprising," HG said, examining the page. "Men like Sir Edmund rarely conduct business with strangers. Their world is rather small, all things considered."

I spotted a leather appointment book beside the typewriter. Inside, Henderson had marked today's date with a single notation: "Z - 4 pm - gym - confirm allegations."

"Z must be Madame Zelda," I said. "He was supposed to meet her this afternoon."

"Which means either she killed him once she knew the game was up," Whipple suggested, "or someone else did for the same reason."

HG closed the diagram folder with a thoughtful expression. "Or perhaps our Madame Zelda knows something vital that Henderson wished to confirm."

"Then we should keep his appointment," I said, checking my watch. "It's nearly four now."

"Indeed," HG smiled. "Though perhaps with a more robust delegation than poor Henderson anticipated."

I led the way to the gymnasium, tucked away on C deck, which seemed designed to discourage its intended use. None of us had set foot there during the voyage.

"I find it difficult to imagine Madame Zelda engaged in

physical exertion," I remarked as we descended a narrow staircase. "She hardly strikes me as the athletic type."

HG chuckled. "Perhaps that's precisely the point, Rex. A gymnasium at four in the afternoon on a transatlantic voyage? One could hardly choose a more deserted meeting place."

"You can say that again," Whipple nodded. "Privacy guaranteed without arousing suspicion."

We went through big wooden doors into a room with no windows, full of shiny machines that looked like torture devices rather than exercise equipment. The air carried the faint scent of liniment oil and polished leather.

In the centre of the room, atop a bicycle-like contraption with articulated handlebars at a particular angle, sat Madame Zelda. She had abandoned her usual flowing garments for what I assumed was an attempt at sporting attire. That said, her signature neck scarf and feather hat remained. The contraption beneath her bucked ferociously as she pedalled, the handlebars jerking forward and backward with each revolution. She clutched them with white-knuckled desperation; her face a portrait of acute distress.

"Oh dear," murmured HG. "She appears to be losing her battle with that infernal machine."

Strange, strangled noises escaped Madame Zelda's lips as she struggled to control the infernal machine. Her scarf whipped about her face like an agitated serpent.

"Perhaps she's having one of her moments," Whipple suggested with uncharacteristic levity. "You know, communicating with the other side."

HG responded in a flash.

"The only 'other side' that lady is about to communicate with is the corridor if that mechanical monster ejects her.

Rex, do please rescue the woman before a third tragedy strikes this accursed vessel."

I approached with caution, mindful of the thrashing handlebars. Reaching for the flywheel, I applied gentle pressure until the pedals slowed. Madame Zelda sagged with relief, her chest heaving beneath her ill-fitting exercise costume.

"Allow me," I offered, supporting her elbow as she dismounted. She collapsed into me, abandoning her usually composed demeanour.

"Perhaps the lady might recover on one of those loungers," HG suggested, showing a row of bamboo recliners positioned against the far wall.

I guided our breathless medium to the nearest one, where she collapsed with an undignified flop. Her neck scarf fell across her face, rising and falling with each laboured breath like a silk curtain in an open window. We watched on as the unexpected tableau of the formidable spiritualist collapsed to exhausted immobility.

We stood around Madame Zelda like junior doctors on the morning hospital rounds, watching her chest rise and fall in a calmer rhythm. The feather in her hat had wilted somewhat, drooping over one eye like a defeated cockerel.

"Thank you," she managed at last, pushing the offending plumage aside. "I must confess that the machine possessed considerably more vigour than anticipated." Her gaze travelled between the three of us. "Though I cannot help but wonder how you came to visit the gymnasium at precisely this moment. Serendipity, perhaps?"

HG offered her most charming smile. "Passengers had been requested to remain in their rooms, Madame. One might wonder what drew you here instead."

Madame Zelda adjusted her neck scarf with nervous

fingers. "I hoped to contact the spirits through physical exertion. Mr Henderson mentioned he was a keen athlete, and I thought, well..."

"Clearly to no avail," HG observed.

The medium's hands continued their fidgeting, twisting the silk fabric into tight coils. Whipple shifted his weight, adopting the casual stance I'd come to recognise as a prelude to sharper questioning.

"When did you last see Henderson?" he asked. "Had you arranged to meet him today?"

Madame Zelda's eyes flicked to the bicycle, as if she was considering a fast getaway.

"Let me answer that for you," Whipple continued. "We have evidence that you were to meet the fellow at this place at four o'clock."

Madame Zelda gazed at Whipple with an expression of sheepish capitulation. "I agreed to the meeting, yes. Though I confess I had no notion of what Henderson wanted with me."

"Why should I believe that?" Whipple snapped.

The woman's shoulders sagged beneath her inappropriate exercise costume. "Very well. Henderson wanted information on Klaus von Ritter and Captain Hardwick."

HG stepped closer, her voice gentle but insistent. "What form might such information take?"

Madame Zelda shook her head. "I don't know, truly. I thought I might turn the tables on Henderson instead, discover what he was really up to."

"For financial gain at some point in the future?" Whipple suggested.

"I deal with the past as much as the future, Detective Inspector," Madame Zelda replied, meeting his gaze with unexpected steadiness. "Though in Henderson's case, I fear he collected the type of futures that lead to tragedy for the naive."

The gymnasium fell silent except for the gentle creaking of the ship's superstructure. I studied Madame Zelda's face, searching for signs of deception, yet her features were unreadable.

We left Madame Zelda to her recovery and emerged onto the promenade deck, where the wind had picked up. The deck stretched before us, almost deserted except for a steward collecting abandoned teacups.

"She knew more than she admitted," Whipple said, tucking his notebook into his jacket pocket. "That business about turning the tables on Henderson. Nonsense."

HG drew her wrap closer against the chill. "Perhaps. Though I suspect she also recognised Henderson as a kindred spirit in the exploitation of secrets."

We walked in silence for several paces, the rhythm of our footsteps punctuated by the slap of waves against the hull. My mind turned over the fragments we'd collected, searching for a pattern.

"Henderson was close to publishing something," I said, the thought crystallising as I spoke. "Or wiring a preliminary story ahead of our arrival in New York. That's why timing became critical."

Whipple paused mid-stride. "Go on."

"Think about it. We dock tomorrow. Henderson would have filed his story the moment we reached harbour." I gestured towards the invisible shore. "Once that happened, there'd be no controlling events. Someone believed there was no more time to negotiate."

"Which suggests they'd already attempted negotiation," HG observed. "And failed."

"Or never intended to succeed in the first place," Whipple added, resuming his pace with renewed energy. Maybe the talks were just to stall, giving time to guarantee Henderson's silence.

We reached the stern rail, where the ship's wake churned white against the grey Atlantic. I watched the turbulent water, thinking of secrets churning beneath equally deceptive surfaces.

"Henderson must have given his killer some indication of his publishing timeline," I continued. "A threat, perhaps, or a deadline for payment. Something that made clear there'd be no further extensions."

HG's hair, styled perfectly, suffered in the stiff breeze as she faced us. "Which means our murderer is someone who had both the opportunity to negotiate with Henderson and access to him in that service stairwell." She paused, her expression thoughtful. "A rather limited circle, wouldn't you say?"

Whipple pulled out his notebook again, flipping to a familiar page. "Limited indeed. And growing smaller by the hour."

"Assuming," I whispered, "that Henderson's killer and Sir Edmund's are the same person."

HG turned from the railing. "I'm inclined to think they are the same person. "Two murders within days of each other seems rather excessive for a simple ocean crossing. Even with Arthur's knack for attracting dead bodies."

Whipple's mouth twitched at the corners. "I assure you, HG, I don't cultivate them deliberately."

"Of course not, dear Arthur. They simply find you irresistible." Her eyes sparkled with mischief despite the gravity of our situation.

I glanced at my pocket watch. "We should speak with Penelope Chase before dinner. She seemed particularly agitated earlier."

We found Penelope at the Royal Bar, nursing a glass of whisky with trembling hands. Her complexion had the pallor of fine porcelain, almost translucent in the afternoon light. When she saw us approach, she sat straighter, composing herself with visible effort.

"Hello, Penelope," I began, "I assumed you locked yourself safely in your stateroom?"

Miss Chase looked crestfallen. "I couldn't bear it. In the end, I thought I might feel safer in one of the public rooms, and I ended up here."

I chose not to enquire further, reasoning there are occasions when every soul needs the comfort of others, even strangers. However, my silence left a void that Whipple soon filled.

"Miss Chase," Whipple began, taking the seat opposite her, "I'm afraid we must ask you some further questions about Mr Henderson."

Penelope's crystal tumbler scraped against her diamond ring as she rotated it in her lap. "Must we? I've already told Rex what little I know."

"You appeared quite upset earlier," I prompted gently.

She drew a deep breath. "Oh, what's the use? He's dead now. Henderson approached me yesterday after breakfast. He knew things about my family that no one aboard should have known."

"What sort of things?" HG asked, her voice softening.

"Financial matters. Private business arrangements." Penelope's fingers twisted around her glass like a serpent.

"He spoke of my father's dealings with Sir Edmund as though they were common knowledge."

Whipple leaned in. "And were these dealings of a nature that might embarrass?"

"Inspector, my father was an honourable man," she replied. "On reflection, naive but honourable, nevertheless. But Henderson implied...he suggested that scandal clings to the innocent as easily as the guilty."

"A rather philosophical observation for a gossip merchant," HG remarked.

Penelope dabbed at the corner of her eye with her handkerchief. "He frightened me. Not physically, you understand, but socially. He said he had proof that would link our family name to Sir Edmund's more questionable ventures."

"Did he require anything for his silence?" I inquired.

"Not directly. He simply mentioned that he would be filing his story upon arrival in New York." Her voice dropped to a whisper. "He said some reputations wouldn't survive the crossing."

"And the card fragment we found in your cabin?" Whipple pressed.

Colour drained further from Penelope's face. "I told you, someone must have planted it."

I scrutinised her, noting the tremor in her left hand, the way her eyes darted toward the exit. She was lying, but about which part?

"Miss Chase," HG began, "we are approaching New York. If there is anything else, you wish to share before matters progress beyond our control, now would be the time."

Penelope's composure cracked. "You don't understand. None of you do. Some secrets aren't ours to tell, even when keeping them destroys us."

She rose abruptly, nearly overturning her whisky. "Please excuse me. I find I'm suddenly quite unwell."

We watched her hurried departure, the rapid click of her heels marking her retreat across the marble floor.

"Well," Whipple said, closing his notebook. "That was illuminating, if not entirely forthcoming."

"Indeed," HG murmured. "The lady doth protest too much for someone with nothing to hide."

Whipple shot HG a curious look.

'Shakespeare," I offered.

Von Ritter approached our table, his pace measured and unhurried, as though he had all the time in the world. He wore evening dress already, though dinner remained two hours away. The black and white of his attire seemed to heighten the chilly detachment in his eyes.

"Ah," he said, pausing beside us. "The amateur detective society holds another convention." His gaze slid from HG to Whipple, then finally rested on me. "Discussing our unfortunate journalist, no doubt?"

Whipple stiffened. "You've heard about Henderson, then?"

"The ship buzzes with little else." Von Ritter signalled to a passing steward for a drink. "Though I find the timing rather convenient."

"Convenient?" I echoed, watching him closely.

He accepted a crystal tumbler of amber liquid from the steward, taking a small sip before answering. "Journalists, young man, are far more dangerous than common criminals. The criminal merely takes what he wants; the journalist creates chaos for sport."

HG raised an eyebrow. "An interesting distinction, Baron. Though I rather thought both pursued their own forms of profit."

"Profit, yes." Von Ritter's lips curled into something approximating a smile. "But criminals operate within predictable parameters. They want money, jewels, perhaps revenge. A journalist? He deals in reputation, which is valueless until someone destroys it or threatens to destroy it.

His cool assessment made my skin prickle. His morality was elusive, like trying to grip wet soap.

"You sound almost approving of Henderson's demise," I suggested.

Von Ritter gave a slight shrug. "I neither approve, nor disapprove. I note that a man who makes a living by threatening others with exposure shouldn't be surprised when those threats return tenfold.

"You speak of justice, Baron?" Whipple asked, his pencil hovering above his notebook.

"I speak of natural consequences, Detective Inspector." Von Ritter drained his glass. "The world has its own balance. Henderson upset it; now, equilibrium is restored."

He bowed from the neck. "Now, if you'll excuse me, I have correspondence to attend to before dinner."

We watched him glide away, his posture immaculate.

"Well," HG murmured, "that was illuminating. I do believe the Baron just confessed to understanding the motive, if not committing the deed himself."

Whipple nodded. "And delivered it with all the emotion of a man discussing the weather forecast."

"The Baron certainly has a unique sense of morality," I said as von Ritter's tall figure disappeared around the corner. "One that conveniently allows him to rationalise murder as cosmic balance."

Whipple frowned, tapping the pencil against his notebook. "Men like him always have tidy philosophies to justify ugliness. Makes it easier to sleep at night, I imagine."

I pulled Henderson's journal from my pocket, flipping through the pages again. Something had been nagging at me since we'd found it, a discrepancy I couldn't quite place. My finger traced the journalist's tight, economical handwriting.

"HG," I ventured, "Henderson's notes from Tuesday morning indicate he was observing Lily de Vere at breakfast, yet I observed no such activity."

Whipple barely glanced up. "Hardly significant, Rex. The man might simply have changed his mind."

"But look here," I persisted, pointing to a cryptic line: *14:30—Saw someone who belonged everywhere. Must verify before print.*

HG's eyebrows rose. "What do you make of that?"

I shook my head. "I'm not certain. It's as though Henderson spotted something, or someone, that didn't fit with their established pattern."

Whipple closed his notebook with a sigh. "Fanciful speculation won't advance our inquiries. We need concrete evidence, not riddles penned by a dead man."

I tucked the journal away, unable to shake the feeling that Henderson's cryptic observation held importance.

"Rex," HG said, interrupting my thoughts, "you've that expression that suggests your mind is wandering down interesting alleyways, while the rest of us remain on the high street."

"Merely trying to see what Henderson saw," I replied.

"Well," Whipple said, rising from his chair, "while you commune with the journalist's ghost, I shall speak with the captain. Docking procedures will provide ample opportunity for our killer to disappear among the crowds tomorrow."

As he left, HG regarded me with curious eyes. "Sometimes, Rex, the most valuable clues are those dismissed by conventional minds. Arthur is brilliant but occasionally blinded by his devotion to procedure."

I nodded, Henderson's words still echoing in my thoughts.

As we returned to HG's stateroom, the corridor remained hushed. Something about the journalist's methodical observations unsettled me more than I cared to admit.

"Do you think Henderson truly understood what he had uncovered?" I asked as HG's steward poured tea. The fellow slipped away, leaving us to our conversation.

"I rather doubt it," HG replied, stirring a dash of milk into her china cup. "Had he grasped the full implications, he might have been more cautious about whom he approached."

She sank into a silk-upholstered chair, somehow maintaining perfect posture despite the ship's gentle roll. "Henderson was gathering fragments, Rex. I suspect he died before assembling them into a coherent picture."

"Which suggests our murderer feared even those fragments."

"Precisely." HG passed me a delicate teacup resting in its intimate saucer. "Consider the change in tactics. Sir Edmund's murder was personal. One blow from someone he likely knew and trusted enough to turn his back upon."

I nodded, recalling the scene. "Henderson met his end in a service corridor."

"Indeed. A more opportunistic killing, yet no less deliberate." She paused, her gaze sharpening. "It demonstrates our killer is both adaptable and calculating."

The realisation struck me hard. "Therefore, neither anger nor panic caused Henderson's death. Someone made a deliberate choice to eliminate him."

"Exactly." HG set her teacup down with a decisive click

against its saucer. "Sir Edmund's murder might have been born of a long-simmering grievance. But Henderson's death proves our killer is not merely angry, Rex, but strategic. They're systematically removing threats to whatever plan they've set in motion."

I contemplated this grim assessment, wondering what other moves this deadly chess player might make before we reached New York.

Chapter Eighteen

ENGINE OF FEAR

I woke early the following morning with a curious sense of unease. The Britannic Star seemed different somehow; quieter, more watchful. As I left the cabin for breakfast, I caught myself double-checking that the door was locked behind me.

The corridor to the dining room felt longer than usual, punctuated by furtive glances from passing passengers. Two elderly women halted their animated conversation as I approached, resuming only when I was far beyond earshot. Their hushed tones followed me like a shadow.

"You've noticed it too," HG remarked when I joined her at our usual table. She buttered her toast with precision, her eyes surveying the room. "Everyone's behaving like characters in a poorly written melodrama."

"The whole first-class section seems to be panicking," I responded, taking coffee from the waiter, who didn't smile.

Across the room, Lady Winthrop pulled her pearls closer to her throat when Matthews passed by her table.

Baron von Ritter sat alone, a fortress of solitude behind his book.

"Two murders have a remarkable effect on social etiquette," HG observed dryly. "Notice how the Perkins-Smyth party cancelled their afternoon bridge tournament? One might think cards had suddenly become indecent."

I nodded, watching a steward deliver fresh orange juice with perfect timing to a couple who ignored his presence. "Yet beneath it all, the machinery of the ship continues without interruption."

"Indeed. The upper class may be terrified. However, heaven forbid their cocktails arrive two minutes late," HG said, her eyes twinkling with that familiar mischief.

Whipple arrived, looking haggard. "Three passengers demanded private guards outside their cabins last night. The captain refused, of course."

A table steward approached with fresh pastries, and the three of us fell silent until he departed. The momentary pause in conversation felt telling, even we had succumbed to the atmosphere of suspicion.

"There's something almost theatrical about it," I mused. "As though we're all playing prescribed roles in some ghastly performance."

"With two genuine corpses to show for it," Whipple added grimly. "Let's hope there are no more before we dock."

HG signalled for another cup of tea as Whipple discussed his plans for the day.

"I intend to interview the crew who work near the service stairwell," he said. "Someone must have seen something, even if they're reluctant to admit it."

Captain Hardwick entered the dining room, his face red and furious, stopping our conversation in its tracks. He marched over to a table where First Officer Grayson sat with another officer I didn't recognise.

"I told you to keep a lid on things by clearing the decks and public areas...yet what do I see? I'll tell you, passengers all over the place!" Hardwick barked, his voice carrying despite his obvious attempt to keep it down. "Now there's talk of a second murder all over the ship!"

Grayson paled. "Sir, we've been following your instructions to the letter. We advised passengers to remain in their cabins, but—"

"But nothing! This is precisely what I warned about." The captain's hand came down hard on the table, causing the silverware to jump. "Do your jobs, or I'll find someone who obeys orders. This matter is not over, do you hear?"

Several diners pretended not to notice, though their sudden interest in buttering toast was unconvincing. Hardwick seemed oblivious to his audience, focused entirely on Grayson's apparent failure.

"I want hourly reports on passenger movements," Hardwick continued, lowering his voice. "And tell Bowthorpe I need to see him immediately."

The junior officer cleared his throat. "Sir, we haven't—"

"Find him!" Hardwick snapped before striding away. He nodded to various passengers as though nothing untoward had occurred.

I glanced at HG, who raised an eyebrow. "Our captain appears more concerned with headlines than homicide."

"Did you notice?" I asked. "He mentioned Bowthorpe as though the man weren't missing."

Whipple frowned. "Either he knows where Bowthorpe is, or he's maintaining a fiction that everything's under control."

"The perfect captain," HG remarked, "standing firm while his ship burns, literally and figuratively."

I watched Hardwick through the dining-room glass partition as he stopped a steward in the corridor, checking something on a clipboard. Even from a distance, I could see the tension in his shoulders, the brittle quality of his smile when a passenger approached.

"That's not the anxiety of a man mourning two deaths," I observed. "That's the fear of someone whose carefully constructed world is collapsing around him."

"HG, do you think the captain is orchestrating all this? You know, Bowthorpe, Henderson's murder, Sir Edmund's death?" I asked, keeping my voice low.

She considered this, dabbing her lips with a napkin. "Orchestrating might be giving him too much credit. I've met many men like Hardwick over the years. They believe their authority grants them wisdom rather than the other way around."

Whipple nodded. "In my experience, captains develop a particular blindness. They spend so many years being obeyed without question that they forget the possibility of being mistaken."

I watched as Hardwick finished reprimanding a steward for some invisible failure of service. The man's practiced smile returned the moment he turned to greet a passenger, like a mask slipped into place.

"I believe it's time we forced the captain's hand," Whipple said, rising from his table doggedly. "His behaviour has moved beyond suspicious."

We followed Whipple as he approached Hardwick as the captain neared his quarters. The doleful solitude of our surroundings matched the mood.

"Captain Hardwick," Whipple began, "I must insist on a formal interview regarding the circumstances aboard your vessel."

Hardwick's smile remained fixed, though his eyes hardened. "Inspector, we've been through this. I've cooperated fully with your unofficial inquiries."

"Let us be clear, Captain. I now possess full authority from Scotland Yard and your Principals to investigate matters. Two people are dead," Whipple pressed, his voice firm yet restrained. "The coal bunker remains on fire. Your chief officer is missing. Yet you continue to behave as though we're experiencing nothing more troublesome than a delayed dinner service."

The captain glanced around. "Come with me."

In Hardwick's office, the atmosphere crackled with tension. Naval certificates and pictures of the Britannic Star decorated the walls, which seemed to watch us as we argued.

"I've made tough decisions to protect this ship," Hardwick began, his fingers almost squeezing an unfortunate fountain pen. "The coal bunker situation required containment, yes. But containment of information, not just fire."

"At what cost?" Whipple asked.

"You have no idea what panic does to a ship at sea," Hardwick said, his voice tightly controlled. "During the war, I watched a perfectly seaworthy vessel capsize because of hysteria and loss of discipline under pressure. Three hundred souls lost because someone didn't do their job."

"That hardly justifies concealing murder," I interjected.

Hardwick's gaze snapped to me. "I never ordered violence against anyone. Sir Edmund was a difficult passenger, yes, but he was worth more to this company alive than dead. As for Henderson, the man was a troublemaker, stirring fear amongst my passengers."

"I have concealed things, yes. I instructed my officers to minimise disruption, to maintain routines, to ensure passengers remained calm." Hardwick's composure cracked. "But I never...I would never authorise harm to any soul aboard my vessel."

"Then who would, Captain?" Whipple asked quietly. "Who aboard has both motive and authority to act without your knowledge?"

Hardwick stared out his porthole at the grey Atlantic. "That, Inspector, is precisely what alarms me."

I sought out Lily de Vere after our unsettling meeting with Captain Hardwick. She sat alone in the library, now restored to its usual pristine state. A book perched on her lap, though her eyes weren't following the words.

"May I join you?" I asked.

She gestured to the chair opposite with a languid movement that suggested I wasn't interrupting anything of consequence. "Rex. How delightful."

"Miss de Vere, I was hoping we might speak candidly."

"I find candour highly overrated," she replied, closing her book. "Though I suppose you've come about poor Sir Edmund or that dreadful reporter."

I studied her face, searching for any flicker of genuine emotion. "Sir Edmund seemed to take a particular interest in your affairs before his death."

"Men frequently take an interest in my affairs, Rex. It rarely ends well for them."

Her voice carried not a threat but a simple observation, delivered with the same tone one might use to comment on the weather.

"He made certain demands of you, I believe."

"Sir Edmund found that suggesting consequences was more effective than vulgar demands." A hint of admiration coloured her voice. "A raised eyebrow, a casual reference to one's past indiscretions over brandy. These accomplish more than shouting ever could."

"Yet you never mention him," I noted. "Everyone else aboard speaks of him constantly, whether in relief or feigned sorrow."

"What purpose would it serve?" She adjusted her pearl necklace. "The dead are beyond caring about our opinions."

"Unless you had reason to fear him."

"Fear is a luxury for those who haven't learned to adapt, Rex. When one understands the rules of any game, one simply plays accordingly."

I found myself impressed and disturbed by her composure at once. Even in discussing murder, she maintained perfect control, her breathing steady, her hands still. Where others sweated or stammered, Lily de Vere observed.

"You don't panic," I said.

"Panic is inefficient." She leaned toward me. "Those who succumb to it make poor decisions. I prefer to weigh my options before acting."

In that moment, I understood what made Lily dangerous; not malice or even ambition, but calculating intelligence that would dispassionately assess any situation, including murder, as merely another move in a complex game of strategy.

I left Lily de Vere contemplating the game board that

was our floating society and sought Penelope Chase. Thoughts of manipulation and calculation swirled in my mind as I knocked on her stateroom door. When she opened it, her tear-stained face provided a stark contrast to Lily's composed demeanour.

"May I come in?" I asked.

Penelope nodded and stepped aside. Her cabin, once well ordered, now bore the hallmarks of distress. Clothes draped without care over furniture; an untouched tea service gone cold.

"I've been thinking about Sir Edmund and Henderson," I began. "Their methods seemed rather different."

"Different?" she repeated, sinking into a chair by the porthole. The mid-morning light caught the redness around her eyes. "They were both dreadful men."

"In different ways, perhaps?"

She twisted a handkerchief between her fingers. "Sir Edmund was terrifying in his quietness. He would speak so softly sometimes that I would have to move closer to hear him, as though he were sharing a confidence rather than destroying my life."

"And Henderson?"

"That journalist was all noise and bluster. He waved that card with Father's handwriting under my nose where anyone might have seen. In the library, of all places." Her voice broke. "Sir Edmund at least had the decency to ruin me privately."

I nodded, understanding dawning. Is that why you trashed it…the library, I mean?"

Penelope's upset turned to rage. "You can't prove it… and why would you want to?"

I offered a smile to show empathy. "I have no desire or reason to expose you. Your current demeanour provides proof. I'm more interested in two dead men. Blythe foreshadowed ruin in whispers; Henderson threatened exposure to the world."

"Yes," she said with a bitter smile. "It's rather ironic, isn't it? I almost preferred Sir Edmund's method. At least it allowed one to maintain appearances."

Shame and fear spread across her features. Anyone looking for a convenient culprit might misread her distress as guilt. Her hands trembled as she reached for her cold tea, then thought better of it.

"What did Sir Edmund want from you?" I asked.

"Information initially. About Father's business associates in New York." She looked up at me. "Then money, always more money."

"And Henderson?"

"A story. He said he wanted the truth." She laughed in a hollow tone. "As if truth matters more than kindness."

I thought of HG's words about those who orchestrate circumstances rather than act directly. "Did you ever consider that someone might have noticed your predicament? Perhaps even wished to help?"

Her eyes widened. "What do you mean?"

"Someone aboard this ship has been systematically removing threats. I wonder if they saw your suffering and decided to act."

"Without telling me?" she whispered. A strange note in her voice pointed to something I couldn't quite place.

"Some people believe they know what's best for others."

Penelope sprang up and went to the porthole, staring at the endless ocean. "I should be grateful, shouldn't I? With them gone, the threats vanish."

She turned back to me, and I was struck by how young she looked in that moment. "But I'm not. I keep thinking about what might happen next. Who decides who deserves to live or die? Today it's someone who threatened me, and now..." She trailed off.

"Anyone who becomes inconvenient," I finished for her.

"That's what truly frightens me, Rex. Not being ruined, but living in a world where someone else decides your fate based on their own whim, or calculation."

I left Penelope's cabin with her words echoing in my mind. To imagine someone judging and killing on the Britannic Star unsettled more than any single brutal act. Such power, wielded without accountability, threatened everyone.

I found Madame Zelda in the Winter Garden, arranging tarot cards with theatrical precision. Her lips curved into a knowing smile as I approached.

"Young man, I wondered when you'd return to me," she said, not looking up from her cards. "The seekers of truth always do."

"Truth seems a rather flexible noun aboard this ship," I replied, taking the seat opposite her.

Zelda laughed, a sound like wind chimes in a storm. "How quickly you rush to blame the mysterious foreign woman with dubious talents. Society adores a convenient villain, particularly when she's female and refuses to bow to convention."

"Your act is convincing," I admitted.

"Is it an act? Or perhaps I simply understand human nature better than most." She turned over the Death card with a flourish; practised yet effective. "When bodies appear, eyes turn to those who speak of mortality, not to those who dine at the captain's table or wear brass buttons on their sleeves."

"You had reasons to fear Sir Edmund," I countered.

"As did half the passengers in first class." Zelda's eyes, dark and unfathomable, met mine. "The difference is that I acknowledge my demons openly while others hide behind their titles and uniforms."

Her argument's logic gave me a moment of doubt. The dangerous seldom announce themselves with seances and dramatic predictions. They smile at dinner, make polite conversation, and wait for the perfect moment to strike.

"You think me guilty?" she asked.

"I think you capable," I answered honestly.

"Such a refreshing change from the usual accusations." She gathered her cards with deliberate movements. "Remember this, young man: guilt doesn't always reside in the exotic or unusual. Sometimes it hides in plain sight, dressed in respectability."

I left matters there, neither adding nor removing her from my mental list of suspects. Even though our talk was short, her act seemed real; however, everyone in first-class acted. The question remained: who was orchestrating this deadly theatre, and what final act did they envision?

I came across Baron von Ritter on the promenade deck, looking out at the featureless Atlantic. He seemed unaffected. The events aboard our vessel seemed to touch him no more than raindrops might affect a well-oiled mackintosh.

"Ah, the young detective," he said as he noticed my form. His accent softened since our departure from Southampton, as though he were shedding one persona for another. "Come to determine if the German is responsible for your shipboard tragedies?"

"I've come to understand your perspective, Baron."

He chuckled, a distant sound devoid of mirth. "My

perspective? How very British. Your Dowager has trained you well."

"Two men are dead," I said plainly.

"Two men who possessed dangerous knowledge." Von Ritter turned to face me at last. "In my country, we understand that certain truths are like dynamite. In the wrong hands, they destroy more than their intended target."

"That sounds remarkably like justification for murder."

"I observe; I do not justify." His pale eyes remained calm. "Some revelations simply cannot be permitted to reach shore without consequence. Particularly when they threaten the stability of more than individual reputations."

I studied his composed features, searching for a crack in the facade. "You speak of consequences with surprising detachment for someone who might be considered a suspect."

"We are all suspects of something or other in someone's eyes, young man." Von Ritter straightened his already immaculate cuffs. "The difference is that some of us understand the natural order of power. Journalists who threaten powerful men rarely prosper. Is this murder, or merely the gravity of influence asserting itself?"

I couldn't determine whether his words reflected a held ideology, cold pragmatism, or the calculated misdirection of a guilty man. The uncertainty left me uneasy, as I suspected was his intention.

"Natural order has a peculiar habit of benefiting those who invoke it," I replied.

"Indeed." A ghost of a smile crossed his lips. "Just as justice tends to reflect the prejudices of those who dispense it."

As he left, with perfect posture, I couldn't decide if von Ritter was the murderer or a noble who thought getting rid of problems was a way to keep things under control. Either possibility made him dangerous, but in different ways.

I found HG waiting for me in a quiet corner of the observation lounge, her elegance a marked contrast to the modest furnishings. A teapot and two cups were on the table, but I noticed she used the good Wedgwood instead of the regular first-class dishes.

"I thought you might be parched after your interrogations," she said, and then poured without waiting for my answer. "Any revelations from our gallery of suspects?"

I settled into the chair opposite her, grateful for the moment of calm. "Each conversation leaves me more uncertain than the last. Von Ritter speaks of natural consequences as though murder were simply an expected outcome of threatening the powerful. Lily observes everything with clinical detachment. Madame Zelda suggests we look to those in uniform rather than those in exotic dress."

HG passed me a cup of perfectly brewed Darjeeling. "And what of young Penelope?"

"That she's terrified, though I can't decide whether it's guilt or genuine fear of becoming the next victim."

"Interesting that fear should be the common element," HG remarked, stirring a precise half teaspoon of sugar into her cup. "Fear of exposure, fear of consequence, fear of being next."

The lounge remained largely empty, passengers having developed a sudden aversion to public spaces following Henderson's murder. Through the large windows, the Atlantic stretched beyond sight, as indifferent to our shipboard drama as von Ritter pretended to be.

"I keep thinking I'm missing something obvious," I admitted. "Something connects these deaths beyond mere opportunity."

HG set her cup down with a barely audible clink. "Perhaps what connects them isn't what they knew, but who they threatened."

"Sir Edmund threatened nearly everyone in first class?"

"Yes, but have you considered the nature of hierarchy, Rex?" She gestured toward a passing steward who instantly altered course to collect our empty cups. "Notice how that young man saw my smallest gesture and responded without question. No one taught him explicitly; he simply absorbed that I occupy a position that commands his attention."

I frowned. "I'm not certain I follow your meaning."

"Hierarchy protects those who commit harm," she continued, her voice muted but carrying no hint of accusation. "We expect danger to come from the top, from men like Sir Edmund and Baron von Ritter, who announce their power through their bearing and manner."

"And rarely from those who serve them," I ventured.

"You have it. Hierarchy also determines who gets noticed and who doesn't, who belongs in a space, and who moves through it without comment. Her fingers traced a pattern on the polished table. "During the war, I observed how generals received credit for victories secured by the blood of nameless soldiers. How easily the powerful claim ownership of others' actions when it suits them."

"And when it doesn't?"

"Then, subordinates become convenient scapegoats." A faint smile touched her lips. "Rather like our missing Chief Officer Bowthorpe, I suspect."

I considered her words, finding them philosophical rather than directly applicable to our investigation. Yet something in her manner suggested she was guiding me toward a conclusion I hadn't yet comprehended.

"You believe the truth lies among the powerful," I said.

"I believe we should question our assumptions about where power truly resides on this floating kingdom," she replied.

As we sat in contemplative silence, a faint unease settled over me I could not yet name. The Britannic Star sailed on to New York, hiding secrets and carrying a murderer.

Chapter Nineteen

ELECTRIC MESSAGES

I left HG in the observation lounge with HG's words about power and hierarchy circling in my mind like gulls around a fishing boat. The sky had darkened to a bruised purple, reflecting my troubled thoughts.

Pacing the corridor toward my cabin, I recalled my last conversation with Henderson. I'd thought little of it, just another journalist angling for scraps of scandal. But now, with the man dead, his questions gained a sharper edge in my memory.

"Who takes inventory of the captain's liquor cabinet?" he'd asked, leaning against the railing as we watched the endless sea.

"I do not have the faintest idea," I'd replied, somewhat annoyed. "Does it matter?"

"Everything matters on a ship, young man. Who cleans Sir Edmund's cabin since Charlie Peabody received a new assignment? Which steward has access to the service keys? Who checks the passenger manifests when they're filed?"

I'd laughed it off. "Rather dull questions for a man of your reputation, Mr Henderson."

"The dullest questions often yield the most interesting answers."

I stopped in my tracks as a thought struck me. Henderson hadn't been fishing for gossip at all. His questions were methodical, specific, almost procedural. He wanted to know who handled certain items, who was on duty in particular corridors. Not who held authority, but who had access.

I thought this was just a journalist being nosy, but Henderson was figuring out how the ship worked; the hidden systems that kept the Britannic Star going without anyone noticing.

"Good evening, sir," a steward murmured, sidling past me with a silver tray.

I barely acknowledged him, struck by a sudden, troubling thought. How many times had I passed this same man without registering his face? How many of the crew moved through the ship like ghosts, seeing everything whilst remaining unseen?

HG's words returned with newfound clarity. We'd been looking at the wrong people; the loud, the obvious, the commanding. Perhaps the truth lay with those who belonged everywhere yet nowhere; those who were simultaneously present and invisible.

I turned on my heel. I needed to find Whipple. We'd been investigating from the top down, when perhaps it should have been the other way around.

The detective inspector poured over Henderson's notebook in the ship's library. Whipple barely glanced up as I approached as his finger traced lines of cramped handwriting.

"I think I've spotted something, Arthur," I said, dropping into the chair next to him. "Henderson wasn't just gathering gossip. He was mapping the ship's service patterns, who went where, who handled what."

Whipple turned to face me, his eyes brightening with interest. "Remarkable timing, lad. I've just noticed something myself." He tapped the notebook. "Henderson's approach changed significantly over the course of the voyage."

"How so?"

"The early entries are speculative, theoretical. *Listen to this: 'Von R possibly involved in currency speculation with B? Captain H seems nervous when B speaks—old debt?' But later,"* he flipped several pages forward, "the tone shifts entirely. *'Steward J.P. enters cabin 18 at 10:05, exits 10:17. Brings fresh towels but takes nothing away.'* Or here: *'First Officer G inspects lower deck 14:30-14:55, speaks with no one, examines coal chute access.'"*

"He stopped guessing motives," I started, "and began tracking movements."

"Yup. Henderson was building an evidence base. Not for a sensational headline, but for something far more significant."

I leaned back, considering the implications. "A journalist who stops speculating and starts cataloguing facts is—"

"Dangerous," Whipple finished, closing the notebook with a snap. "Particularly to someone with something to hide."

"He must have seen something concrete," I mused. "Something that confirmed his suspicions."

"Or someone," Whipple replied. "Henderson writes here about a figure he calls *'the shadow.'* Someone who appears where they shouldn't be, yet never attracts attention."

The library door creaked open, and we both tensed until we saw it was a steward, come to tidy things away.

"Pardon me, gentlemen," he murmured, moving about the room with grace.

I watched him work, struck by how thoroughly I'd forgotten his presence within seconds. The ship was full of such people at all ranks, invisible yet essential, privy to every whispered conversation, every furtive glance.

Whipple didn't draw conclusions aloud, but his eyes followed the steward with fresh interest. Henderson had evolved from a theorist to an observer. And someone had ensured that evolution would be his last.

I observed the steward as he arranged the library's reading materials, his movements precise and economical. When he departed, I turned back to Whipple.

"It still fits our theory about von Ritter, doesn't it?" I ventured. "A man in his position would have much to lose from Henderson's investigations."

Whipple tapped Henderson's notebook. "Perhaps. But powerful people rarely do their own dirty work. They employ others."

"Like Captain Hardwick," I suggested. "He's been acting peculiarly since we boarded."

"Indeed. Though captains rarely move freely about their ships without notice. Someone would remember seeing him. As far as passengers are concerned, a captain is as much a celebrity as responsible for the ship."

We departed the library, proceeding along the corridor. The evening's pre-dinner entertainment had begun in the main saloon; strains of a popular waltz drifted toward us.

"What troubles me," Whipple continued, lowering his

voice as we passed a couple in evening dress, "is timing. Henderson died shortly after arranging to meet Madame Zelda. But how did our killer know about this meeting?"

The answer hit me with such force that I halted abruptly. "Because they heard him arranging it. The walls of these cabins are notoriously thin."

"Or," Whipple added gravely, "because they were in the room."

We rounded the corner to find HG waiting outside her stateroom. One look at our expressions told her something significant had developed.

"You've had a revelation," she stated, unlocking her door. "Come inside before you broadcast it to the entire ship."

Once settled with brandies, I explained our new perspective. HG listened attentively, sipping her drink.

"So you believe Henderson was murdered by a member of the crew?" she asked finally.

"Not necessarily," I replied. "But I think we've been looking at this case backwards. We've focused on who had motive, when perhaps we should consider who had opportunity. Who could move throughout this ship without drawing attention? Who could enter cabins without raising suspicion?"

"The invisible machinery of officers and staff," HG murmured, "forever present yet never seen."

"Precisely," Whipple agreed.

HG gave me an appraising look. "You're learning, Rex. Though I hope you don't intend to suspect every crew member aboard."

Despite the gravity of our discussion, I smiled. HG had a knack for puncturing tension with gentle wit.

"No," I replied. "But I think Henderson discovered

something about one particular member of the crew. Something that got him killed."

"What exactly was Henderson's reputation before this voyage?" I asked, swirling the amber liquid in my cut-crystal glass. "I know he was a journalist, but did he have a reputation for exposing scandals, or simply reporting them?"

HG settled into her armchair. "Henderson appears to have made his name during the war, uncovering profiteering schemes. Not the sensational sort that makes headlines, but the quiet, systematic kind that enriches a few whilst soldiers die for lack of proper equipment."

"How do you know that?" Whipple asked.

HG took a sip of her brandy. "I took the liberty of doing some background work while you two were about your business. A quick telegram to a friend in Fleet Street came up a treat."

Whipple and I shared a sideways glance. HG had a way of surprising us when least expected.

"Systemic corruption," Whipple murmured. "Fascinating."

"But here's what's odd," I said, recalling a detail that had been niggling at the back of my mind. "Henderson told me he interviewed von Ritter at four o'clock on Tuesday afternoon in the smoking room."

HG raised an eyebrow. "And?"

"I distinctly remember seeing von Ritter on the promenade deck at that exact time. He was arguing with Captain Hardwick about something."

Whipple put his brandy glass down. "Are you certain of the time?"

"Absolutely. I'd just checked my watch to meet you both for tea at half past."

HG tapped her finger against her glass. "So, either Henderson was mistaken, or..."

"Or he lied," I finished. "But why would he lie about something so easily disproven?"

"Perhaps," Whipple offered, "he was protecting someone. Creating an alibi."

I shook my head. "No, that's not it. I've probably got the wrong end of the stick."

We fell silent, each contemplating this minor discrepancy. It seemed insignificant compared to our broader theories, yet somehow, we couldn't quite dismiss it.

HG broke the silence with a grin. "Dear Rex, you're developing a positively Whipple-like frown when you're thinking. Be careful, or you'll need to invest in a larger hat to accommodate the extra furrows."

Whipple glanced up with indignation. "I do not frown excessively."

"Arthur, when you're deep in thought, your eyebrows practically merge with your hairline," HG replied with affection. "It's quite charming in its own way."

Despite myself, I laughed. "I'd rather inherit Arthur's deductive abilities than his facial expressions."

"You're well on your way to both," HG remarked dryly.

The call to dinner interrupted our momentary levity.

"You two have ten minutes to change," HG quipped. "Now out with you. Further thoughts about Henderson can wait until the soup course."

I joined HG and Whipple at our usual dining table, somehow aware that tonight our little group had become the focal point of the entire room. The luxurious space hummed with subdued conversation, punctuated by the gentle clink of fine china and crystal. Every so often, I caught furtive glances darting in our direction, then averted when noticed.

"One might think we were the murderers, given the way they're watching us," I murmured, as I sat back to allow a steward to place a serviette across my lap.

Whipple shifted in his chair. His collar seemed tight this evening, though I suspected it was the weight of attention rather than his tailoring causing his discomfort.

"It's normal," HG said, looking around the room with the confidence of someone used to the upper class. "Human nature craves certainty in uncertain times. They look to us, particularly to Arthur, hoping to see confidence that might reassure them."

A table steward appeared at my elbow, serving the first course.

"I've been thinking about Henderson," HG said quietly after he left, keeping her voice low so no one else could hear in the muted room. "His behaviour in the latter days of our voyage suggests he no longer sought proof of guilt, but confirmation of method."

"How do you mean?" I asked, sampling the delicate consomme.

"Journalists typically chase a story, following where it leads," HG explained. "Henderson, on the other hand, seemed to be verifying details of a conclusion he'd already reached."

I nodded. "That makes sense. Good journalism requires methodical confirmation before publishing accusations."

HG gave me the look she reserved for moments when I had missed her point. "Rex, I wasn't offering commentary on journalistic ethics."

The penny dropped late. "You mean he knew who the murderer was?"

"I believe he had a strong suspicion," she replied, dabbing her lips with her serviette. "Strong enough that he shifted from investigation to confirmation."

Whipple joined the exchange. "If that's true, then whatever he discovered in that confirmation process is what got him killed."

"I'm sure of it," HG intoned.

I glanced around the dining room, seeing each face in a new light. "The question remains: what was he confirming, and with whom?"

"I rather think," Whipple said quietly, "that Henderson was confirming how it was done, not who did it."

A chill ran through me as I considered the implications. People around us kept talking, talking about getting to New York and what they planned to do, like shopping or seeing a show. Yet here we sat, discussing a carefully planned double murder.

“About confirmation,” HG said, her voice a little brighter, “I know Arthur hasn’t had a proper holiday for three years.” His sister told me he spent last Christmas cataloguing crime scene photographs."

Whipple's face flushed. "HG, I hardly think…anyway, this was supposed to be a holiday and look how things have turned out."

HG refused to be diverted.

"And the Christmas before," she continued mercilessly, "he volunteered for duty so others might spend time with their families."

"It was the responsible thing to do," Whipple protested.

HG kept changing the subject from the risky topic of murder to the less controversial topic of Whipple’s habit of working too much. She offered us moments to breathe as death menaced our party.

"I suppose," I ventured, returning us gently to the matter at hand, "that Henderson posed a different sort of threat than Sir Edmund."

Whipple nodded, relief clear as we abandoned discussion of his holiday habits.

"Yes," he said, lowering his voice as a steward cleared our soup bowls. "Sir Edmund collected secrets like a miser hoards gold sovereigns. They were valuable to him only in their possession, to be spent sparingly when he held the advantage."

"Whereas Henderson's business was dissemination," HG added, accepting the fish course with a gracious nod to the server.

"That's it exactly," Whipple continued once the steward had moved beyond earshot. "Henderson's danger lay not in what he knew, but in how quickly he could spread it."

I considered this as I sampled the Dover sole. "Then Henderson's murder required an urgency that Blythe's didn't."

"One might even say Henderson's death was preventative," HG mused, "while Blythe's was punitive."

Whipple's fork paused halfway to his mouth. "That's a fine distinction, HG."

"Yet an important one," she replied. "It suggests our killer is both reactive and proactive in their approach. They respond to threats as they emerge but also anticipate future complications."

I glanced around the dining room, noting the captain's absence. "Someone with experience in managing crises, perhaps."

"Or someone accustomed to maintaining order," Whipple suggested.

A thought occurred to me. "What if these murders aren't about personal gain at all?"

HG raised an eyebrow. "Go on."

"What if they're about preservation? Not of a person, but of the ship itself, its reputation, its standing…and by extension, the shipping line?"

"That would certainly explain the methodical nature of both killings," Whipple said thoughtfully. "No passion, just...efficiency."

"And it explains why everyone seems simultaneously frightened and relieved," I added. I said,

HG's smile convinced me I'd done well. "Splendid, dear boy. We'll make a detective out of you yet!"

"Heaven forbid," I replied with mock horror. "I've seen what it's done to poor Arthur's Christmas arrangements."

Whipple almost choked on his wine. "Really, you two."

HG grew serious and asked, "The important question is, who on this ship can move around unseen and also take action?"

"Someone with access to every deck, every cabin," Whipple murmured.

"And who could approach both Blythe and Henderson without arousing suspicion?" I added.

"Also, whose very presence signifies both authority and service," HG concluded.

The three of us exchanged glances as the same realisation dawned. In that moment, the dining room seemed to grow quieter, as if the ship itself held its breath.

"I believe," Whipple said softly, "we need to speak with Chief Officer Bowthorpe."

"If we can find him," I replied, suddenly aware that

none of us had seen the man since that fateful meeting in the captain's quarters.

"Oh, I suspect we will," HG said with certainty. "The question is whether he'll find us first."

As we left the dining room, having eaten the remainder of our meal in convivial conversation, I felt the weight of realisation settle upon my shoulders. We'd been looking for a murderer among the passengers. Someone with the motive, means, and opportunity, when the answer might have been lurking within the ship's own hierarchy all along.

"I still can't quite believe it," I said as we walked towards the grand staircase. "Bowthorpe as our killer?"

"We haven't accused anyone yet," Whipple cautioned, his voice low despite the empty corridor. "But a chief officer would have unfettered access to every part of this vessel."

"And the authority to be anywhere without question. A man in uniform becomes almost invisible, doesn't he? Present but unseen," HG said.

"Like a butler in a great house," I offered.

"True, Rex." HG's approval warmed me despite the chill of our conversation. "People notice the uniform, not the person wearing it."

We paused at the foot of the staircase, mindful of passing stewards. The ornate wood paneling appeared to soak up our conversation, keeping our secrets locked in its smooth finish.

"Henderson had become quite dangerous," I ventured. "But I can't help feeling his danger was directed upward."

"Upward?" Whipple questioned.

"Yes, toward the ship's command structure. His notes focused on movement patterns, service routes, officer rotations. He wasn't investigating passengers; he was mapping the crew's methodical dance."

HG's eyes brightened with understanding. "And what dance is more precise than that of officers aboard a passenger liner?"

"It still feels wrong," I admitted, leaning against the ornate balustrade. "Our solution fits too neatly, like a tailored suit on the wrong gentleman."

Whipple frowned. "You do make the oddest connections, lad."

"I mean, we've constructed a perfect case against Bowthorpe, but it requires such effort to maintain. Why would a chief officer risk everything to protect the ship's reputation? It's not as though he owns shares in the line, or at least I would not have thought so."

"Yet perhaps he does," HG mused. "Arthur, could you make inquiries about Bowthorpe's financial interests when we dock?"

"Certainly," Whipple replied.

A postboy approached, announcing, "Telegram for Detective Inspector Whipple."

Whipple hailed the young man and lifted a small envelope from the tray. His eyes scanned the note at speed. "Scotland Yard has sent information about our missing chief officer," he said after the boy departed. "Lucian Bowthorpe has served on five vessels in the past three years. Three experienced mysterious accidents or passenger deaths."

"Heavens," I breathed.

"Moreover," Whipple continued, "he's not listed in any officer registry prior to 1919."

HG's eyebrow arched. "A man without a past suddenly appears with impeccable credentials after the war. How convenient."

"It says here he's known to associate with a woman

matching Lily de Vere's description." Whipple folded the telegram. "Though never officially."

"So our elusive chief officer and our composed Miss de Vere share a connection," HG said. "And both possess remarkable abilities to navigate social situations without leaving ripples."

"We need to find Bowthorpe," I said firmly. "Before anyone else meets an untimely end."

"I rather think," HG replied with unusual gravity, "that Bowthorpe will find us when he's ready. Men with his particular talents rarely leave loose ends."

"You suggest we wait to be murdered?" I asked, attempting levity although my stomach knotted.

"I suggest," she countered with a gentle pat on my arm, "that we prepare a trap rather than stumble blindly into one."

Whipple acknowledged our dire situation. "First, we must determine if Bowthorpe is still aboard. Unless he jumped...or someone pushed him off. No one just vanishes from a ship at sea.

"Oh, I assure you, Arthur," HG said with a grim smile that held no mirth, "men have been disappearing from ships since time immemorial. The sea keeps secrets better than any confidante."

Chapter Twenty

AN INCOMPLETE PICTURE

The notion of Bowthorpe and Lily de Vere working in concert troubled me as we retreated to a discrete sitting area I had discovered. We each settled into an armchair, my thoughts drifting back to an incident that had nagged at my memory since we began discussing patterns and precision.

"Do you recall Sir Edmund's Will?" I asked. "There was something peculiar in its handling."

HG wore a quizzical look. "What's struck you, Rex?"

"When Matthews first reported to the purser about Sir Edmund's effects, the Will was present among his papers. Yet when you two conducted the formal inventory just hours later, it had vanished?"

"Indeed," Whipple nodded, "causing no small amount of consternation."

"Yet it reappeared the following afternoon," I continued, "tucked neatly between pages where three people had already looked. I assumed it was intimidation, or perhaps incompetence."

"But now?" HG prompted.

"Now I wonder if the timing was deliberate. The will's disappearance created precisely the right amount of disquiet among the potential beneficiaries. Its reappearance calmed matters just as suspicions threatened to boil over."

Whipple frowned. "You suggest someone choreographed even this detail?"

"Consider how it served multiple purposes," I explained. This made Matthews look guilty and confused about who would get the inheritance. It also allowed the actual thief to take Sir Edmund's papers while pretending to look for them.

"Rather like a magician directing attention to one hand while the other performs the trick," HG mused.

"Just so. And who aboard has demonstrated such meticulous attention to timing and detail?"

"Bowthorpe," Whipple said grimly.

"Or someone equally versed in shipboard routines," I added. "That person understands precisely how long papers take to process, which cabins get searched when, and who has access to what areas."

HG toyed with her pearl string "Rex, your mind continues to develop in most satisfying ways. You've identified not merely the presence of manipulation, but its rhythm."

I felt a flush of pride at her words, tempered by the gravity of our situation. "Thank you, but I fear we're still several moves behind in this game of chess."

"Perhaps," HG replied with a slight curve of her lips, but we've finally identified the board on which we're playing."

"The will's disappearance wasn't about the document itself, was it?" I replied.

HG's look of approval warmed her aristocratic features.

"Precisely, Rex. The document matters far less than the reactions it provoked."

"A barometer of sorts," I mused.

"More than that," HG replied. "It created a controlled crisis. Everyone revealed their priorities in those frantic hours. Who sought what papers, who panicked about which clauses."

Whipple nodded, his crumpled features arranging themselves to their liking. "Like watching rats in a burning barn. They'll run straight for whatever they value most."

"Rather vivid, Arthur," HG remarked with a twitch of amusement at the corner of her mouth, "but not inaccurate."

I reconstructed the hours after the Will disappeared. "Matthews nearly wore a path in the carpet pacing outside the purser's office. Penelope Chase kept asking about charitable bequests. And von Ritter..."

"Seemed utterly uninterested," Whipple finished.

"Because he already knew its contents," I suggested.

HG raised an elegant finger. "Or because he knew its contents were irrelevant to his purposes."

The implications settled over us like a fog. One person on the ship was clever enough to set up both a murder and the complicated mystery that came with it.

"We've been looking for someone capable of striking Sir Edmund," I said. "When we should have been seeking someone capable of creating the perfect circumstances for his murder."

"And Henderson's," Whipple added.

HG studied us both with satisfaction. "The question becomes, who aboard possesses the authority to move without suspicion. Also, the subtlety to manipulate everyone aboard without detection?"

I felt the pieces shifting into clearer alignment, though the complete picture remained just out of reach. The killer has always remained one step ahead, like a chess master, as we struggled to solve the crime while they moved closer to winning.

"I suggest we interview the first officer again. His inconsistencies grow more significant by the hour."

Whipple gave me a quizzical stare. "Let's not rush. I know time is short. However, what else have we yet to revisit?"

I hesitated before speaking again. My thoughts had returned to the brooch we'd found in Sir Edmund's cabin, with its Royal Prussian Eagle design. At the time, I'd dismissed it as evidence against von Ritter, considering it far too obvious.

"The brooch troubles me," I admitted. "When we found it, my first thought was that it seemed too convenient, too deliberate."

Whipple raised an eyebrow. "You doubted its authenticity?"

"Not its authenticity, but its purpose. It felt like someone with status and access had placed it there, knowing we would discover it and immediately suspect von Ritter."

"A deliberate misdirection, crafted for investigators rather than passengers. Quite sophisticated," HG intoned.

"Exactly," I continued, warming to my theory. "If von Ritter were guilty, he wouldn't leave such an obvious connection to himself. He didn't drop the brooch. Instead, someone cleverly placed it to guide our suspicions.

"This means the killer knows how investigations work," Whipple said, while running his hand through his brillantined hair.

"Or has watched enough of them to anticipate our

methods," HG added with a hint of amusement. "Arthur, do remember that half the passengers aboard have likely devoured every detective novel published in the last decade."

Whipple grimaced. "Nevertheless, the precision suggests someone familiar with creating false trails."

I considered who might have access to Sir Edmund's cabin and a Prussian eagle brooch. "The brooch itself is distinctive. If someone other than von Ritter owns it, maybe they got it just for this purpose."

"Or borrowed," HG suggested. "Lily de Vere's costume jewellery collection is rather extensive for a touring actress."

The implications were troubling. "So our killer isn't merely opportunistic, but prepared well in advance."

"With materials to implicate multiple suspects," Whipple concluded.

"Rather like a magician with props concealed in various pockets," I observed.

"Indeed," HG smiled, her eyes twinkling. "Though I doubt our conjurer anticipated facing three opponents quite so determined to spot the sleight of hand."

I felt a flicker of optimism despite the gravity of our situation. The killer's elaborate lie, while clever, exposed key details about their personality and tactics. With every false lead, they offered us another thread to follow back to the truth.

As we continued our conversation, Whipple's brow furrowed into a familiar pattern of deep concentration. His eyes took on a distant look, which told me he was reconstructing events in his mind, testing each theory against the cold reality of facts.

"I wonder," he said after a lengthy silence, "whether we might be overcomplicating matters."

"How so?" I asked.

"Consider the physical aspects. Sir Edmund's murder required someone of sufficient strength to deliver a fatal blow. Henderson's strangulation likewise demanded physical capability." Whipple traced an invisible line on the table before us. "Could our primary suspect reasonably accomplish both acts without assistance?"

HG tilted her head. "You're questioning whether Bowthorpe could have managed both killings alone?"

"Precisely. The timing grows tighter when we consider he must maintain his shipboard duties without arousing suspicion."

I hadn't considered this practical angle. "You believe he might have accomplices?"

"Perhaps," Whipple replied. "Though that introduces additional complications. More moving parts in a scheme increase the risk of exposure."

"Rather like adding extra wheels to a clockwork mechanism," I observed. "Each additional element increases the chance of malfunction."

HG smiled. "An apt metaphor, Rex. Though I've known conspirators to maintain remarkable discipline when properly motivated."

"By money?" I asked.

"Sometimes. Often by fear." She adjusted her pearl necklace with elegant precision. "But most reliably through shared purpose."

"If our theory holds, we must consider what binds these conspirators together. What common goal justifies murder?" Said Whipple.

"And whether that goal belongs to all parties equally," I added, "or if someone merely creates the appearance of shared interest."

The conversation fell into another contemplative silence. I admired Whipple's methodical approach. While HG and I had pursued the psychological aspects, he remained anchored to the practical realities of how crimes unfold.

"The wrong suspect could certainly have performed both acts," Whipple concluded. "But only if intermediaries were involved."

"Making our theory more complex," I noted.

"And less elegant," HG finished. "Occam's razor occurs to me."

Whipple gave a grimace. "Is he a passenger I've missed, and what does a razor got to do with anything?"

I had to admit that HG also had me this time.

"Occam's razor offers a philosophical approach to problem solving. It states that, when tested against competing theories, the simplest explanation with the fewest assumptions is often the most likely to be correct."

Whipple shook his head and reached for an Everton mint. "Philosophy has its place, but crime scenes rarely respect logical principles."

HG's eyes crinkled with amusement. "Are you suggesting criminals don't study their Aristotle before committing murder, Arthur? How disappointing."

"I know, who would have thought, HG," Whipple replied with the ghost of a smile.

Their gentle repartee reminded me why I valued their company. Even amidst the gravity of murder, they maintained that quintessentially British ability to find humour in the darkest circumstances.

"If Bowthorpe truly is our man," I ventured, "we must consider whether Lily de Vere is merely his accomplice, or perhaps the true orchestrator."

"An actress accustomed to directing others from behind the scenes," HG mused. "Certainly possible."

"She commands attention whenever she desires it," I pointed out, "yet can become invisible when it suits her purpose."

"A useful talent for a murderer," Whipple acknowledged.

"Or for someone who wishes to appear innocent while others carry out her designs," I suggested.

HG regarded me with approval. "Rex, you are beginning to understand the true nature of influence. The most powerful hand is often the one that never visibly moves."

I pondered HG's words about invisible hands directing events. The Britannic Star now seemed less a vessel of relaxation, than a stage for orchestrated performances.

"There's something else that troubles me," I said. "None of these incidents resulted in any tangible gain. No money changed hands. No accusation stuck firmly to any single suspect."

"Rather curious, isn't it?" HG remarked, tapping her gloved finger against the arm of her chair. "The purpose appears entirely demonstrative."

"Psychological intimidation," I suggested. "The powerful show what happens to those who challenge their position."

"Perhaps," HG replied, a smile playing across her lips. "Though I wonder if we aren't still thinking within the confines they have constructed for us."

Whipple rolled his Everton mint around his mouth. "There's a simpler explanation. What if these murders aren't about asserting power but removing threats?"

"Sir Edmund and Henderson represented dangers to someone," I mused.

"Or to something," HG added. "Perhaps we should revisit the reputational effects on the ship itself, and the company's financial standing?"

I recalled Captain Hardwick's obsession with appearances and schedules. "The coal fire certainly threatened all of those."

"And Sir Edmund discovered it," Whipple continued, "then threatened exposure."

"Which would explain the precision of these crimes," I added. "They weren't acts of passion but calculated necessities."

HG nodded. "You see it, Rex. Not a crime of opportunity, but one of preservation."

"But preservation of what exactly?" I asked.

"Or whom?" Whipple countered.

We sat in contemplative silence for a moment.

"There's another matter," I ventured. "The timing of Henderson's murder. Why kill him when New York was a mere forty-eight hours away? The risk seems disproportionate to any potential gain."

Whipple's face lit up, as if he realised something. "Maybe," he said, "Henderson found something so important that it couldn't wait."

"Something to be acted upon," HG agreed. "Something imminent."

We exchanged glances as the implications settled.

"The coal bunker fire," I whispered.

"Indeed," HG replied. "If it's worsening as rapidly as the stokers suggested..."

"Then we may be sitting atop a powder keg," Whipple added. 'Which means the captain has taken us all for fools."

"It also makes our murderer not merely calculating," I added, "but desperate."

I observed the measured exchange between HG and Whipple with growing fascination. Both possessed formidable intellects, yet approached problems from different perspectives.

"There's something peculiar about these incidents," HG remarked, toying absently with her lorgnette. "Neither the interference with the will nor the planting of the brooch resulted in any tangible gain. No money was taken. No accusation held. Nothing was resolved."

Whipple considered this. "From an investigative standpoint, such acts are terribly inefficient if the aim is profit or revenge."

I listened as they circled the implication without naming it. Each was reluctant to voice the disturbing conclusion toward which we were moving.

"Maybe," HG suggested, "the value of those actions lies in effect, not outcome."

"Rather like a calling card," Whipple agreed, rolling his mint again. This type of display can be more effective than a direct threat, especially if the person watching understands the hidden meaning.

"It's theatrical," I contributed cautiously. "Both incidents forced people to imagine consequences rather than confront them directly. Like a shadow on the wall that appears larger than the object casting it."

HG's eyes sparkled with approval. "Precisely, Rex. The human imagination often conjures far worse scenarios than reality would provide."

Our discussion remained abstract, framed in terms of influence and pressure rather than method or culprit. We failed to identify who might benefit from such demonstrations. Instead, we concluded they functioned to control rather than secure acquisition.

"It reminds me of a case in Cheapside," Whipple mused. "Though thieves broke into the houses, they stole nothing, and yet fear paralyzed the entire street." The culprit wanted to show that locks meant nothing to him.

"A means of establishing dominance," HG nodded. "Particularly effective aboard a ship, where escape is impossible."

"And where people already enforce social hierarchies," I added.

Whipple cleared his throat. "The question becomes, who benefits from this atmosphere of apprehension?"

"Someone who understands that fear is more potent than force," HG replied. "Someone who prefers to let others imagine the consequences of disobedience rather than having to enforce them."

"Captain Hardwick?" I suggested.

"Perhaps," HG conceded. "Though I wonder if his bluster suggests someone less subtle."

"Lily de Vere certainly understands manipulation," Whipple offered.

"As does our elusive Chief Officer Bowthorpe," I reminded them.

Our conversation ended without a conclusion. However, we discovered together that the murders were not aimed at stealing. The goal was to control behaviour, showing that the organiser knew fear was more powerful than force.

While we were thinking, I remembered my time at the children's home. The boys who caused the most fear weren't the ones who hit, but the ones who punished someone to scare everyone else.

"The killer isn't merely eliminating threats," I realised aloud. "They're conducting a masterclass in intimidation for everyone else aboard."

"A demonstration of consequences," HG agreed.

"A warning," Whipple added.

"But a warning against what?" I asked, knowing we were closer to the truth than ever before, yet still unable to grasp its full dimensions.

I left HG and Whipple with a peculiar sense of incompleteness. Our discussion had progressed well enough, but something still troubled me. The incidents with the will and the brooch no longer seemed like clever tricks or distractions. They felt calculated, almost surgical in their precision.

As I walked the deck alone, I considered how effectively these events had altered behaviour aboard the Britannic Star. There had been no loud accusations, no open confrontations, only a subtle shifting of attitudes. Conversations grew guarded. Passengers changed their routines. Even the dinner seating arrangements realigned with no obvious requests for changes.

What struck me most was the proportionality. The missing will made people worried enough to be careful, but not enough for anyone to ask the captain to do anything drastic. The brooch implicated von Ritter just enough to keep him under suspicion, but not enough to stop us considering other possibilities.

"Like applying precisely the right amount of pressure to a wound," I murmured to myself, earning a curious glance from a passing steward.

I paused at the railing, watching the ocean churn below. Even though it seemed possible that the chief officer and Lily de Vere colluded, it would have been difficult for them to coordinate everything. The more I considered it, the more complex and unwieldy it seemed.

"Occam's razor indeed," I muttered, remembering HG's philosophical reference.

But what if we *had* constructed an elaborate explanation when a simpler one would have been more effective? What if the hierarchical structure of the ship itself, the very thing we'd just been discussing, offered a more direct answer?

I recalled how Captain Hardwick bellowed orders that rippled through the ranks. How First Officer Grayson executed commands without question. How even passengers arranged themselves according to social standing.

Maybe we weren't seeking partners in crime, but a system. This system would maintain order by showing increasing levels of consequences, instead of fighting.

The thought was unformed yet, but it nagged at me like a loose thread on an otherwise immaculate garment. I couldn't quite grasp it, but I sensed its importance.

I returned to my cabin to get out of my penguin suit, still turning over these half-formed ideas. The evening stretching before us would be the last but one full night aboard the Britannic Star before we reached New York. Whatever truth we sought needed to be uncovered soon.

As I adjusted my bow tie, I reflected that fear aboard the ship hadn't been allowed to spiral into panic. It had been managed, channelled, directed. Someone orchestrated our emotions, making sure each one was felt at the perfect time and level, like a conductor with an orchestra.

Such control suggested intention rather than accident, design rather than impulse. It spoke of a mind that understood not just the mechanics of murder, but the psychology of an enclosed society.

"Not chaos," I whispered to my reflection. "Control."

The realisation didn't solve our mystery, but it shifted my perspective. We weren't hunting someone who had lost control, but someone who had exercised it with frightening precision. Someone who knew how much fear to generate and how to direct it.

As I left my cabin to join HG and Whipple, I knew we needed to look beyond conspiracies and convoluted plots. The answer might lie in something far more fundamental about authority and the architecture of fear.

Chapter Twenty-One

COMMAND AND CONTROL

I met HG and Whipple at her stateroom as arranged. Whipple had been reviewing his notes on the assault of Charlie Peabody, spreading them across HG's writing desk with meticulous care.

"I've been thinking about Charlie," I said, pacing the room. "The assault never quite made sense."

Whipple looked up from his notes. "Explain?"

"Initially, we thought someone attacked Charlie to silence him about seeing Grayson near Sir Edmund's cabin." But if the killer wanted silence, why not finish the job?"

HG lifted a finger in recognition. "A half-measure seems unlike our methodical murderer."

"Exactly," I said, warming to my theory. "The assault wasn't a mistake or an impulsive act. It was deliberate in its restraint."

Whipple frowned, his forehead creasing with concentration. "You believe the attacker intentionally left Charlie alive?"

"Consider the timing," I replied. "Charlie was attacked just as our investigation gained momentum. The location offered enough privacy, but someone could still find him quickly.

"A warning," HG murmured, "but to whom? To Charlie? To us?"

"Perhaps to everyone," I suggested. "The assault created fear without disrupting the ship's function. Charlie's service was valued, but not essential."

Whipple leaned forward, his chair creaking beneath him. "Are you suggesting the assault was...a demonstration?"

"A calibrated one," I said. "Just enough violence to send a message without forcing the captain to take extraordinary measures."

HG's eyes sparkled with appreciation. "Our killer understands the hierarchy of consequences. Murder for those who pose genuine threats, like Sir Edmund and Henderson. Mere injury for those who are...inconvenient."

"It's rather like a military operation," Whipple mused. "Proportional response."

My thoughts crystallised. "The assault wasn't a panicked attempt to silence Charlie. It was a calculated move in a larger strategy."

"Which brings us back to Chief Officer Bowthorpe," HG said. "Military precision would suit his background."

"Or someone with similar training," I countered. "We're assuming Bowthorpe because he's conveniently missing, but what if that's another misdirection?"

Whipple shuffled through his notes. "Charlie said he saw Grayson near Sir Edmund's cabin, not Bowthorpe."

"And Henderson was investigating the coal fire that

Bowthorpe supposedly inspected," I added. "What if Bowthorpe isn't the killer but another victim?"

The room fell silent as we contemplated this unsettling possibility.

"We need to speak with Charlie again," HG said firmly. "If he's regained consciousness, he might remember more details about his attacker."

"Or about what he saw the night of Sir Edmund's murder," Whipple added.

As we prepared to leave for the infirmary, I offered my thoughts to HG and Whipple. "I believe we've been operating under a fundamental misconception," I said as HG locked her stateroom door. "We've assumed these murders were about silencing specific threats. What if they're about maintaining order?"

"Order through selective elimination," HG replied, her voice low. "A chilling prospect, but one that fits our evidence rather well."

"The ship as microcosm," Whipple murmured. "God help us."

As we headed to the infirmary, I felt sure we were doing the right thing, but also uneasy about what would happen next.

The infirmary was quieter than our last visit. The ship's surgeon, Dr Ambrose, met us at the door.

"Your steward is conscious. In fact, he's bounced back remarkably well. Ready for discharge, I'd say."

Charlie Peabody still looked a little pale against the white walls of the surgery. Still, he appeared to be enjoying his cup of tea and Garibaldi biscuit, as he sat on a bare wooden chair.

"How are you feeling, Charlie?" I asked.

"Oh, you know, my head's a bit sore but otherwise I'll

survive. Charlie touched the surgical plaster covering his wound to reinforce the point.

I could see Whipple itching to intervene, so stepped aside.

"Mr Peabody," Whipple began, his voice gentler than usual, "we won't keep you long, but anything you can tell us about your attacker would be invaluable."

Charlie's fingers fidgeted with his trousers. "It happened so fast, sir. Someone called my name in the corridor, and when I turned..." He pointed to his wound.

"Did you see a face? A uniform?" I asked.

"No, nothing clear. Just a sort of shape."

HG stepped closer to the chair. "Mr Peabody, we believe your assault wasn't meant to kill you, merely to frighten. A warning, perhaps."

Charlie's eyes widened. "A warning?"

"About what you witnessed outside Sir Edmund's cabin," Whipple said. "Your observation placed First Officer Grayson at the scene."

Charlie glanced towards the door as if checking for eavesdroppers. "There's something else," he whispered. "Something I remembered after waking up."

"Go on," replied HG, her voice tinged with curiosity.

"That night, before I saw Mr Grayson, I noticed someone else. A woman."

"Which woman?" HG asked.

"Miss de Vere," Charlie replied. "She was coming from the direction of Sir Edmund's cabin. Looked right through me, she did, like I was part of the wall."

Whipple frowned. "You're certain it was Miss de Vere?"

"Yes, sir. Recognised her perfume. My Bethany saves all year to buy a tiny bottle of something similar for Christmas."

"And you didn't mention this before because...?" I prompted.

"Didn't seem important, sir. Passengers wander about at all hours, night, and day, don't they? But after seeing Mr Grayson acting suspiciously, I thought maybe it meant something."

HG exchanged a glance with Whipple. "It certainly might," she said.

Dr Ambrose cut across our questioning. "I think that's enough for now, Your Grace, gentlemen. Mr Peabody is keen to resume his duties, so if you don't mind, I think a few hours of rest is called for, don't you?"

"Quite right," HG replied. "Mustn't overdo things. Now you finish your cup of tea and follow the doctor's orders, yes?"

Peabody offered a weak smile in acknowledgement.

As we left the infirmary, Whipple voiced what we were all thinking. "This places both Grayson and Lily de Vere near Sir Edmund's cabin on the night of his murder."

"Working together perhaps?" I suggested.

"Or one following the other," HG mused. "The question is, which?"

Whipple tugged at his oversized waistcoat. "Violence like Charlie's assault isn't random. It functions as a warning to the ship's crew."

"But ordered by whom?" I asked.

"That's what troubles me," Whipple replied, his voice low. "In my experience, such calculated intimidation typically flows from a powerful source."

HG nodded. "Which brings us back to the ship's hierarchy. In London's gangland, it flows from the 'Mr Big'. In America, he will be a mob boss. The model is the same; only the context changes."

We rounded the corridor towards the grand staircase, with our footsteps muffled by the luxurious carpet.

"I believe," HG said, breaking our thoughtful silence, "it's time we had another conversation with the First Officer."

"And perhaps," I added, "a more direct approach with Miss de Vere."

"Careful, Rex," Whipple cautioned. "If we're correct about the nature of these crimes, confronting suspects directly could prove dangerous."

HG offered a thin smile. "Then we shall have to be dangerously clever ourselves, shan't we!"

I struggled to plan a strategic approach for our next move. We couldn't make a move against Lily without tipping our hand, but Grayson's connection to her needed to be checked out.

"I suggest," said HG, "that we split our efforts. Rex, perhaps you might engage with Captain Hardwick about Charlie's assault. Observe how he reacts to the news that someone attacked his steward instead of the official story that he was 'taken ill'.

"While we..." Whipple glanced at HG, "track down our elusive First Officer."

I nodded. "I'll meet you back at your stateroom in an hour."

I found Hardwick on the bridge, standing with a rigid posture as he gazed out at the horizon. The steady rhythm of the engines vibrated through the deck plates beneath our feet.

"Rex, you may enter the bridge," he said without turning. "Come to check on our progress? New York beckons, despite our reduced speed."

"Actually, I wanted to ask about Charlie Peabody."

His shoulders tensed almost imperceptibly. "The steward? I understand he's recovering well."

"Yes, from a rather nasty blow to the head. Deliberately administered. He's been lucky. It could have been much worse."

Hardwick composed his expression. He showed no surprise or shock, only the controlled recognition of a man who understands how warnings are issued, even if he did not deliver one.

"Assaulted, you say?" His tone conveyed concern, but his eyes betrayed calculation.

"I thought you might be interested to know he's remembered seeing both First Officer Grayson and Miss de Vere near Sir Edmund's cabin on the night of his murder."

Something flickered behind Hardwick's eyes. "Passengers and crew often traverse the corridors. It hardly constitutes evidence."

"The timing seems rather coincidental."

He smiled. "When you've spent as many years at sea as I have, you'll learn that ships are rife with coincidences. Close quarters, limited pathways."

"And limited places to hide a body," I added. "Like Chief Officer Bowthorpe's, perhaps?"

The captain's face hardened. "That will be all…such nonsense. I have a ship to run."

I turned to leave but paused at the doorway. "One last thing, Captain. The blow Charlie received was precise enough to incapacitate but not kill him. The mark of someone with training, wouldn't you agree?"

"I wouldn't presume to know the techniques of criminals," he replied coolly. "Good day to you."

As I walked away, I heard him bark orders to an unseen crew member about maintaining the watch schedule.

I made my way back to HG's stateroom, where she and Whipple were already waiting. HG poured tea from a silver pot as I related my brief exchange with Hardwick.

"His reaction confirms our suspicions," said Whipple. "He knows more than he's admitting."

"Did you locate First Officer Grayson?" I asked.

"Oh yes," HG replied with a gleam in her eye. "And our conversation proved most illuminating. It seems Mr Grayson harbours considerable resentment towards our missing Chief Officer Bowthorpe. According to Grayson, the fellow appeared from nowhere after the war with impeccable credentials, which led to rapid promotion."

Did Grayson believe someone had falsified the credentials? I ventured.

"That is what the man believes, but most interesting was his slip when discussing Lily de Vere."

"Slip?" I echoed.

"It wasn't what he said, but how quickly he denied knowing her as anything other than just another passenger. Too quickly, I thought. As if rehearsed," HG said.

Whipple fiddled with his notebook. "A man in his position would naturally know the passenger manifest, but his denial suggested a more personal connection he's eager to conceal."

"So we have a web of connections," I mused. "Hardwick, Grayson, de Vere, and the absent Bowthorpe."

"And we have but hours to unravel it all." opined HG.

Whipple gathered his papers, aligning their edges with habitual precision, though I noticed his eyes lingered on the notes longer than strictly necessary. For a moment, none of us spoke.

The discussion had not stalled because we lacked facts, but because we had settled too soon on their shape. The assault on the steward had found its place in our thinking with remarkable speed. It had become an incident rather than a question, a confirmation rather than a complication. Something that pointed upward, toward authority and command, and once it did so, it ceased to invite scrutiny of its own.

I realised with faint discomfort, that sympathy had done much of the work for us. Concern had been expressed, outrage acknowledged, and with that, curiosity retreated. The injured man himself had slipped behind the account we told about him. A victim of someone else's violence. A warning delivered by unseen hands. Evidence that reinforced what we already believed.

HG broke the silence first. "Fear has a way of arranging itself," she said mildly. "Once it chooses a direction, it resents interruption."

Whipple nodded. "People like explanations that behave themselves. Particularly aboard ship."

I leaned against the back of the chair, letting the thought settle. What troubled me was not that the assault concealed something, but that it required no concealment at all. It relied on an expectation. On habit. On the comfort of assuming that violence travels downward from power, never sideways, and never quietly.

We had spoken of the assault as proof of brutality, but not as an act with its own logic. Once framed as a warning, it stopped being examined. Once they placed the steward in the role of victim, his presence in events became incidental, not interrogative. Victims, once accepted as such, are rarely questioned further. It felt unkind, even improper, to do so.

HG watched me for a moment, then turned back to the window. "Speculation is only useful when it leads somewhere," she said. "At present, it does not."

She was right. No replacement for the explanation we'd crafted existed yet, just the realisation that it had settled into complacency. I let the thought go, because there was nothing to be done with it, and because action taken too soon would only harden the very assumptions that troubled me.

Whipple folded his notebook and slipped it into his pocket. "We proceed as planned."

"Yes," HG agreed. "One step at a time."

I nodded, though unease lingered. Whatever truth lay ahead would not announce itself with drama. It would linger, unnoticed, in the spaces we had already decided did not matter.

I jolted awake, my watch displaying four in the morning. Sleep had been a restless affair, filled with fragmented dreams and a persistent, nagging sense of something overlooked. The gentle rocking of the ship, which had been soothing on previous nights, now felt like a persistent reminder of our drifting investigation.

Rising from my bed, I crossed to the porthole. The moon cast a silver path across the dark Atlantic waters. So close to New York now, yet our answers remained frustratingly distant.

Our working theory explained everything, and yet satisfied nothing. Like a suit made from mismatched cloth, it covered what needed covering but hung awkwardly at the seams.

I dressed and made my way to the observation deck, finding it empty save for a solitary steward polishing brass fittings. The air was brisk, carrying a sharp taste of salt.

"Couldn't sleep either?" HG's voice came from behind me. She stood wrapped in a thick wool coat, her silvery hair tucked beneath a smart hat.

"The pieces fit together," I said, "but they don't quite sing."

"Ah yes." She joined me at the railing. "Like a perfect translation that somehow loses the poetry."

We stood in companionable silence for several minutes before Inspector Whipple appeared, looking as rumpled as ever.

"I see I'm not the only one visited by midnight doubts," he said, joining us.

"Not doubts precisely," I replied. "More a sense of..."

"Artifice," HG supplied. "As if we're looking at something constructed rather than something lived."

Whipple nodded. "When I was a young constable, we had a case solved too neatly. Every strand tied up with a bow. My sergeant said, 'Truth is rarely so accommodating, Whipple. It tends to leave loose threads for us to trip over.'"

The morning light was beginning to bleed into the eastern sky, turning the horizon a pale grey.

"It's perfectly sound," Whipple added, though his tone suggested he was reminding himself as much as informing me.

"Of course it is," HG agreed. "Yet one finds oneself moving more carefully around it, as one might an elaborate house of cards."

We fell silent again, watching the strengthening light. Our explanation still held—a conspiracy of power and position, orchestrated through hierarchy and fear. It accounted for every fact, every movement, every relationship we had uncovered.

And yet...

"We shall proceed as planned," Whipple said firmly. "The evidence supports our conclusions."

"Absolutely," I replied, though my voice lacked conviction.

As the sun finally crested the horizon, I couldn't shake the feeling that somewhere, in some small detail, lurked the truth we had yet to recognise.

"There's a pattern," Whipple said quietly, his finger tracing an invisible line across the railing. "It struck me as I reviewed my notes last night."

I turned to him, grateful for anything that might bring clarity to our muddled case. "What sort of pattern?"

"Henderson's enquiries became increasingly precise in the days before his death. His initial questions were broad, scatter-shot. But by the end, he was asking very specific questions about very specific people."

HG nodded. "As journalists do when they've found the scent."

"Yes," Whipple agreed. "But here's the peculiar thing. Charlie Peabody was assaulted exactly twelve hours after Henderson made his first precise inquiry about the activities of certain officers on the night of Sir Edmund's murder."

I felt a chill that had nothing to do with the morning air. "You think the assault was connected to Henderson's investigation?"

"I'm simply noting the proximity in time," Whipple replied, his caution evident. "It's a procedural irregularity that resists simple explanation."

The three of us stared out at the strengthening dawn light, each wrestling with the implications.

"What troubles me most," Whipple continued, "is the nature of the violence itself. I've seen many attempts to silence witnesses in my career. When that's the goal, the violence is typically..." he hesitated, searching for a delicate phrasing, "more conclusive."

"You mean they kill them," I said bluntly.

"Precisely. Yet Charlie was left alive, though unable to speak to us immediately."

HG tapped her gloved fingers rhythmically against the polished wood. "Fear can be applied in degrees, you know. Like heat to metal. Too little, and nothing transforms. Too much, and the whole thing melts away. But applied with precision..."

Her voice trailed off, leaving the thought unfinished.

We stood in uncomfortable silence, watching the horizon brighten further. The connection between Henderson's enquiries and Charlie's assault was troubling, yet it led us nowhere new. Our working theory still accounted for the facts, even as it accumulated these small, nagging inconsistencies.

"We should prepare for breakfast," HG said finally. "The captain has invited us to join him. No doubt to assess our progress."

As we turned to go, I cast one last glance at the vast ocean behind us. Like in our case, its surface appeared coherent and complete, while concealing depths we had yet to fully fathom.

I returned to my cabin to dress for breakfast, my thoughts still tangled around our theory. It hung in my mind like an overloaded bookshelf, not precisely unstable, but requiring constant attention lest it tip forward and spill its contents across the floor. Each new fact we encountered seemed to add another weighty volume to its already burdened shelves.

The explanation sufficed, certainly. It connected Sir Edmund to his enemies, accounted for Henderson's prying and subsequent silencing, explained Charlie's assault. Yet I found myself mentally buttressing it throughout the day, adding small supports here, subtle reinforcements there.

I knotted my tie with mechanical precision, watching my reflection perform the familiar ritual. Our theory required such delicate maintenance now — a mental adjustment before breakfast, a recalibration over tea, another reinforcement with each new conversation. It was exhausting work, this constant shoring up of conclusions against the tide of unease.

"The hallmark of truth," HG had once told me, "Is how lightly it sits in the mind."

This truth, if truth it was, sat heavily indeed.

I smoothed my hair and straightened my collar. We would proceed as planned because we had nothing better to offer. Perhaps this was simply the nature of complex cases; they resisted tidy resolution. Perhaps the strain I felt was merely the weight of responsibility rather than the burden of error.

A knock at my door signalled it was time to join the others. I glanced once more at my reflection, noting the slight furrow between my brows that hadn't been there when we boarded.

"Right then," I said to myself, squaring my shoulders. "Onwards."

I opened the door, prepared once again to take up the weight of our carefully constructed theory and carry it through another day of questioning. Truth or not, it was all we had, and I would bear it until something better presented itself.

I found myself staring at the perfectly arranged breakfast before me without appetite. The morning light streamed through the observation lounge windows, catching the silverware and sending tiny spears of brilliance across the tablecloth. Captain Hardwick sat at the head of the table, his uniform immaculate, his manner controlled despite the strain visible around his eyes.

"We shall dock tomorrow morning," he announced. "I trust your investigation will conclude before then, Inspector?"

Whipple nodded, though I noticed his fingers tightening fractionally around his teacup. "We have a working theory that accounts for the events aboard your ship, Captain."

HG sipped her tea with the serene composure of an empress. "A theory that grows more elaborate with each passing hour, rather like those extraordinary Victorian mansions with their endless architectural additions."

I smiled despite myself. HG had that gift; she could dissect our precarious position whilst making it sound like an amusing observation about someone else's foibles.

"The crew is nervous," Hardwick continued. "Discipline is becoming difficult to maintain."

"Fear has that effect," HG replied. "Even among those accustomed to strict hierarchies."

I watched a steward refill the captain's coffee, noting how the man's hands trembled slightly, how his eyes darted towards the exits. And suddenly, like a photograph coming into focus, I saw the ship anew.

The Britannic Star wasn't simply a vessel with clear chains of command; it was a floating society where influence moved in currents I hadn't fully appreciated. Fear did not behave as neatly as I had assumed. It did not remain contained within rank or title, but drifted, settled, and resurfaced in ways that resisted simple explanation.

I'd been viewing the murders through the lens of a formal hierarchy. I had been assuming control followed rules as dependable as machinery. The ship itself obeyed them. People, I was beginning to suspect, did not. Power applied at one end, movement at the other. But human systems weren't mechanical. They were organic, adaptive.

Our theory still accounted for the facts, but it no longer felt sufficient. It was like trying to explain a storm by describing only the barometric pressure without accounting for the sea temperature, the wind patterns, the seasonal variations.

"Rex," HG's voice cut through my thoughts. "You've gone quite pale."

I composed my features. "Just considering the implications of our conclusions."

Whipple gave me a questioning glance, but I merely nodded reassurance. How could I explain that while our solution still held together, it suddenly felt inadequate, like a map that showed only the major roads but none of the footpaths where people walked?

We would proceed with our plan. We would present our case. But I carried with me now a troubling awareness that from the beginning, we had misunderstood something essential about how this floating world truly operated.

Chapter Twenty-Two

QUESTIONS OF TRUTH

There's a particular calm that settles over a ship when it has decided, collectively, to behave.

The Britannic Star did not soften in any sentimental sense. She did not apologise for what had happened on board her. She simply continued, and that continuation, more than anything, gave people permission to pretend that the worst was behind us.

By mid-morning, the sea outside the portholes was an orderly grey, as if even the Atlantic had agreed to keep its temper. Stewards moved along the corridors with their usual quiet competence. Laughter drifted up from the Palm Court at intervals, smothered, as though the sound itself had learned discretion.

I sat at HG's writing desk with my notebook open, my pen hovering above a page that was already crowded with names, times, and arrows. It had reached that stage of the investigation where the table was full. Not neat, but full. We were no longer trying to find pieces but rather deciding how to arrange them to create something that would not fall apart in our hands when carried ashore.

Whipple stood near the mantelpiece, a stack of papers in one hand, his other thumb pressed against his lower lip in that habit he had when he was thinking hard. He spread his notes on the desk and then put them away, as if this action could bring order to things.

HG sat by the window with her teacup balanced precisely between gloved fingers. Her posture suggested ease, but her eyes were alert, the kind of alertness that did not require movement.

"It will hold," Whipple said at last.

I looked up. "The case?"

He nodded once. "As it stands, if I were obliged to hand it to the New York police, it would hold."

The words should have been reassuring. I had been craving that moment, the one where the investigation could be declared, at least privately, coherent. Yet the relief I expected did not arrive cleanly. It came with a faint, persistent itch of discomfort, like a collar that sat just slightly too tight.

"It's something," I said. "We'd look foolish arriving with nothing but suspicion and anecdote."

HG's mouth curved. "One does prefer to arrive with luggage rather than excuses."

Whipple allowed himself a brief, humourless smile. "I have no wish to spend my first hour in New York defending why I cannot name a culprit."

"And yet you can," I said. "Or rather, you can name several."

"That is precisely the difficulty," he replied.

I glanced down at my notebook. Names sat there like

passengers waiting to disembark. Captain Hardwick, stiff-backed and silent. First Officer Grayson, brisk and evasive. Chief Officer Bowthorpe, absent to the point of becoming a myth. Lily de Vere, composed and guarded. Von Ritter, civilised and unreadable. Madam Zelda, glittering and brittle.

And beneath them all, the persistent presence of the coal bunker fire, the concealed hazard, the buried embarrassment that had become the ship's true wound.

Our theory connected it all. It explained motives. It explained fear. It explained why men might do desperate things in close quarters with land approaching and scandal threatening to leap ashore ahead of them.

It explained everything, and yet it demanded constant attention to keep it balanced.

"You look as if you're about to begin an argument with the furniture," HG observed.

"I was thinking," I said carefully, "how neat it appears on paper."

"Neatness is not always a virtue," she replied, mild as milk.

Whipple tapped the top sheet of his notes. "It's coherent. That is what matters."

A knock came at the door, and before any of us spoke, it opened.

Captain Hardwick entered with a polite certainty that carried the faintest hint of command. His uniform was immaculate, the braid bright and the buttons catching the morning light. Yet around his eyes strain showed, and in the set of his jaw the determination of a man who had decided that whatever happened aboard his ship it could not be allowed to define him.

"Inspector," he said to Whipple. "I understand you wish to interview First Officer Grayson again."

Whipple's expression did not change. "Yes, Captain. There are a few clarifications I require before we dock."

Hardwick nodded. "He will attend to you as soon as his watch is complete."

The phrasing was courteous, but it placed the interview where Hardwick wanted it, in the cracks between duties, not at our convenience.

"Thank you," Whipple said evenly.

Hardwick's gaze moved briefly to HG, then to me. "The crew is unsettled," he added. "Rumours spread quickly at sea. I would appreciate it if you kept your inquiries as discreet as possible."

HG sipped her tea. "Discretion, Captain, is very often the ship's preferred form of religion."

Hardwick's eyes flickered, as if he had not expected quite that. "One cannot run a vessel of this size amid panic, Your Grace."

"No," she replied. "One can hardly run anything amid panic."

Hardwick inclined his head once, then withdrew, leaving behind the faint scent of leather and authority.

When the door closed, Whipple exhaled through his nose.

"He will give us Grayson," I said, "but only when it suits him."

"He is reminding us," Whipple replied, "that he still commands the ship."

HG's gaze drifted toward the window. "Which may be the only thing keeping him upright."

Whipple began gathering his papers again, then stopped, and looked at me with a kind of professional candour.

"When we reach New York," he said, "our difficulties become procedural rather than investigative."

I frowned. "How do you mean?"

He moved to the desk, picked up his pencil, and rapped it against his notebook.

"Here," he said, "we have context. We have proximity, a closed population, and we have been living with the details. Also, we can talk about implication, atmosphere, motive layered upon motive, and it makes sense because we have felt it."

"And there," I said slowly, "you must persuade men who have not been breathing this air."

"Precisely." He glanced at HG. "I will have to present a narrative that survives translation."

HG smiled faintly. "Translation into American?"

"Translation into bureaucracy," he corrected. "Statements. Witness accounts. Chain of custody. The exact timing of Henderson's movements. The handling of his notes. The fact that we cannot produce the missing officer. The captain's concealment of the fire."

He paused, as though tasting the words.

"It can be made to work," he continued, "but only if framed carefully. Too much nuance, and they will think we are indulging ourselves. Too little, and the case will collapse into accusation."

HG gave a delicate snort. "A tragic fate, Arthur. To be misunderstood as verbose."

"I've had worse," he replied dryly.

I felt the itch return, that sense of the case being heavier than it ought to be.

"It is not that I doubt our conclusions," Whipple said, as if reading my face. "It is that explaining them requires effort. Consider what we must account for. Sir Edmund's blackmail. The coal bunker fire. The captain's desire to avoid scandal. The missing chief officer. Grayson's ambitions. Miss de Vere's secretive movements. Henderson's deadline. The assault on the steward."

He turned a page. "Each element makes sense. Together, they require a certain willingness to accept complexity."

"And why should they not?" I asked, irritation rising. "Crimes are messy. People panic. They improvise. That is the whole point. The world is not tidy."

HG's eyes rested on me. "No, Rex, the world is not tidy. But good crimes, like good stories, tend toward economy."

I felt myself bristle. "That sounds like philosophy, HG."

"It is not philosophy," she replied. "It is observation."

Whipple lifted a hand, as if to soothe the edge off the exchange. "We needn't quarrel. The case is complex because the circumstances are complex."

"Exactly," I said, grateful for his intervention. "We are not the ones who have made it so."

HG's smile suggested she was unconvinced, but she did not press.

Another knock came, and this time, after a brief pause, the door opened to reveal Grayson.

He stepped inside with the controlled stiffness of a man who understood he was being measured. His uniform was pressed, his hair neatly combed, his expression prepared. He glanced from Whipple to HG to me, as if gauging which of us was most dangerous.

"You wished to see me, Inspector," he said.

"Yes." Whipple did not offer him a seat this time, and Grayson did not ask for one. "I will not keep you long, Mr Grayson, but I require clarity on several points."

Grayson's jaw tightened fractionally. "Of course."

Whipple opened his notebook. "Your movements on the night of Sir Edmund Blythe's death."

Grayson's gaze did not waver. "I have already accounted for them."

"Then you will not mind accounting for them again," Whipple said.

Grayson recited his schedule with practised ease. Duties, inspections, a brief visit to the officers' mess. He used the language of routine because routine sounded innocent. He described his movements as though he were describing the turning of the engines, inevitable and automatic.

Whipple listened without interruption, then asked, "At any point did you enter the passenger corridors near Blythe's cabin?"

Grayson's eyes flickered for an instant. "No."

"Did you speak with Blythe that evening?"

"No."

"Did you send anyone to him?"

Grayson's mouth thinned. "No."

HG's tone remained mild. "Mr Grayson, you understand that absolute denials have an unfortunate way of eroding trust."

Grayson inclined his head. "I understand many things, Your Grace."

Whipple continued, unhurried, his questions precise.

"Mr Henderson. Did you meet him privately at any point in the twenty-four hours before his death?"

"No."

"Did you discuss the coal bunker fire with him?"

"No."

"Were you aware he intended to transmit a report before docking?"

"I would not know," Grayson said, though his voice tightened on the words.

Whipple's eyes remained fixed on him. "The wireless operator confirms Henderson booked transmission time just hours before we found him."

"I cannot speak to what journalists do," Grayson replied.

"You can speak," Whipple said quietly, "to what you did."

Grayson's hands remained clasped behind his back, but his shoulders had drawn tighter, as though bracing.

Whipple turned a page. "You told us earlier you had not seen Henderson on the day before his death."

Grayson's nostrils flared. "I said I had not met him."

"And yet witnesses place you in the officers' mess at four o'clock," Whipple said, "with Henderson present."

Grayson hesitated. "He approached me. I dismissed him."

"About what?"

"About rumours," Grayson said. "He wanted a comment. I gave none."

"Did he mention Sir Edmund Blythe?" I asked.

Grayson's gaze snapped to me. "The man was dead. Of course he mentioned him."

"Did he mention the coal fire?" I pressed.

Grayson's jaw worked. "He mentioned everything. That is what journalists do. They throw a net and hope it catches something."

"And did it catch something?" HG asked.

Grayson stiffened. "No."

Whipple let the silence sit long enough for Grayson to feel it.

"Mr Grayson," Whipple said at last, "I will be plain. If

you are withholding information, you are doing so at your peril. When we dock, outside authorities will become involved. Your career will not be protected by your uniform."

Grayson's face reddened faintly. "Inspector, I have told you what I know."

Whipple studied him. "Then you will not object if I ask you once more about Chief Officer Bowthorpe."

Grayson's eyes narrowed. "Mr Bowthorpe is indisposed."

"Indisposed," HG echoed softly.

"He has been unwell," Grayson insisted. "The ship is large. There are many places."

"Not so many," I said, "that a senior officer can vanish entirely."

Grayson's gaze flicked toward the door, just once. "If that is all, Inspector, I must return to duty."

Whipple closed his notebook with a crisp snap. "For now."

Grayson inclined his head to HG with stiff politeness, offered me a glance that was almost contemptuous, and left.

As soon as the door shut, Whipple's shoulders dropped fractionally.

"He's hiding something," I said.

"Undoubtedly," Whipple replied. "But whether it is murder or mere negligence remains to be seen."

HG set her teacup down. "He is frightened," she said. "Not in the theatrical way of a guilty man, but in the practical way of one who understands how quickly reputations sink."

I nodded, though the itch of unease remained.

We sat for a moment in silence, the ship's steady vibration beneath our feet. Then Whipple began again, not with suspects, but with process.

"I will have to produce statements," he said. "Signed accounts. Times. Witness lists. The precise chain through which Henderson's notes were handled, and by whom. I will have to explain why we suspect a conspiracy of several actors rather than a single impulsive killer."

"Because it is what the evidence suggests," I said.

"Yes," Whipple replied, "and I will say that. But I will also be asked whether the evidence suggests it, or whether we have built the narrative because it feels plausible."

HG's eyes glittered faintly. "Does it feel plausible, Arthur?"

Whipple's mouth tightened. "It feels…defensible."

I did not like the word.

Before I could respond, HG rose. "Come," she said. "Remaining in here will not change the ship's determination to continue pretending it is civilised," she said. "Let us see that pretence in motion"

We stepped into the corridor together.

The Britannic Star at mid-morning was a theatre of routine.

A steward moved past us with a tray of coffee cups balanced perfectly, his gaze lowered, his footsteps measured. Two ladies emerged from a cabin in matching coats, laughing softly as they adjusted their gloves. A maid pushed a trolley with fresh linen, her face expressionless, her eyes fixed on the path ahead. Somewhere down the corridor, a child's voice rose and was hushed immediately by a nanny's murmur.

We passed the lounge where breakfast service was

ending, the tables still scattered with plates and silver. A waiter moved between them with practiced speed, collecting napkins, restoring order. There was no sense of panic, no visible fracture. Only the faintest tension, like the knowledge that too much laughter might be considered vulgar.

"It is remarkable," I murmured.

"What is?" HG asked.

"That it continues," I said. "Two men dead, and still the tables are laid as if nothing happened."

"It is not remarkable," Whipple replied. "It is policy."

HG glanced at him. "Do not flatter yourself, Arthur. It is not only policy. It is habit."

We moved toward the stairwell. On the landing, a steward polished the brass rail with slow, careful strokes. When he finished, he stepped back and inspected his work with the solemn concentration of an artist. Then he moved on, leaving the rail shining as though murder were incapable of leaving fingerprints on metal.

"Order is comforting," I said.

"Order is useful," HG corrected. "Comfort is merely the excuse given afterward."

Whipple did not speak, but I could feel his mind turning, gathering.

We returned to HG's stateroom, and the moment we re-entered the enclosed space, the air changed. The outside routine had steadied me, but it had not eliminated the itch. If anything, it made it sharper. The contrast between the ship's calm and the violence that had occurred aboard her felt almost indecent.

Whipple resumed his preparations, stacking papers again, and I realised he was rehearsing, silently, for a room full of unfamiliar men.

"I will have to decide," he said, "how much of this to present as motive and how much as circumstance."

"What do you mean?" I asked.

"If I lead with the fire," he said, "I risk them thinking this is about negligence, not murder. If I lead with Blythe's blackmail, I risk them thinking this is melodrama. If I lead with Henderson's deadline, I risk them thinking this was an opportunistic killing rather than a planned one."

"And what is it?" I asked.

Whipple's eyes lifted. "It is both."

HG's smile was faint. "A tragedy in two acts," she said. "Act one, leisure. Act two, urgency."

That, at least, I understood. Blythe's death had been quiet. Henderson's had been rougher, hurried.

"The methods differ," I said. "Blythe was dispatched in his cabin, private, controlled. Henderson died in a more functional manner."

Whipple nodded. "Circumstance dictates method."

"Exactly," I said, pleased to have something solid. "The killer adapted."

HG's gaze sharpened. "And adaptation requires competence."

"Competence," I repeated, feeling the familiar pull upward. "Which suggests training. Discipline. Hierarchy."

Whipple did not contradict me, but he did not agree either. He simply gathered his papers with renewed care.

It was then that HG's earlier comment returned to me.

Good crime tends toward economy.

I felt that bristle again. "Crimes are not stories," I said, as if answering her from across time.

HG looked at me. "No," she said. "But people tell themselves stories about crimes. That is how they endure them."

Whipple cleared his throat gently. "Captain Hardwick

may not endure a story in which his authority is revealed as fragile."

"And yet his authority is fragile," I said.

HG's mouth curved. "Everything is fragile at sea. Even the illusion of control."

I found myself pacing, unable to keep still. "For our theory to work," I said, "the chain of command must function efficiently. Orders passed, acted upon, repeated. No delay. No hesitation."

Whipple watched me. "That's what troubles you?"

"It doesn't trouble me," I insisted. "It is simply… demanding."

HG regarded me steadily. "Demanding is another word for heavy."

I stopped pacing, annoyed at myself for being lured into metaphors. "It is plausible," I said.

Whipple's expression remained neutral, but his eyes held something like fatigue.

"It is plausible," he agreed. "But I will be asked why it required so much."

"Because they were under pressure," I said.

"Yes," he replied, and the word sounded almost like concession.

A message was delivered then by a young steward, who knocked, entered, and handed Whipple a slip of paper with the careful solemnity of ritual. Whipple read it, then folded it neatly.

"The captain requests my presence briefly," he said.

HG's gaze held his. "To assess your progress," she murmured.

Whipple did not deny it.

"I'll accompany you," I said.

We found Captain Hardwick on the bridge, standing

with his hands clasped behind his back, gaze fixed on the horizon. He did not turn when we entered, as though to look would be to admit vulnerability.

"Inspector," he said. "Mr Manning."

Whipple's tone was procedural. "Captain."

Hardwick turned. "We dock soon," he said. "I would prefer this matter settled before then."

"That is our intention," Whipple replied.

Hardwick's eyes flicked over us, assessing. "The crew is nervous."

"Fear is natural," Whipple said.

"Fear is dangerous," Hardwick corrected. "It breeds looseness."

HG was not there, and I felt her absence in the air. Without her, the bridge seemed more purely an instrument of command, less a stage for social subtleties. The smell of polish and oil, the quiet discipline of officers moving in their stations, the restrained voices. It all emphasised Hardwick's world.

"I wished to ask you," I said, "about Chief Officer Bowthorpe."

Hardwick's posture stiffened. "You have asked me before."

"Yes," I said. "But matters have progressed."

Hardwick's eyes narrowed. "Progressed?"

"We are attempting," Whipple said evenly, "to understand the full context of events aboard your vessel."

Hardwick's jaw tightened. "Bowthorpe has been indisposed."

"The same word Mr Grayson used," I said.

Hardwick's gaze flicked to me. "It is a reasonable word."

"It is also vague," I replied.

Hardwick did not rise to the bait. "Mr Manning," he

said, "authority at sea is not a philosophical abstraction. It is survival. A captain does not discuss every internal difficulty with passengers, no matter how well connected."

"I'm not asking out of curiosity," I said. "I'm asking because his absence has become part of the pattern."

Hardwick's mouth thinned. "Patterns are often imagined."

Whipple stepped in, tone quiet but firm. "Captain, I am not asking you to satisfy my curiosity. I am asking you because if Bowthorpe is missing under circumstances you have concealed, it will become my duty to treat that concealment as relevant."

Hardwick's eyes hardened. "Inspector, I concealed a hazard to prevent panic. I did not murder anyone."

No one had accused him in that moment, and yet he defended himself as if the accusation were already present.

"I understand," Whipple said.

Hardwick's voice remained controlled. "Do you?"

Whipple did not answer immediately. Then he said, "When we dock, you will be answerable to your company and to the authorities. I suggest you consider whether it is wise to allow questions to be answered for you."

Hardwick's mouth tightened. "Is that a threat?"

"It is a statement of consequence," Whipple replied.

Hardwick looked away, back at the horizon. "Good day, Inspector," he said.

We left the bridge without further exchange.

As we walked back down the corridor, my mind returned to Hardwick's words.

Authority at sea is survival.

It wasn't a confession or evidence; it was a worldview. The conviction could justify almost anything if framed as necessity.

Back in HG's stateroom, HG was waiting. She poured tea as if we had merely been out for air.

"Well?" she asked.

"He believes in command," I said.

HG smiled. "Most captains do."

Whipple set his papers down with a tired precision. "He is frightened of being made to look weak."

"And that fear," HG said softly, "is often more motivating than guilt."

I sat again at the writing desk, my notebook open before me. The page was full, but my mind felt crowded rather than satisfied.

Whipple resumed speaking, more to himself than to us.

"I will have to state, plainly, why Henderson's death could not be delayed," he said. "The booked transmission time is crucial. It indicates urgency. It indicates a narrowing of options."

"And yet it does not tell you who acted," I said.

"No," Whipple agreed. "Only that someone did."

"And when people are hurried," she said, "they become crude."

"That is not always true," Whipple replied, though without heat. "Some people remain methodical under pressure."

"Which makes him dangerous," HG said.

I found myself staring at a point on the carpet, thinking of Henderson's last days, his questions growing sharper, his tone less playful. Thinking of Blythe, comfortable in his cabin, believing himself safe because he controlled other people's secrets. Thinking of the ship continuing, brass polished, cups poured, laughter carefully rationed.

Our theory held. It held stubbornly, like a heavy piece of furniture that could not be moved without effort. It accounted for everything, but it demanded too much coordination to do so. Too many people acting in step, too many motives aligning at the precise moment required.

I felt the need to defend it again, as if defending it would make the itch stop.

"Complexity does not mean falsehood," I said.

"No," HG replied gently. "It means effort."

Whipple looked at me, eyes quiet. "Rex, do you know what I dislike most about this case?"

I hesitated. "The lack of sleep?"

A faint smile touched his mouth. "That as well. But no. What I dislike is how much it requires us to persuade ourselves."

I frowned. "That's unfair."

"It is not unfair," he said, patient. "It is simply... unusual. Truth does not always arrive elegantly, but it rarely requires constant maintenance."

HG's eyes rested on me. "The hallmark of truth," she said softly, "is how lightly it sits in the mind."

I bristled again, because I did not want philosophy. I wanted facts.

"Perhaps," I said, "this is simply the nature of modern crimes."

HG's smile was faint. "Do not blame modernity for the human appetite for complication."

Whipple glanced down at his papers. "We proceed," he said firmly. "Also a defensible case and suspects. Motive and opportunity. This must not drift into doubt merely because our minds are tired."

"Yes," I said, grateful for the firmness. "We proceed."

HG lifted her teacup. "How splendidly procedural," she murmured.

The ship's bell sounded distant in the corridor, marking

another segment of the day. Somewhere nearby, a steward moved past with a tray, his footsteps muffled by carpet. The Britannic Star continued to behave as though she were innocent.

I looked down at my notebook again, at the neatness of lines and arrows, at the confidence of ink.

It would hold. Whipple was right.

And yet, as the morning slipped toward afternoon, I found myself aware of how carefully we were holding it. When I finally closed my notebook, my hand lingered on the cover as if reluctant to release it. The case was ready to be carried ashore, presented, defended, and believed.

But I could not shake the suspicion that somewhere beneath our narrative, something simpler waited. Not to be discovered yet, but to make us feel, later, that we had been labouring to keep the wrong thing standing.

Chapter Twenty-Three

SILENT NOTES

A curious stillness had settled over HG's stateroom, not the hush of silence, but the restraint that follows when words carry weight. Tea sat cooling in its cups. Whipple's notebook lay closed beside him, his pencil aligned along the spine, as if placed there. HG sat opposite, hands cupped in her lap, composed yet alert, like a woman listening for something she half expected to hear.

What struck me was not what they were saying, but what they were no longer saying.

We no longer discussed potential suspects, motives, or opportunities as we had before. Instead, they spoke in generalities, almost abstractions, as if discussing principles rather than people.

"Pressure has a way of simplifying behaviour," HG remarked, adjusting the pearls at her throat with an absent touch. "Whatever complexity one cultivates tends to collapse beneath it."

Whipple inclined his head. "Training remains. Habit.

Whatever a person falls back on when deliberation becomes a luxury."

"And what remains," HG added, "is usually rather ordinary."

"Ordinary," Whipple repeated thoughtfully. "Which is often the most disappointing discovery of all."

They exchanged a brief glance, unremarkable in itself, and yet weighted with something unspoken. I watched them rather than listening, aware of a faint irritation building behind my ribs.

"You're both sounding unusually philosophical," I said at last. "Are we to solve this murder by quoting Montaigne at one another?"

HG smiled. "The nearness of land has that effect on me. One reflects when a journey draws toward its conclusion."

"Or one prepares," Whipple added, gathering a small stack of papers into his leather portfolio with methodical care.

I poured myself more tea, noting how naturally their movements aligned. When HG reached for the sugar bowl, Whipple had already nudged it within reach. When Whipple frowned at a particular notation, HG supplied its context without prompting. There was no conspiratorial air to it, no sense of secrecy. And yet I could not shake the feeling that something had shifted while I was looking elsewhere.

"Have you two reached a conclusion I've missed?" I asked.

They looked at me then, both of them, neither indulgent nor dismissive.

"Not a conclusion, Rex," HG said gently. "Merely a narrowing of perspective."

"The evidence will determine our path," Whipple added. "Nothing more. Nothing less."

"Terribly procedural," HG said, though her tone suggested the word carried more weight than it appeared.

I leaned back, unsettled. It felt as though the field of play had been reduced while I was still pacing its former boundaries.

"I rather thought we were still exploring possibilities," I said.

"Oh, we are," HG replied. "But some possibilities now require a great deal of effort to keep alive."

Whipple nodded. "A theory that demands constant reinforcement is rarely as stable as it first appears."

"Meaning," I said, "that you think I have been reinforcing something."

HG's eyes softened, though her voice remained brisk. "Meaning only that you are conscientious, which is both admirable and exhausting."

Whipple cleared his throat. "Rex, no one is accusing you of inventing facts. We are discussing economy."

"Economy," I repeated. "A charming word. Do you mean thrift, or do you mean elegance?"

HG's mouth curved. "If you like. The best explanations, like the best manners, waste nothing."

"And if a matter cannot be explained elegantly?" I asked. "If it is untidy and inconvenient?"

"Then it is untidy and inconvenient," Whipple said. "But it may still be true."

That ought to have reassured me. Instead, I felt again that faint exclusion, as if I had wandered into a conversation already underway.

"You two," I said, with a faint smile, "are becoming alarmingly alike."

"Perish the thought," HG replied. "Arthur still insists on neat handwriting, and I still insist on comfort."

Whipple's mouth twitched. "I concede I will never have Your Grace's taste in upholstery."

The moment passed, but the unease did not. It had shifted shape, becoming less pointed, more pervasive.

I kept going back to the crimes, rather than the people involved or their reasons. Believing men and women capable of murder was one thing. Figuring out how a murder could occur on a lively ship full of people, without anyone noticing, was something else.

"There is something rather peculiar about these deaths," I said at last. "Not who committed them, but what minor disturbance they caused."

HG glanced up from her notebook. "Go on."

"Sir Edmund's cabin showed no sign of forced entry," I continued. "No overturned furniture. No evidence of a struggle. Everything was orderly."

"Order can be arranged," Whipple said. "But yes, go on."

"And Henderson was found in a service stairwell," I said. "Yet no one reported hearing anything unusual. No raised voices. No sounds of alarm."

Whipple considered this. "The absence of witnesses does not necessarily imply the absence of opportunity."

"No," I agreed. "But it does suggest that whatever occurred blended easily with the ship's ordinary business."

"Certain presences discourage questioning."

"The privileges of rank," I said. "If one belongs somewhere, no explanation is required."

Whipple nodded. "Authority discourages questioning."

It was a neat phrase, perhaps too neat, but it put words to something that had been pressing at the back of my mind. A captain on the bridge, an officer in a corridor, a person of standing entering a cabin, such things raised no eyebrows. The Britannic Star ran on deference as much as it did on steam.

"A person of sufficient position could move about without being challenged," I said. "They need not be furtive. They need only be certain."

"Certainty," HG murmured. "Yes. It can be very persuasive."

Whipple's gaze met mine, then returned to his notebook. "Let us test that thought against Henderson."

He opened his notebook and reconstructed Henderson's last hours, and adopted the precision that had earned him his reputation. Times, locations, brief encounters, each arranged into a sequence that felt inevitable.

"Henderson left the bar shortly after nine," Whipple said. "He spoke briefly with von Ritter. The baron claims it was trivial, an exchange about politics and weather, which is often how men avoid saying anything at all."

HG gave a small sound of amusement. "Civilisation's great talent."

"After that, Henderson went to the library," Whipple continued. "He remained there for some time."

"Forty minutes," HG said.

"Approximately," Whipple agreed. "He was then seen by a steward delivering cocoa, by Madame Zelda returning to her cabin, and by Miss Chase."

I frowned. "Penelope tipped her hat story again."

Whipple nodded. "She said he was polite. Quiet. Not at all like a man who believed he was in danger."

"He wasn't alarmed," I breathed.

"No," Whipple replied. "He was curious."

HG leaned back. "Which suggests he was not confronted, but invited."

The thought sat uncomfortably in the mouth, like a sweet that turned bitter after the first taste. To be invited to one's death had a particular cruelty to it. It implied trust, or at least expectation.

"He believed he was following a lead," I said.

"Precisely," Whipple replied. "Someone offered him information he believed credible."

"And valuable," HG added.

Henderson's notebook lay open on the table. The final entries were measured, analytical, even optimistic. He had not scrawled frantic warnings or half-finished sentences. He had written as though his world remained intact.

"He expected a conversation," I said. "Not a confrontation."

"Journalists are vulnerable to that," HG observed. "Curiosity is both their instrument and their weakness."

I turned the pages, unsettled by how little would have been required. A suggestion, a hint, a promise of proof. Henderson would have pursued it with dogged interest and determination, just like a dog following a scent, sure that the effort would pay off.

"Very little force was needed," I murmured, "at least from Henderson's point of view."

"And timing," Whipple added. "Always timing."

He tapped his pencil against the notebook, once, as if to anchor the thought.

"Consider how different this is from a street crime," he continued. "A man is attacked in a dark alley. He shouts, he runs, someone hears. Here, the environment does half the work for the criminal. Narrow corridors, muffled carpets, a culture of discretion. People do not wish to see trouble. They step around it."

"Or pretend they have," HG said.

"Indeed," Whipple replied. "And there is another point."

He turned a page and glanced at me. "Henderson's movements were not random. Each step took him closer to the stairwell."

"You make it sound as if he were guided like a dog on a lead," I said.

Whipple did not smile. "Not like a dog. Like a man who believes he is choosing freely."

HG's voice remained mild. "The most effective inducements do not feel like coercion. They feel like opportunity."

That landed. I felt it settle somewhere behind my sternum, not as a conclusion, but as a discomfort. Opportunity was not a word one wished to associate with murder.

We might have continued in that vein, were it not for the sound of life outside HG's door. Footsteps, muted by carpet. A gentle knock. The rhythm of the ship asserting itself, as it always did, regardless of what lay beneath.

"Come," HG called.

Her steward, Graham, entered carrying a silver tray with sandwiches arranged with practised precision. Cucumber. Egg and cress. A little pot of mustard for the ham, as though murder was a mere inconvenience, not a condition of life aboard.

"Your luncheon, Your Grace," Graham said. "Cook mentioned you had not attended the midday service."

"Thank you, Graham," HG replied. "You are always thoughtful."

He bowed and withdrew, closing the door without a sound.

I watched him go, then caught myself watching. Aboard a ship, it was easy to disregard the humanity of the staff. They came, did their part, and disappeared quickly, just like stagehands switching the scenery in a play.

"Reliable fellow," I remarked, mostly to fill the space.

"The backbone of service," HG replied.

Whipple glanced at his watch. "Routine breeds familiarity."

I accepted that without question. On a ship, faces repeated. Paths crossed. Nothing remarkable in that.

Still, as we ate, I noticed the little repetitions of the day in a way I had not previously bothered to. Not as clues, simply as texture. The ship was a machine, yes, but it was also a society, and societies ran on predictable movements.

After luncheon, we shifted to procedural work. Whipple read aloud a line from Henderson's notes, not as evidence, but as context.

"He wrote that a ship is a place where privacy is always conditional," Whipple said. "He called it a floating town with fewer exits and more secrets."

"That is rather melodramatic," I said.

HG's eyes glittered. "And yet, not entirely wrong."

Whipple turned a page. "He also wrote that certain men behave as if they are untouchable simply because they are unchallenged."

"There's your authority again," I said.

Whipple nodded. "Authority can make people careless."

Or confident, I thought, though I did not say it aloud. Confidence often proved perilous.

The assault on Charlie Peabody returned to my mind, as it had every day since it happened. I remember him hurt but alive, leaning against the wall, and not letting the ship make him just another thing on board.

"It had the effect of silencing him," I said, more to myself than to them. "Without provoking panic."

HG looked at me. "In what sense?"

"The crew were unsettled," I said. "But the ship continued. No alarms. No disruption. It frightened them, but it did not stop the machinery."

"A measured outcome," Whipple murmured.

"Yes," I agreed. "Restraint, rather than excess."

I left it there. I avoided talking about Charlie's attack because it could change in people's minds, becoming more about its meaning than the event itself. Meaning was a dangerous appetite. It consumed facts and left you with a certainty that might not deserve the name.

HG's gaze rested on me for a moment, as if she had heard the shape of my thought rather than the words. Then she looked away and returned to her notes, allowing me the dignity of my reasoning.

The afternoon wore on. The ship's rhythms continued with stubborn indifference. A steward knocked to collect tea things. Another arrived with a message for Whipple from the purser. A piano started playing a song down the corridor, the same song it had played before, maybe hoping that repeating it would stop something bad from happening.

At four o'clock, tea was served in the Palm Court. We did not attend, but the scent of it drifted, anyway. The faint sweetness of pastries. The tell-tale aroma of bergamot. Outside, the ocean rolled on, patient and implacable.

"You see," HG said at last, looking toward the porthole as though she could see beyond it, "this is why ships are so useful to storytellers. They create the illusion of control."

"The captain would appreciate that," I said.

"Perhaps," HG replied. "Or perhaps he would object strongly. Captains are unsympathetic to the word 'illusion'."

Whipple kept his eyes on his notebook. "Control is not an illusion, Your Grace. It is a necessity."

"Yes," HG said softly. "And that is exactly why it is dangerous."

I frowned. "Dangerous?"

HG's mouth curved. "Dangerous to those who require it most. When control becomes the highest virtue, certain acts begin to look, to some minds at least, like practical solutions."

It was an uncomfortably intelligent remark, and I did not know what to do with it. So I did what I often did when uneasy; I pushed back.

"Human behaviour isn't a parlour game," I said. "People are messy, illogical creatures. Their motives twist and turn. One can hardly expect murder to follow tidy principles."

HG raised her eyebrows, mildly amused. "How fortunate for us that humanity is so delightfully unpredictable."

Whipple cleared his throat, as if hoping to prevent the discussion from turning into a debate. "Rex has a point. Crimes can be complicated."

"They can," HG agreed. "But they are rarely complicated in the way we imagine. Complexity often arrives after the fact, when we begin to explain."

That landed, though I disliked admitting it.

We continued working until HG excused herself to fetch a book. Her absence created an odd quiet. Sitting with Whipple among papers and cooling tea, I saw how much I relied on HG to keep the conversation stable, especially when it got awkward.

Whipple spoke first.

"Rex, something has been troubling me about our theory."

I looked up. "Our theory that the ship's hierarchy is driving this, that the violence flows down from authority."

He nodded. "Yes. It explains the facts."

"That's a strange way to say it," I replied. "Surely explaining the facts is the whole point."

"It explains everything," he said again, and now I heard the concern beneath it. "And that is what troubles me."

I waited.

"It requires perfection," he said carefully. "Timing without error. Coordination without hesitation. A sequence of actions passing cleanly through several hands."

"That isn't impossible," I said.

"No," he agreed. "But it is improbable."

He hesitated, then continued in the tone he used when being fair.

"In fifteen years at the Yard, I have never seen such faultless execution. Criminals err. They misjudge. They leave traces. Even trained men leave traces."

"And here?" I asked, my throat dry.

"Here, everything aligns," he said. "Too neatly."

I sat back, uneasy. "You think we've mistaken coherence for truth."

"I think," Whipple said, "that we may be asking too much of too many people."

The thought was not a conclusion. Pressure slowly crushed the chest.

"But the evidence," I began.

"The evidence fits," Whipple said. "That is precisely the point. It fits without resistance. It behaves as though it wants to be placed where we are placing it."

I stared at him. "You are suggesting someone arranged it."

Whipple held up a hand at once. "No. I am not

suggesting that. I am suggesting we are leaning on assumptions we have not tested properly."

"Such as?" I asked.

"Such as the idea that authority can coordinate murder without friction," he said. "That orders can pass downward without distortion. That no one hesitates. That no one talks. That no one makes a mistake."

"You're describing the army," I said.

"And even the army makes mistakes," Whipple replied.

I had no answer to that. I felt something shift beneath my certainty, like a floorboard that creaked not because it was broken, but because it had loosened.

HG returned then, book in hand, her arrival breaking the intimacy of the moment. Whipple's expression smoothed into neutrality, and I did my best to appear as though nothing had happened at all.

"You two look positively conspiratorial," HG remarked, settling back into her chair. "Have I missed something delicious?"

"Shop talk," Whipple said lightly.

"Arthur fretting over plausibility," I added, forcing a smile that felt stiffer than it ought.

HG glanced between us, her eyes sharpening for a fraction, then softening again, as if she had chosen not to press. "How very responsible of him."

The evening brought a shift in atmosphere aboard ship. The nearer we drew to New York, the more the passengers behaved as though the Atlantic had been nothing but a brief inconvenience. Trunks appeared in the corridor. Stewards hurried with lists. A woman in first class complained loudly that her evening gown had not been pressed to her satisfaction, as if that were the true crime of the voyage.

From HG's door we could faintly perceive the sound of

laughter from the lounge. The orchestra was practising again, the same waltz they always practised at this hour. Familiarity reasserted itself, stubborn and polished.

"Remarkable," I murmured, looking toward the corridor.

"What is?" HG asked.

"The ship," I said. "Two men are dead. The chief officer has vanished. A fire has smouldered in the bow for far too long. And yet the beds are turned down, the silver gleams, and someone somewhere is arguing about the correct temperature of tea."

Whipple's mouth tightened. "The shipping line will not permit standards to slip merely because trouble has boarded."

"But trouble has boarded," I said. "And it has walked about in the open, if only we knew how to recognise it."

I heard myself say it and disliked it at once. It sounded too close to certainty. Too close to the sort of remark Henderson might have written with satisfaction.

HG studied me. "You are tired, Rex."

"Possibly," I said, though I did not feel tired. I felt awake in a way I had not been earlier in the voyage, awake to discomfort rather than clarity.

Whipple closed his notebook with care. "We are all tired. Which is why we must rely on procedure."

"Procedure," HG echoed, her tone neither approving nor dismissive. "A comforting word."

"It is more than a word," Whipple said. "It is the only thing that prevents us from seeing what we wish to see."

I held his gaze. "And what do we wish to see?"

He sidestepped the answer. "A neat ending."

HG's mouth curved. "We are a narrative-minded

species. We prefer an ending that flatters our understanding."

I thought of the wrong solution, the framework we had been building, brick by brick. It did not feel false, not exactly, just heavy. Every new fact needed extra support, and soon the supports were more noticeable than the primary structure.

"Perhaps we are expecting murder to announce itself," I mumbled.

HG smiled. "It rarely does."

"Perhaps it requires very little disruption at all," I continued. "Only minimal effort."

She regarded me for a moment. "Or perhaps," she said, "it requires nothing more than people behaving exactly as they always do."

I had no answer to that. The remark was too broad to be useful, and yet it had a chilling plausibility. People behaving as they always did, that was the ship's great talent. It continued, because it must.

That night, on the ship heading to New York, I thought about how easily everyday life can include amazing events. How much could happen without altering the surface at all?

Our theory still stood. It accounted for all the facts we possessed. And yet it sat more heavily in the mind than it ought to have done, requiring constant care to keep upright.

If the truth were simpler, I could not see how.

But I was no longer certain that complexity was the virtue I had assumed it to be.

Chapter Twenty-Four

READY OR NOT

Graham cleared the table, collecting the china and silver, erasing all traces of our meal, and the door had closed behind him without a sound.

For a moment, the stateroom felt empty. Not of people, for the three of us remained, but of momentum. The discussion stopped after Whipple admitted that our system required a huge amount of effort from everyone. His words still hovered, not as an argument, but as a weight.

HG sat with her teacup resting between her hands, gaze angled toward the window where the sea slipped past in long, dark folds. Whipple had returned to his notebook, though his pencil did not move. I watched them, and their similar, thoughtful expressions struck me, as if they both needed a private moment to think.

I fidgeted as though I were waiting for something that my will could not summon.

"You're doing it again," HG observed without looking at me.

"Doing what?"

"Staring at us as though we've mislaid a piece of you somewhere," she said mildly.

I gave a short laugh that did not quite contain amusement. "Perhaps you have."

Whipple glanced up, expression guarded. "Rex—"

"I know," I said. "It's not a complaint. Only…you two have been speaking as if the case has begun to behave differently."

HG's mouth curved. "Cases do behave differently when they feel the approach of land. So do people."

Whipple emitted a subtle sound that suggested agreement, a mere breath. He set his pencil down with care.

"The closer we come to the end," he said, "the less forgiving a mistake becomes."

"That sounds like a threat," HG replied, serene.

"It's a fact," Whipple returned. "We dock soon. Once we reach shore, other men will have questions. Less patience than ours, and fewer scruples about how they ask them."

The remark should have comforted me. I should have remembered we weren't just guessing but dealing with a murder and its results. Instead, it sharpened the unease that had been growing in me since the previous night.

We had on paper, a coherent explanation, assembled it like a structure supported by careful beams of motive and opportunity. Yet now, when I looked at it in my mind, I saw how many supports it required. How much we had to assume not about what people wanted, but about what they could do together without friction, hesitation, or misstep.

The ship's gentle movement seemed to underline the thought. It endured. Unquestioning. All momentum directed forward.

HG spoke again, still watching the sea.

"Tell me, Rex," she said, "what is it you cannot quite settle in your mind?"

I opened my mouth, closed it, and then tried again. "It's not a single fact," I said. "It's…the way the facts sit together."

Whipple's gaze sharpened. "Meaning?"

"Meaning that they fit," I said, and then, because it sounded foolish, I added, "and yet they do not feel as though they ought to."

HG's eyes caught my attention. "An elegant discomfort."

"Yes," I admitted. "Exactly that."

Whipple shifted in his chair. "Discomfort is not evidence."

"No," I said, "but it can be a warning when it persists."

For several seconds, no one spoke. The silence was not awkward, attentive, as though we were listening for something beyond the walls of the stateroom. Outside, the corridor carried the faint murmur of passing footsteps, a trolley wheel rolling, a distant bell.

The ship continued.

And then, quite without my intending it, an old remark returned to me.

The recollection lacked drama. Clarity did not dawn, and no triumphant thought snapped into place. Henderson, once more. Reclined, radiating smugness, and spoke as though his profession granted him special insight.

The memory irritated me first because it felt irrelevant. Henderson had been full of remarks that sounded clever in the moment and proved empty on reflection. I had no desire to indulge him now, dead though he was.

Yet the remark would not go away.

"If you want the best secrets on a ship," he had said to

me, “don’t watch where the powerful sit. Watch where the ordinary moves.”

Something like that. I could not swear to the exact wording. Only the emphasis remained, and the faint, unpleasant sensation of having laughed it off.

I realised I had gone still.

HG noticed at once. “There it is,” she said.

“What?” Whipple asked.

I hesitated, reluctant to give the memory shape. “Henderson said something,” I murmured. “Earlier in the voyage. The sort of thing I dismissed because it sounded like Henderson.”

Whipple’s expression tightened with professional interest. “What sort of thing?”

“About…where information travels,” I said.

HG inclined her head. “Go on.”

I stared at my own hands for a moment, annoyed that the words felt childish even as they pressed to be spoken.

"He implied," I said, "that the most useful things aboard ship don't stay still. People expect them, so they go unnoticed.

Whipple did not react, but I saw his posture shift. Not alarm, not excitement. Attention.

HG's gaze rested on me with that peculiar steadiness of hers, not pushing, but holding.

“The remark irritated you,” she said.

“Yes,” I admitted. “It does even now. Because it has the temerity to feel relevant.”

Whipple reached for his pencil again, then stopped himself, as though writing too soon might damage whatever was forming.

HG set her cup down. “Then let us not be sentimental about Henderson,” she said. “Let us be practical.”

I swallowed. "Very well."

We sat like that for several minutes, the three of us not quite speaking, but no longer resting. Something had shifted. Not toward a new theory. Not toward a name, but a different way of looking.

I thought once more about the issues on the Britannic Star, but I didn't have any clues about the people or their reasons. I considered instead what each incident required to occur without breaking the ship's surface calm.

The will that vanished and returned. A thing removed and reinserted at the right moment to cause agitation. The brooch appeared, diverting suspicion in a more colourful direction. Sir Edmund's death, quiet and contained. Henderson's, urgent and ill-suited to ceremony. Charlie's assault, calibrated violence without fatal consequence.

Each event depended, in its own way, on the same assumption: that some presences do not register. That some movements do not become memorable. That the ship can absorb disturbance and continue smiling.

I shifted, uneasy. I felt as if I were approaching a truth that I couldn't speak aloud without changing the room.

Whipple spoke first, his tone procedural.

"Two murders," he said. "No obvious cries, commotion or remembered interruption."

"And an assault," HG added, "which produced fear, but not chaos."

Whipple nodded. "If the intention were to remove a witness, murder would have been simpler."

"Yes," I said. "Which means the assault was not simply a failed murder."

HG's eyes narrowed, approving. "It did precisely what it needed to do."

"Which was?" Whipple asked.

I felt a faint flush of discomfort. "It turned Charlie into a victim," I said. "And once he was a victim, we stopped examining him."

That honesty was unsettling. It sounded unkind, but factual. Charlie had ceased to be a person in our minds. He had become an incident; injured, the warning. The signpost pointed upward toward authority.

HG said, "Victims, once accepted as such, are rarely questioned further."

I frowned. "It feels improper."

"Exactly," HG replied. "And that feeling is itself useful to anyone who understands social habits."

Whipple's pencil moved once across his notebook, a short line. Then he stopped again.

"If we are correct," he said slowly, "then sympathy did some of the work for the attacker."

I looked from him to HG. Neither of them sounded triumphant. Neither sounded accusatory. It was all stated with the same restraint one might apply to discussing the weather, though it felt far heavier.

"I don't like the direction of this," I admitted.

"Truth is often discourteous," HG said mildly.

The ship creaked as if in agreement.

Whipple rose and moved to the window, looking out at the sea as though distance might assist his thinking.

"Let us be careful," he said. "We are not naming anything, not accusing anyone, but clarifying what the circumstances allow."

HG nodded. "That is all we must do today."

Whipple turned. "Rex. In your mind, who aboard this ship can approach a cabin at an odd hour without it being remembered as strange?"

The question made my stomach tighten, not because it

invited a name, but because it invited the wrong sort of answer.

"Someone of rank," I said at once, because it was safe. "An officer. The captain. Anyone who can command rather than request."

HG's gaze sharpened. "And yet Henderson did not walk into danger because someone commanded him, did he?"

"No," I admitted. "He walked because he believed he was meeting someone with information."

"Because he expected," Whipple said quietly, "that such meetings occur."

I hesitated. "Yes."

HG turned her head, as though listening for something beyond the walls.

"Expectation," she said, "is more persuasive than authority. Authority invites resistance. Expectation invites compliance."

The remark landed with an unsettling smoothness.

Whipple did not press. Instead, he returned to the desk and, with care, gathered his papers into a more orderly arrangement.

"I want us to proceed," he said, "as if we still believe what we have believed."

I stared at him. "You mean the wrong solution."

He did not react to the phrase. "I mean," he said evenly, "that we do not alter our manner. We do not change our habits. We give no one any reason to think we have shifted our attention."

HG's eyes brightened with understanding. "Quite so. Nothing alarms a careful person like the sudden sensation of being looked at differently."

I felt my throat tighten. "So, we pretend we still look upward."

Whipple met my gaze. "We are still behaving as though people will accept our current conclusions," I said.

"And," HG added, "we arrange a last piece of civility."

She spoke as if discussing dinner invitations rather than strategy.

"A small gathering," she continued. "A farewell of sorts and a chance to settle rumours, to show calm, to reassure those who need reassurance."

Whipple's expression did not change. "And in doing so, we create conditions."

I understood then what they meant, though still without naming it. A gathering is a form. A ritual, which brings people together. It makes movement deliberate, and therefore noticeable. It draws attention not through accusation, but through the ordinary expectation of social proximity.

HG turned to me. "Rex, you will attend," she said, "as you would attend any polite gathering. Observant, charming, and entirely unthreatening."

"Unthreatening," I echoed.

HG smiled again. "Yes. One must not look like a man about to witness something important."

Whipple closed his notebook. "We are not staging theatre," he said. "We are simply allowing the ship to reveal itself."

The phrase sent a small chill through me.

We spent the next hour discussing practicalities. Who would join us? Those whose names had clustered around the case like moths around a flame. Hardwick, Grayson, Lily, Penelope, Zelda. Von Ritter. Perhaps others would join, but a smaller gathering would allow us to keep the meeting more controlled.

HG organised everything for the event as carefully as she did with all social gatherings. She paid attention to the chairs, drinks, and the right topics to avoid arousing any doubts. Even the timing would make the invitation feel natural.

Whipple curtailed his contributions, focusing on containment and procedure. He made no speeches, offered no dramatic declarations. The man simply ensured he could control any moment of disorder.

I found myself both impressed and unsettled by how calmly they handled it.

HG observed the late afternoon light diminish, stating, "Politeness manifests when land nears."

"You said that once before." I stated.

HG's smile was soft. "Did I? Perhaps the ship encourages repetition."

Whipple looked at her. "It encourages forgetting," he said.

HG nodded. "Yes. And forgetting is often what people want. It makes them pliable."

I imagined the passengers praising the Britannic Star's superb service. Not least the delicious food, music, and fancy activities. For most, the murders would become a grim story, an unfortunate event they could sum up as an 'incident'.

The ship would arrive, gangway lowered. Everyone would step ashore into new routines, grateful to leave the floating claustrophobia behind.

And somewhere within that transition, truth might vanish if not secured now.

"Arthur," I said quietly, "do you truly believe we are ready?"

Whipple's eyes held mine for a moment, steady and unromantic. "We are ready to see what happens," he said. "And that is the most one can ever be."

The way he said it did not sound like doubt. It sounded like discipline.

As evening approached, I left HG's stateroom to dress, as she instructed. The corridor outside felt no different from any other evening aboard ship. Lights diffused behind shaded glass. Somewhere in the distance, laughter drifted, polite and controlled.

I passed a young maid pushing a trolley of folded linen; her face blank with routine concentration, and she did not look at me. She did not need to. The ship's pedestrian areas were filled with people who seemed to know where they were going, making everything seem easy.

I paused for a moment at a junction, allowing a small stream of passengers to pass. A man in evening wear, arm linked with his wife, discussing tomorrow's docking arrangements. Older ladies murmuring about customs and trunks. Children tugged at a nanny's sleeve, asking when they would see the Statue of Liberty. Their voices were light and free of care.

I walked on, the earlier irritation at Henderson's remark replaced now by a different discomfort. Not revelation, nor certainty.

Back in my cabin, I dressed, choosing a tie that looked as though I had made no special effort. The mirror showed me a young man attempting calm, although inside told a different story.

When I returned to HG's stateroom later, I found my co-conspirators composed and dressed as though for an ordinary evening of conversation, rather than the culmination of a murder investigation. HG wore understated jewellery. Whipple's jacket sat firm, his collar precise. Both had the same quality of outward ease that people who are in control of their own nerves can achieve.

"You are late," HG observed with mild reproach.

"I am on time," I replied. "You are simply early."

"Being early is one of the few moral virtues left in society," she said, and her eyes warmed slightly. "Sit."

I did.

Whipple looked at me across the room. "Rex," he said quietly, "whatever happens this evening, you must resist the urge to speak too much."

I blinked. "That is a tall order."

"It is necessary," he said. "Words shape attention. Attention shapes behaviour."

HG added, "We want behaviour without interference."

I nodded, though my stomach tightened. "And if something goes wrong?"

Whipple's gaze was steady. "Then we contain it."

The doorbell sounded. The first guest arrived.

For the next half hour, the stateroom filled with the murmur of polite voices and the soft clink of glass. HG received everyone with her usual composure, as though hosting a farewell gathering were the most natural thing in the world. She did not look like a woman preparing to expose the truth. She looked like a duchess offering civilisation one last chance to behave decently.

I noticed how people's seating/standing spots showed their connections, fears, and habits. Some clutched their drinks. One or two smiled too soon. Several avoided looking at Whipple.

Nothing dramatic occurred. No one blurted out a confession. No one fled. The ship continued to hum beneath the gathering, indifferent to the human drama played out in its compartments.

And yet, even without overt disruption, I could feel something tightening, like the drawing of a thread.

It signalled readiness.

We had reached the point where the truth did not require further invention. It required only that we stop interfering with it.

HG's gaze found mine. It held no triumph. Only muted instruction.

Hold steady.

Whipple shifted nearer to the door, his posture relaxed to casual eyes, purposeful to mine. He looked like a man attending a social occasion. He also looked like a man who had already decided what he would do if someone attempted to leave.

I understood then why they had named nothing aloud, even in private. Naming invites response. Response invites adaptation. Adaptation invites error, and error invites danger.

Silence was not hesitation; it constituted strategy.

As the conversation flowed around us, I felt an odd stillness settle in my mind. The old explanation, the one built of rank, motive, and coordination, remained intact. No one had disproved it.

Something else waited beneath it; simpler, quieter, more consistent with the ship's own habits.

I could not yet say it.

I did not need to.

The ship would say it for us.

As evening approached, polite laughter faded into muted tones; I knew with absolute certainty that no questions remained.

Nothing new needed to be found.

Only shown.

I looked around HG's stateroom, at the shaded lamps, the positioned chairs, the glasses on the sideboard. At the faces assembled under the pretext of civility. The vessel continued its steady progress toward land as though murder were another passenger who would disembark and leave no mark.

And I understood, at last, that the truth would not come from accusation.

It would come from exposure.

HG's voice drifted across the room, light and perfectly placed.

"We are so close to the end of our voyage," she said pleasantly, "and it seems a pity to arrive with unpleasantness unresolved."

Her words were mild.

But the air shifted, almost imperceptibly, as though the ship itself had drawn a careful breath.

And I knew, with a calm that surprised me, that we were ready.

Chapter Twenty-Five

FIRST CLASS JUSTICE

There is a particular politeness that settles over a ship when land draws near.

It is not kindness, precisely. It is relief practising its smile.

The ship cut through the harsh Atlantic Ocean, its engines sounding sure of themselves and their course. Beyond the windows, the sea lay smooth and opaque, like black silk drawn tight. New York waited ahead, no longer an abstraction but an inevitability. One could feel it in the lounges where passengers relaxed, the upbeat music, and the emphasis on style. A sense had taken hold that whatever discomforts the voyage had contained would soon be left behind, tidied away like deck chairs after a squall.

It was easy to imagine safety at sea once land was visible.

Yet the voyage had not healed.

Two men were dead. Sir Edmund Blythe, found lifeless in the cabin he had believed himself master of. Henderson, the journalist, silenced before his pen could reach shore.

And between them, the steward, struck down with calculated restraint, removed from circulation just long enough for fear to do its work.

That final detail, I believed, was what compelled HG to act now.

Her invitation had arrived with the muted certainty of a command disguised as courtesy. A small cocktail in her private saloon, before we docked. A chance, she wrote, to enjoy a civilised moment together before the inevitable dispersal.

No one declined.

I had arrived early, as requested, and found her saloon arranged with a tact so deliberate it might have been mistaken for tenderness. Lamps shaded to soften faces rather than illuminate them. Chairs drawn into a loose, conversational arc that suggested intimacy rather than interrogation. The heat sat low, warmth implied rather than required. A decanter and glasses waited on the sideboard, not ostentatious, but present enough to signal that this was to be a social occasion, at least in form.

Whipple was already there, standing near the mantelpiece. His jacket buttoned, posture easy to the casual eye and alert to mine. He had the look of a man who'd identified where he'd stand if anyone moved against his wishes, and where his hands would go if restraint became necessary.

HG sat with her gloved hands resting in her lap. Calm as stone. Not cold—never cold—but steady in a way that suggested the room would move before she did.

"They will expect you to name one of them," I murmured as I took my seat beside her.

Her mouth curved faintly. "People prefer their villains to be visible, Rex. It makes the world feel manageable."

Whipple did not turn when he spoke. "No one leaves the saloon until we are finished."

I nodded, though my throat tightened. A ship nearing port ought to feel like release. Instead, it felt like someone had sealed the windows against more than the cold sea, enclosing the air.

The guests arrived in quick succession. No conversation, just suspicious glances.

Captain Hardwick entered first, uniform immaculate, expression neutral. He carried himself as a man attending a hearing disguised as a social call. Lily de Vere followed, elegant and unhurried, her gaze already measuring the room, noting exits and alignments as if by habit. Penelope Chase came next, pale and anxious, her chin lifted with an effort that did not quite conceal her nerves. Madam Zelda swept in with theatrical grace, jewellery chinking, her smile bright enough to serve as armour. Baron von Ritter arrived last, calm as a winter lake, silver-topped cane in hand, as though this were an intellectual exercise rather than a reckoning.

A steward circulated with drinks.

He was not the anonymous, interchangeable figure first class often imagined when it thought of service, though we had trained ourselves not to see. The fellow moved among us, tray balanced with professional ease, and spoke only when spoken to. He belonged to the furniture as much as the lamps and the curtains.

Only tonight did a difference register.

The steward carried himself with care, as though mindful of his balance. Bruising remained at his temple, imperfectly concealed. The sort of discolouration one might attribute to a mishap in a narrow corridor. He moved in a restrained manner, as if someone had instructed him to be gentle. Light duty, I thought. The ship could not afford to waste a pair of hands, not even battered ones.

No one commented. No one asked after him.

I realised then how quickly first class could absorb a man's suffering into the background, provided it did not interrupt their comfort.

HG waited until everyone settled.

"I am grateful to you all for indulging me at such short notice," she said. "We are nearing the end of our voyage, and it seemed appropriate to speak plainly about what has occurred aboard this ship."

Zelda lifted her glass. "How refreshing. Rumour is such an exhausting companion."

"Truth can be more so," HG replied mildly.

A hush settled. Even the Atlantic's impatience seemed to withdraw.

"We have endured two murders," HG continued. "Sir Edmund Blythe and Mr Henderson. We have also endured a violent assault on a steward. Fear has been allowed to ferment. In such circumstances, it chooses its targets wisely."

Captain Hardwick's jaw tightened. Lily's smile thinned. Penelope clasped her hands together. Von Ritter watched with courteous detachment.

"I do not propose to accuse anyone this evening," HG went on. "I intend only to ask questions. You may answer as you see fit."

The absence of overt threat rendered the room more dangerous than any declaration could have.

HG rotated her glass slowly, watching the lamplight catch it.

"We are taught," she said, "that power announces itself. That it wears fine clothes and commands the space. That when something terrible happens, responsibility must sit where authority resides."

Her gaze moved deliberately around the circle.

"And yet," she continued, "the most consequential influence is often quiet. It moves through routine. It hides in plain sight. Being taken for granted is how it persuades."

Zelda laughed in a low tone. "You offer us a philosophical discourse, Your Grace?"

HG regarded her evenly. "Only insofar as you are having a practical one."

Whipple spoke then, his voice measured. "We dock soon. If the truth is not settled before we reach shore, it will be settled by gossip. Gossip is an untidy form of justice."

Hardwick set his glass down with controlled precision. "Then ask your questions, Detective Inspector. I am a busy man."

HG inclined her head.

"Captain," she said, "how long have you commanded vessels of this size?"

Hardwick blinked, clearly expecting accusation rather than chronology. "Fifteen years."

"And in that time," HG asked, "have you found authority to be a blunt instrument, or a subtle one?"

Hardwick hesitated. "Authority is only effective when it is controlled."

"And when control is threatened?" HG asked.

"One contains the threat."

Whipple's eyes did not leave him. "You contained the fire."

A faint ripple moved through the room. Fire aboard ship was not a subject raised lightly. The ghost of it was felt by all, though no one claimed it.

Hardwick's colour rose. "Yes."

"You kept it from the passengers," Whipple said.

"Yes," Hardwick repeated, sharper. "To prevent panic."

HG's voice remained mild. "And when Sir Edmund Blythe discovered it?"

Hardwick's gaze flicked to her. "He was curious."

"Curious is not the word you used earlier," HG observed.

Hardwick's nostrils flared. "He was dangerous."

Penelope made a small, involuntary sound.

HG tilted her head. "Because he threatened exposure?"

Hardwick's jaw worked. "Yes."

"And what did you do?" HG asked.

"I told him he would be heard. In due course."

Whipple's tone was quiet. "You attempted to manage him."

"Of course I did."

HG let the silence stretch, then asked, almost conversationally, "Did you order his death, Captain?"

Hardwick's shoulders went rigid. "No."

No one declared him cleared. Suspicion shifted without lifting.

HG turned from him without comment, leaving the Captain to sit with the weight of the room's attention.

"Miss de Vere," HG said next, "you have been described as a woman who understands influence."

Lily smiled. "Influence is persuasion exercised well."

"And persuasion does not always require honesty," HG replied.

"Nor does it require violence."

Whipple's focus narrowed. "Sir Edmund applied pressure to you."

"He attempted to."

"He threatened exposure."

"Men threaten women daily, Inspector. Most live to regret their arrogance."

Penelope's eyes widened. Zelda leaned forward, avid.

HG's tone did not change. "And Mr Henderson?"

Lily's gaze flicked briefly to the fire. "Henderson was tiresome."

"Did he threaten you?"

"He insinuated."

"And if he had published?"

"I would have dealt with it."

"How?" HG asked.

"I meander around inconveniences."

"Not through them?" HG enquired.

Lily's fingers tightened around her glass.

The steward passed behind her chair, refilled it with steady hands, and moved on. She did not look at him.

HG turned then to Penelope, her voice gentler.

"Miss Chase," she said, "you have been under considerable strain."

Penelope nodded, swallowing. "Yes."

"Sir Edmund frightened you."

"He did."

"And Henderson?"

"In a different way."

"How so?"

"Blythe threatened quietly. Henderson publicly."

Whipple's tone remained procedural. "Did either give you reason to wish them dead?"

Penelope shook her head, tears rising. "No. To hide, perhaps. Not to kill."

HG allowed that fear to sit in the room before moving on.

Madam Zelda deflected with brittle charm. Von

Ritter answered with civility that revealed nothing and concealed much. Each spoke, and each avoided the obvious danger: the desire of the room to be given a villain.

HG rose at last, moving toward the false fire grate, as though warming her hands.

"We have spoken," she said, "as if power resides only where it is seen."

She paused.

"But aboard a ship," she continued, "the most influential people are often those who move everywhere without being noticed."

Zelda scoffed. "You mean servants."

HG looked at her. "I mean the unseen machinery of society."

The air changed. I felt it in my chest, like a door opening onto a colder corridor than any we had yet explored.

And still, no one understood what was about to be taken from them.

HG let the silence do its work.

It was a thing she did better than anyone I knew. She allowed it to settle, to stretch, to make those seated within it aware of their own breathing. The ship's engines vibrated, as if a basic force was pushing against the idea of a civilised place.

"Sir Edmund Blythe," HG said at last, "was not merely a blackmailer. He was a man who delighted in proving that other people's privacy belonged to him."

Captain Hardwick's jaw tightened, though he did not interrupt.

"He did not shout," HG continued. "The fellow did not bluster. He spoke calmly, casually, as though the consequences he described were as inevitable as the weather. And that is what made him effective."

Whipple nodded. "Miss Chase told us as much. Blythe did not threaten directly. He implied. He allowed the imagination to do the work."

Penelope's throat worked as she swallowed. I remembered her earlier account, the way she had described Blythe's voice. Measured. Certain. A man who never needed to raise it because he assumed obedience.

"He tested people," HG went on. "He did not immediately demand. He demonstrated reach."

Zelda lifted her glass. "You speak as though he were a magician."

"In a sense, he was," HG replied. "But not with tricks. With access."

She turned her gaze briefly to me. "The will."

I felt heat rise to my face, remembering the unease that discovery had stirred. The codicil. Its loss and reappearance. I had treated it as provocation, as psychological pressure applied from above.

"The will was not simply about inheritance," HG continued. "It was about intrusion. About proving that private spaces were not private at all."

Whipple added, "And the brooch."

Von Ritter's eyes sharpened.

"That, too, appeared conveniently," HG said. "Just when it would redirect suspicion. Just when it would nudge attention toward a particular narrative."

Zelda snorted. "You are describing coincidence with a flourish."

"Incompetence does not return missing property at the precise moment it will cause maximum disruption," HG replied.

Whipple's voice stayed low. "The point is not the objects themselves. The point is what they demonstrated."

HG took up the conversation. "That someone could enter cabins, handle personal effects, and leave no trace. They could move through first class, and people would forget them as easily as they overlooked them.

The steward continued his circuit, refilling glasses. His presence barely registered.

"Sir Edmund learned from these rehearsals," HG said. "He learned who could do such things safely."

Penelope whispered, "Who?"

HG did not answer.

"Henderson," Whipple said, taking up the thread, "was different. He did not hoard secrets. He scattered them."

"And he was close to transmitting his findings ashore," HG added. "His notebook made that clear."

Lily's eyes narrowed. "You searched his cabin."

"Yes," Whipple said simply.

Zelda laughed. "How democratic. Everyone rifling through everyone else's drawers."

HG ignored her.

"Henderson began asking questions," HG said. "Not gossip. Not innuendo. Precise questions."

"And precision," Whipple added, "is dangerous when someone depends on blur."

Hardwick's hands tightened on his glass. "Henderson threatened panic."

"Yes," HG agreed. "But more than that, he threatened to connect threads."

Whipple inclined his head. "Sir Edmund's death and Henderson's demise are not separate crimes. They are two acts within the same protection. One to stop blackmail. The other to stop exposure."

Von Ritter's mouth curved . "The second is always riskier."

"Because it invites disorder," HG said. "And institutions fear disorder more than guilt."

Whipple shifted, and I recognised the moment he decided it was time to speak not only of motive, but of method.

"Sir Edmund Blythe died in his cabin," he said. "No one heard a struggle. There were no obvious signs of violence. Dr Ambrose could offer only opinion. A man of Sir Edmund's age. A sudden collapse. Easy to accept as natural."

"It looked like apoplexy," Hardwick said stiffly.

"It looked like many things," Whipple replied. "But it was convenient."

HG asked quietly, "What would you require to kill a man in his own cabin without alarm?"

Whipple did not hesitate. "Access. Time. The ability to approach him without raising suspicion. And something to lower resistance. Not melodrama. Not poison in the theatrical sense. A sedative. A draught. Something a gentleman might accept without question."

Zelda's eyes widened. "Laudanum."

"Any sedative," Whipple said. "Available aboard ship. Medical stores. Spirits."

"And then?" Penelope whispered,

"A sleeping man does not struggle," Whipple stated calmly. "A man who does not struggle makes no noise. A cabin can be tidied until it looks as it always does."

The words were plain. Their simplicity was worse than any flourish.

HG turned to matters concerning the dead journalist.

"Henderson would not accept such a thing," HG said. "The man was wary. He pried; believed himself important."

"Or invincible," von Ritter murmured.

"So you lure him," Whipple said. "You offer information. Proof. Something he wants more than caution. You choose a place where sound does not carry. A service stairwell. A pantry."

"And you strike quickly," HG said.

"Yes. Urgently. Because time had run out." Whipple added.

The contrast hung there. Blythe's careful death. Henderson's hurried one.

"And the assault," HG said.

The room tightened.

"The steward was struck from behind," Whipple said. "Hard enough to cause concussion. Not enough to kill."

Penelope whispered, "Why leave him alive?"

HG answered gently. "Because a corpse invites questions. A battered man invites assumptions."

Whipple nodded. "It shaped our thinking. We assumed violence flowed downward. Power frightening weakness."

That was how it had felt. How easily I had accepted it.

Whipple turned to me. "Until Rex remembered something Henderson said."

Every eye came to me.

"Henderson told me," I said, my voice steadier than I felt, "that the best secrets on a ship do not sit in first class. They travel on trays."

The sentence sounded absurdly simple in the warm saloon. Yet it landed like a dropped plate.

HG watched the room register it.

"We were not defeated by secrecy," I went on. "We were defeated by assumption. We looked upward because it was comfortable to do so. We mistook authority for capability. The will, the brooch, even the assault, all showed the same thing: access. Movement. Acceptance."

HG inclined her head, inviting me to continue.

"We forgave what moved quietly," I said. "We accepted sympathy where we should have asked questions. We believed a bruise meant innocence. And because of that, two men were allowed to die before we understood that the most dangerous thing on this ship was not power at all, but invisibility."

HG let the silence stretch.

Then she lifted her glass.

"Could you top me up, please?" she asked. "Mr Peabody, is it not? Bravo to you for returning to duty so soon. I want you to know we all very much appreciate your sense of duty."

The steward stepped forward with the decanter.

For the briefest instant, his composure slipped.

HG's compliment appeared to take him by surprise.

"You have a family in Southampton," she said with a smile.

"Yes, Your Grace."

"A wife. Children."

"Yes."

"You mentioned them to Rex earlier in the voyage," Whipple added.

Peabody's gaze flicked to me. For the first time, I truly saw him. Not as part of the ship's furniture, but as a man holding himself together by habit alone.

"Sir Edmund Blythe noticed you," HG said softly. "He noticed that you moved everywhere. That you heard everything. That you belonged in corridors and cabins without anyone questioning why."

"I'm a steward," Peabody said hoarsely.

"Exactly," Whipple replied. "And that is what made you valuable."

Peabody shook his head. "I didn't know him."

"But he knew you," HG said calmly.

She turned, addressing the room as though explaining a social principle rather than accusing a man.

"Sir Edmund's method was intimidation through implication. He did not need to claim responsibility. The victim believed he could make consequences happen—because they did."

Penelope's face drained of colour.

"The will. The brooch. Those were not accidents," HG said. "They were demonstrations. Proof of reach. And once Sir Edmund identified the safest pair of hands aboard this ship, he applied pressure."

Peabody's breathing quickened.

"Not to a duchess. Not to a diplomat," HG continued. "But to a man whose entire life could be destroyed with a whisper."

Peabody's voice broke. "He threatened my family."

The words escaped him, raw and involuntary.

The room froze.

The words hung in the air like a dropped glass that had not yet shattered.

"He threatened my family." Peabody repeated, louder this time.

No one spoke. Even Zelda, who so often filled silence as a reflex, held her tongue. Penelope's hand flew to her mouth. Captain Hardwick stared at the carpet as though he had discovered a fault line running beneath it.

HG did not soften. She permitted the truth to stand.

"And you believed him," she said quietly.

Peabody's jaw clenched. "Because men like him always win."

HG inclined her head a fraction. "Until they do not."

Whipple's voice was calm, ironed flat by years of professional practice. "What did he threaten, Mr Peabody?"

The steward's gaze flicked around the room, then dropped. "He said he knew things about me. About before. He said he could make sure I never worked again. That my wife would have to beg. That my children would grow up knowing what their father was."

Lily's mouth tightened, not with pity, but with disdain. Hardwick shifted, the sound of his chair faint against the carpet.

"You killed him," Whipple said.

Peabody jerked his head up. "No."

HG did not argue. She shaped the truth until it could not be escaped.

"You killed Sir Edmund Blythe," she said, "because his blackmail reached a place you could not survive. He was not threatening your comfort. He was threatening your future. And he did so in a way that gave you no dignified exit."

Whipple stepped closer, though not threateningly. "You had access. A steward's presence in a corridor is invisible. You could approach a cabin with a tray, deliver a drink, fetch a tonic. You did not need spectacle. You needed quiet."

Zelda whispered, appalled, "And then you clobbered him over the head."

Whipple did not flinch. "Yes, he did."

Penelope made a small, broken sound. I felt something twist in my chest, not sympathy, but the terrible understanding of how easily this had all been allowed to happen.

"And then Henderson," HG said.

Peabody's face changed at the name. Fear, not rage.

"Henderson learned about the will. The brooch," HG continued. "He began asking who had handled them."

"He wouldn't stop," Peabody said hoarsely. "He said he was close. He said it would all be public by morning."

Whipple nodded. "Blythe threatened you privately. Henderson threatened you publicly."

"And you had no time," HG said. "So you acted urgently."

Peabody's shoulders slumped. "I didn't mean to kill him."

HG's voice remained steady. "Few people ever do."

Whipple added, "You lured him. Offered proof. Led him somewhere he would follow willingly."

Peabody said nothing.

"And the assault," Whipple continued.

Peabody flinched.

"You tried to protect yourself," HG said. "After Blythe's death, you hinted that you could speak. About the fire. About what you knew. Someone found out and decided you needed reminding of your place. Yet you recovered in time to strike Henderson before he could transmit his story."

Hardwick's face tightened. "You are making assumptions."

Whipple did not look at him. "I recognise patterns."

"Captain," HG asked mildly, "did you order a warning?"

Hardwick did not answer.

The silence answered for him.

Peabody's gaze flicked again to the door.

"You believed," HG said, "that we would never look

past first class. That sympathy would protect you. That a bruised steward is always a victim, never a culprit."

Peabody's face twisted. "You don't know what it's like."

HG's tone did not change. "You had choices."

"I had a family," Peabody snapped.

"And you chose to make two men die for your fear," HG replied.

Something in him broke, not tears, but panic.

He ran.

The movement was sudden, shocking, as though the polite theatre of the room had torn and revealed the animal beneath. A small table clipped his hip. A glass toppled and shattered, the sound sharp as a gunshot. Penelope cried out. Zelda recoiled. Lily rose, eyes wide, alert rather than afraid.

Whipple lunged, but Peabody slipped past him with the desperate agility of a man who had lived by disappearing.

Von Ritter intervened.

He did not shout or grab. He adjusted his stance with exquisite economy and extended his foot into Peabody's path.

Peabody stumbled, arms flailing, then went down hard against the doorframe. The decanter shattered beside him, liquid spreading across the carpet like a stain that would never quite fade.

Whipple was on him in seconds, pinning him with controlled force.

"Charlie Peabody," he said clearly, "you are under arrest for the murders of Sir Edmund Blythe and Mr Henderson."

The struggle went out of Peabody as quickly as it had come. He sagged, breath rasping, the habit of invisibility finally stripped from him.

Penelope stared as though the world had rearranged itself while she was not looking. Zelda's mouth moved without sound. Lily watched with cool contempt. Hardwick stood rigid, the knowledge of his own failures settling like lead.

HG stepped forward, composed.

"The most dangerous influence," she said softly, "is the influence no one believes exists."

Whipple hauled Peabody to his feet and led him toward the door. Von Ritter adjusted his cane.

"The trouble with invisibility," the baron remarked, "is that it encourages people to believe they are untouchable."

The door closed behind them.

The room remained, filled with the aftertaste of truth.

I stared at the dark stain on the carpet and understood, at last, why we had been mistaken for so long.

We had been looking at power.

Not at access.

Power does not always sit at the table.

Sometimes it moves quietly, on soft shoes, carrying a tray.

And if you do not look properly, it can kill twice before you ever notice it has entered the room.

Epilogue

The easterly wind had been sharpening its claws all day, and by evening it rattled the windows of HG's Norfolk home with determined malice. Inside, however, the fire roared as though it had taken personal offence at the weather, and the cosy library glowed with lamplight, leather bindings, and the unmistakable scent of well thumbed books and easy comfort.

I had been persuaded, against my better judgement, to relinquish my greatcoat at the door.

"You look like a half frozen stork," HG had observed briskly. "Sit nearer the fire before you begin to molt."

I obeyed, extending my hands towards the blaze.

Whipple, already installed in a high backed chair, allowed himself the faintest smile.

"I warned you about the east wind," he said. "It has no respect for enthusiasm."

"This," I said, "is precisely why civilised people winter abroad."

HG snorted. "Nonsense. Cold builds character. Besides, you would only complain about the food."

She handed Whipple a glass of something amber and restorative, then settled opposite him with her own.

"To our safe return," she said.

"And to England," Whipple added dutifully.

I raised my glass last. "And to trains. I am exceedingly fond of trains. They do not pitch and roll at the oddest angles."

HG regarded me over the rim of her glass. "You survived the Atlantic."

"Barely," I replied. "And I maintain the sea only tolerates humanity out of professional courtesy."

Whipple leaned back, studying the fire.

"It was a most instructive voyage," he said. "Though I confess I prefer crimes that do not require lifeboat drills."

"Ah yes," HG said lightly. "You do prefer your murders on solid ground, Arthur, do you not?"

Whipple made a sound that , in another man, may have resembled laughter.

"I like clarity," he said. "You, on the other hand, seem to enjoy ambiguity."

"I enjoy truth," HG corrected. "Ambiguity merely turns it into a puzzle."

She turned to me.

"And you enjoy noticing things no one else finds important."

"A gift," I said. "Especially when it irritates professionals."

Whipple raised an eyebrow. "It does not irritate me."

"It absolutely irritates you," HG said pleasantly. "You simply pretend it does not."

He did not deny it.

For a moment we sat in companionable silence. The fire popped, as if eavesdropping.

"At least," I said, "we may hope our next adventure does not involve a ship."

HG smiled. "Have you been talking to Madam Zelda again?"

"Oh, don't," Whipple sighed.

I looked from one to the other and felt, for the first time since New York, that everything was as it should be.

Outside, the wind howled. Inside, the fire held fast.

And between the three of us, I suspected, there would always be enough warmth to keep the darkness at bay.

Also by Keith Finney

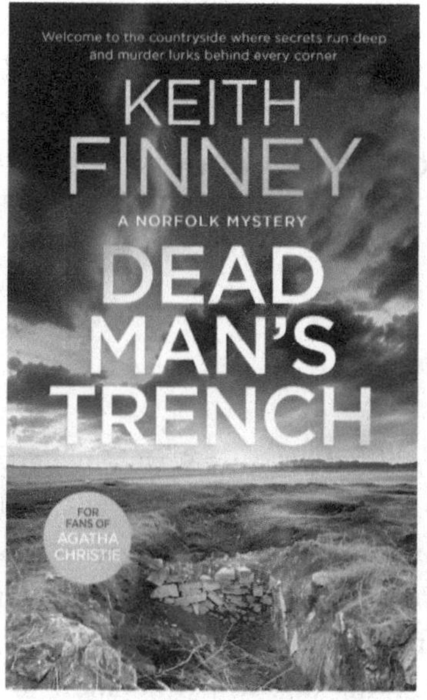

vinci-books.com/deadmanstrench

A quiet village. A deadly secret. Two unlikely allies racing against a killer.

When a suspicious death is brushed aside as an accident, landowner Ant Stanton and headteacher Lyn Blackthorn dig deeper—unearthing buried grudges and a murderer who's not done yet.

Turn the page for a free preview…

Dead Man's Trench: Chapter One

IN A HOLE

Alan Fairchild's blood pressure wasn't in a good place.

Getting the head of archaeology at Cambridge University to meet Stanton Parva's history group was a coup.

Why on earth turn up if they won't listen? Alan fumed in his thoughts. Did no one care that he'd sweated blood to secure a private tour of the dig, which he knew to be of national importance?

"May I emphasise again," said Professor Pullman, as heads swivelled and old friends chatted, "on no account interfere with the excavations you will see this morning."

It was an unequal battle. The gentle waters of Stanton Broad, glistening in the morning sun, had much more appeal than a dusty academic. Add in a golden carpet of Norfolk reed swaying rhythmically in the breeze, and the result was inevitable.

"Our hypothesis is that this vast Roman villa complex was wantonly destroyed. All the signs point to Boudica, queen of the Iceni tribe. In around AD 60 she led a revolt against the Roman legions. Also…"

The professor's words failed to impress one section of the group as they soaked up the latest village gossip. First amongst equals was Phyllis Abbott, a sprite eighty-two-year-old whose loss of hearing caused her to shout then accuse others of not speaking the queen's English.

Alan tried a flanking manoeuvre to work his way around the rebels so he could get close to Phyllis, who was in deep discussion with her best friend, Betty.

Phyllis was lamenting the post office's move from the village shop, which she'd run until she was age seventy-one, to the petrol station on the outskirts of Stanton Parva.

"Modernising the post office is what they call it. How can making things worse be better for the customer? And what Her Majesty must think about it, well, I just don't know. What do you think, Betty?"

Betty nodded as she attempted a reply. "Well, yes… I suppose…"

Phyllis was having none of it. "There's no supposing about it. How do I get to Flatley's petrol station with my leg? Then there's the price of a first-class stamp. Shocking, that's what I say."

By now, Alan had sidled up to the pair and knew from Betty's scowl that she'd given up any hope of challenging her friend's views on the subject.

"Shush," said Alan, a wobble in his voice letting slip that his nerves were getting the better of him.

Phyllis shot Alan a cold stare. "Who are you shushing, young man? Just like your mother, you are." The old woman dismissed Alan with an imperious wave of her hand before turning back to Betty. "And you know what?"

"No. What, dear?" offered Betty, pleased to be asked her opinion.

"When I went to pay for my Jiffy bag, that stupid boy

asked which pump I was using. Well, I thought he was talking about the thing Dr Bridlington prescribed me. I told him to mind his own business. Then…"

The rest of the group were torn between Boudica chasing out the Romans and Phyllis' medicinal pump.

Alan had had enough. "Er, excuse me, Phyllis, but I'm sixty-five, and my mother's been dead for fifteen years."

Half turning, she switched conversation from Betty to Alan without missing a beat. "I remember you when you were in shorts. They called you Snot-Sleeve, didn't they? And your mother still owes me for a pint of milk," said Phyllis, before once more engaging Betty in the thorny issue of Jiffy bags.

Alan withdrew, trying hard to act as if his run-in with Phyllis hadn't happened.

Keen to regain a measure of control, he turned to the professor. "May I ask if the expanse of open water had anything to do with the villa's location ?"

It was a question to which he already knew the answer, but anything was better than another rebuke from Phyllis.

"Ah," replied the professor, pleased once more to be the centre of attention. "In fact, the Broads weren't dug until the twelfth century when the growing population needed peat for cooking and heating."

Alan's relief was palpable as the academic gave a positive response to his question.

Professor Pullman waxed lyrical about the abandoned peat diggings being filled over time by rising water levels to form the Broads, until the manic laughter of a Minions mobile ringtone interrupted his flow.

Alan strained to see where the sound was coming from and meandered through the group until he came across

Angela Simms, who was rummaging through her enormous shoulder bag to silence the din.

"Can you manage?" asked Alan, sensing Angela's embarrassment.

"Never you mind this lot. They can tut all they like."

Alan shook his head in admonishment at two male members of the group. "You can moan all you like, but just think, what if someone was trying to get an urgent message to you? Until you take the call, you don't know why they're ringing, do you?"

The two men half turned from Alan, shrugging their shoulders like two naughty schoolboys.

Alan turned back towards Angela just in time to see her retrieve the mobile and scurry from the group, her face etched with concern.

As Professor Pullman seized his opportunity to round off his introduction to the site, he turned from the group, lifted his right arm, and urged the assembly to follow as he set a blistering pace towards a small mound in the middle distance.

It took a couple of minutes for Alan to realise Angela hadn't rejoined the group. Fearful she had received bad news, he scanned the field to see where she might be.

He noticed a hundred yards or so to his left the young woman standing ramrod straight, frozen to the spot.

Alan quietly backed away from the group and ambled towards the woman, not wanting to draw attention to himself—or to Angela.

As he neared, he noticed Angela held both arms to her sides. Her phone hung limply in one hand.

Oh Lord, he thought.

"Is everything okay, Ang?" said Alan in a low, quiet tone, keen not to startle her.

She didn't respond.

Alan slipped the mobile from her hand and raised it to his ear. Angela offered no resistance. He turned and walked a few paces back towards the distant group.

"Ang, are you still there? How's the signal? Can you hear me?"

Alan spoke into the handset, trying his best not to alarm the caller. "Hi, she's fine but tied up for a minute or two. I'll get her to give you a ring back. Is that okay?"

Alan didn't wait for a response. Instead, he ended the call, switched the mobile to silent, and slipped it into his shirt pocket.

He retraced his steps towards Angela and both now stood at the edge of a deep excavation.

Alan saw what she saw.

The body of a man.

Dead Man's Trench: Chapter Two

THE WALLED GARDEN

The eyes were open, face drained of colour. A trickle of congealed blood puddled in the dusty ground to the side of his head.

"I knew that bugger would come to a sticky end one day."

Alan, startled at the sudden sound of voices, turned to see Phyllis at the head of a small group of club members who had wandered over, curious at Alan's earlier departure.

The old woman showed no sign of shock. It wasn't the first time Phyllis had observed violent death. War service had seen to that.

Alan instinctively moved closer to Angela, who hadn't moved a muscle.

He looked across to Phyllis, admiring her composure but puzzled by her comment. "What do you mean?"

"Well, they don't… or should I say, didn't, call Fred Collins 'Narky' for nothing. He was a bad-tempered bully, that one."

"Mrs Abbott," Alan responded, not sure of how to

finish the sentence. Simultaneously, he turned Angela away from the horror. She offered no resistance.

"It's true," Phyllis continued, her voice quiet now yet still lacking any trace of sympathy for the dead man. "He always picked on the young'uns from the 'big house'. He knew they couldn't answer back."

Alan returned to the edge of the excavation. He shook his head. "What a waste."

Phyllis fumed. "Waste? What do you mean? He thought he was God's gift to women. Always trying to paw them. I've seen him do it. Given him a piece of my mind more than once, I have."

Phyllis kicked some loose earth into the trench, watching it settle like unwanted confetti on the dead man's exposed cheek and shoulder.

Alan recoiled, at last summoning the courage to challenge the old woman. "For the love of God, Phyllis. Show some humanity, will you? No one deserves to die like *that*."

The old woman tilted her head upward and sniffed the air, dismissing his show of sympathy for the dead man.

She pointed a spindly finger towards the corpse. "Seen this in the war. Men who lord it over other lads. Try it on with their girlfriends. When a jealous man gets his blood up, he can do anything. And from what I know, plenty had it in for that fat sod."

Before Alan could respond, he noticed the remainder of the group approaching and headed them off before they reached the excavation.

"There's been a terrible accident," said Alan. "We need to call the police. I'll try and get through on my mobile, but as backup, I need someone to run over to the big house and raise the alarm."

All eyes descended on Sid. He was the youngest by decades.

"I'll do it," replied Sid, making off at a sprint towards Stanton Hall.

Enjoying the solitude of the Hall's walled garden, Anthony Stanton filled his lungs with a riot of heady scents. As the dew lifted into Norfolk's big sky, the effect seemed all the stronger.

This place is about as far from work as I can get, he thought.

Anthony kicked a spray of gravel from the pathway, which cut its way through blazing beds of late-summer flowers.

He flopped onto a rickety, cast-iron bench and tilted his head backwards. A warming sun had the desired effect.

For the first time in a long time, he pushed painful memories to the back of his mind.

The quiet didn't last long. Reacting in an instant to the sharp crack of a rusty gate latch lifting, he hunched over as if to make himself as small as possible, his attention focused on a dark outline filling the gate opening.

Anthony squinted at the silhouetted figure of a woman.

"Excuse me, this area is private." The voice was assertive. He expected compliance.

Ignoring his words, the woman continued to close the distance between them. "So it's true. You're back, Anthony… and in one piece too. Lucky for you they couldn't shoot straight."

He recognised the voice. Using the long form of his first name was a giveaway. She always did that to provoke him.

He chose not to react. "Military training has its uses."

"Hello, you," said Lyn.

"Hello, you," he replied.

The ease of their exchanges had all the familiarity of a long-married couple, relaxed in each other's company.

"Still breaking the rules, Lyn. Just like at school… and the Hall still isn't open to the public today."

Lyn smiled, unmoved by his halfhearted rebuke. "Just as well I'm not Joe Public, then, isn't it? And as for school, we couldn't all be the class swot, could we?"

Lyn's barbed comment rolled back the years to a time when they were at Stanton Primary together.

He gave a throaty laugh. Time had passed, but the constant ribbing he got from his classmates had stayed with him. He'd always seemed to come top in exams, but it wasn't the only reason he stuck out. Ant spoke differently and lived in "the big house".

His smile widened as he recalled how she was the one who controlled the others. A talent, he suspected, Lyn still possessed, judging by the confidence in her voice and the way she held herself.

"Wasn't my fault my parents bought into that swinging sixties hippie thing, and sent me to the local primary school for oiks instead of public school."

Lyn gave him a sideways look and shook her head in that dismissive way only she could get away with. "Playing the victim doesn't suit you, Ant, and anyway, you wouldn't have suited pinstriped trousers or a straw boater. At least your parents spoke to each other in words with more than one syllable and lived in the same place."

"Things any better now?" Ant responded.

Lyn let out an almost inaudible sigh. "Let's put it this way, at least Mum has stopped throwing things at Dad. Mind you, living at opposite ends of the village helps."

Ant didn't pursue the point and broke eye contact, knowing the damage went deeper than Lyn would ever admit.

"Anyway, I popped over to drop off a chocolate cake to your parents. It's their favourite, you know. I bring one over every Saturday."

Ant smiled as Lyn flopped next to him on the bench.

"I didn't think you'd come back after Greg's death."

Ant rolled his head as if to make sure his exposed skin captured every ray the sun had to offer. His arms hung across the back rail of the bench. Lyn didn't try to avoid contact as she settled back.

"I didn't intend to stay away for so long. At eighteen you think your parents will live forever. I'm still not sure if I'm back for good, even though…" Ant faltered. He shuffled his feet in the gravel.

Lyn stared into the distance, looking at nothing in particular. "A flying visit, then? Your brother's been dead a long time, and the estate seems to run itself from what I can see."

Ant gave a short, sharp laugh. "That's just the problem, Lyn. You know better than me how frail Mum and Dad are. They've both suffered bad luck with their health for years, and I don't suppose it helped that they had Greg and me comparatively late in life because of all the travelling they did. But still, to tell you the truth, it was a shock."

He stopped, sensing Lyn's reaction.

Another telling-off coming.

"For heaven's sake, Ant. They're both in their seventies, and the man had a heart attack a few months ago. What did you expect?"

Ant shrugged his shoulders and changed tack. It was easier than thinking about his parents not being around forever. "The thing is, Lyn, the estate's in a right mess, and I'm not cut out to fix it."

Lyn sensed his unease.

"That was Greg's job. And what happens? He flips his car into Stanton Broad, and goodnight Vienna."

"Sounds like you're feeling sorry for yourself again, Anthony."

There she goes again.

"Not at all," replied Ant. "I'm just stating a fact. It was Greg's inheritance, not mine. Turns out the estate income has been slipping for years, and the Hall is in a hell of a state. You've seen the water damage. Dad's tried, but it's too much. To make things worse, the people paid to look after the place just haven't done their jobs."

Lyn's expression softened.

Ant settled back into the bench, his head once more falling backwards as the sun bathed his face.

"Isn't it strange, Lyn? You know, when you're a kid, you look up to your parents and assume they know it all. Then whether it's poor health or just getting older, you realise they're not invincible after all. You must see it all the time." Ant opened an eye and squinted into a bright Norfolk sky. "Dad mentioned you started as head teacher at our old school in September. Spooky or what!" He let out a throaty laugh.

"Come to think of it, it's kind of strange, dealing with stuff in classrooms I sat in as a child," replied Lyn. "But you're right. I see kids affected by things at home. There's a familiar look in their eyes when voices are raised—a rabbit caught in the headlights type of look. Despite working like stink, sometimes we can't fix things. But we try. That's all anyone can do."

Ant sensed her sudden nervousness and could have

kicked himself for making her remember her own childhood traumas. “Sorry, Lyn. Didn’t mean to do that; I know you had it tough at home.”

After a few moments of uneasy silence, Lyn gave Ant a sideways glance as she playfully pinched the skin of his arm between two fingers.

Ant winced in mock pain but made no move to distance himself from the attack.

“That’s something else you did in class, remember?” said Ant. “I never understood why.”

Lyn smiled. “Let’s just say it was my way of toughening you up,” she replied.

Ant had to admit Lyn had got him out of several sticky situations with Jezza, the class bully.

“Of course, there’s another explanation.”

Lyn gave Ant a puzzled look. She was at risk of overacting. “And that would be?”

“Affection, Lyn. I asked my father once why you kept hitting me when you spent most of your time fending off Hillier and his thugs. Dad was clear about it, and seeing as I didn’t have a better explanation, I believed him!”

Lyn waved at Ant dismissively. “In your dreams, Anthony Stanton. My older brother used to pinch me, so I took it out on you. One snotty boy was just the same as any other to me. Anyhow, you sat next to me and were daft enough not to fight back.”

Both laughed, the interlude having served as a convenient pressure valve for less happy memories.

“Right. Time for a piece of chocolate cake and a cup of tea with your parents.” As she spoke, Lyn sprang from the rickety bench and launched herself towards the gate.

“Haven’t I endured enough pain for one day without being exposed to your baking?” moaned Ant as he sprinted to make up the distance between them. "Remember that nut caramel toffee you made with salted peanuts in year four? Yuck!"

Without stopping, Lyn bent down, scooped a handful of gravel and tossed it over her head. "And before you say anything, if I'd have wanted to hit you, I would have. You're not the only one who's a crack shot."

The levity didn't last long. As Lyn reached out to lift the latch of the gate, it moved towards her at speed, causing Lyn to cry out in pain as the heavy construction smacked into her.

"Oh, er… sorry, miss. Only…"

Ant's instinct was to shout at the lad. The look of panic on the youth's face stopped him from doing so.

The boy didn't wait for either a welcome or reprimand. "It's your land agent, sir. He's, er… sort of… dead."

Ant felt a swell of frustration at the youth's nervous ramblings. "What do you mean, 'sort of'? Either someone is dead, or they are not dead."

Ant glimpsed Lyn's look of disapproval and knew he'd gone too far.

Sid looked no less frustrated as he tried to make himself understood. "Up at the dig site. He's in a ditch. They told me to fetch the police."

Ant pointed towards the elegant columns fronting the imposing entrance to the Hall. "The phone's in the hallway. And you'd better ask for an ambulance."

About the Author

Keith's fascinating novels skillfully combine the heart of a retired assistant principal with the imagination of a gifted author, taking readers on a captivating journey through Norfolk's scenic landscapes and rich history.

www.ingramcontent.com/pod-product-compliance
Lightning Source LLC
LaVergne TN
LVHW030915080826
845145LV00013B/2904

9781036716479